Discard

Discard

Meddlin' Madeline Mysteries

Sweet on You

Chautona Havig

ISBN-13: 978-1533041876
ISBN-10: 1533041873

Chautona Havig lives in a small, remote town in California's Mojave Desert with her husband and eight of her nine children. When not writing, she enjoys paper crafting, sewing, and trying to get the rest of her children educated so that she can retire from home education.

Fonts: Times New Roman, Alex Brush, Eterea Pro
Cover photos: Masson/shutterstock.com, marekuliasz/shutterstock.com, Caesart/shutterstock.com
Cover Art: Chautona Havig
Edited by: Haug Editing
Connect with Me Online:
Twitter: https://twitter.com/Chautona
Facebook: https://www.facebook.com/pages/justhewriteescape
My blog: http://chautona.com/blog/
Instagram: http://instagram.com/ChautonaHavig
My newsletter (sign up for news of FREE eBook offers):
http://chautona.com/chautona/newsletter
All Scripture references are from the KJV.

Christian Fiction/Mystery

Dedicated to:

Ashley. You've inspired me, kicked my butler, encouraged me, terrified me, and made me a better writer simply because of your expectations of me. Your comment about me proved true with this book, didn't it? You said, "You buy stock photos like most women buy shoes." And here we have a six book series beginning, and because I fell in love with a series of pictures. Who knew she'd become one of our favorite characters? Oh wait, you did. Then again, that's your job.

But more than being the world's best publicist and marketing guru, you've been a beautiful friend to me. I thank you. Here's to being old ladies rocking on a porch together with a box of See's between us. You'll have an ice-cold super-soaker squirt gun on your lap ready to pop any smart-alecky kids, and I'll have my laptop ready to record it all. Or will they have electrodes that connect to my brain by then. Can you imagine? Books while I sleep! Wheeee!

ONE

Gaslight, although it affords a pleasing and warm, amber glow about a room, has the distinct disadvantage of another kind of warmth—a much less pleasant kind. Madeline Brown sat on a plush settee, her skirt spread out just enough to ensure no one sat too near, and merely observed those around her. The unusual oppressive temperatures for a May evening, combined with her dislike for the heat of gaslight, kept her sipping at a glass of cordial in an attempt not to have to remember to smile. Mr. Merton should accept that electricity is not a passing fancy.

Mid-mental rant, Ida, the Mertons' maid, offered her a small sandwich from an equally diminutive tray, but Madeline declined. "No thank you, Ida. As you can imagine in this heat, I have no appetite." The girl's grimace told much and prompted Madeline to ask, "Is your tooth better this evening?"

"Well enough, miss. Thank you."

Bankers and their miserly tendencies. Your maid needs not to fear for her position if she has her tooth taken care of, Mr. Merton. The listless way that Edith fanned herself prompted further mental rebuke. Edith will exceed her allowance until the day she leaves your home on another man's arm, so you might wish to reconsider the extent of your hospitality if you hope to hasten that day. Madeline's lips turned upward at that thought. A lickpenny like Jonas Merton— generous? The idea was almost as ludicrous as the idea of Edith ever exerting herself enough to encourage a man.

But just as Madeline entertained that thought, Ida showed a young man into the Merton parlor. Interesting. *I believe Vernon Smythe attended the last social that Edith held.* The man greeted Edith with much more warmth than Madeline had expected, piquing the young woman's curiosity further. *Dark coat, wing-tip collar, teck tie, and derby. Methinks Mr. Smythe attempts to present himself as tres chic, non?*

Regardless of the man's intentions, Madeline could not help but notice his overt attentions to her friend. *In the span of less than two minutes, he managed to pay a compliment—what, she could not hear—and receive most definite encouragement in the form of smiles and—could it be? It is! Edith Merton actually lowered her lashes and blushed. I revise my opinion. It seems that, with proper inducement, Edith can be prevailed upon to exert herself indeed. Does this mean her apparent diffidence is merely a ruse, or is there something more intriguing afoot?*

"Madeline, how did I miss seeing you here?"

A smile—a warm, genuine one, if the truth be known—formed as Madeline shifted her skirt enough to allow the speaker to sit. "I hadn't seen you arrive, Russell."

"I've been at billiards with some of the others," he admitted. "You must have come after I arrived."

"I was late." Madeline laughed at the unspoken question in Russell's eyes. "Yes, it was not unintentional, I suppose, but I admit nothing and therefore confess even less." She nodded in the direction of Vernon and Edith. "Did Mr. Smythe join us at the May Day soiree?"

"I believe so. I...."

What else Russell had to say flitted in the general direction of Madeline's ear, but whether it bounced off again or dissolved in her thoughts may never be determined. Madeline, schooled in fine social graces, had long mastered the skill of being an "excellent listener" while hearing nothing. She nodded at the proper inflections, frowned when tone required it, and even offered a light laugh—all without consciousness of her actions.

Indeed, her attention was more interestingly occupied. As Russell spoke of something—likely a new invention he'd heard of and wanted to see in operation—she watched Vernon and Edith. A certain intimacy in Vernon's manner proved a catalyst that spun Madeline's life into an entirely new direction, but she did not know it—not then.

As Flossie Hardwick spoke to Edith, Vernon took a sip of his cordial. Something at that precise moment startled him. Madeline observed, fascinated—and saying, "oh, really!" at all the wrong moment as well—as she watched him nearly spill the drink on himself. *That is peculiar. I wonder....* But Madeline's wonder became astonishment as she watched the scene play out before her. Every movement, every shift of the eye or hand, stunned her—particularly the way Smythe brushed Edith's cheek in full view of every person present!

"Did you see that?"

"I did, and that is why I agree that your bicycle riding days should be at an end."

Madeline's throat went dry, wondering what she'd missed in the conversation. "I—"

"You should have seen your face." Russell's eyes twinkled in spite of the dim lighting. "Admit it. You didn't hear a word I said."

"I didn't," she confessed.

"I've often wondered if you truly listen to what people say or not."

Madeline slid one hand over the other in a deliberate attempt to remind herself not to cross her arms over her chest. "And what made you wonder that?"

"Because when you are unquestioningly interested in a conversation, I don't think you ever repeat a word and add, 'really'

9

to it." Russell peered at her as if to determine how accurate his assessment might be. "Do you?"

"May I have an example?"

Without skipping a beat, Russell said — and in a fine imitation of her, she had to admit, "Example? Really?"

Embarrassment flooded her, tinging her cheeks and making her even more uncomfortable in the overheated room. "I — I never reali — oh, dear."

Russell leaned forward as if to pick up something from the carpet, but as he did he winked. "I doubt anyone else has noticed it. I wasn't certain myself until you turned all rosy."

"Well, you must credit those horrible lamps as well as my mortification."

"But I am curious what caught your attention. You were listening — at first." Ida brought a tray again, and Russell availed himself of three little sandwiches before the girl left. "Would you like one?"

"No, thank you." It took every ounce of self-control not to lean forward and whisper what she'd witnessed. Instead, forcing herself to look as calm and relaxed as if she discussed nothing more interesting than the length of ribbon she purchased that afternoon, Madeline sipped her cordial and said, "I saw something peculiar, but I wouldn't care to be overheard."

"Is your father calling for you on the way home from a meeting perhaps?"

A slow, coy smile appeared as she shook her head. "I must brave the streets alone, I'm afraid."

"All one of them?" Russell tisked and began to say something — offer to take her himself, she suspected — but Madeline didn't have time for formalities. She jumped to her feet and tugged at his arm.

"So thoughtful of you to offer, Mr. Barnes. Let's go now, shall we?"

"You're up to something," he muttered as he swallowed the rest of his sandwich and gulped down the cordial.

But Madeline didn't wait to explain or to demur—didn't wait at all. She simply crossed the room to where Edith and Vernon spoke in low undertones as they examined something on Vernon's wrist. "Edith, I'm afrai—oh, what has happened? Cordial?" Even as she asked the question, Madeline saw that it was not cordial at all, but her friend's gaze flew to Vernon's face and the man nodded. "I am clumsy tonight it seems."

"You should take it to the kitchen and let Ida rub lemon and salt on it before it sets." Madeline gave Edith an apologetic smile. "I'm sorry to leave so early, but—well, you understand." She glanced over her shoulder. "Russell has kindly offered to escort me home."

A round of goodbyes followed, each friend stopping her long enough to chat and make plans for the summer. By the time she made it outside, exhaustion tinged her tone. "I thought we might say goodbye until time to say hello again to Edith. Goodness!"

"You do know that Smythe now thinks that we've sneaked away to do a little canoodlin'."

"He what!" She glanced over her shoulder as if she could see through brick and flesh into the mind of the now infamous Mr. Smythe.

"Your cryptic message, quite brilliant by the way. There's moonlight; shall I compliment you in some way? I'm accustomed to telling you about your superior and non-existent bicycling skills, but it's hardly fit for romantic conversation."

"Oh, do be serious. This is dreadful. Edith thinks I am indisposed with a feminine ailment, and her mysterious suitor thinks I am flirting with my childhood friend's brother. Could things be any more annoying?"

"Thank you."

Never had the distance from Madeline's eyes to Russell's face seemed so far. "You are far too tall, Mr. Barnes. I cannot see if you are mocking me or the situation—not in this light."

"Or lack of it." Russell laughed. "Now tell me. What has you looking so curious?"

"Cordial—or lack thereof."

"Behavior or refreshment?" Russell asked as he remembered to offer her his arm. "My apologies."

"Certainly." Madeline looped her hand around his arm and continued as if she hadn't been interrupted before she could begin. "Refreshment, if you must know. That is not cordial on Mr. Smythe's cuff." Taking Russell's arm brought her nearer to him, and on a warm evening, it was not the sort of closeness she appreciated. It is my hypothesis that social conventions are created to test our fortitude.

Russell broke through her musing with another question. "Then what is it? I'm sure you have a suspicion."

"It is lip color. I've seen that stain before on Stanley Wakefield's collar once. Mrs. Wakefield had vapors about it for days."

"How can you be sure it's not cordial?"

Madeline's head shook with a decided snap. "I am quite certain. I've spilled enough of the stuff on my clothing to know the difference between complete liquid and a salve."

"Well, no one can argue with the expertise of experience." They paused at her gate. "I suppose you suspect him of dastardly deeds then."

"Not at all. I'm just surprised at Edith. I hadn't noticed her wearing any sort of cosmetic, and she has always said she does hate that kind of thing." Madeline opened the gate. "He brushed a crumb from her cheek—did you see? He must have gotten it then. And there's something more, but I cannot remember what it was. How frustrating." Although she started to close the gate behind her, Russell stepped through. She gave him a curious glance before realizing he likely couldn't see it. "Are you coming in?"

"With such a warm invitation, how could I refuse? Alas, I must not. Still, I see people milling about down at Edith's and did not want to make Miss Merton or Smythe question the sincerity of your words. She will surmise that I am being solicitous of your health. He will congratulate me on my good fortune as to bring you to the door." He paused under the arched, gingerbread encrusted entrance to Mayor Brown of Rockland's home. "And will assume all kinds of intimacies that would likely get me sore shins if I dared."

"You know me well." Madeline squeezed his arm before stepping inside. "Thank you — for walking me home. Papa will be pleased that I didn't ignore convention or inconvenience Ida. It is so much better that I inconvenience you."

"I do have to walk to the trolley anyway."

"Which is in the other direction, but it was a kind thought anyway." As she closed the door behind her, she called, "Goodnight, Russell."

"Oh, I forgot."

She pulled open the door again. "Yes?"

"Have you received a better offer, yet?"

Madeline manufactured a woebegone expression and sighed. "I'm afraid not."

"So sorry to hear it — for your sake, of course. Perhaps next week." He turned away, jogging down the steps with an air that one could only describe as "jaunty" and called out, "Goodnight, Miss Brown. I hope you'll be feeling yourself tomorrow."

With the door shut and a bit of privacy, Madeline allowed herself full enjoyment of Russell's joke. Excellent word choice, my dear Russell. Anyone overhearing you will assume that I am not myself now, but you didn't say that I wasn't, did you?

Lights blazed downstairs, meaning either that her father had not returned or that he left them alight for her. As if I could not manage to scale the heights of the stairs without the lights on in every downstairs room. Silly man. Room by room, she plunged the house into near-darkness before making her way up the slightly curved staircase.

13

The door to her father's bedroom stood ajar as she passed. "I'm home, Papa."

A glance at his pocket watch produced a frown. "You've returned early, haven't you?"

Madeline stepped into the room and smiled at the picture of her father still in his suit, his watch hanging from a fob, and not even his collar button unfastened. He sat in his old, leather armchair, a book perched on his rotund belly, and peered at her over half-spectacles. He's such a stereotypical political figure—if one can call a mayor of a place like Rockland such. Round belly, bald head with those adorable puffs of hair on each side. She ran her fingers through the curled, snowy tufts and smiled. "I do believe you need a haircut."

"I'll see the barber tomorrow, but you didn't answer my question."

"Oh—what question was that? I'm afraid my mind is elsewhere." The moment the words left her lips, Madeline regretted them. Oh, please don't ask me if I walked home alone. You'll just suppose some romantic interest, and you couldn't be more wrong.

"I—well, I suppose it was more of an observation. I just remarked that you are home early."

Madeline moved to turn down her father's bed. "It was so hot in there, Papa. Mr. Merton really must consider electric lighting soon, or Edith will end up back up in the mountains for the summer." Her fists fluffed the pillows as she eyed him. "The expense of that alone would cover the fixtures, surely."

It worked. Albert Brown possessed few defined flaws of character, but enjoying a moment of superiority over a wealthier man was one of his personal and private hobbies. He smiled, stood, kissed her cheek, and sent her off to bed, much gratified to be proven wiser than the great Jonas Merton.

Madeline slipped into her room and began the tedious task of unpinning her hair, brushing it out, undressing, and putting on nightclothes. At times like this, having a personal maid might be a blessing, but then what about the rest of the time? How annoying to have someone hover. I don't know how Edith tolerates it.

Edith. The memory of the tête-à-tête still niggled in her mind. Something about it—I forgot something. What is it? First Edith's vicissitude and now this foray into the use of cosmetics. Positively inconceivable.

The pillow called her. Madeline curled beneath the blankets, reached for her Bible, and read the daily Psalm. With the words of the Psalmist soothing her mind, she soon drifted off to slumber, while across town, a man scrubbed vigorously at his shirt cuffs, a lemon wedge and a bowl of salt at his side.

$\mathcal{T}$wo

She walks though humid is the day, of thickened air and sun-filled skies, and all that's wretch'd of... endless rays.... The rest of the parody almost refused to form, but a slow smile lit Madeline's face as the final words danced in her imagination. *Show in her carriage and her face.*

Jonas Merton's fine, if a bit pretentious for such an infamous miser, home loomed before her. Their boy, Jimmy Higgins, swept the front walk with careful diligence. *I should hire him on occasion. The gutters likely need inspecting or some such task of dubious consequence. He seems a multi-eloquent lad.*

"Mornin', miss. Hot enough to drive you stir-crazy, ain't it?"

"That it is, Jimmy." Madeline paused and watched with feigned interest and admiration before she asked, "Do they keep you busy here *all* day?"

"Nope. I just gots to clean up after Miss Edith's party—stuff outside, y'know—and then I'm off."

Excellent. "Well, what would you charge to do odd errands and chores around our house?"

"Miss Merton pays me a jitney an hour, miss."

And likely out of her pocket allowance to prevent her father's expostulations over the household accounts. Madeline smiled at Jimmy as she nodded. *As if a nickel per hour would break anyone. It's almost shameful.* Her plan formed and morphed at dizzying speeds. She fished a nickel out of her purse and passed it to him. "I'll pay you a nickel up front...." She fished out a quarter as well. " —if you'll be so good as to run to the grocer and fetch a pound of butter when you're done here. By that time, I should be home. I believe we have gutters in need of cleaning and various other odds and ends."

"I'll hurry. And thanks!"

"Please don't, Jimmy. Mary won't know what to have you do if you arrive before I do. Just take your time."

The boy stopped mid-swipe of the broom and stared at her. Madeline arranged her face into as placid an expression as she could manage. Then it happened. A slow smile formed on the boy's freckled face. He nodded and went back to work again.

Just as she stepped past him, Madeline would have insisted she heard him mutter, "Never know what a fella might learn by takin' the time to do a job right."

You'd never know indeed.

Ida opened the door with such pain in her eyes that Madeline didn't hesitate. "I brought you clove oil, Ida. My aunt is plagued with tooth problems, and she swears by its healing properties. Just pour a little on a clean bit of cloth and bite down on it. She also says a good brushing will hurt but then take it away."

"Thank you, Miss Brown. I will."

"You really should see a dentist."

The girl's eyes dropped. "Can't afford the time off."

Translate that to, "Mr. Merton won't allow me the time off," Madeline growled to herself.

"But my sister's husband is going to try to pull it tonight."

Translation: Mr. Merton will dock me if I'm not there on Monday, so I'll have to miss Mass tomorrow while I recuperate from a clumsy extraction.

Ida led her into the grand entryway and gestured around the staircase. "Miss Edith is practicing the piano. Would you care to come through?"

"I would. Thank you. Do try the clove oil right away. I think you'll find it helps."

A sour note greeted Madeline as she stepped into the Mertons' music room. *Why can she not possess the talent she so desires. I know of no one who expends more effort in the pursuit of something so important to happiness.* Another sour note punctuated her next thought. *And despite hours of practicing, she's little better than mediocre.*

Edith looked up just at that moment and rose to greet her. "Madeline! You're feeling better, I trust?"

The girls met in the middle of the room and greeted one another with a quick embrace and a kiss that never quite reached the cheek. "I am, thank you. I came to apologize for leaving so abruptly."

Edith's sweet smile belied the girl's words. "I told Papa that the heat is just too obnoxious to bear. I'll be forced to withdraw to the mountains soon if it doesn't break."

She didn't have the heart to remind her friend that summer had not yet even begun, so instead, Madeline chose a seat on a bench near an open window and patted the spot beside her. "So tell me what I missed. Is Flossie still not speaking to Warren?"

Edith's eyes lit up as she leaned closer and in a conspiratorial whisper said, "He came in with an assumed air of nonchalance and began talking to Milty Grueber. He fooled no one, of course. He hadn't been here for ten minutes before I saw him corner her by the Aphrodite in the dining room."

"Oh, I missed that. Considering she sat with you later in the evening, I assume his apologies were for naught?"

"That's just the most confusing thing. Mr. Smythe said Flossie would have forgiven him had he actually *asked* for forgiveness. He says that any man of sense would know this. But since Warren didn't, he thinks Warren is innocent."

There is some sense in that.

"What do you think, Madeline?"

"I think Mr. Smythe makes an excellent point. Just as you said that, my first thought was that I've never observed Warren to be above apology. I wonder that she's so set on the idea of him having gone to that burlesque show."

Edith glanced around her as if anyone *could* overhear, even if they chose to, and murmured, "Stella's brother insists he saw Warren entering with a few other young men — no one else of our acquaintance, of course."

"Of course...."

When she didn't respond, Edith leaned a bit closer. "What is it, Madeline? I can see you have an idea brewing."

"It's just," she began hesitantly. "It's only that I find it curious as to why Flossie would give weight to Stanley Wakefield's account. He could only make such an accusation if he were present at that time, wouldn't you think?" With an arch smile, she added, "And why else would Stanley be in that particular place at that exact moment unless...."

"Ohh! You are so clever! I must ask Vernon what he thinks about that!"

Vernon, is it? Why, Edith, I believe I greatly underestimated you. She started and gave herself a little shake. "Did Mr. Smythe ever get the stain off his cuff?"

"I don't know. I tried to encourage him to allow Ida to take care of it, but of course, he wouldn't. He said...." Edith's eyes scanned the room as if spies might be lurking about, ready to hear her deepest secrets. She leaned close and whispered, "He said, 'I wouldn't care to leave you alone with so many unattached gentlemen in the room. You might find you preferred someone else's company.'"

Hope welled up in Madeline's heart. Marriage would be the best thing for her friend — out from under the harsh rule of a father such as Mr. Merton often was. "Well, he seemed most attentive to you. I know so little of him. Where is he from again?"

"He has family in the East — Boston, I believe. He came here from Chicago on business and found it so congenial that he stayed."

It would appear that he found your company satisfactory, anyway. "And just what is his occupation? I don't believe I've ever heard anyone say."

"He's in finance. I think that's why Papa enjoys his company so much." Edith dropped her gaze to her hands. "That's how I met him, you know. He came to dinner one night and...."

And somehow found the banker's daughter fascinating, I'm sure. Madeline, as much as she ached to, did not allow herself to finish the thought. Whatever Edith's deficiencies in the beauty or vivacity departments, no young lady of their acquaintance had a kinder disposition or a more generous heart. *And there are men who find those qualities far more attractive than a mere pretty face or stimulating conversation.* But whatever internal concessions Madeline made, she couldn't help but be surprised that a man such as Vernon Smythe would be one such fellow. *I would have imagined him much more of a Romeo than Galahad.*

The conversation had lapsed too long. Madeline offered an opening. "Well, you don't seem averse to him."

And with those words, Edith nearly erupted in a gushing geyser of information about the man's compliments and dreams. "He plans to settle here, you know. Well, unless he is fortunate enough to marry and his wife would 'prefer a little distance from her family.' Then he'll be content to move to Philadelphia or some other eastern city."

Ahh... the man is no fool. Spoken that way, he has ensured her agreement not to live too near Rockland should they marry. I would not wish to live near Mr. Merton if he were my father-in-law. But despite her understanding of the man's objections, the idea of Edith moving such a distance predisposed her to dislike the idea.

"I should miss you if *you* were to marry and leave Rockland."

"But you could visit me, couldn't you? I know how much you enjoyed your travels to Boston and New York."

Except that New York City was not nearly as delightful as I'd

21

expected it to be. Interesting, to be sure. But instead of forests of trees, it seemed as though the place was a forest of buildings, and the people grew up like weeds about them.

"Madeline?"

"Oh, yes. Sorry. I was remembering New York. I am pleased to hear he—I mean *you*—have no intention of settling there." At the sight of Edith's rosy cheeks, Madeline smiled. "You are so lovely when you blush, Edith dear."

"Did you ever imagine a man such as Vernon Smythe showing any interest in someone like me? I have only Papa's money to recommend me, and Vernon doesn't seem interested in it."

He is likely wise enough to know that Mr. Merton will see a marriage as a savings rather than an opportunity to be generous. Her conscience smote her as the thought faded. *I am quite unpleasant today. I wonder at such recalcitrant thoughts. For shame, Madeline! Be pleasant.*

So, properly self-chastised Madeline turned her attention to soothing Edith's sensitive spirit. "Well, as I said, you are lovely when you have color in your face. Why, last night I noticed the faintest touch of it in your cheeks and lips. No one I know uses rouge or lip stain so perfectly. No one would ever have—"

"Madeline Brown! I never! You know how I feel about such things. Vulgar in the extreme! How could you even suggest something so unladylike?!"

Her apologies formed, soothed, and in less than a minute, Edith's characteristic pleasantness returned. "And this is why any man would be fortunate to secure your affections. You are so kind, so amiable. It's why we all love you so dearly. I'm sure Mr. Smythe would say as much as well."

Before Edith could reply, Ida stepped into the room. "Pardon me, miss, but you did ask me to remind you...."

"Oh, yes! Thank you, Ida. Is your tooth quite well now?"

"Thanks to Miss Brown's oil, yes. Thank you." With that, Ida skittered from the room.

"I'm sorry, Madeline. Papa has Mr. Smythe coming for luncheon. Would you care to stay or...."

The temptation nearly overrode her common sense, but Madeline sighed. "You know how much I would love to. I haven't spoken much to Mr. Smythe. I think it would be pleasant to become better acquainted with my friend's favorite. But Papa has that dinner tonight. I'm needed at home to make sure all is well. So, I'll satisfy myself with soup and bread while you enjoy yourself without me."

At the door, she kissed her friend's cheek. "I'm very happy for you. I hope he proves to be everything you could hope for."

"I knew you would be, Madeline. Flossie is jealous, of course, so she said some rather unpleasant things." Edith gave herself a little shake, as if admitting such unpleasantness was more than she could bear. "Thank you. And I'm glad you are feeling so much better."

Madeline walked with a light step down the long walkway to the street. She waved at Jimmy who now stood at a precarious angle on a ladder, soaping up one of the windows on the side of the house. "I'll see you later, Jimmy!"

The Brown dining room had been endowed with the convenience of electric lights but without the pleasing aesthetic of a lovely chandelier. As forward thinking as Mayor Brown was, his pocketbook hadn't yet allowed for the expense of the purchase and installation of a more attractive light fixture than three bulbs strung together over the table. So, Madeline and Mary had spent the better part of an hour draping and securing flowers and greenery over the bulbs and wires in an attempt at camouflage. The results, as seen in the light of the trio of candelabras on the long cherry wood table, proved quite satisfactory, and the heat of the bulbs near the blossoms helped perfume the room with floral fragrance. However, as she sat in her seat at the foot of the table, Madeline's eyes watched the decor with grave concern.

That lilac droops lower with every passing second. If Providence doesn't intervene post-haste, Mrs. Estershire will likely enjoy a garnish to her veal. Would the other ladies feel deprived, I wonder.

"—feel better today." Russell's voice snapped Madeline from her ponderings and into the moment again.

You did that deliberately, Mr. Barnes. Beware my retaliation. Of course, she would never say anything of the kind. Rather, her smile as she took another bite of her creamed peas warned of coming repartee. With fork down, creamy linen napkin at the ready to dab imaginary dribbles at the corners of her lips, Madeline turned full attention to him and smiled. "Better, really?" At his amused smirk, she added, "Why, yes. I do feel quite well today. The heat was, of course, unbearable while I walked to Edith's house, but an afternoon of preparation for the party this evening ensured I was rested and cool again."

It almost worked. Russell managed to stifle a choked response and instead, leveled a penetrating gaze on her—watery eyes and all. "And how is Miss Merton today?"

Do you not ever weary of the tediousness of polite conversation? While Papa and his friends discuss things that make a difference in our world, I, as a young lady, am relegated to discussions of parties and other outings. I want to tell you about my conversation. But how?

An idea formed and Madeline allowed it to emerge full bloom before she answered his question. "As you can imagine, she was in good spirits after the party. I found her practicing her piano and waiting for a luncheon guest."

"I see. You did not stay, I presume?"

If you do not take heed to what I say and read between the lines, as it were, we'll have little more than a dialogue de sourds. *Pay attention, Russell, or I shall inform Amy that her brother has grown unobservant in her absence. Imagine the fun she can have without you to prevent her.*

24

Madeline tried again. "As much as I would have enjoyed meeting with and talking to the guest of honor, I did have this party and its preparations to attend to."

At that moment, a floret fluttered to the table, missing Mrs. Estershire's hand by a fraction of an inch. Russell, once more, stifled his amusement. His eyes twinkled at her in the candlelight. "Oh? Do I know her guest? I spent so much time at billiards last night that I wasn't able to visit with the others for long."

At last! "Mr. Smythe was expected just as I left. I would have delayed to inquire about the success of his stain removal, but...."

"I suppose Miss Merton didn't know yet either." He leaned close and murmured, "Was she aware of the full extent of the stain?"

"I'm afraid not, and only her claret can be blamed for it. As to the other...." Madeline allowed her words to trail off, waited for those around them to speak, and added, "I did so want to hear about his financial interests. Little Jimmy Higgins said he'd overheard something about an interest in electricity." She hesitated, choosing each word carefully, before finishing her thought. "Although. Edith is a dear girl; I doubt she paid much attention to that sort of thing."

Madeline's eyes rose as yet another floret fell. The lilac now remained connected to the floral arrangement by what appeared to be a single thin stem. *Oh, help.*

The alderman's wife, Mrs. Bletchley, turned to Madeline with an expression on her face that surely meant some embarrassing comment or question. Everyone has a talent for something. Adeline Bletchley's was to mortify anyone within earshot of her garrulous voice. "Miss Brown...."

Providence indeed watches over the smallest details. From the hairs on our heads to the tiniest of sparrows as they crash to the ground in death, He notices and intervenes. Just as Mrs. Bletchley spoke, the precariously perched lilac blossom plopped unceremoniously into Mrs. Estershire's plate. The woman jumped, squealed, and then fanned herself with such vigor that Madeline

25

would have suspected it would warm her more than cool her.

"Oh, Mrs. Estershire!" Madeline dropped her napkin in her seat and hastened to the woman's aid. "I do apologize. Our skills with aerial floral arrangements are clearly lacking." Mary appeared, hands out and ready to take the woman's plate. "Let Mary replace your dish. Did it splash your dress? Do you need—?"

"Please, my dear. Please don't give it another thought." Just as Madeline bent to pick up the florets that had preceded the excitement, she heard the woman murmur, "It's the most exciting thing that's happened at one of these dinners in an age."

Madeline gave the woman a small smile and hurried back to her seat before her father's dinner was any further interrupted. *When one asks help from Providence, one should be prepared for the consequences. Still,* Madeline mused, *I am grateful.*

Beside her, Russell once more stifled a snicker or a chuckle. He must have sensed her mortification, because he turned to the others at the table, waited for a lull, and asked, "Has anyone heard much about Vernon Smythe's electrical ideas? I overheard something about it recently, but I'm not privy to the details."

Overheard.... That's stretching the truth, isn't it, Russell? You heard directly only moments ago.

But Russell's query produced exactly the response he'd intended. The table erupted in animated discussion—almost evenly divided on the subject. Madeline listened, trying to piece together the details of the idea. As information flowed in the short snatches that she heard, Madeline turned to Russell. "Do you really think it can be done? Electricity in every home at such an affordable rate? I can't imagine!"

Russell's eyes lit up—whether because of the topic or some impending joke, she couldn't tell—and he leaned forward, his food forgotten. "Absolutely. It's simple economics. If you have to make just enough cable for one house, it'll cost significantly more per foot than if you manufacture enough for five hundred homes. I can't determine much from the few details I've heard, but it sounds like a feasible idea. If such a scheme became a reality, and if I had the money, I would be tempted to invest myself."

Electricity in every home.... Her eyes rose to the floral arrangement covering the bulbs that hung above the table. *I wonder if such a plan would include attractive ways to provide lighting. Now that would be worth investing in.*

But despite her curiosity over the feasibility of such an idea, one thought overrode it all. *And would this sort of endeavor, should Mr. Smythe undertake such a scheme, be enough to secure him financially? Perhaps make it possible for him to marry?*

The guests milled about the Brown's understated terrace, but Madeline hung back, watching, listening. From a nearby column, Russell Barnes had the advantage of seeing all and hearing more than might be supposed.

Just what has you lost in thought, Miss Madeline? Amy would know. Indeed, if I could capture this moment and mail it to her across the ocean, Amy could tell me exactly what you were thinking or feeling.

" — Barnes, how goes the architectural business? Are you vying for that arts center project?"

Despite the interruption of his thoughts, Russell turned to Mr. Estershire and gave his full attention to the man. "We are at that. I think we have an excellent design planned. I hope we will be awarded the project. My employers have promised that I'll be assigned to it if we are." Russell couldn't help but take the opportunity to try to inveigle a little information from the man. "I haven't yet heard if we will be trying a more modern approach with glass and steel or if we will be focused on a more classic design. There are advantages to both, of course."

Thankfully, Herbert Estershire proved eager to discuss it. "I often wonder if there isn't some way to combine both classic and modern aesthetics. If it could be done, and done well, it would appease both the traditionalists and those who are more, shall we say, *avant-garde* in their tastes."

"Or, would it perhaps be a means of ensuring that no one liked it?" Russell allowed his words to settle in for just a moment before he added, "However, that thought appeals to my *personal* aesthetic. I see much beauty in the newer, cleaner lines, but I can see the logical progression to sterility in architecture, and that would be a shame."

"An excellent observation, Mr. Barnes. I cannot say that I've considered the idea. But I think if you can combine both, and do it well, your firm is well set to be awarded the project. I happen to know...." Mr. Estershire lowered his voice and stepped a little closer. "That the head of the committee is not keen on Fuller and Blum for the job, and that leaves only two real candidates. Zimmerman and Hague have, of course, an excellent reputation, but their lines do fall quite sharply on the modernist side of things."

What the man said next, Russell never heard. He left the man staring after him with a confused expression, but that almost didn't register in Russell's consciousness. Madeline had overheard or seen something that intrigued her, and this he needed to investigate.

When Amy asked me to watch over you while she is away, I didn't mind too much, but I did expect it to be a bit tedious at times. I should have known better. Now what has you so intrigued...?

He made his way to her side and stood just behind her. "What amuses you so, Madeline?"

"Amused?" An impish quality filled her tone as she repeated, "I look amused?"

Her head turned as she looked up at him. Once in a while, and particularly at unguarded moments such as these, Russell caught a glimpse of the woman she would become. *You are going to be a beautiful woman — not classically stunning like Flossie Hardwick or*

Elizabeth Denton. No, much like the building Mr. Estershire and I discussed, you will be an interesting blend of classical and modern beauty. I wonder which one will take precedence.

" —ssell?"

His thoughts evaporated in the intensity of her gaze. "I apologize, Madeline. I don't have your talent for hiding my lack of attention to a conversation."

"Well, as we saw last night, my purported skill is not as great as I would have wished. Now tell me, why do I look amused?"

"Perhaps that's the wrong word. I saw something in your face that hinted you were interested in something you'd seen or heard."

"How observant of you." She turned back to gaze out over the terrace — or was it the yard? — before adding, "I've found that many men aren't."

Several possible explanations presented themselves, but Russell chose the one he assumed she would expect. "I've had to learn to be, or Amy would decide to cut her trip short and return home to tell me exactly what she thought of my lack of attention to your welfare."

"Poor, dear Russell. He cannot have the carefree bachelor life he so desires, because his little sister plagues him with duties to her dearest friend. I shouldn't allow it." She stiffened at something, but her words never faltered. "But, of course, I miss her a little less with you to torment."

"And what has you ruffled now? I saw it. You froze for a moment."

Madeline turned to face him. "Now, really, Russell. You will become obnoxious if you observe more than you ought." But seeing his interest provided all the encouragement she needed to continue. "See my Aunt Louisa over there?"

"Yes...?"

"I am almost certain I just saw her mention Mr. Smythe's electrical idea. And then she looked directly at *me*. Now why would she do that? I wonder."

The woman in question did indeed seem to be trying to observe her niece. After several seconds of watching the scene, the woman's eyes met his and held for a moment before she turned back to her conversation again. "Well, I would have presumed she had been discussing Edith and naturally glanced your way, but the look she just gave me...." Russell smiled down at her confused expression. "I do believe she is now considering the wisdom of you forming an attachment to your dear friend's older, rakish brother."

Madeline snorted. Her hand flew to her nose to stifle it, but too late. "Rakish—*you*? That is...." She shook her head. "No, I'm afraid there are no words."

"There." He nudged her elbow with one finger. "She was eying us again. You will have to admit your lack of interest in the matrimonial department, or she will be setting up dinner parties with us as partners."

Madeline turned to him, folded her arms over her chest, and jutted out her chin in that way that always preceded a pert comment. "And that is exactly why I will appear to flirt with you, if you don't mind." She leaned closer and whispered, "I do so prefer Auntie's parties when I am not saddled with yet another eligible bachelor who either wishes to be as far away from me as I wish to be from him, or worse...."

"Decides to propose at an impudent pace?"

She rocked back on her heels and nodded. "Precisely, my dear Russell. You, on the other hand, would be more likely to save a lady from an unwelcome proposal rather than offer one."

"I will take that as a compliment." Russell glanced at Louisa Farnsworth, but the woman had moved indoors. *And you could learn a lesson or two about managing your niece, Mrs. Farnsworth.*

"You should." Madeline waited for him to come back to the present and look at her before she added, "It was meant as the very best."

As much as it annoyed him to do it, Russell nodded toward the doors leading out from the dining room. "I see a few people behaving as though they are ready to leave. Why don't I wait out here until everyone is gone? We can take a walk through your delightfully cool garden."

"I'll be back as soon as I can." A few steps away, she turned back. "Thank you, Russell."

And as he watched her disappear into the house, Russell couldn't help but wonder why Madeline's thanks always held a deeper note than anyone else's. *Perhaps because she wouldn't offer them unless she meant them. If she could avoid it, that is.*

*T*HREE

The trolley wound its way down streets, around corners, and into downtown Rockland. At Waterbrook Avenue, Madeline stepped off the car and wandered up the street in search of the perfect gift for her aunt's upcoming birthday. *I should buy her a hat – something with heavy netting....* A new idea prompted a smile that, had anyone paid attention, could only have been described as diabolical. *And in black. No one would blame me. Especially after that last atrocity she foisted on me.*

As she knew would happen, Madeline found herself wandering into Gardner & Henley's Booksellers. She'd been waiting weeks for the next edition of *The Strand,* and while she could no longer hope to find Sherlock Holmes stories in it, she did enjoy Arthur Conan Doyle's other stories. The mere thought of the author's name sent a wave of outrage through her. *He had no business killing off his best character.*

The clerk stood on a high shelf, dusting the tops of cases. "Miss Brown! I hoped you would come in soon. *The Strand* arrived just the other day. There's a new 'Strange Studies from Life' story in it."

With a happy wave, and a lilt in her step, Madeline hurried to where the display of magazines would be. *I should have noticed it in the window. How odd that I didn't.*

The clerk moved to her side and pointed out a new puzzle and the story. "Business is bustling, miss. Why, here we have this humdinger of a new magazine and haven't had a moment to fix it in the display yet." The young man raised his voice to a snooty falsetto—quite a fine imitation of the owner's wife. "'We must keep the shop clean and tidy. Ignoring basic housekeeping in favor of financial gain is *vulgar.*'"

"Well, I'm happy for my part." Madeline didn't even look up from the pages as she turned them. "You might have been sold out by now!"

"The boss always keeps one for you, Miss Brown. We can't have the *mayor's* daughter waiting for her copy of her favorite magazine; can we?"

Madeline smiled at him, but a man passed by the magazine-less display window—a person she very much desired to speak with. Quick as she could, Madeline fished a dime from her purse and handed it to the young man. "I—have somewhere to be. So sorry."

Without waiting for him to wrap the magazine, Madeline stepped outside the shop and strode after Vernon Smythe as quickly as propriety permitted. At the corner, she saw him step up to a taxicab and ask the driver to take him to the "Dry Docks."

Now what business do you have down there? As she mused, she raced to the next taxicab. She climbed in before the driver could hop down and open the door for her. "Please follow the taxicab there— that one with the black horse."

Though not easy, she watched from the window as the horses wound through the streets—streets that grew narrower and dirtier the farther into the city they rode. The noise level grew with each passing street, and as if a byproduct of the din, odors grew more and more pungent. *Papa would not like to see me down here, but why is that man coming this way? Surely, Mr. Smythe doesn't have business in this part of town. He's in finance. Isn't he?*

Just as the taxicab ahead turned a corner, her driver pulled up short. "I'm sorry, miss, but I cannot take you any farther."

"Indeed, why not? I have the fare, if that is your—"

"I don't want your money, nor do I want the responsibility of bringing a young lady into this part of town. Your father wouldn't wish to have you here; I'm sure."

It took two hard swallows before Madeline trusted her voice. "And how would you know what my father would or wouldn't wish? I *need* to speak to that man. Please drive on!"

The driver refused. Furious, Madeline stumbled from the taxicab and pulled out her pocketbook. "Just how much—"

"Miss, put that away. Do you want to have it pinched?"

"I insist on paying you. Wha—?"

The driver spat out the price of the fare with an oath Madeline suspected he usually wouldn't utter in the presence of ladies. And, by the way he didn't beg her pardon, she also suspected he didn't realize he'd done it. The moment his fingers closed around her coins, Madeline turned and dashed up the street, heedless of propriety. She held her skirts almost to her calves to keep them out of the filth, and picked her way around dubious looking puddles and deposits left by other horses.

There shouldn't be puddles. We haven't had rain in over a week.

At the corner, Madeline peered around one side and scanned the area for the taxicab with the glossy black horse. It came straight toward her. Madeline's heart raced as she tried to hide behind a tower of wooden crates, but as it passed, it appeared empty. *Is he reclining back in the seat, or did he send it away again?*

It would be impossible to follow now, so Madeline crept forward, her eyes still surveying the area. Dirty children raced through the streets with matted hair and patched clothing. Clean children also played and worked among the rest, wearing clothing just as patched but looking infinitely less ragged by their mere cleanliness. Men worked, carrying heavy loads off wagons and into warehouses or out of them. The stench of stale sweat permeated every square inch of air.

Madeline pulled a handkerchief from her purse and used it to try to mask the stench of unwashed bodies, manure, and sulfur. *Why is there such a sulfuric odor down here?*

She should have turned back. Nothing in the area hinted at Mr. Smythe's presence, but morbid fascination with horrors she'd only heard vague references to kept her picking her way through the streets.

Then, ahead, she saw Mr. Smythe talking with a woman. Instinct demanded she hide—this time beside a horse as it stood waiting for its driver to return. *I wonder what would happen if I went up to him and asked for his assistance? After all, I was abandoned by my driver.* The moment she thought it, Madeline dismissed the idea. *Such a deliberate deception. I cannot do it.*

As the thoughts swirled in her mind, another woman stepped from the building—younger, prettier than the first. She curtsied. Mr. Smythe slipped an arm around her waist and turned to enter the building. The moment they disappeared inside, Madeline bolted from her hiding space and rushed across the street. In her haste, she nearly stepped directly in a fresh pile of dung. Alas, a last second jog to one side turned her ankle somewhat but kept her from destroying her favorite shoes.

The first woman stood on the porch and watched with initial amusement, but as Madeline stepped forward, her expression changed to concern. "What are you doing here?"

"I just thought I saw a man I know—well, I don't *know* him. I met him at a friend's house the other evening, and...." Madeline blinked twice. "What was the question again?"

With a grip that would leave a mark, the woman jerked Madeline off the porch and dragged her across the street. "You need to get out of here. It's not safe for a girl like you—"

She couldn't help but query, "But it's safe for a woman like you?"

"I have my... protectors. No one would dare molest *me*, but you with your lace and your gloves...." She eyed Madeline's purse. "Tuck that away! You would be safer to wave it about and offer it to the first person who knocks you down."

Indignation welled up in her, and Madeline resisted. The attempt, however, proved futile. The woman's iron-grip held fast as she dragged Madeline around the corner again. "There—see that taxicab?"

Madeline nearly screamed in vexation at the sight of "her" taxicab waiting just a few dozen yards ahead. "Yes…?"

"Get in it and get out of here. Don't ever come back. Stay uptown where your kind belongs."

"I—"

The woman stared at Madeline for a moment before her features relaxed. "I—I'm sorry. I don't mean to be harsh. I'm fearful for your safety. That's all it is. Please, go home. Stay away from this place."

"But my friend, Mr. Smythe—or rather—"

The woman interrupted with a stern, unyielding look and tone. "Your friend's, friend. I know. If he's truly down here, I suspect it's on business, and you know how men are about business. They don't care to be interrupted. Talk to him the next time you see him, but don't follow him or anyone else into the Dry Docks again."

Madeline turned to go, but the woman called out to her again. "You have a lovely sense of style, my dear. That burgundy check and poplin skirt—beautiful combination."

The compliment seemed odd for the situation. *First you warn me of the malevolent dangers lurking behind every corner, every pair of eyes, and then you tell me I have a "lovely sense of style"? I can't comprehend what could possibly prompt such… flattery.* But as she stepped toward the taxicab, Madeline smiled at the woman, taking note just how weary the woman looked when she took the time to notice. "Thank you."

"Now go. *Please*."

Once settled in the taxicab and on her way out of the district, Madeline closed her eyes, pressed her handkerchief to her nose, and mulled over the brief but intriguing events of the afternoon. "I'll have to see what Russell thinks of Mr. Smythe's visit down there." Though murmured under her breath, the words reverberated in her mind until she wanted to cover her ears with her hands to drown out the noise. *On the other hand, why bother him with something that is likely nothing? As the woman said, if it* was *Mr. Smythe, he likely was there on business and wouldn't appreciate learning that one of Edith's friends followed him. Yes, I wouldn't care to be the cause of discomfort for Edith.*

That thought settled the idea in her mind. Mr. Smythe had been in the area on business—assuming she had not mistaken someone else for him—and she did not need to risk a breach in Edith's budding romance because her curiosity overrode her good sense.

The woman spoke to him. If it were Mr. Smythe, she surely would have shown some sign of recognition at the name. She showed none. However, if it was business, why did he have his arm around that young woman's waist? It is curious.

Only a wisp of wind off the river afforded the residents of southern Rockland any relief from the evening's stifling heat. Russell mopped his forehead with his handkerchief as Mary led him through the parlor. "She's out in the yard, Mr. Barnes. It's cooler out there."

"I'll see myself outside, Mary. Thank you."

From the terrace, he spied her seated on her old swing and using the tips of her shoes to push her in slow, lazy sweeps. *That must create a pleasant breeze as well.*

As he neared, he expected her to turn and make some comment—perhaps about visiting too often and the impression it might make on others. *I can't ignore it is likely, but neither will I leave her to her own devices. Even if Amy would forgive me, I don't believe I could forgive myself.*

But lost in thought, she didn't notice him at all—something Russell found most unusual. He couldn't resist. As he took a step or two closer, he spoke aloud. "I believe you have the most pleasant yard in town—so cool and refreshing."

Madeline whirled, twisting the ropes on the swing as she faced Russell. "You startled me!"

"Then I succeeded. Excellent." He gestured his offer to push her, and as inappropriate as it might be for a young lady of her age, Madeline nodded.

"Thank you, Russell."

She didn't speak for some time, and if she were more like other young ladies, Russell might have suspected that the heat left her without the inclination toward conversation. But something in her carriage, the way she didn't relax as the swing carried her through cooling breezes—these things told him that something occupied her mind. *But will she tell me, or must I inveigle it out of her?*

"Russell, have you much business in the Dry Docks quarter?"

Of all the things you could ask about — why that? Russell gave the swing a great shove before moving to stand in front of her. Despite every effort to read her expression, Madeline's face remained blank—almost *too* blank.

"Well...." Again he gave her a pointed look before continuing. "I suppose I *could* be hired by one of the companies with warehouses down there. I can't imagine why, but it seems possible. If they needed a specific building design?" He knew he rambled, but despite every effort to hide his discomfort with the question, he continued talking until he found an answer that might satisfy. With any luck, and a liberal dose of Providential care, she would assume he had to work through the idea. "I believe it is possible, yes. But I don't believe it's likely. Why?"

"I just wondered *who* might have business there." Madeline jumped from the swing and began walking along the path toward the house. "For example, Papa. Today, I realized for the first time that Papa might have cause to go down there. Isn't it considered quite dangerous?"

This isn't a casual question is it, Maddie? There's something to it. But how do I get you to tell me? If I'm not careful, I'll give away my purpose.

Madeline's voice broke through his thoughts. "And if it *is* such a terrible place, why isn't something being done about it?"

In the Brown's bright, spacious kitchen, Mary met them with arms full of clean kitchen linens. She jerked her head toward the dining room. "I put mincemeat pie in there for both of you." As Madeline thanked her, she added, "That Jimmy Higgins was just here. He brought word that Mr. Brown won't be home till late."

"Thank you, Mary. Would you bring in coffee as well, please?"

"Of course, miss. I'll just put these away. Cook's already gone home."

Russell smiled his thanks before following Madeline to the table. His eyes scanned the long cherry wood table and marveled at how different it looked when nearly empty. He held her chair as she seated herself and sensed something. How, he couldn't have explained, but he sensed it. She would wait for him to take his first bite before she spoke — deliberately wait.

"Just what *is* so awful about the Dry Docks, and who gave it such a ridiculous name?"

His reluctance to discuss the unsavory nature of the area dissolved in a question he *could* answer without delving into topics her father wouldn't appreciate, even had he been so inclined. "Well, it's named that because it's somewhat comparable to a shipping port. Trains and wagons — the Wells Fargo Company, of course — send their shipments of things there. Then they're stored and sent out to the stores in town and the area. It's like a shipping port — a dock without water."

"I see...." Russell heard much too much interest in her tone than fit the question. "It is such a simple explanation. I mistakenly assumed that I was mistaken."

And you just gave yourself away there. You added in the question about the name to get me talking. Unsure how to extricate himself from further discussion, Russell jumped up, nearly knocking over the Queen Anne chair in his haste. "I think I should help Mary. Without Cook here, she's probably busy. I can at least carry a tray."

His explanation—ridiculous to his own ears—brought an amused smile to her lips. However, it did seem as if it worked. When he returned, she poured their coffee—even allowed him to take a drink—without a word. Russell relaxed just a few seconds too soon.

"You see, I overheard one of the girls talking." A hint of pink tinged her cheeks, leaving him to wonder if it was modesty or disingenuousness. "I won't say whom, to avoid a charge of gossip—and she showed concern for someone in our set being seen down there."

Russell almost choked, causing his eyes to bug a bit, but he managed to take another sip of coffee and stifle the urge. Madeline waited with almost nonchalant patience until he answered the implied question. "Well, some of the fellows do have shipping interests." His mind shuffled through a dozen names before the most logical one appeared. "Chester's father, for instance."

Madeline latched onto that statement with great eagerness. "Let's just say it *was* Chester." She gave him an enigmatic smile. "It wasn't, of course, but let's assume it was. Why would Chester enter that area in the company of a young woman if it isn't *safe* for a young woman down there?"

Oh, Madeline. I can't answer that. If you thought about it, of course, you'd know. I can't imagine who we know that—unless Stanley Wakefield…. He's been a bit fast lately.

"I imagine it's possible," Madeline began as she speared a piece of the pie, "that he knows a young woman down there who needs help." She gave him a curious expression. "I imagine some young women without family might find themselves in difficult circumstances—forced to do things I can't and don't *want* to

41

imagine."

Russell stared at her, trying to read her expression, filter her words, translate them into understandable sentences. *What are you – ?*

But once more, Madeline shifted the subject just slightly. "Oh, well. I suppose that if there is something our league can do to help, someone will inform us. Until then, I imagine all we can do is pray."

Relief washed over him—likely visibly—but Russell didn't care. *As long as you think that, we'll both be more comfortable.* He set his fork on his empty plate and nodded. "That is, of course, one of the best things you can do in situations such as these."

She invited him into the parlor to help with her jigsaw puzzle, but something in her eyes, or perhaps it was her carriage—something hinted that she only had *more* questions unanswered. *I believe you need something to occupy your time. If I can't get you on a wheel, perhaps some other hobby.*

$\mathcal{F}$OUR

Do be a dear and call the meeting to order, Flossie. Someone will notice that I'm in a swivet, and that will undo everything I hoped to accomplish. If I must endure such tediousness as this committee, I'd like to attempt to make it useful.

"Did you have something to say before we begin, Madeline?" Flossie Hardwick's tone implied that the girl had become piqued — likely about Madeline's supposed impending interference with the meeting.

Realizing she must have been staring intently at something or another, Madeline dropped her eyes in front of her. "Not at all. I think we should begin immediately."

It began. Roll call, the reading of the minutes from the past meeting, updates from subcommittees, ticket sales. *Can our plans become any more asinine? Why won't people simply subscribe to the children's charity and be done with it? Why must everything require an event?*

The question presented itself at every meeting. As far as Madeline knew, it had one answer — only one. *Because, without these ridiculous committees, we're all quite useless creatures.*

"Madeline, have you contrived to convince the ladies auxiliary to help with the effort?"

Oh, yes, my token usefulness. "My aunt has promised to do so. She says she can guarantee their wholehearted support. 'Who could deny the children?'"

"Who, indeed?" Flossie's agreement received nods of approval that made the room look like hens bobbing at worms.

But, at last, the meeting drew to a close. "Is there any other business?" Just as Flossie reached for the gavel, Madeline raised her hand. "Madeline? What have we missed?" Her eyes scanned the room. "Trust Madeline's thoroughness. We can always count on her not to forget anything."

"Oh, but you've done a lovely job, as usual, Flossie. I just had a harrowing experience last week, and it has weighed heavily on my mind. I wondered...." Madeline counted to three—just one second shy of Flossie urging her to continue, if experience applied. "You see, I thought I saw a friend in a taxicab and impulsively jumped in one myself—to follow, you know." By the looks of the others, they did *not* know, but no one seemed to be surprised that *she* would do such a thing.

"Go on."

"Well, I found myself just inside the Dry Doc—"

A gasp erupted somewhere in the room and created a domino effect. One after the other, her friends gaped at the horrifying idea of being found anywhere near such a rough place. Flossie, on the other hand, seemed rather intrigued. "Did you really? What was it like? My brother refuses to speak of it with me."

I didn't know you had any kind of an adventurous spirit. Well done, Floss! But aloud, she transformed her near-jubilation to semi-feigned sadness. "Its reputation is well-earned. I can't tell you how many half-dressed, dirty children I saw. And even the clean ones wore clothes that had long outlived their usefulness. It's truly one of the saddest things I've ever witnessed."

And there she left her words—just a well-timed show of concern and someone would come to her after the meeting. *I wonder who here knows what the rest of us don't. We shall see.*

Ruth Parsons found her first and immediately asked how they

could best help those children. "I thought the orphanage was in dire straits, but children with homes —"

"We assume."

The young woman's eyes widened so far that Madeline feared they'd fall to the floor. "You don't think —"

"I can only hope not, but if you saw how fil —"

A snide, sniveling voice interrupted Madeline. "*My* father says the area is a disgrace. He blames Mayor Brown, of course."

Before Madeline could hope to reply, Edith's quiet voice reached her ears. "I'm sure he does, Prissy. Your father has made criticizing Madeline's a full-time occupation. It is easy for spectators to criticize the game, but could they play any better?" And with that, Edith turned and strolled from the room as if nothing unpleasant had just occurred.

Madeline knew better. The rigid set of Edith's shoulders, the way she didn't pause to speak to friends — it all gave away her friend's true state of heart and mind. *I do wish you wouldn't be quite so quick to take up an offense for others, dear Edith. Some of us are quite capable of becoming annoyed without your help.* Resigned to a wasted committee meeting, Madeline waved at Ruth Parsons and followed Edith from the room.

As they stepped from the building, she slipped her arm through Edith's and murmured, "Don't mind anything Prissy says. She is just jealous because her father lost the election."

"I know. She so wanted her father to win — for *her* social advancement, of course. I know you only cared for your father's ambition." Edith wiped away a rogue tear and assembled a feeble attempt at a brave smile. "I don't know how you endure the criticism."

The truth spilled from her heart and through her lips before Madeline could consider whether it would be wise to speak it. "But you care for how people think of you, Edith. I don't. I've never been particularly interested in most people's opinions of me or anyone

45

else." Before Edith could reply with some self-disparaging remark, Madeline qualified her statement. "And I don't necessarily consider that a virtue. It is just as it is, though. I'm afraid I can't force myself to care."

They ambled down the street in relative silence, but the moment the girls rounded the corner, Edith started. "Oh! I meant to tell you! Prissy had me all flustered and I quite forgot! Mr. Smythe has business in the Dry Docks quarter. He spoke of it last evening, in fact. He described it much as you did—dirty, ragged children and young women of ill repute. Perhaps he might have an idea for you. He's dining at our house on Thursday evening. Would you care to join us?"

And here I thought the afternoon was wasted. Well done, Edith!

Though she made a show of consideration, as if anything would have kept her away, Madeline eventually capitulated. "That is very kind of you. I can't help but think he would prefer *not* to share you with such a sordid conversation, but it is for the children's sake...."

Well, Madeline Brown, that one most definitely crosses over the line into prevarication.

Madeline floated through the rest of that week on a cloud of anticipation and, if truth be told, relief. As she told Jimmy while they attacked the weeds in the flower garden near the terrace door, "I expected Russell Barnes to come and scold me, of course."

Jimmy hadn't learned that fine art of not questioning his employers about their personal affairs—much to Madeline's amusement and delight. "Why's he goin' to scold you, miss?"

"Well, if he discovered that I inquired about the Dry Docks, he might. He's set himself up as honorary big brother—Amy's doing—"

"And who's Amy, miss?"

Madeline grabbed the boy's wrist. "No, not that one, Jimmy. That's a snapdragon. We like those. Who is...? Oh, yes. Amy. Amy and I have been dearest friends since we were in primary school." The boy's eyes pleaded with her to continue, and it occurred to Madeline that weeding in the sweltering heat might be exceptionally tedious for a curious boy like Jimmy. "Now, Amy has an uncle who is quite wealthy and a bachelor. So when she graduated from high school, he promised her a year of travel abroad. They're in Switzerland right now. She says it's beautiful — all that snow still on the Alps."

"That's in Europe, isn't it, miss?"

"Very good! Yes. Well, Mr. Barnes is Amy's brother. He used to torment us dreadfully when we were little girls — likely getting back at us for pestering him. But after he went away to college, he came home quite a different fellow. He laughed and joked with us — took us out on the river and to various games. He's the closest thing I have to a brother, I imagine. As Amy always says when I wish for a brother like hers, 'I'll just loan you mine.'"

Jimmy nodded. "Sounds like a real humdinger." A moment later he murmured, "I've got a little sister — Clemmie. She was named after my granny."

Madeline fixed an approving smile on Jimmy. "I bet you will be as wonderful as Russell is to his sister. Do you share treats with her?"

Shame filled the boy's face as he shook his head in slow, wagging movements. "No... don't get many treats." Resolve — she saw it the moment it entered Jimmy's heart. "But I will now. I want to be a *good* big brother."

"We'll start with today. I'll go see if Mary can pack you a little cake to take to her."

If she had expected to receive a request for one for himself, Madeline's disappointment would have been keen. However, the boy's determination to be a "good big brother" like Russell Barnes had taken root. *And you'll be rewarded for it.*

Mary met her at the kitchen door. "I just passed the dining room window and saw Mr. Barnes coming up the walk. Do you think he'll stay to lunch?"

"Just plan for it, please. Oh, and will you make sure there's enough for Jimmy?"

"Certainly. He seems a nice boy."

Madeline couldn't help but play with the word. "I think he'd say he was a 'real humdinger' — if he were me, of course."

"My little brother speaks that way. Drives Mother to distraction trying to stop him." She'd taken a few steps to return to the kitchen when Mary turned back again. "Did you come inside for something in particular? You seemed elbow-deep into that flowerbed and then poof! You were inside."

Her mind retraced her steps until Madeline remembered just why she'd come inside after all. The door buzzed just as she remembered. "I'll get that, Mary. And yes, I came in for something. Will you please wrap two little cakes for Jimmy. If you can do it, please make one larger than the other." Without waiting for an answer, Madeline skipped off toward the door, pulling one of her gloves from her hand as she did.

Now, if he's here to scold.... But the smile on Russell's face and the little string-tied parcel in his hand hinted that her concern had been for naught. "Why, Russell! What brings you here this fine, intemperate morning?"

Russell stepped inside and presented his package. "I came to bring you this, but you're correct. It is a beautifully miserable morning, isn't it? What have you been doing?" Even as he asked, Russell's eyes slid to her single-gloved hand dusted with dirt from the garden. "Planning a new fashion? The dirty, single-gloved craze?"

"Working in the garden with Jimmy. I thought I'd teach him how to weed." The memory of a snapdragon saved from destruction at the last second sent her scurrying toward the kitchen door. "Come with me, Russell! The snapdragons may be in peril!"

Their laughter turned Jimmy's head as they approached. "Something wrong, miss?"

"We just came to see if you'd left any snapdragons, or if they've all been slain by Sir Jimmy of Rockland."

The boy ducked his head as he rose. "I did pull one, but I put it back. It's a little limp, but maybe...." His eyes traveled to the box she carried. "That's a big cake, Miss Brown. You didn't have to—"

"Oh! My package! I quite forgot in my quest to rescue the snap-damsels in distress! This is a gift from Mr. Barnes." She turned to Russell. "Do you know Jimmy Higgins? He's often at the Mertons'."

Russell offered his hand to the boy. "I've seen him there, but I've never made his acquaintance. Nice to meet you, Jimmy."

Dirty hands flew up and looked amusingly like a surrender. "I'm all dirty, but thanks. Nice to meet you, too. Miss Brown says you're a good big brother. I'm going to try to be, too, I reckon."

She almost doubted she saw it—a tiny fraction of a change in Russell's expression. He gave her a smile, one she'd often seen him bestow on his beloved little sister, and winked. "Good big brother, am I? That's a fine thing to hear. But this good big brother wants to see what the little sister thinks of his gift."

The words sounded just like him, but something in the tone.... Madeline filed it away for later consideration and pulled the other glove from her hand. Her fingers tugged at one end of the string. The other end. Jimmy fairly danced in place as he anticipated what hid beneath the wrappings. Russell just beamed. Then she saw it, that impatient twitch to the corner of his mouth. *He's as anxious as Jimmy. Alleviate his misery or intensify...?*

"Madeline...."

She couldn't do it. Whenever Russell used her name in that exact tone, she found herself incapable of thwarting him. She dropped the string into his outstretched palm and slowly unrolled the papers. Her eyes widened. "A Brownie? Really?"

She hadn't hugged him impulsively for years, but Madeline couldn't help it. "I've wanted one, but of course, Papa hasn't been able to look at them. He never wants to purchase something like this unless he thinks it's his idea." Her mind whirled with the possibilities. With a Brownie, she'd have a perfect excuse for going anywhere in the city she wanted.

Alas, when she gazed up at Russell, something in his expression changed. Her heart raced and her stomach flopped. *He will try to impose conditions; won't he? Well, he can just take it ba —*

"I thought perhaps if you had one of those, it might just keep you out of trouble."

Her face flushed.

"And I'd feel much better if I never saw photographs of the Dry Docks quarter. The architecture down there isn't anything worth preserving for posterity."

Translation: keep your fingers busy with safer pursuits than your current obsession with the city's seedier side.

Jimmy peered at the case, asked questions about how it worked and even how much the camera cost. At hearing it was only a dollar, he promptly decided to begin saving. But all the while he chattered, Madeline watched Russell. His eyes held hers with a silent plea.

I can't promise what you want to hear, but…. Aloud, she spoke what truth she could manufacture. "I can assure you that I have absolutely no interest in photographing the Dry Docks area. It's a filthy, dirty place. I'd rather see if I can capture that new Waterbrook Building." She dropped her eyes. *Well, it's true. I'm interested in photographing the people down there, not the buildings.*

"Why am I not reassured by that?"

As she looked up at him, Madeline saw genuine concern and something else—was it fear?—in his eyes. Madeline swallowed a lump in her throat. "I haven't any idea; I'm sure."

$\mathcal{F}$IVE

The Brown dining room always felt a little grandiose to Madeline — their long, cherry wood table, the silver candlesticks, the fine china. Rich drapes and matching chair covers provided such elegance that, even after seven years, still left her in a little awe sometimes. *It's quite a change from the solid oak table and chairs in the old house.*

However, sitting at the Mertons' table in a room half-again as large as the Brown's, with everything just that much more resplendent than anything the Browns could afford, Madeline couldn't help but compare. *And to think, Mr. Merton is so penurious. What would their home be like now if Edith's mother were still with us to influence decisions? Was he such a lickpenny in those days?*

As Ida served their meal, Madeline noted the generous portions, the hothouse flowers — everything. *One can't help but wonder if you consider this an investment in the future welfare of your pocketbook.*

Edith's voice broke through her musings. "Mr. Smythe, Madeline is concerned about the state of the Dry Docks. I knew you had business there, so I thought perhaps you might have an idea for how to help her."

I never imagined I'd be grateful to Edith for opening a delicate topic with such innocence.

Vernon Smythe finished chewing, wiped his mouth, and dropped his hands in his lap. "You do well to be concerned, Miss

Brown. One of the reasons I'm interested in seeing electricity in all homes—even those in the Dry Docks—is for that very reason. Perhaps if it is readily available, new inventions to aid in cleanliness and health will become affordable to everyone."

"I'm sorry, Mr. Smythe, but I have little idea of what your idea fully entails. Just what do you hope to accomplish?" Madeline picked at the roast beef on her plate, focusing just a little too intently on cutting a perfectly sized piece.

Even without looking at Vernon, Madeline sensed the change—the eagerness and excitement—that comes over a man when he discusses some passion of his. "I believe that electricity is the key to radical change in this country. If every home had access to affordable electricity, poverty could become a thing of the past."

"But electricity is so expensive—to install, I mean. How—"

Smythe's eagerness interrupted Madeline before she could finish the question. "That is precisely the point. You see, almost everyone can afford to pay the low cost of electric usage, but the wiring and the fixtures are prohibitively expensive. The only way to 'get around that', as they say, is to purchase everything needed in bulk. That will reduce costs by a significant amount. Then...."

What he said next, Madeline never knew. She nodded at proper inflections, asked vague questions such as, "And that will mean...." and generally appeared to be properly fascinated by the man's words. Unfortunately, her mind was much more disagreeably inclined. *Which all sounds wonderful, but it does not adequately explain your... closeness... with a certain young woman in the Dry Docks. I wonder what you would say or do to explain that.*

Madeline almost started as Smythe described a house of ill repute. "I have spoken to one brothel madam who wishes to bring electricity to her establishment. She says that with a means for her ladies to make a legitimate living, they will be able to leave the life of sin that holds them in its grip."

The words sound so lofty—so charitable. Look at the beatific expression on Edith's face. Even Mr. Merton seems impressed. Why do I feel as though they are disingenuous? What about electricity in a brothel would suddenly offer legitimate work for such women? It doesn't make sense!

To her right, Edith sat up with an eager expression on her face. "Oh, wouldn't that be wonderful! I can't imagine being reduced to such *unsavory....*" Her hand grasped her throat as her eyes sought Smythe's.

"Your concern for the less fortunate does you credit, Miss Merton. Too often, those removed from the seedier side of life forget that there are fellow humans trapped in it."

Excellent touché, Mr. Smythe. Propose an idea that would bring more money to Mr. Merton's coffers, flatter his daughter, and jab the dissenter in the process. Yes, excellent indeed.

"My life has been so protected. Madeline's too, of course. So, as you can imagine, I am eager to help the less fortunate."

"The Lord helps those who help themselves," Mr. Merton insisted. "It does not do to make the less fortunate dependent on others for their sustenance."

"But, Father, surely —"

Mr. Merton interrupted with an impatient, dismissive gesture. "Edith, you cannot allow sentimentality to overrule good sense. Doing *for* others teaches them only to expect others to do *for* them. Teaching them to do for *themselves* relives the burden on them *and* on the coffers of those with the means to do so."

Only you can be absolutely correct about the plight of the poor in such a way as to make you sound insensitive, callous, and completely boorish. Charities are stretched beyond their ability to cope in their extreme desire to avoid any connection with you.

"I can't help but think," Vernon Smythe began, "that there shouldn't be a compromise that allows one to show charity without removing dignity, as well as restricting the limits of that charity in order to aid people out of the need for it."

From her place, she could only watch two of the other table's occupants at once, but she saw Mr. Merton stiffen and Vernon Smythe smile—at her. A glance Edith's direction showed the young woman looking quite besotted. However, as she turned back to Vernon, his smile changed from a smile to a challenge—a threat.

I know that look, she mused. *I accept.*

As he sliced through roast beef, Vernon Smythe spread a layer of diplomacy over the conversation before flattering Edith and issuing a challenge to the obnoxious Miss Brown. *And you accept, I see. Very well.*

Edith's tone shifted and her eyes pleaded with her father as she bemoaned the plight of the "poor children in that dreadful place." She set down her fork and stared at her plate. "As terrible as it may be that the parents haven't provided better, it isn't the fault of the children. If they aren't—"

"That is the kind of sentimental nonsense…."

What Jonas Merton said about her theory, Vernon didn't hear. Instead, he mentally admonished her as he wished he had the right to do audibly. *My dear girl, if you do not learn not to cross your father, you will only find yourself hurting twice—first for the children, then from his rebukes.* Just then, Edith's eyes met his and he smiled. *Then again, if it provides me the opportunity to console….*

Madeline spoke up in Edith's defense—of course, she *would.* "I think Edith makes a fine observation. If we do not help these children, they will only learn a life similar to that which they've always known. Few escape their upbringing, we're told."

"I did. I started out as a factory worker making pennies an hour. Now look at me!"

Yes, Mr. Merton, and I am sure if this country could support a few hundred thousand more banks, everyone could have such success. As it is,

54

we may need to find other alternatives.

" — comparable to the orphans? By that I mean," Madeline's eyes met his as she continued. "Are we not to feed orphans? Are we not to clothe and educate them? Should *they* be left to fend for themselves?"

"I didn't say *that*, Miss Brown. The sacred texts are quite clear on this point. We are to provide for widows and orphans — if the widows are widows *indeed*. Able-bodied widows, we are told, are expected to work for themselves." Mr. Merton sawed at his roast beef with unnecessary vigor for such tender meat. "But we were discussing the poor, not orphans and widows."

Vernon cleared his throat. "But Miss Brown makes an excellent point, Mr. Merton. While there is a delicate line between proper charity and unhealthy generosity, if we do not provide a means for those trapped in the horrors of poverty — a means for, or at least the vision of escape — how can we expect these children to ever imagine it could be so?"

Few would have noticed it. Indeed, had Vernon not looked up at just that precise moment, he doubted he would have. But Madeline Brown's eyes widened just a bit in evident surprise. *You expect me to side with him. Why? Do you doubt my sincerity toward your friend or toward the poor?*

"I managed to see that others had what I didn't and determined what needed to be done to get there. I did it."

"But not everyone has — "

"Edith, you must cease this revolting habit of contradicting me!" Mr. Merton lowered his voice. "It's unseemly in a young woman."

The temptation to remind Mr. Merton that lashing out at his daughter for being sensitive to the needs of others was also unseemly nearly overrode Vernon's good sense. *And what will it get either of us? I will likely find myself unwelcome, and she will be further disgraced in his eyes.* Instead, he gave her the most sympathetic — nee, *caring* — smile he could and tried to change the subject. But before he could voice anything, a flash of surprise in Madeline's eyes caught his attention. *So, you do doubt my interest in your friend.*

Edith's pink cheeks gave her a lovelier countenance than usual—one he couldn't help admire. *If you would only consider the slightest bit of rouge, my dear. I see nothing immodest in it, but it does you credit that you are cautious of your reputation.*

"Have you chosen a dress for the Midsummer's Ball, Edith?"

Vernon turned his attention to the ladies and the newest topic of discussion. "I can't imagine Miss Merton wearing anything that didn't look lovely on her."

"Scarlet." Edith flushed at the outburst, but she explained regardless. "I do look quite horrid in scarlet. Poison green as well. Those bold colors...." She gave Miss Brown an indulgent smile. "But Madeline can wear them. She looks lovely in vivid greens and blues and reds."

"Not reds, Edith. With my hair...."

Perhaps he shouldn't have done it. In fact, there was no "perhaps" about it. But the temptation proved too great. Vernon gazed at Miss Brown with frank appraisal and nodded. "I imagine it clashes with the red in yours. It isn't quite carrot colored—nor is it auburn. What *do* they call your color, Miss Brown?"

"That depends on the person. I've heard 'deep red' and 'light auburn.' And, in the middle of summer as a girl, I often heard ginger. My Aunt Louisa is always quick to inform me that it *will* darken as I age."

"I often wished that I had Madeline's hair as a little girl. It was so much more interesting than my blonde. But then a child would tease her, and I would decide—for another week or two—that boring blonde was better than interesting red."

Vernon waited to catch Edith's eye before he smiled. "I happen to think blonde the loveliest hair color. It suits you in a way that no other could."

Before anyone could respond, Ida stepped in with a tray of strawberry shortcakes. Still flushing pink from the indirect compliment, Edith thanked Ida for taking away the cakes and bringing their empty plates. Madeline stifled a smile. Mr. Merton dropped his fork in exasperation, but Vernon sat in self-satisfaction.

She is becoming attached. I couldn't have hoped for it anytime sooner. A glance at Madeline twisted his lips before he could stop himself. *If you disapprove of me, I fear you may find yourself disappointed. I am not dissuaded so easily*

SIX

The uncharacteristic heat wave passed and left perfectly spring-like temperatures in its wake. After church let out that Sunday, Madeline accepted an invitation to a picnic down by the river with Edith, Flossie, Russell, and a few of the others from their set. With any luck, and likely due to what Madeline suspected was the formation of a nasty, suspicious mind, Vernon Smythe would make an appearance as well.

The young men spread picnic blankets out under the shade of a great oak, and the girls took turn unpacking hampers of food. "Found the chicken!" Madeline called out to the others.

Flossie dropped the lid of one basket. "Mine is nothing but desserts — tempting though they may be, I really hoped for something more substantial at first."

Madeline pointed to Russell. "Would you mind setting up a makeshift table on the back of the wagon? I believe we've found all the dishes."

A glance that way showed the arrival of Vernon Smythe, speaking to someone she couldn't see. Madeline jumped up and retrieved her Brownie from beneath a wagon seat. "I meant to take a picture."

Russell bent low and murmured, "Of food? And what is the inducement?"

"I thought it might be wise to try different things in different lighting to learn how best to capture the perfect photograph. The first are likely to be terrible. I need practice before I try to take one that I desperately want and ruin because I haven't mastered operation of the thing."

Somehow—and how, she'd never be able to determine—her words didn't set off alarm bells in Russell's features. He nodded and helped her check the viewfinder, rearranged a few things, and then stood back to get out of the line of "fire." At the last second, Madeline shifted just slightly, re-centered her viewfinder on something else, and snapped the picture.

"Now, do I turn this to advance the film?"

It worked. The suspicious look in Russell's eyes changed to interest as he followed directions and helped her turn the dial the proper number of times. "I think that's correct. I suppose we'll see when the film is developed."

Inside ten minutes, Madeline sat on a blanket with Russell and a young woman she didn't know well. "Miss Denton—"

"Please. I prefer my given name, Elizabeth. The formality here surprises me."

"*Elizabeth*, how are you settling into Rockland? Is it much backward after Philadelphia?"

The young woman set down her fork and wiped at her lips. "Not at all. I expected it to be," the lovely, young lady confessed. She wiped at rosebud lips of a shape and color that novelists would rhapsodize over in the pages of their books. Madeline noticed that the napkin bore not even the slightest trace of color.

Something about the affair tickled a memory—one she couldn't see clearly. *Why is that important? I wonder....*

"I found Philadelphia to be a beautiful and friendly place when I was there a year ago," Russell interjected. "I understand your father purchased a great deal of the Dry Docks."

"He did. He's in commerce, you know. All that buying and selling. I don't really understand it all, but at the crux of what he intends to do are the warehouses down there. I believe he's speaking to your firm about an office building he wishes to commission," Elizabeth added with a smile that bordered on flirtatious. "I do hope you'll submit a design for the project."

"I've already begun one, yes. Thank you."

This is interesting. You said nothing to me about that when we discussed the Dry Docks the other day. Very interesting, indeed.

As if he read her thoughts, Russell added, "I know Madeline is particularly interested in the Dry Docks quarter. She considers the conditions there disgraceful. One never knows just why she takes such an interest, but when she does...."

At that moment, a call came for badminton players, and Elizabeth jumped up with evident relish. "Oh, I do love a good game of badminton. You'll both join, of course?"

"I think perhaps later," Madeline began. "I would like a walk first. I'm afraid I've eaten too much for such rigorous activity."

Elizabeth turned to Russell. "Shall we?"

That borders just a bit on the brazen. Philadelphia must be a little more progressive than Rockland... unless.... Madeline stood and turned to go but stopped short. "Elizabeth, I understood that you're part of the temperance, and by association, the suffragette movement. Is this correct?"

"I am passionate about suffrage, it's true. And, of course, the temperance movement is such a vital element to arresting the moral decline of the nation." Elizabeth smiled up at Russell. "Wouldn't you agree, Russell?"

I don't recall him pressing you to use his given name. How will he respond to that? I wonder.

"I have not studied the issues sufficiently to answer that without possibly misrepresenting myself."

A smile formed on Madeline's face as she turned away. *His overly formal speech tells me that Russell finds not reacting quite difficult.* "Well, I hope Rockland provides you adequate support for your causes. Good luck with your game."

She hadn't made it a hundred yards before she heard someone—Russell most likely—jogging up behind her. "Nicely extricated, Miss Brown."

Madeline smiled up at him. "Do you think so? I found myself thinking of a dozen ways I could have been less overt in my evident dislike."

"I still do not understand why suffrage isn't a passion of yours. You seem suited to the cause, with your dislike of convention and your desire to break free from it."

"I support a woman's right to fight for it if that's what *she* desires, I suppose. But why any woman would want to be involved in politics is beyond me. Why, Papa's campaign alone nearly cured me for a lifetime."

Russell slowed their pace considerably with that ease that only he possessed. She'd never seen anyone quite like him for taking charge of a room. *If I only had his abilities, I'd find myself much more able to learn things.*

"I hear you thinking. Should I be concerned?"

Her laughter rang out across the meadow. "I suspected you'd say something like that." Madeline gave him a sidelong glance before she asked the next and most obvious question. "What do you think of Mr. Smythe?"

"As a person or as a businessman?"

Madeline pointed to a rowboat tied up on a pole in the ground. "Care to row me out on the pond? I'd rather not be overheard." Russell's nod and proffered arm prompted her to answer his question in an undertone. "I don't know which I mean. I'm trying to understand him."

Russell led her that way as he explained his reservations. "Well, he is considered to be quite the electrical expert. I have heard people discussing his electricity to combat poverty theory. People seem to like him. I haven't heard any reservations regarding his character."

He started to ask why, but Madeline preempted him.

"I had dinner with him at the Mertons' home the other night. He was quite charming—showed what seemed a genuine concern for the plight of the children in the Dry Docks quarter."

Speaking in low tones, Russell suggested something that surprised her. "Should his concern be disingenuous, it would still be in his best interests to pretend to be. After all, the need of that area for electricity is at the core of his pet project. He would be wise to demonstrate at least a show of compassion."

Madeline considered his words as Russell un-looped the rope from the pole and held it fast. She found herself climbing in, but her mind was otherwise engaged. "Interesting idea." Other ideas swirled in her thoughts. "Do you think it is easy to feign interest in someone?"

The water lapped at the side of the boat, and a dragonfly darted about the bow as Russell pushed off into the pond. She'd almost decided he hadn't heard her when Russell began speaking again. "Well, like the reverse, I imagine eventually one's true feelings would out. A person can successfully pretend *not* to care for some time, but eventually something will reveal the heart. You can't hide those things indefinitely. And, as I said, I would assume the reverse to be true. As Shakespeare reminds us—in your favorite play, no less—truth will out."

The words swirled in her mind as Madeline allowed her fingers to slide over the edge of the little dory and trail along in the water. Russell paddled further and further out across the pond. "Do you think one is harder than the other? Pretending *to* care or pretending *not* to?"

His eyes pierced her as he nodded. "I would imagine it would be infinitely more difficult to hide feelings than to manufacture them." He held the oars steady and observed her for a moment. "What is your interest in it?" Russell leaned forward, "Surely *he* hasn't made you an offer?"

"Oh, don't be silly! That would be even more ridiculous than Mr. Jackson!" A quandary lay before her—to answer frankly or merely truthfully. Madeline opted for both. "He has shown interest in Edith." A pointed nod toward the shore where Edith and Smythe walked arm-in-arm is all it took for Russell to nod his agreement. "He has shown every evidence of sincerity, but she is so easily led. I wouldn't want to see her hurt if he is, for example, only interested in some business venture with her father."

"I see your point." Russell pointed to the camera at her feet. "Why don't you hand that here? I'll take a photograph of you."

The idea sparked a new one, and Madeline set it up. "After I take you."

Despite his best intentions, Russell found himself involved in a game of croquet while Madeline and a few of the girls strolled away from the picnic site. Others, such as Elizabeth Denton and Margaret Rodgers, played the game. Twice Miss Denton tried to catch his attention, but both times Russell managed to divert it. Had he known what was coming, he might have endured it—for Madeline's sake.

"Margaret, did you hear about Madeline's foray into the Dry Docks?"

Confusion filled Margaret's voice as she tried to respond. "Well, yes… she did mention it at the meeting the other day. Didn't you hear her?"

A cough ripped through him—one created in his attempt *not* to laugh at Miss Denton's evident irritation. "Oh, you were there, weren't you? I'd quite forgotten." When Russell didn't take the bait and ask the obvious question, Miss Denton tried again. "I wonder at her father permitting such foolishness."

"Madeline has always been a little fearless." Margaret glanced around her in search of support, but the others either weren't paying attention or preferred to avoid the subject. She tried to catch Russell's eye, but he stepped up to his ball and aimed his mallet. "No one would fault her for following a friend in there, though. It could happen to anyone—even without realizing it."

Madeline.... You didn't say you'd gone in there. I should have known, of course. Now who—Smythe. It would have to be him. So, when you asked about why a young man would be with a young woman, were you speaking of actually seeing *him with someone, or seeing a woman and putting two and two together?*

"Well, I do fear for her reputation. Any young lady being seen in such a disreputable area would have her character called into question. Why, my brother says there are *brothels* in there."

It wasn't wise, but the snider Miss Denton's voice became, the more Russell didn't care. "I didn't realize George frequented the area so much. Do brothels have much use for accountants? I suppose like any business—"

"Oh, that is too funny, Russell! I'll have to tell him about that. No, of course George isn't in the habit of visiting brothels for *any* reason, but as a man, he can't but help hear about these things."

The temptation to argue that point—to insist that 'of course' wasn't a just assumption. Not every man heard of such things, surely. He did. In his line of work, if buildings were involved, he had a good idea of what happened in them. But an accountant or a teacher wouldn't likely have a need for that kind of information. The words sat at the tip of his tongue, daring him to let them fly, but Russell resisted. *It will only leave her to infer that I think her brother does frequent such establishments.*

And that thought gave him a new idea. "I imagine Miss Brown's experience has increased your own interest in the area? For someone so committed to the moral climate of Rockland, I would assume...."

"You are right, of course. We will have to take it up at our next

65

meeting. Why, if there are brothels, there must be saloons. Both are inextricably linked, you know. This is why the temperance movement is so vital to the moral climate of our country." Miss Denton stood as close to him as she could without risking the accusation of immorality herself, and murmured, "Won't you join us in our quest, Russell?"

"I'm afraid not." He swung and his ball missed by the proverbial mile. "But I do wish you well in your endeavors." He pointed with his mallet. "If you'll excuse me, I need to finish my turn."

As he measured his shot, Milty Grueber came and stood beside him. The moment he swung, Milty murmured a warning. "I'm not saying that Denton girl isn't full of bunk, but she's only saying what a lot of folks are. The word is Madeline's going down there as some plug for her father's next campaign. You might want to tell her to give it a rest."

Russell stared at the ball and then at Milty. "I wasn't aware that I was Madeline's keeper. If you are truly concerned, perhaps a word with her or her father…."

Hands in the air, Milty backed away a little. "Look, I'm not saying read her the riot act, but she's going to give the mothers of Rockland the vapors, and you know what that means. Just a friendly warning. She's a nice girl…."

When Russell didn't respond, Milty turned to go. Russell watched as he sauntered away with one last glance back. *Why, of all people, are you the one telling me to warn Madeline off an area that, by all appearances, she wandered into without premeditation?*

He swung and made his shot. Another glance back at Milty showed him talking with Vernon Smythe. *Now that Madeline would probably find interesting. Unfortunately, I have no idea why.*

SEVEN

Packet in hand, Madeline stepped off the trolley and made her way to the Rockland Post Office. *Ten days. Russell says it'll take a week to ten days to get the photographs back.* That thought would have depressed her had she not been so excited about her new "toy."

Her feet skipped up the steps of the large building, and a gentleman held the door for her as she reached the top. "Thank you."

Something in the man's eyes hinted that perhaps he might speak further, so Madeline arranged her features into a blank look and made her way to an open window. Seconds later, a glance back showed the man gone again. *Phew. Men are so forward these days.*

The clerk weighed the packet, accepted the coins she offered him, and commented on the recipient. "I've seen quite a few parcels sent to the Eastman Company lately."

"It's the film for my new Brownie. I'm sending it off for development. I look forward to seeing if I managed to take any photographs of recognizable subjects. The exposure process can be a bit intimidating. Too short and it could be a black square, I'm told."

"I've been wanting one of those. Do you like it?"

Madeline's enthusiasm bubbled over and she chattered about the process until she'd paid for the parcel and received a receipt. "Have a lovely day. And do get one. I understand the price is quite reasonable—only a dollar."

With that errand complete, Madeline hurried from the post

office and down the street. A group of suffragettes passed, bearing signs calling for the vote for women, and several of the young ladies applied to her to join them. "No, thank you." The reply seemed to echo around her every time she answered. *As much as Papa might like the added votes, I would not like yet another "committee" to join. No, indeed!*

At the corner of Waterbrook and First Streets, Madeline waited for a passing wagon to clear the streets before she crossed, and as she waited, her eyes scanned the area. *Such a stark contrast between here and the Dry Docks. This is as clean and tidy as city streets can be. Passersby don't leer, and I never feel unsafe.*

At just that moment, almost as if in defiance of her observation, Madeline noticed a man at the corner diagonal from her. He seemed to watch her for a moment, but after the wagon finally passed and she had the opportunity to look again, the man had vanished. *Handlebar mustache, flashy suit, and no hat. Interesting….*

Rockland's downtown area afforded much to observe and little to do. After wandering around the area for the better part of an hour, Madeline found herself outside City Hall. Mayor Brown rarely had a free moment to chat with his daughter, but Madeline always took the time to stop in and say hello.

She found him at his desk, examining papers as if of the greatest import. "Are you busy, Papa? Should I come some other day?"

Albert Brown jumped, and his eyes flew up to meet hers. "Oh! Maddie, dear. You startled me. I almost thought you were your aunt, Louisa. She does like to stop in to complain about *something* on a regular basis."

"What fascinating things are you working on now?" Her eyes scanned the desk, but reading upside down had never been one of her finer skills. *However, I should learn. It might be an advantageous skill someday. Perhaps when I have children.*

He began explaining—the long, rambling stories that he so loved when he hadn't made a decision yet—and as she listened,

Madeline peered out the third floor window and into the courtyard where a fountain sprayed water into the afternoon air. That same man—the one without the hat and wearing the plaid suit—sat along the edge of the fountain. Waiting, it seemed.

"—expansion project. The trolleys would go right to the edge of the Dry Docks quarter, which would be a way for those who work there to move to nicer neighborhoods."

Though she'd missed his first words, the project was one she'd heard discussed often. *If it were as simple as a yes or no, you would have decided.*

"Well, what do you think?"

"About the trolley line?" Madeline gazed out the window once more before pulling up a chair next to him and settling herself in it. "I'm certain you've weighed all the advantages and disadvantages...." She peered at the papers spread out on his desk as she rambled. "Of course, transportation to the area must be considered progress, but at what cost? What part will the city have to pay for it? Is it in the budget? How long will we have to settle the bill?"

His sigh ripped through her heart. "Those are the questions that will make or break the decision. If everything goes well...."

"You always taught me to make decisions based on sound logic rather than wishful thinking."

For a moment, the rigidity in his shoulders made her prepare for a rebuke, but it never surfaced. "You're right, of course. The trolley company will have to shoulder the expense. The city budget simply cannot meet it."

With a kiss to his cheek, Madeline turned to go. "I think I'll ask Cook to make a lemon cake. Someone could use something to sweeten his day."

As her hand reached for the door, her father called out to her. "Maddie?"

She steeled herself against the news that he wouldn't be home for dinner. "Yes?"

His features softened at the sight of her face — or perhaps it was the tear that escaped just then. *He's thinking of Mama again.*

"Thank you. Many young ladies would have tried to sound intelligent and progressive and encouraged me to take the risk for the 'good of the city.' You spoke sense."

Though Madeline knew she should go, she returned, wrapped her arms around his neck, and kissed his cheek. "Papa, if I spoke sense it's because you taught me to. I echo that which I learned from you."

The memory of her father's thanks and the smile he gave her filled Madeline's mind as she skipped down the stairs to the bottom floor with a lighter heart and step than she'd anticipated. That all crashed in a heap at her feet when she saw a man — *that same man* — slip around the other side of the fountain and into a group of pedestrians.

Madeline called out — ran after him. But despite crashing into half a dozen people and earning as many sharp reproofs, the man had gone. Vanished. *Coincidence or concerning?* The question filled her thoughts all the way back to the trolley *and* all the way home.

A flash of blue with narrow gold braid — Louisa Farnsworth would recognize the dress and its perfect confection of a coordinating hat anywhere. *Whatever are you doing, child? It's quite —* Shock cut her thoughts off before Louisa could hope to finish them.

Madeline dashed past without seeing her and nearly knocked her down. "Madeline Brown!"

But the girl didn't notice — didn't notice and seemingly didn't care that she left a string of disheveled pedestrians in her wake. "Well!"

"Young people these days!" A woman nearby tried to straighten her askew hat. "I think the mayor should do something about it. You can't leave the house without being accosted by heedless boys and girls—always in a rush."

And you would be alarmed to discover that this was the mayor's *daughter. Well, you won't hear it from me. I can do that much for my poor Lily.*

Once Madeline disappeared from sight, Louisa readjusted her own hat and strode into City Hall. The stairs that led to Albert Brown's office produced a satisfactory click to her shoes as she stepped on each one in perfect time to an unsung melody. Several people smiled as she passed them on the way to the office, but other than a pleasant nod, Louisa did not allow herself the possibility of distraction.

She stepped into the anteroom, dismissed the clerk who assured her Mr. Brown was "unavailable," and pushed open the door. "Good afternoon, Albert!"

Dismay—he couldn't hide it if he tried. The one thing that would destroy Albert Brown's mayoral career would be his inability to hide his thoughts. *At least I don't have to worry about you taking up gambling. You would fail at cards, and you know it.*

"Louisa. You just missed Madeline."

"Yes, I know. This is why I've come."

He would take offense. Men always did when people questioned how they governed their children, but Louisa wasn't one to play at insincere pleasantries unless quite necessary. Even as the thought formed, Albert's face screwed into a frown.

He stood and moved a chair to the opposite side of his desk. "I don't know what you mean, Louisa, but you might prefer to sit before telling me."

"Thank you." She waited until he'd seated himself before she began. "Your daughter just plowed through a crowd without regard for anyone's safety. Why, I nearly lost my own hat!"

71

"That doesn't sound like my Madeline. She can be impulsive, but to show disregard—"

But Louisa cut him off before he could continue. "I believe she was *chasing* someone. At her age! Albert, she's *nineteen!* She needs to be thinking about marriage, not dashing after a friend or acquaintance in the middle of town!"

"How do those relate at all?" Albert's confusion grew visibly with each passing minute. "And she's still just a girl. I will not have her pressured into some antiquated idea of early marriage to avoid the stigma of spinsterhood. If she's forty and unmarried, you may, of course, try your hand at matchmaking, but until then, I won't have it!"

"Without a house to manage, she's—"

"She has a house, Louisa!" At her shocked expression, Albert's voice dropped. "I shouldn't shout. Please forgive me. You alarm me with your ideas, however. I *won't* have her pushed into a marriage simply out of the fear that she'll reach twenty-five and still wear the name of Brown. It's a good, solid name—good enough for Lily, if you recall, and that was long before we ever moved into the city."

His mention of her sister wrenched Louisa's heart—as it always did. "Lily would want the best advantages for her daughter. Madeline won't find those if she allows her friends to snatch up the most eligible young men. Which is why I've come—or rather, was my original purpose. I've planned a dinner at my home Friday evening. There are a couple of young men I want Madeline to meet."

"Louisa...."

She stood and waited for him to acknowledge her. "Have you another engagement?"

Albert's evident disappointment answered long before he shook his head. "Not that I know of, but I can't speak for Madeline. You know these young people—parties and socials at every turn. I can't hope to guess if she is otherwise—"

"She'll be there, Albert. As will you. I don't do these things for my own advancement. Heaven knows it's not how *I* care to spend an evening, but even if neither of these gentlemen are the one for her, she may make an acquaintance that leads to another — and to the right one. She cannot be too cavalier with her future, you know."

But Albert rubbed the top of his head until it shone, all while trying to divert her plan. "This isn't our day, Louisa. Young people have many more opportunities available to them nowadays. Why, young women work in offices and even as tellers at the bank. They are nurses and teachers. Some attend medical colleges and become doctors!"

The words sent her fumbling for her chair. Louisa sank into it and stared at him, jaw agape. "You wouldn't—you *couldn't* encourage her to do something so inappropriate! She's the *mayor's daughter* — not some laborer's — "

"You've grown snobbish as the years have passed. Our parents were good, kind, modestly educated farmers. My father never finished primary school, but he could read, write, and quote entire books of the Bible."

Louisa felt herself relax a little. "Mr. Brown was a fine man." She softened her tone and added, "Your mother — a lovely, godly woman. No one could grow a garden better than Mary Brown. But, we've come up in the world, you and I. Don't you want better for your daughter than a hundred acres and a passel of children? Do you really want her in an office where men can be forward and brash with her? Is that what you *truly* want for your girl?"

"I want her happy." He folded his hands over his belly and added, "What I don't want is her pressured into a life that society demands simply because it *is* expected."

He wouldn't listen, not then. However, seeds planted, the invitation issued — her plans would go forward as expected. That's all she could hope for at that moment. "And I want her happy as well. I just fear that you foolishly dismiss how *un*happy she will be if she flaunts convention one too many times. People only forgive to a point." Louisa strolled to the door and turned the knob. "Marriage to a respectable man is her surest guarantee of happiness, Albert. Think about it."

With that, she stepped into the anteroom, nodded at the clerk, and sailed out the door and down the steps.

$\mathcal{E}$IGHT

The next afternoon, Madeline strolled the streets of Rockland in an aimless pursuit of nothing. She tried several shops, but nothing tempted her. Even Gardner & Henley's new detective novel, featuring an amateur detective confined to a wheelchair, "aided only by his keen powers of observation," didn't tempt her. However, when she found herself in a millinery shop trying on a *hat*, of all things, Madeline decided perhaps she just might need to reconsider her position in life.

I didn't want college, but now I'm not as certain. Papa would agree....

At that moment, two things occurred simultaneously. First, she spied Vernon Smythe walking down the street only a couple of yards ahead of her and in an evident hurry to get somewhere. Madeline scurried after him, trying both to keep up and remain inconspicuous. And just then, the second thing happened. A group of women rounded a corner carrying leaflets and signs that extolled the virtues of sobriety and the horrors of alcohol.

Madeline tried to push through the crowd, but one particularly large and well-dressed woman blocked her way. "Why, if it isn't Madeline Brown. You know, this is quite fortuitous. I had hoped to call on you about our cause."

It's anything but fortuitous!

" — see, we do need the Mayor's support for our cause, and who better than his daughter?"

"Except that his daughter has no interest in the temperance movement. Excuse me."

The woman pressed her further — detained her until Madeline had no hope of catching up to or following Vernon Smythe. "It's your *Christian* duty, Miss Brown, to support the cause of morality."

"It's my filial duty, and therefore also my *Christian* duty to respect my father's wishes. He does not wish me to be a part of this kind of radical movement. Now please excuse me."

The woman's next words sent an icy, burning chill through her. "Your mother would be—"

"Don't you presume to imagine *what* my sister would have wanted for her daughter, Elvira Evanston. I believe Madeline has informed you of her lack of interest. I would have thought your cause would appreciate personal conviction, or does that only apply when the conviction is yours, I wonder?"

Louisa Farnsworth hooked her arm through Madeline's and led her around the crowd and down the street. "I do believe Elvira becomes more obnoxious with every pound she gains. It must be connected somehow."

Though perhaps she should have, Madeline didn't even try to stifle her giggle. With an apologetic smile, she changed the subject. "I don't know how to thank you, Aunt Louisa. I was just about to say something I should very much regret."

"Then it is a blessing I happened along." Her aunt bestowed a benevolent smile upon her before asking, "And what brings you downtown today?"

Answering that question would likely earn her a lecture on why she needed to find a nice young man to marry. *And I can't desire that — not yet.* The words flowed from her lips before she could consider the wisdom of them. "There's a new detective novel at Gardner & Henley's." Once the words began, she couldn't seem to stop them. "I just thought perhaps I would be wise to...." She swallowed. "—take a constitutional before curling up with a book."

Her conscience added, *And perhaps spend a few minutes in prayer confessing the sin of lying to your aunt.*

"Those novels can't possibly be appropriate for someone your age." Louisa Farnsworth flung one hand aside as if to sweep a row of imaginary books off a shelf. "Dime novels — the lot of them."

"You know very well that Papa is careful of what I read. This isn't some lurid potboiler. It's not quite the caliber of Mr. Doyle's work, but from what I saw of it, I expect it to be a good story. Anyway, it'll drown out the moralistic jargon from Mrs. Evanston and the like."

Louisa stopped and cupped Madeline's face in her hands. "It does my heart good to hear you say that. I've worried about you. A young lady without a mother's care could be easily led into fanaticism."

The memory of having her plans thwarted by the temperance league's interference sent Madeline's temper flaring once more. "I don't think you need be concerned about that. I pray, of course. I read the text on Sundays. I even read a Psalm or Proverb during the week sometimes, but I am not in danger of wearing my religion on my chest as some sort of badge of honor."

"I'm very glad to hear it. Religion is beautiful, in its place, but displayed as an ornament, it becomes vulgar."

The women parted ways at the entrance to the store. Madeline went in to retrieve the book she'd lied about, determined at least to make her words true *after* the fact. Louisa murmured something about a trip to the milliner's. Devotion to one's faith suddenly seemed less oppressive and more essential as Madeline braced herself for another hat after her aunt learned she'd been in there that morning.

I fear I'm becoming duplicitous in many areas of my life. It's most disconcerting.

Louisa Farnsworth's home would have been a perfect example of the benefits of electrical lighting if Vernon Smythe had been of a mind to use it as one. However, seated across from Madeline, a hapless victim of an obvious matchmaking scheme, Vernon ignored the opportunity and turned his attention to the young man at his right. "Mr. Gray, I understand you are studying medicine."

The look of relief on Madeline's face made the sacrifice in asking about those studies worth it. *I cannot blame you for finding him tedious. I suspect he's a temperance man as well. Edith did say you don't think much of the movement. I wonder....*

As soon an appropriate moment came, Vernon turned to Mrs. Farnsworth. "Did you say you had leanings toward the temperance movement?"

The answer shone in the woman's indignant eyes, but his suspicions proved correct. Before Mrs. Farnsworth could answer, Mr. Gray spoke up. "It's a worthy cause, isn't it? I've been studying the effects of alcoholic spirits on the livers of indigents, and it's appalling—"

Mrs. Farnsworth looked ready to choke on her veal as she listened, and Vernon decided to do something about it. "I can only imagine." He leaned close and murmured, "I don't think the ladies have the stomach for such discussions."

Apologies flowed from William Gray's lips. "Pardon me. I have so immersed myself in my studies that I often forget not everyone spends their days..." He cleared his throat. "Doing what I do."

"Do you think the damage is comparable in a man who drinks only a small amount each day—say, a glass of wine with dinner?" Madeline's curiosity belied the look of revulsion Vernon felt sure he'd seen only moments earlier.

"I haven't made a deliberate comparison, but I don't recall

seeing that."

Vernon hadn't anticipated the purpose of the question, but when Madeline's lip twisted just a little, he suspected what she'd say next. He wasn't disappointed.

"Yet you are of the opinion that rigid adherence to temperance will greatly benefit society — medically speaking, of course."

I hadn't realized just how sharp your mind is, Miss Brown. Score one for you.

But William Gray didn't catch the subtle, mocking undertones of Madeline's words. "No one can argue that you cannot destroy your body with liquor if you don't partake of it."

"The same could be said of food, could it not?" Madeline blinked at the man.

Anyone watching you might suppose that you had no idea of the challenge you just issued. I wouldn't like to underestimate you.

At Mr. Gray's raised eyebrows, Madeline offered a sweet, seemingly innocent smile. "One cannot become a glutton if one doesn't eat."

Gray objected. "Yet food is essential to life. Without it, we die. Even Jesus was called the 'Bread of Life.'"

Her parry — Vernon couldn't have done better had he tried. "Yet, Jesus Himself said that man cannot live by bread alone. And, later in the New Testament, Paul instructs Timothy to drink a little wine. Furthermore," Vernon struggled to stifle a snicker at the dismayed looks on Mrs. Farnsworth's and Mr. Gray's faces as Madeline continued. " — several places in the Old Testament, we are told of how wine gladdens the heart."

"'Wine is a mocker, strong drink is raging, and whoever is deceived thereby is not wise.'"

Madeline's smile belied the flash Vernon saw in her eyes. "It's a pity our Lord didn't remember that verse when He turned water into excellent wine at the wedding at Cana." She turned to her aunt. "Aunt Louisa, this is the most delicious meal I've enjoyed in ages.

79

You must have Sarah tell Cook how the veal was prepared."

Albert Brown—Vernon had forgotten the man's presence—nodded his agreement. "Truly fine cooking."

Mr. Gray, however, did not take the gentle hint. He waxed eloquent about the effects of inebriation on the mind and body, until Vernon expected someone to snap. *Who knew an unwelcome matchmaking scheme could be so entertaining. And it never hurts to cultivate the friendship of the mayor's sister-in-law and daughter.* Another jab from Madeline and the conspiratorial smile she gave him prompted yet another thought. *Miss Merton will be pleased as well.*

Everything changed in an instant. Mr. Gray flung a bit of the sauce that covered the asparagus on his sleeve, and as he dabbed at it with his napkin, Madeline's attention shifted from annoyed to intrigued. "Those are unique cuff links, Mr. Gray."

The young man beamed. He gave Madeline an expression that, if the girl had any intuition at all, would signify genuine interest. Vernon leaned back just a little and prepared to watch the show.

"They are, aren't they? I found that I couldn't resist them."

"Where *did* you find them? You see, my friend Milty Grueber had a pair *just* like them commissioned by one of the jewelers downtown. Well...." She cocked her head as she considered her words. "I should say his father did—for his eighteenth birthday."

Red stole up Mr. Gray's neck. "I did find them downtown. Strange that they should be so similar to a special commission."

She leaned as far over the table as she could and peered at them. "WG. They're even your initials. Milty's looked like that—like it was WG instead of MG. His father asked for the M to be upside down so that from either direction one letter would be upright. He thought it *tres chic.*"

At those words, Vernon leaned forward. *Are you implying...?* He couldn't resist the temptation. "We'll have to compare them at the next social. It'll be amusing to note the differences."

All red drained from Mr. Gray's face. In fact, all *color* drained.

He coughed, grabbed for his wine glass, and gulped down two swallows before realizing what he drank. "Pardon me," he gasped. "May I trouble you—for some—water?"

Mrs. Farnsworth didn't wait to ring. She stood, retrieved the water pitcher, and poured a tumbler for Mr. Gray. "Are you quite all right?"

"I'm well now, thank you." He stared at the wine glass in dismay. "I apologize, Mrs. Farnsworth, Miss Brown." Though he spoke to both women, Mr. Gray raised his eyes to gaze at Madeline. "What hypocrisy I've shown. It was reflex rather than a desire for…"

"No one would assume otherwise," Madeline assured him.

Vernon saw it—a flash of disappointment in Madeline's eyes. *You are annoyed that the discussion changed. Why…?* He decided to try something. "I was just thinking how unfortunate it is that Mr. Grueber isn't here this evening. While young women rarely enjoy arriving in dresses of similar style and color, I believe men would find matching custom cuff links… interesting?"

Gratitude—it filled Madeline's eyes before she spoke. "Before Mr. Gray's unfortunate choking, I had been ready to explain that it wouldn't be possible. You see, Milty's cuff links have gone missing. He can't imagine how. They aren't the sort of thing one removes often—like a coat or hat."

"That they aren't. Did he play billiards somewhere? Perhaps he rolled up his sleeves?" Vernon turned to Mr. Gray. "I believe Mr. Grueber is particularly fond of Snooker. Have you ever played?"

After another cough, another gulp of *water*, and a nervous clearing of his throat, Mr. Gray shook his head. "I've watched, but I don't play. You do have a good theory there. Perhaps Mr. Grueber should ask around houses where he's played—or at local clubs?"

"I'll do that!" Madeline positively beamed at the man. "How clever you are. I'll also reassure him that replacement links can be found downtown. Where did you say you found yours?"

Oh, Miss Madeline. You do have a wicked sense of humor, don't you?

81

And as I have already observed, you seem to hide a sharp mind. A bit fearless, as well. However, a glance her way showed the girl's face blank—lacking all hint of extraordinary intelligence. *Is it deliberate, or are you truly so artless? I can't decide.*

"—didn't like to admit it, but I purchased these near Fordyce Square." Mr. Gray waited for polite nods of understanding, but Mrs. Farnsworth looked confused, Madeline intrigued, and Albert Brown narrowed his eyes in suspicion. When no one responded, Mr. Gray choked out, "At a pawnbroker's. I couldn't afford the quality I wanted, so...."

Mrs. Farnsworth now looked ready to choke on the dill-roasted potatoes, and Mr. Brown tossed her a glowering look. Madeline looked positively smug until Mrs. Farnsworth turned toward him. "I understand you're interested in electricity, Mr. Smythe. My niece has often said that she thinks the heat radiating from electrical light is less oppressive than that of gaslight. What do you think?"

I can oblige, Mrs. Farnsworth, but you will find that your niece and I are not congenial. His eyes met Madeline's for just a moment before he answered. "I couldn't agree more. While there is some heat with electricity—how could there not be?—gaslight has an actual flame. It can't help but produce much more heat than electric lighting."

The woman turned to Madeline. "I believe you've been proven right, my dear, but I still can't help but think my gasolier is a much more attractive piece than Albert's wires and bulbs."

If he hadn't seen it himself, Vernon would never have believed it. Madeline snickered. "And safer for the veal." She smiled at Vernon before continuing. "Why, at our last dinner, Mary and I decorated those wires and bulbs with as many flowers as we could—for aesthetic purposes, of course. Alas, we do not have the skill with twine and flowers that we thought we did. One guest managed to have a lilac garnish on her veal before the dinner concluded."

With an embarrassed clearing of his throat, Albert Brown tried to explain their lack of proper dining room accoutrements "I've been told that electrical fixtures will drop dramatically in price as well as have fewer power failures if I wait a year or two."

"I must agree with your advisor, Mr. Brown. I believe it is only a matter of a very short while before we will see great improvements in electrical fixtures and reliability. The more widespread the use, the better." Vernon stared down at the plate of half-eaten lemon cake before him and wondered at when it had arrived and how he'd eaten so much. "This is delicious cake, Mrs. Farnsworth."

She beamed at him. "It is Madeline's favorite."

"I am particularly fond of lemon as well, Miss Brown." Mr. Gray's eagerness to interject himself into the conversation proved only to make him look quite desperate.

"Is that so?" Madeline set down her fork and sighed. "I think I'll excuse myself for a moment, Aunt Louisa."

"We'll be having coffee on the back porch, Madeline. Please join us out there when you can."

And you'll be sure to have me inside on some pretext, won't you Mrs. Farnsworth? Vernon's supposition proved true. No sooner had they seated themselves on the porch furniture than Mrs. Farnsworth glanced about her. "I've left my fan inside. Do excuse me."

Despite the words, the implication rang clear. Vernon glanced at Mr. Gray and found the young man examining his saucer with great interest. *Well, that will work. An excellent maneuver, ma'am.* He stood. "Allow me, Mrs. Farnsworth. Would it be by your chair at the dining table or…"

"Or perhaps on the credenza? I don't remember if I picked it up and laid it down again or if I left it there. How silly of me."

"I can get it for you, Louisa." Albert Brown started to rise, but Vernon waved him back. "I'm happy to do it, sir."

Madeline found him scouring the table, the credenza, even the *floor* for the missing fan. "What have you lost, Mr. Smythe?"

"Your aunt has mislaid her fan. I offered to find it, but…."

A knowing smirk twisted her lips. "I assure you, she has it with her. She often thinks she's *forgotten* things that she hasn't."

Courtesy demanded he offer his arm. Her chagrin would make it amusing, at least. And, a few well-timed words might put him in favor with Miss Merton. "Shall we join them and see if they've recovered it yet?" Vernon offered his arm before adding, "Miss Merton has a charming habit of mislaying her things as well, doesn't she?"

"Yes, but where Auntie usually 'forgets' to a purpose, Edith is genuinely distracted—usually because she has considered someone else's needs above her own."

"It is one of the things I admire most about her—that selflessness of character."

Madeline paused just inside the door to the porch. "I'm pleased to hear it. I wouldn't like to see my friend hurt."

His smile, his nod, the quiet tones he used—each seemed to soothe the concerned lines that tried to etch themselves into her features. "I wouldn't either."

NINE

Nearly a week passed—a week in which May slipped into June with little notice by anyone in Rockland. Blue skies clouded for an hour or two every few days and gave just enough rain to keep crops and gardens healthy and happy. The temperate weather affected all in Madeline's circle of friends, including Madeline herself.

So, when she heard masculine voices in Jonas Merton's home study, Madeline didn't seem to notice or care about who might be in there and discussing what. She strolled past on her way to the washroom and made a mental note about the unusualness of Mr. Merton being home at that time of day. Once inside the washroom, she stared into the mirror, straining her mind in an attempt to discover why something seemed off.

You didn't even pause in case you overheard something interesting. Then again, what can one expect to hear in Mr. Merton's office? The current rate of interest, perhaps? I'll pass on that scintillating opportunity.

Madeline dawdled as long as she could justify and strolled back through the house to the music-room-turned-meeting-room. A crowd of young ladies sat in smaller groups, giggling about the latest *faux pas* of one of their beaux or the new vaudeville act in town. Madeline inched her way close to Edith and murmured, "Is everyone here, do you think?"

As expected, Edith rose and stood near the piano. "Ladies, can we come to order, please?"

No one heard, or perhaps they didn't listen. Regardless, Madeline elbowed Margaret Rodgers and murmured, "It's shameful when someone sweet like Edith has to resort to yelling to capture everyone's attention *in her own home.*"

It worked. Margaret clapped her hands a few times and the room quieted in response. Edith tossed Margaret a grateful look and opened the meeting. As usual, Edith began with Madeline—a distinct benefit to being one of Edith's closest friends. "Can you update us, Madeline? Do we have news regarding the speaker?"

She opened her mouth to announce that yes, they had managed to secure a popular elocutionist, but another idea flowed from her lips almost of its own accord. "While I did manage to arrange for Hortense Montbatton to recite for us, I do wonder if we shouldn't vary the program. We could have her recite something, have another speaker lecture on some current event, and then have Mrs. Montbatton conclude the evening with another recitation."

"Wouldn't that just complicate things?" Sally Penworthy stood as she spoke. "I don't understand the purpose."

Madeline kept her voice quiet, soft, but firm. "I just thought we might have a larger number of men attending if there was something of interest to them. Most men hold the purse strings, so it only makes sense that the more we can entice to attend, the larger the donations would be. But if you think it's a poor idea, then it's all settled as it is."

Low murmurs filled the room, and Edith's eyes darted about as she tried to determine what to do. A twang of guilt plucked from Madeline's heartstrings made her regret causing the impending ruckus—almost. *You'll forgive me in a moment, Edith, dear.*

And it happened. Edith called the room to order and asked Madeline's opinion on just what kind of speaker they should consider. "Perhaps if we had an idea of what you meant, we'd know if it's the direction we wish to take the event."

This time, Madeline stood and moved nearer the front. "When the idea first came to me, my initial thought was someone political.

You know how men love their politics." Madeline wrinkled her nose. "But after the recent elections, I think Rockland is weary of the subject."

Cheers—much less decorous than one would have expected from a group of proper young ladies—erupted from every corner of the room. Madeline stifled a smirk and continued. "But then I remembered our discussion at the meeting at the Hardwick's—after my unfortunate foray into the Dry Docks quarter. I thought perhaps a lecture on the purpose of the area and how it can be improved. Mr. Smythe seems to be well versed in the area's strengths and weaknesses. It would be such a civic-minded speech, wouldn't you think?"

As she saw Edith's eyes light up, Madeline couldn't help but feel yet another twinge of guilt. *It was almost too easy, Edith. The moment I mentioned Vernon Smythe, no one had a chance to object, did they?*

"Can we even secure Mr. Smythe for that date?" Margaret's voice rang out over the growing squeals of excitement. "This all sounds just the thing, but really, ladies. Aren't we being a bit premature?"

"Why don't we ask him?" Edith beckoned Madeline to come closer. "Vernon is in Father's study, discussing something about the project. Would you? Perhaps ask if he'd address us now for a moment to give an account of what he'd discuss?"

Madeline blinked, glanced around the room, and turned back again. In the quietest whisper she could manufacture Madeline suggested, "Surely if *you* requested...."

"I couldn't leave." But despite the words, Edith flushed and cast her eyes downward.

"I'll be right back with him, then. Oh, can you imagine the admiration on his face when he sees you leading such an important committee!"

It worked. Edith's entire demeanor changed. Before Madeline

could reach the doorway, her friend had managed to call the room to order. *Excellent rally, my dear. Excellent.*

The study door stood slightly ajar, and the men's voices reached her with perfect clarity. "—spoke with a woman down there. The conditions are worse than I first thought."

Mr. Merton's voice rang out with his usual gruffness. "I don't see what that has to do with our purpose. Let the bawdy houses stand. They aren't hurting anyone but the fools who go there without care for the diseases they may catch."

Madeline's throat went dry and her breath caught. *What could you be talking about?*

"If we're seen as capitalizing on the misfortunes of others...."

"That's preposterous! Why, I—"

Though she ached to listen further—see what response Mr. Merton would make—Madeline forced herself to rap on the door. *They sound too close for them to be across the room. If they opened that door—*

And at that very moment, the door flung open. Had she not been inches away from him, Madeline wouldn't have trusted herself to believe it, but most definitely did his eyes narrow for just the merest fraction of a second. "Miss Brown! I did not hear your knock."

"I did. How could you not?" Mr. Merton sounded more put out than he should have in Madeline's estimation.

"I'm sorry. I must have been concentrating on our discussion." Smythe gave a curt nod. "I'll leave you to speak with Mr. Merton."

He tried to slip beside her and out the door, but Madeline took a slight sidestep and flashed her most innocent smile. "Oh, please don't. I came to speak to you. You see, we're holding a meeting downstairs. We're in need of a speaker for our upcoming event, and I thought we could convince you to lecture on the Dry Docks—propose ideas for improvement, perhaps?"

Of all the responses he could have given her, reluctance—nay, *resistance*—would never have crossed her mind. Smythe protested, thanked her profusely, but insisted he couldn't possibly consider it. "I'm sure you understand that my contacts in that area would likely feel betrayed by any public discussion of their misfortunes. I cannot hope to do any *good* if my presence in the area is called into question."

As Smythe spoke, Jonas Merton went from the appearance of protest to nodding his agreement. "I must agree. This sounds like a dangerous proposition. We must preserve their pride and our relationship at all costs."

Relief—it oozed from Smythe, despite the grave expression on his face. Madeline nodded, praised their forethought, and turned to go. *I think a debate over how best to improve conditions down there might just be a better idea anyway.*

As she relayed the news, the room split between sighs of disappointment and sighs of relief. She'd hardly made the proposition of a debate before Jimmy Higgins' freckled face appeared over the bottom of the music room windowsill. "I'll leave it to everyone to consider while I make inquiries. We can finalize the idea at our next meeting. As it is, we still have Mrs. Montbatton regardless of any other addition to the program. Now, I really must go. I have an important meeting in a few minutes. I'm afraid I couldn't get out of it. You understand."

Questions followed her all the way to the door, but Madeline ignored them and strode down the walk. At the corner of the Mertons' yard, half-hidden by a rhododendron, Jimmy waited. "I saw you talking to that Vernon Smythe fellow. Miss Edith is sweet on him, but he's just a bonehead wisenheimer who's trying to catch the banker's daughter 'cause he's loaded."

Madeline's head spun in dizzying circles, but whether it was the string of slang or the jumbled pronouns, she couldn't say. "Everything I've seen showed a genuine interest in her, though. How could you be sure of that assessment?"

"Maybe he's just one of those fellas that likes a girl on each arm.

I don't know. But I do know I saw him smooching with some girl in the park last evening. Miss Edith deserves better than that."

After fishing out a penny from her purse and handing it to him, Madeline gave Jimmy a grateful smile and moved on her way again. *She does indeed, my dear Jimmy. She does indeed.*

Six photographs lay on the desk before her. Madeline gazed intently at each two and a quarter inch square. Four of the pictures had developed nicely. The images were reasonably crisp and the lighting good. Unfortunately, the two she had most anticipated turned out dark and somewhat blurry. Still, under direct sunlight, she could just make out the wagonload of food and Vernon Smythe in the distance. As she'd suspected, his head had been turned away from the group, looking over his shoulder. In the other one—the one of Flossie Hardwick and her brother—Vernon Smythe stood off in the distance talking to a woman.

Why does everything about that look familiar? It isn't the young woman I saw him take into that building. She's much too tall for that. And Jimmy said the woman he saw Smythe with was very young. Something about this woman implies maturity – in her stance, if nothing else. So –

Mary stepped into the room just as she stepped closer to the window. "Miss Madeline, Mr. Barnes is here. Shall I show him in or would you like to—"

"Send him on back. He'll want to see these, and the light is so much better in this room. Papa chose his study wisely."

She picked up a magnifying glass and used it to stare at the photo of Flossie and Frank. *That is disconcerting. Why can't I recall what is so familiar?*

"I see you received your first photographs." Russell moved closer. "They are rather small, aren't they?"

Madeline gave him a bright smile and passed the photograph and the magnifying glass. "This one is just exceptionally dark. I was trying to see who else was in the picture. I know Frank and Flossie are in there, but who is back behind? There's something familiar about that lady, but I can't determine what."

Russell turned the photograph in his hand, angling for the best light, and stared. "Well, I don't recognize her at all, but that hat.... I think the man is definitely Vernon Smythe. Does that help identify her? She looks too tall to be Edith, but...."

"Edith wore white that day. This is more of a medium shade of some color—cornflower or rose, perhaps."

The minute she spoke the word, "rose," Madeline's mind whirled. *Is that... no, it couldn't be. But how curious.* Her fingers played with the edge of another photograph until Russell put down the one he held and picked up another—the one he'd taken of her in the boat.

"Now this one I remember. It's a fine picture of you, Madeline. It captured you quite well, don't you think?"

She leaned over his arm to peer at it closer. The photograph hadn't interested her at first. But at Russell's praise, she gave it a thorough perusal. "I think it is a good likeness, isn't it?" She picked up the magnifying glass and stared at her face. "Is it the lighting, or do I have a rather thin nose?"

Russell took the glass from her hand and examined the photograph. "Well, I think perhaps it's a bit of both." His head turned and he gazed into her face for a moment before nodding. "Yes, your nose isn't exactly wide, but the photograph does thin it a little. Perhaps the shadow here...." He pointed to the darker side of her face. "See?"

"I'll have to remember that next time I try a portrait. I may be able to balance the shadows and lights better."

With a dismissive air, she shoved the photograph aside and pulled hers of Russell off the desk. "How do you think the camera captured your likeness? It looks as though these people behind you have created a single horn on the left side of your head. How unfortunate."

Once more, Russell took the magnifying glass and stared at it. "I think those are the same people in the one of Flossie and Frank. That's certainly Mr. Smythe."

"Well, it's quite inconsiderate—and rather vain of him, don't you think? To insert himself into nearly *every* picture?"

"He does seem to enjoy being the center of attention." However, despite his words, Russell watched her with what felt like a suspicious eye.

Changing the subject seemed the best option. "Well, I'm sorry my pretty picnic spread came out so dark. I had hoped to share it with Amy. I can send her your photograph instead. She'd probably like that best anyway." She stacked up the little photographs with the picture of Frank and Flossie on top. "It's a shame this isn't a nicer one as well. Mrs. Hardwick might have liked to have it."

Russell picked up the photograph of Madeline and started to hand it to her. "You missed one." But as she reached for it, he pulled it back. "Then again, might I have this one? You didn't seem particularly fond of it, and...." He gave her a small smile before adding in a rush, "Your idea about sending one to Amy is a good one. She'd like to have this of you. I'll be the thoughtful big brother if I send it instead of you."

I can't imagine what the difference is, Russell, but by all means. Take it. It took her a moment to realize that she hadn't spoken aloud. "Of course. Do whatever you like with it. I'll have to have you take another of me in different lighting. Papa might like something a little less formal than my eighteenth birthday portrait."

"Amy still insists that she wants to paint you a 'proper' portrait. She does love photographs, but...."

"'Nothing produced by a machine ought to be called a portrait. It's a disgrace to the art.'" Madeline laughed. "Sometimes when I think she's heading into melancholy, I 'accidentally' mention photographed 'portraits.' It pulls her right out again."

Mary stepped into the room. "Excuse me, miss, but I wondered if you would like to eat on the terrace or in the dining room?"

"Is the kitchen over-warm today?"

The young girl nodded. "Cook's making bread, and you know how that is."

"Then we'll eat on the terrace—if Russell can stay, that is. Otherwise, I'll brave the kitchen."

Just a hint of hesitation preceded Russell's agreement. "I'd like that. Thank you, Mary." To Madeline he added, "I actually came to see if you'd like to join Flossie and Warren for a drive out into the country. Warren's uncle loaned him the carriage for the afternoon. You know how he's been trying to get back in her good graces. He thought perhaps if *you* came...."

"I am happy to. As far as I know, Warren is an upstanding young man. I understand Flossie's concern, but one must take a person's entire character into account when considering what seems an out of character action, don't you think?"

His eyes sought hers. "I understand a theory of yours is what softened her in the first place—something about how Stanley would have known where Warren supposedly was if...."

A slow smile spread across Madeline's face. "It did seem relevant to the situation."

Not until they were seated with cold chicken and potato salad before them did Russell speak again. "I overheard Elizabeth Denton express concern about you the other day. She seems to think you are quite obsessed with the Dry Docks and some scheme to improve it." He took a bite and chewed it thoughtfully before adding, "I can't help but think there is more to it than simple curiosity or concern."

I suspect her "concern" has more to do with her desire to ingratiate herself with you than a desire to protect my virtue or whatever that so-called concern is. Of course, Madeline couldn't say such a thing, so she concentrated on Russell's theory. "I don't know what scheme she has attributed to me. I'm merely *concerned* with what I saw while down there that day. It really was quite… unsettling."

Russell's expression hinted that he knew she'd been deliberately evasive, but he just nodded. "I see."

I suspect you do, my friend. But even you have to admit it was a particularly fine choice of words.

$\mathcal{T}$EN

Once again, Madeline sat on a settee, her skirt spread as wide as she could manage, and fanning herself against the oppressive heat of the Mertons' parlor. Stanley Wakefield, heedless of her skirt and the instant discomfort he would bring, plopped himself down beside her. "Blasted heat. We'd all be more comfortable outside."

"I believe some of the fellows are playing croquet by lantern light...."

"Boring game, that."

What else he said, Madeline missed. Her mind was more interestingly occupied by something she saw across the room. Vernon Smythe sat next to Edith whispering something into the young lady's ear. *Likely those 'sweet nothings' that the fairer sex tends to enjoy.*

But what riveted her attention wasn't the closeness of Smythe's lips to Edith's ear, or even the way his hand covered hers in broad view of all present. No, her eyes remained firmly on the ground—so to speak. *What about those shoes...?*

"—things become more and more tedious every week. Stella thinks Edith only holds them as an excuse to invite that Smythe fellow."

She's likely correct, but it wouldn't do to say so, would it? Madeline folded her hands in her lap, in a deliberate attempt at self-control, before answering. "I expect it has as much to do with Mr. Merton as it does with dear Edith. I believe they are working together on some project in the Dry Docks." Just as he began to reply, Madeline's eyes widened. "I wonder if it is quite safe."

"I don't know much about the business," Stanley admitted. He called out across the room to ask that very question. "Hey, Smythe. Madeline was wondering how safe an improvement project to the Dry Docks would be."

Vernon Smythe's eyes darkened just before a few chuckles escaped. "It seems to me that if it *isn't* safe, that is all the more reason to consider such a project."

"I see. Thank you. I hadn't considered that. I would recommend sanitation to be a first step. Why, I must have asked Mary to brush my shoes half a dozen times before I felt willing to walk through the house in them after my sojourn into the area." Her heart raced to hear her own words, and she glanced at Smythe's feet again. Madeline shifted her expression from thoughtful to curious. "Do you find the cleanliness to vary during different times of the day or on different days?"

Smythe gave a brief shrug. "I couldn't say. I haven't spent enough time down there. It isn't the sort of place one would wish associated with oneself. A man's reputation, while not as fragile as a woman's, is his livelihood."

"But you've been there more than once, surely? The last time compared to the first, perhaps?"

"They were reasonably similar, yes, but you do pose an interesting question. I'll have to inquire. It might help in determining *how* such a project could be attempted."

Madeline turned to Stanley and paused. Smythe had almost resumed speaking with Edith, when she spoke out again. "You've piqued my curiosity. The first time you went down there, was it a weekday? Early in the day or late?"

He didn't want to answer. It showed in his posture and the way his eyes almost glared despite the smile he wore. Still, Smythe considered her question for a moment before answering. "I believe it to have been a Tuesday or Wednesday afternoon."

"That is comparable to my trip." She described the sights she saw—all but the ones of *him*. "Is that much like you've experienced?"

"I would say so, yes." Smythe swept the room with an indulgent smile. "Our Miss Brown has a reputation for being uninterested in temperance and suffrage, but I believe we've discovered her passion this evening."

A small ripple of laughter designed to embarrass her echoed through the room, but Madeline dismissed it. "I don't see how anyone who has experienced the Dry Docks could be immune to the horrors of it." Before he could reply, she added, "Oh, and the last time you were there?" Her mind pleaded with him to mention a Saturday or Sunday.

"I believe it was last... Sunday. Yes. After church." He turned to Edith. "Is that correct? We spoke of it."

"Yes. You said you overheard some sort of meeting." Edith smiled at the recollection. "That's right! Because, remember, there was that little boy walking past singing, 'Bringing in the sheeps.'" A ripple of laughter—loud and unrepressed this time—filled the room.

Satisfied with new information to chew on, Madeline sat back and sipped at her lemonade. Seconds later, she looked up to see Russell leaning against the parlor doorjamb. His arms were folded over his chest, his eyes riveted on her, and an amused smirk lifted one corner of his mouth. He raised his eyebrows ever so slightly and nodded.

Deduced my scheme, did you, Mr. Barnes? Very good. Excellent. Now, to determine if there is some financial gain in improving places such as the Dry Docks quarter. Mr. Merton owns quite a bit of property around the city. And for someone who hasn't been in the Dry Docks since Sunday, your shoes do look quite similar to how mine did that day. I wonder.

What are you doing, Madeline Brown? As interesting as "Madeline the Crusader" might be, I happen to know you have no such ambition. So, that begs the question, "What is your true motive to this inquiry?"

He had intended to persuade Madeline to take an early stroll home—the long way. With fine weather and a gentle breeze, the walk would have been pleasant. If nothing else, it would have rescued her from Stanley Wakefield's boorish behavior. However, everything shifted when she met his frank gaze and smirked.

Edith rose and a moment later, Madeline followed. The opportunity proved too perfect to allow to pass. Russell seated himself in Edith's vacated seat and pretended to fuss with his watch. "Have you the correct time?"

The watch Smythe produced was just fine enough to suit a man of his supposed status but not expensive enough to be considered flashy or pretentious. *Why doesn't she trust you? I can sense it. Can you?*

"It's just a few minutes until ten o'clock."

"Thank you." He pocketed his watch and glanced around him. "The girls are still gone, so I'll sit, if you don't mind. It's been a long day." Smythe looked anything but pleased, but before he could protest, Russell continued. "And please do warn me if the girls return without my notice. If I know Edith, she'll seat herself on that settee beside Madeline, and I know how overwarm she gets over there."

Smythe murmured something that sounded like an agreement, but when he spoke, his tone shifted—almost to suspicion. "Have you known Miss Merton long?"

"A good portion of her life. Madeline and my sister, Amy, are very close, and Edith joined them in their play often enough." He forced himself to look a bit taken aback. "I'd forgotten you aren't from here. Baltimore, is it?"

"Boston. Family has been there since it was founded, or so my grandmother liked to insist." He lowered his voice. "I wouldn't be surprised if the stories were grossly exaggerated. Grandmother was known for *embellishing* her stories to suit the occasion."

And did you inherit that talent? Though tempted to ask the question, Russell ignored that temptation and opted to ask another. "How are you enjoying Rockland? I believe Madeline said you'd found it congenial enough to stay?"

"I do. The people are open and friendly, and I've found several promising business opportunities."

"Would one of those be this Dry Docks project Madeline is so enamored with? I've never seen her take such an interest." He swallowed hard and inwardly begged Madeline's forgiveness should she overhear him. "I can't help but be concerned of your influence if you can stir her to such out-of-character behavior." Though he smiled as he spoke, Russell couldn't smooth *all* of the edge from his voice.

A grave, concerned expression wiped away Smythe's previous look of disinterested curiosity and he sighed. "I can well understand your concern. However, I don't believe I've had any influence over her at all. I believe Miss Brown's concern came from her own experience rather than mine."

Every word held a note of sincerity. His expression showed nothing to infer anything else, but Russell also noted a distinct chill in the conversation. The girls entered the room and Russell stood. "It was nice having a moment to talk, Mr. Smythe. I think I'll see if I can convince Madeline to leave." He leaned a bit closer. "Her father appreciates it when I can walk her home, but I'd prefer an early night."

As Smythe stood at Edith's arrival, the men shook hands. "Madeline, I was just telling Mr. Smythe how I thought to convince you to leave a little early. It's been a long day."

"Of course! I'll just say goodbye to a few people." She gave

Edith a parting hug and stepped away. "Shall I meet you at the door in five minutes?"

It'll be ten, if half your friends have a say in it, but I can stomach that. Aloud, Russell merely agreed. He thanked Edith for a fine evening and made her promise to join them for their next drive into the country. "I'd thought to hire a buggy sometime in the next week or two."

"That'll be lovely. Thank you, Russell."

Will it irk or inspire Madeline, I wonder. Russell nodded to Smythe. "You're welcome to join us, of course."

"Depending on the day, I'd enjoy that. Thank you." Before he could ask for an address, Smythe added, "You'll find me at the boarding house on West Charles Street, but advance notice would be appreciated and would make it more likely that I can join you."

The happiness in Edith's eyes couldn't be denied. *You care about him, or at least his interest in you. Which is it?* But before he could ponder the question, he spotted Madeline standing by the door—waiting. "It appears Madeline has proven me wrong once again. She's waiting. Goodnight. Thank you for inviting me, Edith."

They stepped out into the night and sighed in perfect unison. Madeline gave a lighthearted giggle. "I wonder how many others will leave early in an attempt to escape the oppressiveness in there. Edith does so love her lights, but the *heat*...."

At the gate, he turned left instead of right. "Let's walk the long way round."

She waited several seconds—at least a dozen yards, in which Russell grew nervous—before she asked, "What am I to be scolded for tonight, Russell?"

"Should you be scolded? I wasn't aware. But if you just confess your wrongs, I promise—"

"Oh, no! If you are as clueless to them as I am, let's just keep it that way. Speculation only serves to ensure that I reveal something you didn't know."

Russell pulled her arm through his and led her down the street and around the corner. *What is there that I shouldn't know, Miss Maddie?*

But before he could conceive of a way to ask without prying, she stomped her feet on the sidewalk and grinned. "I do so love these paved walkways. Papa says he grumbled at the added expense when he moved in, but I remember the little house on Oak Street. The streets were so dusty and my shoes and stockings were always filthy."

"I have often admired them. I understand your father has raised the funds to pave some of the side streets downtown. I think the business owners will appreciate that."

She turned and walked backwards as they strolled, her eyes flashing with excitement in the occasional light of a street lamp. "Papa says that anytime a path ends abruptly, people look for it to continue and follow it. So, if the sidewalks go around all the corners, people will be predisposed to follow them if they are out for a ramble. That will bring new customers to businesses that usually must wait for someone who *needs* their services."

"He's correct. In fact, I overheard Mr. Thurgood predicting that Jefferson Avenue will become an even more important thoroughfare than Whiting Boulevard."

"Does he really think so?" Madeline spun and slipped her arm through his again as they neared the next corner. "That is so exciting. Can you imagine telling our children someday, 'Why, I remember when no one went down Jefferson Avenue unless they must'?"

Madeline, any man who didn't know you would take your words as a hint of the kind of affection that I know you don't feel for me. But how to warn you? The answer came in an unexpected moment of genius. *Amy, I'll be writing another letter on the heels of the last one.*

"—don't you think?"

He turned and confessed he hadn't been listening. "What did you say again?"

101

"Nothing." She nudged him just as she might any fellow might his buddy. "I just saw you were a mile away in your thoughts, and I had to tease you."

"I deserve that, I suppose." He waited until he felt her relax again and asked, "Why are you so curious about Smythe's Dry Docks interests?"

She didn't answer. One step after another, they strolled along Verdigris Lane. Russell waited, knowing her tendency to share all with him wouldn't fail. And just as they turned yet another corner, she spoke. "I noticed something, I had a theory, I tested my theory, and I proved that I was correct."

"And that was…." Surprise and concern swirled together as she shook her head, refusing to answer. "Madeline…."

But she remained obdurate. "I only proved a theory true, Russell. The *why* behind it may be perfectly innocent. If it isn't, however…."

"I don't understand." To himself he added, *And I'm not sure I want to, but Amy would never forgive me if I didn't* attempt *to dissuade you from anything that sounded dangerous.*

Madeline slowed her walk—a good sign, he thought—and sighed. "It's only that I've seen things that trouble me, but you know how the most innocent actions can appear to be quite the opposite when observed out of context. I wouldn't want to misjudge someone, but neither do I wish to see people I care about hurt because I kept silent when I should have spoken."

She gave an impatient shake and folded her arms over her chest—a leftover childhood habit when piqued. "Growing up is such an inconvenience. I think I prefer days of chasing each other through the back yards brandishing swords or rescuing each other from dastardly fiends who sought to make us work in diamond mines or sell us to be servants in the Orient."

"Well I, for one, am thrilled that you've grown older, and hopefully wiser. Those escapades of yours earned me no small

102

number of scoldings—for allowing them to happen, of course."

"As if you could have prevented us!" Madeline giggled. "Do you recall when I found that man lurking about the place—right after we moved here? I was certain he was some sort of spy. Of course, I didn't know who he was spying for and what kind of secrets he hoped to find. You nearly broke your neck trying to prevent me from making my suspicions known to him."

And you nearly got yourself killed with your sneaking around. If that man had realized what you were doing.... But Russell didn't say it. Instead, he reminded her that she had been proven correct. Though not a spy, he had been scouring the neighborhood for likely places to burgle. "My mother still remarks on your keen powers of observation. She's convinced that you single-handedly saved the silver."

"And I've never forgotten the dollar your father gave me. No other dollar I've ever possessed ever held as much meaning to me as that one still does."

"You still have it?" That kind of sentimentality in Madeline—unexpectedly delightful. "I think I'll have to send Father a letter and tell him."

"I could take a photograph of it. Wouldn't that be an interesting one to try to capture?"

He couldn't help but be intrigued. "You'll wait until I can watch, won't you? The light will have to be just right, or you won't see the detail in the coin."

At her gate, she smiled up at him and nodded. "Come after church on Sunday. Have lunch with us. And we'll play with it all afternoon if necessary."

She invited him inside, but Russell pulled the gate shut behind her. "I said I wanted to go home early. I'll go to keep my word, but I accept your invitation for Sunday. Father will appreciate the photograph."

The moment she stepped in the door, Russell turned and

walked past the Mertons' once more and to the trolley line. *Sleep well, Madeline.*

$\mathcal{E}$LEVEN

A rumbling outside sent Edith and Madeline to the window. Edith blanched. "Is that—surely not!"

Vernon Smythe removed a pair of gloves and tossed them onto the seat as he climbed down. "It looks like an automobile." Madeline peered at her friend. "Did you know he planned to purchase one?"

From the horrified expression on Edith's face, Madeline surmised the answer to be a resounding, "No!" Edith merely shook her head. "Aren't they quite...." She dropped her voice to a hoarse whisper. "*Dangerous?*"

"I don't know. I've always found the idea quite fascinating. Papa would never purchase one, of course. Well...." A small smile formed as she reconsidered her thoughts. "I suppose he might if it became *the thing* to do. There's still no stigma against a trolley or hired carriage. He does need to keep up appearances."

Ida led Smythe into the parlor, and Madeline enjoyed a moment of amusement at his discomfiture. *You most definitely did not expect or desire to see me here. I wonder.*

"Is that your contraption, Ver—" Edith hesitated before finishing. "—non?"

"It was just delivered an hour ago. Isn't she a killer?"

It took every bit of her self-control for Madeline *not* to laugh at Edith's blank expression.

Edith looked out at the automobile and back up at Smythe. "Did you say she's a killer?"

Oh, my. Even I know slang a bit better than that, Edith dear.

"The machine," Smythe repeated. "She's a 'killer'—a real lollapalooza."

When her friend still couldn't seem to grasp his meaning, Madeline took pity—on *both* of them. "It means it is a fine piece of machinery, Edith." But the words intrigued her. *I don't believe I've ever heard you use such slang. Interesting.*

"Oh! Is it? I don't know anything about these new-fangled things. Whatever made you decide to buy one?"

"The convenience. I can dash about town without waiting for trolleys or taxicabs. The convenience alone is incomparable, but I also admit to liking the privacy of it."

I imagine you do. It would be much harder—and easier, I suspect—for someone to follow you into an unsavory area of town if you didn't choose to be followed.

"Well, you must take us for a ride, Mr. Smythe. I've never had the opportunity, and I know Edith hasn't." When he looked ready to object, Madeline threw out her only hope of further inducement. "Of course, on that little seat, we might be a bit crushed. I would offer to stay behind, but I would so like to see what it's like. Would you mind terribly?"

It worked. Smythe flashed a smile at Edith and asked, "Are you game? Just a short trip around the neighborhood, perhaps?"

"But if I should fall out...."

Oh, Edith. You just ensured that we'll be motoring around in no time.

"Perhaps Miss Brown wouldn't mind sitting on the outside then? That way you'd be safely wedged between us—no possibility of falling out." Madeline stepped away in hopes he'd take the opportunity to press her. And he did. She strained to hear but smiled when he added, "You could hold onto my arm, of course—if it made you feel better."

"If you're sure it's safe...."

"Would I risk your safety for anything, Edith dear?"

Dear is it? And look, she barely blushes. She's heard that from you before, I think.

Edith slipped toward the door. "Let me go find a couple of driving scarves—one for Madeline too, of course."

As much as she ached to stay, Madeline made a show of following her friend. "I fear she's a little more nervous than she cares to show. I'll settle her. And thank you. I've never ridden in an automobile before. Is it gasoline or steam powered?"

"It's steam—a Locomobile. Your knowledge does you credit, Miss Brown."

She ducked her head as she stepped through the door. "I'm afraid that is the extent of it. I've heard arguments about the superiority of both machines, and it all seems to hinge on that one thing—steam or gasoline. Now, if I only knew what significance that held!" She called back as she hurried upstairs. "We'll be down directly."

Less than ten minutes later, Madeline led Edith back down to the front steps where Smythe waited with the engine still running. Hats tied down with large chiffon scarves and shawls on their arms should the great speeds of fifteen miles an hour produce a chill— Madeline nearly laughed at the idea—the two young women climbed up into the vehicle and waited for Smythe to check something on the boiler and climb up beside them. Edith clutched at his arm in a display of true terror. Madeline's conscience ordered her to put a stop to the excursion, but the very real probability that Edith could *marry* the man she now clung to silenced her misgivings.

She must get used to modern times and inventions if she's to marry him. Vernon Smythe seems to be quite obsessed with all things modern. In that, he's not so unlike Russell. I wonder if it's a masculine trait. Then again, I enjoy them as well. Perhaps not....

"—deline!"

Madeline started. "Yes? I'm sorry. I was just anticipating the

107

journey."

"Vernon wanted to be sure you were ready for him to drive now."

"Very solicitous of you, Mr. Smythe, but I am quite ready, yes." Madeline leaned forward and gave the man a warm smile. "It is so very kind of you to do this for us."

By way of an answer, Smythe released a brake of some kind, how she couldn't say, and the Locomobile rolled forward.

The anticipated thrill didn't materialize. In fact, it was quite a disappointment. Horses trotted at a quicker clip, and the boiler directly under their seat made the ride a bit rougher than she'd expected. Still, to imagine they rolled along at comparable speeds to that of a horse without the need for the animal, Madeline couldn't help but find it intriguing.

"Are you ladies game for a bit more speed? We can take the Longmire Road out to Westbrook Boulevard. That is usually quite free of carriages and wagons at this time of day." He leaned close to Edith's ear and murmured something—something that sounded suspiciously like, "I had to find the quickest route to *your* house, of course."

His words rang true, despite their overt flattery—an odd combination if she'd ever heard one. Once on the boulevard, he cranked up the motor and the machine zipped down the road at a speedy clip. The engine whined as he pushed it faster for a little bit before reducing speed back to a more moderate pace.

Madeline beamed. "Oh, now *that* was thrilling. I've been in a carriage that raced down the road a time or two, but this was much more exciting. Do you think we were going faster, or was it the fact that the scenery ahead wasn't obscured by the backside of a mare?"

"Both, I should imagine!" Vernon's voice sounded farther away than she expected.

As they raced—at a moderate speed—down the road, Madeline felt Edith relax. They rounded a corner and encountered a pair of bays pulling a grocer's wagon. The horses balked, the driver shouted rough words that left the girls blushing and Smythe equally red with rage. "Scoundrel doesn't know how to speak appropriately in the presence of ladies."

One has to credit him for a certain gallantry. Perhaps the lip color was an innocent thing — a young lady distraught over something. He could have offered a handkerchief. Her mind whirled in half a dozen directions in an attempt to riddle out a way he could have managed to get lip color on his sleeve. *And, of course, even if it were an innocent thing, after Flossie's overreaction to the affair with Warren, any young man would be eager to hide any hint of impropriety. Why, he could have been helping the woman in the Dry Docks that day. Perhaps she was concerned that a clean-up project would serve only to take away her means of making a living without replacing it with something more reputable.*

That thought prompted a question. "Who would be most injured by changes to the Dry Docks quarter, Mr. Smythe?" Her voice rang out a little louder than necessary, but Smythe didn't seem to notice.

"That is difficult to say, but the obvious answer is those in illegal activity — gambling… things like that." Edith leaned forward to tuck her skirt more firmly behind her legs at just that moment. Smythe's gaze met hers across the short space that separated them, and he raised one eyebrow. "You are quite taken with the project, aren't you, Miss Brown?"

Just then, the Locomobile sputtered, wheezed, and rolled to a stop. Smythe hopped from the machine and examined it. "I think we're out of water. Of course, I should have been paying attention. They send it with only a couple of gallons in it — just enough to get you home, you know. I forgot to add more at Ed — Miss Merton's house as I'd planned."

"What shall we *do?*" Edith's panic-stricken tones would have indicated a near tragedy compared to a simple issue of procuring a bit of water.

Smythe showed every solicitation for Edith's welfare and comfort. He led them to a nearby tree and promised to return quickly. "You'll be safer here than riding on a trolley into town or wandering the streets. Just enjoy a moment in nature and I'll return presently."

Madeline smiled at the pointed look he gave her and waved him off with assurances that they'd enjoy a few moments gathering wildflowers. "It's almost fortuitous, isn't it, Edith?"

Though Edith didn't answer, she did smile at him and turn back to follow Madeline's example in picking a few flowers. They'd near-filled handfuls inside a few minutes. "Come up by the road with me. I think I saw black-eyed-susans up there before the mishap."

"I think I'd rather sit by the tree, if you don't mind. I still feel a bit shaken from the ride. I found it terrifying to see the machine just zip along with nothing to control it!"

Well, Madeline mused as she wandered closer to the road, *I suppose you aren't ready to accept that man controls the machine, much as man controls a horse. Although, with a horse you can see what is being controlled.*

She found the black-eyed-susans as well as a few bluebells. Engrossed in the bouquet she'd begun, she didn't hear the crunch of Smythe's shoes on the road until he'd nearly overtaken her. "Where's Edith, Miss Brown?"

Interesting. You'll defer to convention in her presence – except when no one else is around, of course – but away from her you're more familiar. Very interesting – and unusual.

"Miss Brown? Edith? Where is she?"

"Oh, I'm sorry. She's back near that tree where you left us. We picked flowers, but she didn't care to walk anymore, so I came to gather enough for both of us." Madeline thrust the flowers under Smythe's nose. "Aren't they lovely?"

He managed *not* to sneeze, but it took a great effort, even from her perspective. "That they are. However, I am sorry you didn't think your friend's comfort more important than a bunch of weeds."

"She was not averse to me leaving, I assure you. I am of an inquisitive nature, Mr. Smythe. I enjoyed exploring." Madeline nodded at the bucket he carried. "I see you found water."

"I did. We'll return this and finish filling it up at the house just around the bend there."

They'd gone another half dozen yards or so before Madeline spoke again. "This was quite the adventure, wasn't it? I appreciate you taking me. Edith could have kept you all to herself, but I did so wish to go." A second passed—three. Then, just as he'd begun to speak again, she added, "Then again, I don't know that you could have convinced her to come if I hadn't pressed for it. She is a bit timid, you know."

"Yes, it's a lovely quality in a lady such as Miss Merton." He stopped and waited for her to turn and face him. "But I assure you that had I not wished to give you a ride, you would not be here. I am not a man who is pressured to do that which I do not wish to."

A smile formed on Madeline's lips before she could stop it. "I can well imagine."

"And," he added, "I do not allow *anyone* to get in the way of that which I *do* wish to do."

Madeline met his gaze, held it, and nodded. "A good trait for a man in business, I should think."

His dumbfounded expression amused her as she skirted him and took off toward Edith's seat beneath the tree. *And what will you do with that, I wonder.*

"*A good trait for a man in business, I should think.*"

The words, delivered without artifice or even a trace of malice, still left him unsettled. *There's a double meaning in that. I know it. But* what?

"I was always taught," Vernon began, "that steadfastness in purpose was a trait everyone should strive for."

Edith overheard them and stood. "Did you find water, Vernon?"

"I did. And we're set to go. We'll get more just around the bend."

They strolled through the grasses and up to the road, Edith leaning on Vernon's arm, apparently lost in thought. He offered her a penny for those thoughts. *I'd give you a hundred if you'd share them only with me.*

"I've been thinking about Madeline's question—about those most hurt by an improvement project. There are ladies down there, aren't there? Ladies who will need other... *employment*, but may not have the skills to qualify for positions open to them."

"That is very true. It is the one thing that makes me hesitate in putting my support behind such a project. As unsavory as some of their businesses are, it keeps humans fed, clothed, and sheltered. Until they have other means of support, I cannot see how leaving them starving in the streets is any kind of improvement."

Madeline spoke his next thought before he could. "Some might call it an improvement in the moral atmosphere of the city, but I would disagree. It is just as immoral to turn people into the streets to forage as it is to participate in their... *professions*."

"Surely not, Madeline! They aren't required to *stay* in the streets. There are charities and—"

"No charity I've ever heard of would provide for a woman of ill-repute. They would tell her to repent. They would *tell* her to find legitimate work. But none that I've ever seen would *help* them. Even as generous as my father is, if I brought home such a woman to help her until she could learn to be a dressmaker or clerk—a shop assistant—he would insist she leave."

"But, Madeline!" Edith looked properly horrified, and Vernon couldn't help enjoying the little disagreement. "Your father has a reputation to uphold. If he allowed something so...." She shuddered. "Why, he'd be discredited, I'm sure." Edith turned to him. "You agree with me, don't you, Vernon?"

Oh, how he ached to say he did, but Madeline would surely call him out on the discrepancies in his words. "I find myself agreeing with both of you. While it is unfortunate, Edith is correct. Your father cannot do the kind of good that this city needs from him if he damages his reputation. However, the kind of charity you espouse is exactly what is needed if we can hope to make an improvement project successful."

"Would there be support for something like that?" Madeline leaned forward to watch him as he released the brake again.

Vernon shook his head. He didn't mean to, but his eyes slid to Edith before he answered, "In fewer quarters than you'd think. I'm always surprised at the men who care more about profit than people."

But Madeline didn't answer. Her eyes returned to the road and, it seemed, she pondered his words. *Did I give myself away there? If Merton's opinions became public....* Again, Vernon glanced her way and relaxed the faintest bit. *She could have me at the meeting that day, but she seems oblivious enough. No one could ask an intelligent question one minute and appear utterly dull the next.* Another glance her way showed Edith smiling at him.

"Are you more comfortable now, my dear?" he murmured as loudly as he dared.

Edith must have heard him, because her eyes lit up and she nodded. "You're a fine driver."

Another glance over Edith's head showed Madeline staring out over the countryside. *And I think I made the right choice in companion. Mayor Brown's influence cannot be undervalued, but his daughter doesn't have the sweet, gentle qualities her friend possesses. In that sense, Merton is a much better choice.* The memory of Jonas Merton's broad hints at his approval of Vernon's suit sent a wash of satisfaction over him. *I'll have the advantage of a lovely, well-respected young lady* and *a father-in-law of influence. What more could a man ask for?*

$\mathcal{T}$WELVE

Brown skirt, blue shirtwaist, nondescript chapeau with enough netting to half-hide her face worn atop hair pulled back in a tight bun. Madeline gazed at her reflection with satisfaction. *Almost unrecognizable. If you looked closely, of course, I would be me. But I don't think anyone would look twice. Now, if I can only get someone in the vaudeville troupe to help me.*

More than a little disappointment filled her as she rolled back two layers of the netting and re-pinned the hat back further on her head. Even with the severe hairstyle, she looked herself again. Madeline, with an eye to the clock and some reluctance, pulled on a short, lightweight, matching jacket. *It really is over-warm for the jacket. Still, it might help.*

She picked up the hopelessly out of date reticule she'd spent the past two days sewing and tucked it inside her jacket. With one final appraising look in the mirror, Madeline turned to go. *I am not certain of what I will do once I am down there. But it seems that the Dry Docks is central to Mr. Smythe's interests.*

The walk to the trolley—never had Madeline felt so conspicuous. The ride into the downtown area—equally awkward. But each step that led her to Rockland's most popular theater increased her unease beyond anything she could have imagined. Her palms grew damp and clammy, and her forehead beaded with nervous perspiration.

The building loomed before her. Tall, blond brick, bustling activity at the stage entrance door. Her knees weakened as she crossed the threshold. A girl wearing only a wrapper and her hair in a turban almost knocked Madeline into a wall as she rounded a corner. "Oh! I'm sorry. Gotta step lively."

"Would you—" But the girl was gone before Madeline could finish the question.

She applied for help to several others, but each person just moved past at a frenetic pace without acknowledging her—well, unless to order her out of the way. Still, Madeline stumbled through the melee, trying to stop each person in hopes of a single answer.

Twenty minutes passed at the very least before Madeline decided the trip had been futile—worthless. *I can do it without the glasses. It just would have been nice.*

Perhaps it was the theatrical air about her, or maybe just her location, but Madeline couldn't help but feeling a trice melodramatic about the loss of her plan. Shoulders slumped, face downcast if it reflected her heart at all, she stumbled through the theater trying to reach that side door once more. Just as she saw the light shining in as yet another person crowded into the room, a hand gripped her arm.

"What are you doing in here?"

Her heart attempted to race right out of her chest and lodged into her throat. "I—"

The man pulled her out of the way of an oncoming trunk and glared at her. "Spit it out. I could have you arrested for trespassing!"

Much to Madeline's mortification, tears sprang to her eyes. "Please...." Her plea erupted from her in a rasped, panicked gasp. "I'll go. Just—"

The man crossed his arms over his chest as his eyes narrowed and focused on her. "What are you doing here?"

"I just—" She swallowed the rest of the words. *Oh, do develop a bit of backbone, Madeline Brown. Honestly, this is mortifying and ridiculous. It's not a crime to attempt to purchase theatrical property.*

"I could just call that policeman we discussed." Though the man's tone sounded almost menacing, she saw a glimmer of amusement in his eyes.

"I don't think you'll do that, Mr....."

Someone interrupted with a question before the man could return to her. "Now where — oh, yes. You don't think I'll call the police. And you're correct — *if* you are so gracious as to answer a simple question."

Spirit buoyed, Madeline stepped closer. "I was hoping to purchase a pair of false spectacles. I thought perhaps you might have an old pair you'd like to sell for a small price — something you don't use any longer?"

"Spectacles, eh? And just why would a young lady such as yourself want something like that?"

Her elaborately concocted story about trying to fool her friend fizzled the moment Madeline opened her lips. "I'm trying to discover something about a young man — someone courting a friend of mine. He doesn't seem... *genuine* in some respects. But...." She fidgeted with her hands. "Well, I know that innocent things *can* seem untoward."

Everything changed with those words. The man led her through the bustling backstage area without mishap. Indeed, the people seemed to part before him as if he carried Moses' staff. In a small office just upstairs, with the door open, presumably for her comfort, he gestured for a chair. "I'm Tim Smallwood — manager of the Imperial Theatre. Tell me more about your scheme."

A glance over her shoulder prompted assurances that they could not be overheard without first knowing someone was coming. Madeline picked at her sleeve and gathered her wits before meeting the manager's gaze. The story from the first evening through the automobile ride spilled out. The man looked skeptical, and it unnerved her, but she continued.

"Well, the lip salve on a gentleman's sleeve — now that can be an innocent thing or it could mean more, couldn't it? And when you consider that his business in the Dry Docks quarter could be innocent or nefarious as well... well, I needed to investigate more. But, people sometimes recognize me. And with that man turning up everywhere I go, I thought a disguise might be just the thing. So I pulled out one of Aunt Louisa's frights."

Smallwood watched with undisguised amusement as she pulled the pin from her hat and readjusted it on her head. She rolled down the pieces of netting once more and pulled off her jacket. The reticule dropped to the floor. "So with this...." Madeline stood and spun in a small circle. "—combined with a pair of spectacles, I thought perhaps I might not be recognized. I haven't worn this skirt and shirtwaist in over two years, so I doubt any acquaintance, should I pass one, would recognize me. I'm certain the gentleman in question wouldn't."

"You thought this out well." Admiration filled the man's eyes. "And you decided to come here to see about spectacles. Whatever made you think of that?"

"Because I wouldn't know where to find such a thing, and surely someone would recognize me if I inquired about them." Impatience overrode her desire to keep the man in good humor. "I don't wish to be contrary, but if you have no intention of selling me the spectacles, I need to leave."

He stood and beckoned her to follow. Once more she navigated stairs and through a swarm of people until he came to a stop beside a tray of various eyewear. Spectacles of several sizes, monocles, pince-nez—they all lay out before her. Smallwood retrieved a very small pair of eyeglasses with a bent arm and handed them to her. He tugged her arm until she stood before a large mirror and smiled at her. "Good luck in your sleuthing."

"What do I owe you?" Even as she asked, Madeline squeezed the spectacles onto her face. They pinched a bit, and the bent arm dug into her head, but Madeline couldn't have been more pleased at her reflection in the mirror.

"A promise that you'll prove this man innocent or guilty. I don't really care which, so long as you do it."

She passed him the little jacket and returned his smile. "Then keep this for a costume or a rag. And thank you. I can't imagine what would make someone so helpful, but I'm grateful."

Without Smallwood to make a way for her, Madeline earned a bruise or two in her attempt to weave through the crowd to the door. Just as she stepped through, the man's voice arrested her escape. "And if you ever decide you'd enjoy theater, I think we could create an exciting act for you."

Something in the man's eyes, his tone, everything about him hinted he might not take no for an answer. Against everything she thought she approved of, Madeline decided to end the discussion before it began. "As flattering as that is, Mr. Smallwood, I'm sure Mayor Brown wouldn't like to see his daughter on stage, but thank you."

It worked. Whether he'd taken her seriously or her words had shocked him into silence, Madeline made it around the corner and down the street without further entreaty. *Well, it worked! This is exciting. Now, should I test my disguise, or do I – ?*

Her thoughts were frozen by the sight of a man, mere feet ahead of her. Despite an unfamiliar hat, something in the way he held himself, the way he eyed each person passing, Madeline recognized him. *And there you are again. I wonder if you'll recognize me.*

Madeline knew better. Her wiser-self insisted that any move in the man's direction would ask for exposure of her plan, but the temptation proved too great. She dodged pedestrians and closed the gap between her and the man who seemed intent on knowing where she went and what she did *anytime* her foot stepped off a trolley into the commercial areas of town. *Does he watch near home, too? Does he know where our home is?*

A squeal almost escaped as she passed him, dropped her

reticule, and picked it up again. He looked directly her way and didn't hesitate for a moment. Instead, he continued on his way, around the corner, and still appeared to be looking for someone. *Looking for* me, *that is. It worked!*

"Madeline?" Her heart sank at the over-loud interrogatory exclamation from Sally Penworthy. Madeline tried to keep going in what she knew would be a feeble attempt to hide her identity, but Sally reached her side. "What are you doing wearing that ridiculous hat? *Spectacles?* I'll say! Why, Madeline Brown. If I didn't know better, I'd think this was some attempt at a disguise!"

Her face flamed. "You're correct, Sally."

"Why ever would you do such a thing?!"

The lie flowed from her lips before she could stop it. "I've read of people doing similar things in novels. I wondered at the plausibility of the storyline. Clearly the authors have not done their research."

"Well, it might have worked had you not chosen that hideous skirt. It was particularly ugly two years ago. I would recognize it anywhere. And that hat! Your Aunt Louisa outdid herself with that monstrosity! Why would you try to disguise yourself with something that couldn't help but draw attention?"

Why indeed, Madeline muttered in her heart. Meanwhile, she pulled the spectacles from her eyes, rolled back the heavy netting, and turned to go. "Thank you for your help with my experiment, Sally. Have a lovely day."

"But—"

Despite Sally's protest, Madeline hurried down the street toward the trolley. Just as she climbed on, she saw the man in the checkered coat. He nodded at her as she passed. *Oh, bother!*

All through dinner, Vernon watched, *waited* for the perfect moment. The true dilemma hinged on question of whether to say something in Mr. Merton's presence. He opted for private. So, when Jonas Merton went to his office on pretext of "important paperwork", Vernon suggested a stroll through the lovely Merton gardens. "The moonlight is perfect tonight."

Edith didn't hesitate—unusual for her. "I think that would be lovely. Allow me to bring Father some coffee, and I'll join you by the arbor?"

Vernon caught her hand in his as she passed and pulled her close. "I'll wait, but I won't like it."

Her blush—it always made her look lovelier than she truly was. "You say the nicest things."

"You should hear nothing else." He strolled out the French doors, through the wide porch, and onto the terrace.

Ida followed behind and lit a few of the outdoor lamps. "Can I get you anything before I go inside, Mr. Smythe?"

"I think we'll be fine for a while, but perhaps you would bring us some claret when we return to the porch?"

"Of course." The girl scurried away with more pep than she had in weeks.

That tooth must have finally healed. Each minute that approached took an hour to pass, but he heard Edith's feet on the stone path at last. "Edith…."

"It is lovely out here tonight, isn't it? Why, it's hard to imagine that just a couple of weeks ago the heat was so beastly!"

Vernon slipped her arm through his and covered her hand with a squeeze. "At least you won't be uncomfortable if I step a little closer…."

It worked. She sighed, relaxed, and followed his lead as they strolled through the roses, and around the giant willow that created a canopy that, had he been a little surer of himself, Vernon might have used to gain a little privacy. *There will be time enough for that. Now, I need to concentrate on her influence over Miss Brown.*

"You seem unsettled, Vernon. Is everything well with you?"

He stroked the back of her hand with his thumb. "You're always so surprisingly observant." He paused at the little bench where he'd first called her "darling" and seated himself beside her. "I'm concerned for your friend, Edith. I...."

"Which friend?"

"Madeline Brown."

A rush of air escaped as Edith sagged. "Oh, dear. What has she done now?"

Premature? Perhaps. But Vernon chose to take the opportunity while he had it. He slipped his arm around her waist as if to support her. "Are you well? I shouldn't have spoken. I—"

"No, truly. If Madeline has made herself unpleasant...." Her forehead wrinkled as if not able to believe it. "But, surely not."

Strong censure to put Edith on her guard? Sincere concern to ensure Edith's cooperation in warning Madeline? Or both—somehow. *It must be both. But how?*

"Vernon?"

"I wouldn't like to be excessively severe, but I am concerned that she will be censured if someone does not convince her that these forays into the Dry Docks quarter are ill-advised. Today I heard of her on that end of town—quite far away still, you understand."

Edith blinked as if confused.

You're often confused, my dear. But that is one of your charms. A clever wife is a plague to a man of business — always presuming her ideas to be better.

"But, Vernon, there are shops on that end that are quite respectable. Madeline could have been there—a stationer, a dry goods that sometimes gets the loveliest shawls, and of course, her father could send her on an errand. It doesn't signify that if she is on that side, she must be returning to that unsavory area. I know she's concerned, but...."

He hesitated—the exact truth or hint at the possibility of doubt? "Of course, it could be a mistake, but I understood that she was seen at that end of town dressed in what can only be described as a *disguise*."

"Surely not!" She grew stiff and shifted away from him. "Vernon, I cannot imagine why you would say such a thing. Madeline is my dearest friend!"

Oh, how he ached to argue—to insist she listen to reason, but Vernon dropped his arms to his legs and clasped his hands together. He stared at his fists, waiting, hoping.

"Vernon? Why would you say something like that? I thought you liked Madeline. You said she had a keen mind, didn't you?" Her voice dropped in a whisper. "I was quite jealous of her over that. No one would say such a thing about me."

He took the risk, reached for her hands, and held them fast in his own. "And she is a very clever girl. But she hasn't your sweet disposition and kind heart. Please forgive me, Edith. If I spoke out of turn, I take it back. I was merely concerned that her reputation might be impacted, but perhaps I misunderstood Miss Penworthy."

"Sally?"

He managed to stop the grin that tried to stretch across his face. "Yes. She's who told me about it when I saw her this afternoon. She was quite shocked. I just...."

Edith's hands squeezed his, and to his delight and surprise, Edith kissed his cheek. "I understand now. It's kind of you to mention it. I'll talk to Sally tomorrow. We'll sort this out, I'm sure."

The temptation to kiss her—*really* kiss her—almost overwhelming. Alas Edith was the sort of girl who wouldn't kiss a fellow before their engagement, and Vernon refused to risk her rebuff. Instead, he leaned close and whispered, "Thank you for understanding. And for such a sweet kiss. I'll be thinking of it until I fall asleep."

There it was again—a blush, a smile, and her fingers clinging just a little tighter to his. *Perhaps six months isn't necessary.*

The novel—the one she'd neglected since purchasing it— proved more interesting than she'd expected. So, when the heat of the afternoon made working in the rose garden quite uncomfortable, Madeline made herself comfortable on the Chesterfield sofa and lost herself in a world of murder, intrigue, and a clever detective who outwitted the criminals at every turn. *It is a shame that there are no excellent novels showing women in the role as detective. Would women approach the science differently? Do we have a unique perspective to offer? Perhaps intuition?*

Madeline's mind revolted at that thought. *Intuition may be well enough to raise questions, but rational, logical, methodical deduction is a far superior way to discern the truth.*

Her musings disappeared with the turn of a page as the novel drew her back into its depths. In fact, Madeline became so engrossed in the tale that when the door buzzed, only the fringes of her consciousness recognized the sound. *Russell, go away. I want to read.*

"Miss Merton is here to see you." Mary's voice almost mirrored the words on the page. "Miss?"

Madeline jumped. "Oh! Mary. I'm sorry. Did you say...?" Her mind raced to retrieve the information. "Edith is here?"

"Yes, miss."

Edith stepped into the room. "Wha—oh. Another book. Did Sherlock Holmes return from the grave?"

"Unfortunately not." Madeline tossed the book aside and rose to greet her friend. "But, Detective Reynold Surat is an adequate substitute."

"Surat? That sounds rather... exotic."

Edith should have known better than to inquire about

Madeline's reading. Madeline began pacing as she regaled Edith with a summary of the plot and the detective's mental prowess. "He's from India, of course—I believe we'll discover he's the illegitimate son of an English gentleman. He has some unpronounceable surname, so he changed it to the city of his birth. But his keen eye—he notices things that most of us wouldn't consider worth noting if we did see it. And all of those clues build upon each other until he paints a picture of the murder. It's fascinating!"

Edith just stood and gaped at her.

Sensibility returned in a rush of apologies. "I'm sorry, Edith. You know how engrossed I become in a good story. Would you like to sit in here, or perhaps the terrace is in shade now?"

"Here would be fine." Edith glanced around her. "Are we quite alone?"

He's proposed. A bit sudden, don't you think? You've hardly known him four months. But Madeline didn't voice her opinions or concerns. Instead, she crossed the room, slid the doors out of their pockets, and latched them to prevent even Mary from stepping in and overhearing something she shouldn't. "There. Perfect privacy."

"Is it really?" Edith seated herself on a side chair, folded her hands in her lap, and gazed into Madeline's eyes with earnest sincerity. "Madeline, we need to talk."

Oh, dear, you are *engaged. Well, at least the odds are that I'm making molehills into mountains. There is that comfort.*

"—seen walking around downtown... *in disguise!*"

Madeline blinked. "Pardon me? I missed something you said."

"I *said*...." Edith's voice had never sounded so loud, so stern. "Sally Penworthy just came from my house describing how she found you walking around downtown the other day, dressed in old clothes, a heavy netted hat, and spectacles—a disguise! What were you doing?"

Though she had originally felt a pang of guilt at "lying" about her reasons for being downtown the other day, in the interim, she'd managed to justify every word as truth. *Just because they weren't true to the situation does not change the veracity of them. I have always wondered about the feasibility of changing one's appearance to deceive others.* So, with those thoughts in mind, Madeline reiterated her story about how she'd tested the idea of the likelihood of effective disguises. Unfortunately, Edith's concerned expression kept her talking until she'd spilled the whole thing—almost.

"So, you know how hurt our friend might be if her beau was truly at a place of ill-repute, and you know how happy she would be if she learned of his innocence." Inwardly, she added, *And I know that you would be crushed if you knew that I spoke of you instead of Flossie.*

Edith's features softened for just a moment, but almost immediately, she assumed a sterner air again. "I understand your motivation, of course. It is commendable, but Madeline...." Her entire body shifted forward. "It isn't *proper!* You cannot wander the streets dressed as someone you aren't. And if you were planning to visit an area with a place of ill-repute...."

Well, I hoped you hadn't considered that. Exasperation may have had a role to play in her next words, but if Madeline were honest with herself, she would have admitted that irritation overrode it. "Edith, I have broken no laws, moral or legal. I simply sought to discover the truth about a friend's beau. This is hardly a reprehensible occupation."

"Leave it to the men, Madeline. Don't interfere."

Oooh, could anything be more infuriating? Why must women be relegated to radical opinions or trapped by conventional ones? Why can there be no moderation?

Edith hadn't finished her mission of propriety—not by far. "Madeline, you must see how inappropriate it is. A young lady traversing the streets? Why, I've heard you comment on the impropriety of young ladies peddling their temperance message! How is this any different?"

Had she not contrived to find a way to control her temper, Madeline's friendship might have been severely damaged. However, thanks to a touch of self-control and the mercy of Providence, she managed to bite her tongue just in time. "I've never lectured on impropriety, Edith. I don't consider having an opinion and sharing it with others to be improper. I just consider their message to be misguided. They are allowed their opinion on the subject, as am I."

"Maddie...."

Oh, don't. Once you resort to nicknames, I can't possibly hope to argue with you. "We won't agree, Edith. I see no difference in—"

"Well, there is a difference. If for no other reason than your father." Edith stood and tried to hide her hurt. "He doesn't need his daughter branded as a 'meddlesome young chit.' That's what she called you, you know. Sally Penworthy." Edith turned to go, but as she unlatched the doors she added, "Think about that before you do something else that could irreparably damage his position."

Long after Edith had gone, Madeline sat on the Chesterfield, hands gripped tightly in her lap, and fought to contain her frustration. "*...branded as a meddlesome young chit.*" The words reverberated in her mind.

"Well, if people would attend to their own affairs and leave others alone...."

Madeline's eyes slid to the book beside her, but the joy had gone from the story. Still, a rebellious side of her demanded she pick it up again. *I refuse to allow Edith's meddling....* A smile formed at the use of the word. *–her meddling to take from my enjoyment of this book. Detective Surat has much to teach me, and I, his willing pupil, will observe and learn.*

$\mathcal{T}$HIRTEEN

It took three days for Edith to return to the Brown home to apologize. Had it taken another, Madeline suspected she would have made the first overture. *After all, though I did nothing to cause this breach, friendship must prevail over conviction. But our propinquity should, it seems, create these little moments of discord. And I must remain in her good graces if I hope to be able to observe Mr. Smythe further.*

"Madeline, I needed to take some papers to the bank for Father. I found them on the desk this morning, and I know he'd planned to bring them. I heard him mention it to Vernon last night. So I thought we could take them up to the bank and then go to the Newcastle Hotel for luncheon."

Containing her excitement—nearly impossible. Madeline hugged her friend and dashed for the stairs. "Help me choose *something* else to wear. This silly shirtwaist is barely appropriate for the house."

Inside twenty minutes, the two girls strolled up Beaumont Street to meet the trolley. "That Venetian green is just the perfect shade for you, Madeline."

She glanced at her sleeve, admiring the sheer gauze, and nodded her agreement. "Thank you. I think it's a lovely shade myself. Miss Ada does know how to take a lovely fabric and turn it into a remarkable creation."

"No amount of skill can make a color suit a complexion,

Madeline."

The trolley appeared before Madeline could reply, but the moment they were seated, she hooked her arm through Edith's and murmured "I'm thankful you chose to forgive me for being so obstinate. I missed you."

Their eyes met, and in a matter of seconds, silent apologies and forgivenesses filled the space between them. Edith spoke first. "Have you taken any more excursions?"

Nothing could have healed the breach more thoroughly than that question. As a response, Madeline recounted the details of her novel all the way to their stop just outside the bank doors. "I must return to Gardner & Henley's to see if Winthrop Randley has written any more novels. If this book is indicative of his usual work, I may have a reasonable substitute for my beloved Sherlock."

"I'm pleased for you. Truly." Edith waved the string-bound bundle of papers. "Let's get these to Father—oh! I see Mrs. Atherton. Would you mind?" Edith inched toward the woman. "I've been meaning to call on her, but I was a bit out of spirits, and...."

"Of course not. I'll wait by your father's office." She hesitated, her conscience demanding her silence, but Madeline heard herself say, "Let me hold that for you. You know how inquisitive she can be. There's no reason to give her reason to delay you further."

Though not a strictly accurate assessment of the woman's general character, it could not be denied that Mrs. Atherton *could* be quite nosy if the notion struck her. Edith handed the packet over to Madeline with a conspiratorial smile and hastened off to speak to the unwitting Mrs. Atherton.

Madeline, on the other hand, moved closer to the office—the one with "Jonas Merton, Banker" engraved on a brass plate mounted to the door. With her back turned to the main lobby of the bank, she picked at the corners of the wrapper. It held fast. She slid the string to one side—or rather, she tried. As usual, Edith's thoroughness left no chance for anyone to see anything "accidentally."

Voices inside the office rose and fell with the ebb of conversation. The thickness of the door ensured that Madeline couldn't make out more than half a dozen words, but it was not for lack of trying. A glance over her shoulder showed Edith in rapt conversation with Mrs. Atherton and the arrival of her Aunt Louisa.

Oh, dear. Don't notice me. How you could miss this hat, I don't know. It's so conspicuous! The temptation to pray for her to remain concealed presented itself, and Madeline promptly stifled it. *What an inappropriate waste of the Almighty's time – just to prevent a minor annoyance.*

Still, she moved behind a large rubber plant and tried to blend into the mahogany paneling. Louisa Farnsworth had obviously come to withdraw the monthly household allowance. Nothing would divert her from that mission until she had the funds tucked safely in her pocketbook. After that, however....

Hurry, Edith. We must be on our way before Aunt Louisa notices my presence.

And at that moment, Edith waved at Mrs. Atherton, strolled across the lobby, and rapped on her father's door. A voice inside called out to them. "Enter!" But before either of them could reach for the doorknob, it swung open and revealed Vernon Smythe.

How did I not recognize his voice? Interesting.

"Vernon! Why, I didn't know you were here!" Edith pulled Madeline forward. "As you can see, I took your advice and made up with Madeline. We're headed to the Newcastle for luncheon once we give these to Father." She took the papers from Madeline and passed them across Mr. Merton's desk. "I heard you say you needed to bring these, but they were still on your desk...."

Smythe eyed Madeline with a suspicious expression on his face. His eyes darted between the perfectly wrapped package and her until Madeline wanted to shout, "I didn't read your precious papers!" A thought prompted a small smile. *But I do wish I had.*

Mr. Merton stood and moved to kiss his daughter and thank

her. "I was just about to send Vernon for them. Thank you, my dear. We need them before we can—"

"Your daughter's thoughtfulness does her credit, I think. I see why you are so fond of her."

Must you distract him? The moment the thought came, Madeline's heart raced. She followed the man's gaze and settled the notion for herself.

But Edith ended the conversation prematurely—to Madeline's thought anyway. She kissed her father's cheek and beckoned Madeline to follow. "We must go or we'll wait for a table until supper time."

Vexation grew with each step toward the door. Madeline searched her mind for any pretext to return, but Edith created one for her. "Oh! I forgot to ask Father for the donation to the orphanage project. He's always forgetting to bring it home. I'll be right back." Edith blushed as Madeline began to offer to follow— "I think he would prefer I ask alone."

In other words, my dear, Edith, your father is likely to grumble at the expense.

Vernon Smythe stepped out of the office a moment later, and his eyes locked onto hers. In her determination not to allow him to intimidate her, Madeline missed the approach of her aunt. In fact, she stepped a bit closer. So did he. Just as her foot moved another inch or two in the direction of Mr. Merton's office, Madeline heard her aunt call her name. "Madeline!"

Smythe's eyes mocked her as she stifled a groan and turned to greet the woman who had just thwarted any hope of seeing if she could confound her friend's beau. "Aunt Louisa."

How it happened, she couldn't say. In a blur of activity that only comes when widowed aunts decide to address an issue with their beloved nieces, Louisa Farnsworth half-dragged Madeline behind a pillar and hissed at her in a futile attempt at subtlety. "What are you doing *here*, Madeline? Hasn't this investigation of yours gone far enough?" When Madeline couldn't repress her surprise, Louisa nodded. "Oh, yes. I've heard all of it. Why, the town is all a-buzz about Madeline Brown and her trip into the Dry Docks quarter. They can't stop talking about her obsession with it. And now, it seems, you've taken to putting on disguises and... what? Following people? It has to *stop*, Madeline! You can't imagine what people are saying!"

"I don't really care what people say, Aunt Louisa...." The words faded into the echoing cavernous lobby of the bank. *Those were an unfortunate choice of words, Madeline Brown. You know better.*

Aunt Louisa pulled her further away from any hope of being overheard before she scolded again. "You will bring shame to your father and destroy his future political aspirations. Even if you have no respect for your own reputation, do you not care about his — about *him*?" Defiance welled up in Madeline, but pain filled her aunt's eyes. "If my sister could see...."

Oh, don't. Must you always throw Mama's presumed disappointment at me? She might have been proud that I care enough about my friend to protect her from heartache — even if at the risk of my own reputation. However, her father's face, accented by the little white tufts of hair above his ears, filled her mind and heart.

Madeline took a slow, steadying breath, hugged her aunt, kissed the woman's cheek, and whispered, "I'll be more careful, Aunt Louisa. I promise."

She expected an admonition of, "See that you do," or "I should hope you would." Instead, Louisa held her cheek and smiled into Madeline's eyes. "I admire your spirit, Madeline. Just direct it to more appropriate endeavors, and you can't go wrong. Meanwhile, let's go shopping on Friday. We need to find you a dress for the Midsummer's Ball."

Edith appeared just then. "Oh! Mrs. Farnsworth! I didn't see you there. I wondered who Madeline was talking to. And yes, she does need something new. I just saw her wardrobe today, and well...."

133

You don't have an aunt who likes to insert her sense of fashion into every clothing purchase you make, Edith. There is a reason I avoid the nuisance.

"Well, then you'll have to collect me on Friday afternoon—unless you'd rather I meet you at Miss Ada's?"

"I'll collect you, of course." Louisa leaned close and whispered, "And think about what I said. Please."

How could I forget, dear auntie?

Though not as grand as the Merton parlor, and certainly not as cool as the Wakefield's, down by the river, the Brown parlor held one advantage over most of the homes in Madeline's set—a recent addition, one might say. Russell remarked on it as he entered their parlor a few nights later.

"That new fan hanging from the ceiling, I didn't think much of your father's idea of installing it, but I have to say it is a fine addition."

"Well, unlike those gas-powered atrocities, this doesn't *add* to the heat before trying to remove it." Her hand rested on his arm for a moment as she added, "Thankfully, Mr. Merton is too frugal to consider such an... *improvement*. A gas one? Edith would never survive."

The Hardwicks entered, and Madeline moved to greet them. Russell, seated in his favorite chair—the one Amy had called his "Knightley" chair—watched her. *Are you aware of the latest gossip, Miss Brown? Do you know how your friends are defending you, and your petty "enemies" are using your recent actions as an excuse to voice their so-called "concerns"?*

Frank Hardwick came and plopped down in the chair beside him. "Flossie made me promise to help steer the conversation away from Madeline's disguise the other day."

"I had similar ideas." He waited for it—Frank's opinion that it wouldn't be necessary if Madeline would stick to more feminine pursuits—painting, cycling, or raising funds for new hymnals.

It never came. Instead, Frank growled, "It's a sad day when a girl can't walk around in some old clothes and spectacles to see if something in a book could really happen. Who cares where she went or why? If she were a man, people might applaud her."

Russell couldn't help but laugh. "What your mother would say if she could hear you."

His ears turned red, but Frank sat up and looked a little enlivened, despite his slight embarrassment. "I heard a debate the other night—a man in favor of suffrage and temperance against an Episcopal clergyman. Most of what he said, I disagreed with, but that, I had to admit...." Frank glanced toward his sister and sighed. "Flossie wouldn't be nearly as fretful about Warren if she were *permitted* to behave as she wished. Every move she makes is dictated by Mother's antiquated ideas of propriety and decorum. What about the state of her mind? Why does that not matter?"

"I see what you mean. I've often thought similar things, but then I imagine Amy...."

Once more, Frank leaned close—even closer than before—and whispered, "I wonder if these cases of 'female hysteria' aren't *caused* by the very conventions that we must assume were created to prevent them."

Now that is an interesting thought. If Madeline tried to follow all societal expectations—tried to be like Edith or Flossie, for example—she might just lose her mind!

But before he could respond, Madeline moved their way. She bent low and murmured, "Help! We need some amusement. I'd considered night bowling, but I forgot to have Jimmy mow the lawn shorter."

"There are too many here." Russell's eyes swept the room, and

135

a few faces reminded him of some of their more entertaining evenings. "Charades?"

A game of charades—something that would have been miserably uncomfortable at Edith's home—transformed the evening party from a banal affair to something more interesting. Warren Osborne acted out the death scene from Romeo and Juliet. The entire room tried to hold back so Flossie could guess it, but one of the girls finally blurted out the answer in a desperate attempt to keep the evening from dragging.

Not to be outdone, Vernon Smythe took the floor. He folded a paper and inserted it into his hatband. The tall, rectangular shape completely transformed the hat into something of a couple centuries earlier. The pantomime began. He spoke earnestly with someone. He darted to one side, got down on one knee, and spoke earnestly again. Off came the hat! His hands held out an imaginary skirt as he curtsied and clutched at his breast.

A voice rang out from the other corner of the room. "The Scarlet Letter—Dimmesdale?"

Smythe's eyes narrowed and his voice dropped to a low growl. "Different Puritan—"

The crowd called out several suggestions, each further from Smythe's charade as they could be, if his infuriated expression meant anything. Russell held back and watched the others, and at almost the same time, he saw that Madeline had discerned it, and her opinion read clearly on her face. *You think Dimmesdale suits him better, don't you? Why is that, I wonder?* Then he saw it—that saucy expression she always stifled just before being particularly pert. *Madeline, you shouldn't do it.*

But Madeline clapped her hands and called out. "Of *course*, a *different* Puritan! You're Chillingsworth!"

"John Alden!" Vernon's flashing eyes swept the room and landed on Madeline. Fury flared. "Longfellow. Not Hawthorne. Don't you see?"

136

A silent room answered him. Madeline shrugged. "I apologize. I think we became caught up in the idea of tragedy from Romeo and Juliet." She turned to Stanley Wakefield. "Would you like to go next? Maybe Stella?"

Stella stepped forward. "You've all inspired me. I must act while I remember the idea, or I'll be struggling to think of something the next time my turn comes around." With that, she reached for something on the ground and held it. Shuddered. Eyes closed, she held it to her bosom, shuddered again, and dropped to the floor in an impressive show of theatrics.

It does call into question some of your infamous fainting spells, Stella. It might not have been prudent to disclose that talent to all of us. Before someone said something and embarrassed the girl, Russell called out, "Cleopatra and the asp."

"I should have known that Russell would get that. He has always been so clever at these things."

Across the room, he watched and mentally applauded as Madeline managed *not* to snicker at Stella's overt flattery. *I've often wondered if your compliments were indicative of something... more. Anyone who knows me knows of my love of Egyptology and history.*

"Go ahead, Russell. It's your turn." The rest of the room picked up Frank Hardwick's urging.

With an encouraging smile, Madeline nodded. "Yes, Mr. Barnes. You've stumped us before. Let's see if we can riddle out your charade."

Russell nodded and gave her a pointed look. *This one's for you, Madeline.* The challenge rang through the room as clearly as if he'd vocalized it.

He sat for some time in an empty side chair. It took a moment, but it became evident that he smoked a pipe. Then, he jumped up, held something in front of him, and with exaggerated movements, moved around the room. A glance at Madeline showed her with eyebrows drawn together as she watched him move, pause, and move again. *You can do it. No one else is even trying anymore.* He knew the moment she riddled it out.

"I believe that Russell is portraying Sherlock Holmes. First he smoked a pipe and now he's investigating."

"That might explain Madeline's sudden taste for wandering all over the city," someone behind them said—someone who sounded suspiciously like Stella Wakefield.

But Russell didn't continue the teasing. Instead, he bowed as the room clapped—the first charade to receive applause—and moved behind Madeline. He bent low and asked, "So, if you are assuming the role of Sherlock Holmes in Rockland, will we soon see you with a pipe?"

"Perhaps...." When he didn't act at all surprised, she added, "I've already scandalized half of Rockland. I might as well do a thorough job of it and shock the rest."

Russell might have replied, but one of the other girls stood and began to act out Paul Revere's ride—obviously inspired by Smythe's charade—and the moment passed. Though the rest of the room laughed at Annabeth's pantomime of the ride, Madeline looked decidedly disconcerted that she'd lost the opportunity. Her laughter rang out with the rest as Milty Grueber called out the correct answer, but her laughter rang hollow.

Do you wonder, as I do, why you are disappointed not to hear what I had to say? Would you be even more disappointed to hear that I meant only to tell you that your true friends think well of you regardless of your unorthodox pastimes?

$\mathcal{F}$OURTEEN

Many people considered the bustle of Rockland to be a bit overwhelming, but Madeline found the hubbub invigorating. While trips to the dressmaker's for such things as fittings could be tedious, at least the environment gave her much scope for mental stimulation.

She and her Aunt Louisa had found the perfect rose colored gown on a mannequin—that precise shade of dusty pink that suited her auburn hair in ways that any other pinkish hue would make her look ill. However, not unexpectedly, the dress needed alterations. *If I weren't as vain as the next girl, I might be content with it a little over-large. Alas, what joy is there in attending such a grand occasion looking dowdy?*

So, with that thought in mind, she wove her way through the streets and stepped inside Miss Ada's shop just minutes before her appointment. The woman grimaced at her—a likely effect caused by trying to smile around a row of pins protruding from compressed lips. *I hope you never get a sudden case of the hiccoughs. You could swallow one or more of those.*

Another dress hung on a mannequin—cornflower blue with embroidery on the bodice—crystal encrusted embroidery, no less. If any other color suited her better than cornflower, Madeline didn't know what it was. She shook herself. *I don't need another dress, and I already purchased the rose.*

No matter where she went in the little shop, the dress caught her eye and tugged at her desire to look well at one of Rockland's biggest affairs. Miss Ada stepped up to Madeline, pulling the pins from between her lips. "I thought of you when I finished that. It just seemed made for you. I didn't think of it as I was working on it, but completed...."

"If I hadn't already purchased the rose...."

Miss Ada moved to where a curtain separated the front room from the workroom and returned with Madeline's dress draped over her arms. "Look at it again. I haven't made adjustments yet, of course, so if you'd like to change your mind...." Her voice dropped a bit. "The cornflower is a little higher, but not significantly. I don't think you would find the difference extreme."

"May I try it on first?" Why she asked, Madeline didn't know. She had no doubt that she would arrive at the ball resplendent in blue and crystals.

"Of course. Let's get you out of that street ensemble and into this. I'm quite confident you'll find it to your liking, and, if I'm not mistaken, it shouldn't need as much alteration."

I would almost suspect that you made it closer to my measurements intentionally.

Anyone seeing her in the dress would have surmised the same. Aside from a couple of small adjustments to the bust line and a new hem, the dress fit perfectly. "You know I'll take it. I suspect you knew before you made the first snip into the fabric."

Madeline hadn't expected a confession, but Miss Ada's ability to keep her countenance placid and free of guile proved impressive. The woman rehung the rose gown on the mannequin but did not remove the sold tag from it. A new idea prompted her to ask, "Should it still be marked sold?" Her fingers flipped the tag for emphasis.

The woman began to assure Madeline that she would take care of it later but laughed instead. "Well caught, Miss Brown. I did have another client in mind. I would not have thought of it had I not seen this fabric and immediately thought of you." When Madeline didn't respond, the woman added, "Of course, I wouldn't have offered the dress to anyone else until you decided against it."

The words—Madeline did not doubt them. But something in them didn't ring true either. She considered them as she redressed, as she smoothed her hair, and even as she paid the difference in gown price and left the store with Miss Ada's assurances that the dress would be delivered on the Friday following by three o'clock. But even by the time she'd crossed several streets, on her way to City Hall, Madeline hadn't uncovered what about them felt off.

She passed a haberdashery—the one her father frequented—and froze before a display of men's bowler hats. Russell's taunt about the pipe resurfaced, and on impulse, she opened the door and strode into the shop. A young clerk—hardly older than her, if at all—stepped forward and offered to assist her.

"That bowler in the window. The one with the brown satin binding and band? I'd like to try that on, please."

Though the young man blinked, he brought her the hat and steered her to a tabletop mirror. Madeline set the hat on her head, marveling at how perfectly it fit. *Papa's hats are always much too large, but this is perfect. Room enough for my hair but not sloppy.* She stepped back over to the window to look over the others and paused before a deerstalker. *That looks somewhat like that hat described by Watson. Something about an "ear-flapped" cap of some kind?*

Madeline shook herself and returned to the bowler, her fingers sliding along the satin-bound trim. The clerk, eager to make a sale, asked, "For a brother, miss? It looks well on you."

She gave it one last glance and nodded with satisfaction. "I'll take it." Just then, the young man's words struck her. "Oh! For a brother? No... no, this is for me. And a friend. I believe it will definitely amuse a friend."

141

Mayor Brown was known for indulging his daughter, though most of the city had no idea just how rarely Madeline used that to her advantage. On that afternoon, with bowler atop her head and a spring in her step, Madeline hurried to visit her father and inform him that she had managed to exceed her clothing allowance — for the first time in her life. So, as she walked, she concocted a case worthy of Mr. Holmes himself.

City Hall bustled with businessmen, city officials, and even, or so it seemed, Russell had business there. She saw him at a clerk's window, but he didn't notice her. *Unfortunately. What would you say to this hat?*

She couldn't help it. What more perfect way would there be to show it off than to walk past where he'd have to see but couldn't tease her? It simply was too perfect for words. That thought in mind, Madeline ducked behind a post, waited until he appeared to be finished with his business, and then strolled past. The timing couldn't have been better. He turned and walked straight toward her. Madeline kept walking but smiled at him.

He passed without a word, without a hint of acknowledgment, without a flicker of recognition.

Well that was... anticlimactic.

Her father greeted her at his office door. "I thought we'd go have tea at that little room around the corner. Russell Barnes might be meeting me there — if he's finished filing his blueprints."

Oh, really...? Madeline hooked her arm through his and smiled up at the dear old man. "Well, then we shouldn't keep him waiting. I saw him leaving just as I came up to see you."

"Did you really? And how is he today? Did he mention meeting me?"

Her laughter echoed in the stairwell. "I said I *saw* him, Papa. We didn't speak. I don't know if he saw me, or if he was just being a little ornery. You know how he loves to tease."

At that moment, Albert Brown noticed his daughter's hat. "Or, perhaps he was confused by your conflicting attire. I've heard of young women wearing these bowlers, but I equated them with the suffrage movement. You haven't joined?"

"Of course not!" The words reverberated around them — much louder than she'd intended them to be. In more dulcet tones, she added, "I have no interest in politics — if you'll pardon my frankness. One politician in the family is sufficient for me. No, Russell teased me about taking up the pipe. He seems to think I'm trying to ape Sherlock Holmes. So, when I saw this, I thought it could be *my* signature accessory. Madeline Brown, detective story reader. It has quite a ring to it, doesn't it?"

"As long as you stay a *reader* instead of a *doer*. There are rumors about town that my daughter has taken up meddling in affairs that are none of her business."

"Meddling?" Madeline leaned against him and squeezed his arm. "Investigating interesting things among my friends? Definitely. However, I haven't done anything to open me to an accurate charge of meddling." She cleared her throat quietly. "But, I *am* open to the charge of exceeding my clothing allowance."

This stopped him short on the last step. His eyes met hers. "Have you? Whatever — oh, the hat. Was it really so expensive?"

"Not at all." Madeline tugged his arm to allow someone behind them to step past and into the lobby. As they reached the door, she tried to explain. "Aunt Louisa —"

"I think that explains everything right there." Albert's voice softened. "I'm sorry, my dear. I know she can be tiresome, but your aunt does love you."

"I'm afraid I can't hold her accountable for this one, Papa. You see, we went and found the perfect dress for the Midsummer's Ball. Today was my fitting."

"And you ruined the dress. Tea stain?"

Oh, Papa! Sometimes I want to shake you — just a little. Let me tell the story! Of course, Madeline wouldn't say something so disrespectful,

143

but the thoughts did tend to form, despite her best intentions. "No... vanity. I saw a prettier one in the shop today — one that will require almost no alterations. It was a bit more expensive, but well within my allowance until...."

She waited for him to make the connection. His chuckle told her he found the situation amusing — just as she'd expected it to. "So, my daughter then finds a hat she must purchase to tease a friend, and there's an end of it. Well done." He pulled out a few dollar coins and passed them to her. "I won't have it said that my daughter has to scrimp on the rare occasion she indulges *herself.*" He led her past the fountain and flipped a penny into it as they went. "But don't make a habit of it, my dear, Madeline. Indulging you is *my* responsibility and privilege."

Madeline almost didn't hear him. As her eyes followed the spinning coin, they landed on the man in the plaid suit — the *same* plaid suit. Most definitely the same man. This time he too wore a bowler. *A chance to mock me or coincidence?*

When he turned to look in the other direction, Madeline tugged her father's sleeve. "Papa, do you know that man?"

"What man?" Albert's eyes scanned the area.

"The one in the plaid coat. I've seen him around town — often. Is he possibly a detective in everyday wear?"

Her father led her down the walk and around the corner. "A plain clothes-detective. You've been reading too many of those novels, Madeline. I don't recognize him. He's likely some sort of salesman if you've seen him around often."

With a final glance back — one that showed the man watching them from the corner — Madeline followed her father into the tearoom and tried not to think about it further. *Papa is likely correct. Salesman. He even dresses like one. But still, that hat....*

" — hat, Madeline."

Madeline's head whipped around so fast it nearly made her dizzy. Russell stood waiting for them in the anteroom, and by the amused expression on his face, she suspected he'd teased her. *And I missed it, of course.* Impatience laced her words as Madeline formed a reply. "I'm sorry. I'm afraid I didn't hear you. Something about a hat?"

"Yours. It's quite... fetching."

Her father stepped aside to speak to someone, which gave Russell the opportunity to speak with some privacy. "If I hadn't recognized the dress, I wouldn't have known you in that hat. It suits you, though."

"I thought it could replace the idea of a pipe. Nasty, smelly things. This hat is quite distinguished."

"And here I thought you had tried to *disguise* yourself—not make yourself conspicuous."

She couldn't help a small laugh. "Well, since that plan failed, I decided on this. Who knows, perhaps it will induce a better offer, or at the least, discourage another unwelcome one. I'm quite sure that Mr. Jackson never would have if I'd been wearing something so modern. Do you know, I think he thought I was docile and tractable?"

"You can give that impression if you aren't careful. It can be disconcerting to those of us who know you."

Her father joined them, and all unpleasant talk about her one and only, most unwelcome, proposal ceased. *We must be more careful. If Aunt Louisa heard that I had turned down any man, much less one as well off as Mr. Jackson....*

Seated at their little table, Madeline allowed herself a full smile—a grin of sorts. "Now isn't this a lovely way to end a successful shopping trip? Refreshment with the two most important men in my life—my father and the brother I never had to torment me. I'd say I am richly blessed."

Albert Brown beamed at his daughter, pride shining in his eyes. But despite Russell's laughter, something seemed off with him. She quirked an eyebrow at him in question, but he just smiled again and

145

said nothing. *How strange.*

$\mathcal{F}$IFTEEN

Just as the door buzzer reached her ears, Madeline hopped up from her dressing table and reached for the hat she usually wore with her checkered shirtwaist and skirt. With pocketbook in hand, she dashed for the door and to the stairs, but a new thought stopped her in her tracks. Two seconds—it took two seconds for her to race back into her room, sail the hat across to her bed, and snatch up the bowler. *Won't Flossie be surprised!*

Frank and Flossie stood just inside the door, waiting for her. Flossie's lips formed into a perfect O and her eyes widened until she looked squeezed from the middle and ready to pop. "Where did you get that hat?"

I bet people will ask me that every day. "Isn't it nifty? It absolutely *called* to me, so I had to buy it—as a joke for Russell, of course. But now I quite like it."

"It's a humdinger!"

Flossie threw her brother a look that could have meant anything from, "Slang is vulgar" to "Don't encourage her." But before she could make a comment, the parlor clock struck the quarter hour. "Oh!" Flossie urged them out the door. "We'll be late if we don't hurry. Frank hired a carriage or we'd never make it."

"I have a vague memory of your cousin. Didn't he visit when we were still in primary school? For the summer, perhaps?"

"Yes. He was sickly then. His family had planned a trip to

Europe, and so he came to us. Most miserable summer of our *lives.*"

A scene flashed in her mind and illuminated her memory. "Arrogant, self-important fellow. Always spouting facts to look intelligent — or to make us look like imbeciles. I never knew which."

"Probably both." Flossie muttered the words with uncharacteristic malice. "But Mother thinks, from his letter, that he's improved now that he's well and more mature."

"One can only hope." Madeline had presumed her memory had been faulty, but hearing the description of Henry Hardwick hinted that she had a perfect mental picture of him. *Then again, it could be interesting. I wonder if he is one of those intelligent sorts who can't grasp innuendo or if he would find them amusing.*

The streets of Rockland were particularly congested that afternoon, due to a fire on one of the main streets. Black smoke hung over the area they were forced to travel through to reach the station, and by the time they arrived, all three found it difficult to speak or breathe without choking.

"Need — water." Flossie looked ready to double over in pain, and her eyes bugged out once more.

Why, Flossie. I've never noticed that tendency before. I've never heard it mentioned — even by the most poisonous of the committee members. It's strange. But Madeline didn't wait to ask. The moment the horse was tied, she sprang from the carriage and went in search of a dipper.

A clerk called out to her, insisting that she not remove the dipper from the barrel, but Madeline ignored him. By the time she arrived with it, poor Flossie was ready to collapse from the coughing. "Here, drink this. I'll get more in a moment."

The clerk arrived, and whether he'd heard of the fire or could smell the smoke on them, apologized and hurried to retrieve yet another dipper of water. Everything jumbled into a confused cacophony. Frank disappeared, Flossie clung to Madeline, and the clerk made several trips to provide them with water.

By the time Frank arrived with Henry Hardwick, Flossie stood

148

limp but stronger, and Madeline wanted nothing more than to be far away from the train station. Henry hugged his cousin and offered his hand to her. "Hello. I'm Henry Hardwick."

Frank stepped up and introduced them properly, but something in Henry's forthright introduction appealed to her. "It's nice to meet you again, Mr. Hardwick."

"Oh, no!" Henry turned to Frank and Flossie. "How could you bring someone who remembers what an obnoxious kid I was? My mother will be mortified."

Why she did it, Madeline couldn't decide, but she found herself saying, "Did I say again? I'm sorry. I'm sure we've never met. I would remember an affable fellow like you, wouldn't I?"

Silence—as much silence as a busy train station could provide. Among the whistles, the conductors' calls, the press of the crowd, and the joyful cries of reconnecting people, the small quartet stood there without saying a word. Henry found his voice first. "I—" Well, he found it but he couldn't quite *use* it.

"Oh, let's go. Frank, you must drive upwind of the smoke—even if it takes twice as long. I simply cannot go through that again."

Henry helped Madeline into the back seat of the carriage and went to help Flossie, but she stepped back. "I'm sorry, Henry, but I still feel ill from riding in back. I'll sit up here with Frank, if you don't mind—especially on an extended trip."

Surprise, confusion, and a hint of intrigue and admiration filled her as Henry paused and asked, "Will that be all right with you, Miss Brown?"

"Well, I'll *try* not to bite, but self-control isn't my best virtue."

"Oh, we have a live-wire here."

Flossie frowned and cocked her head. "Whatever is a live-wire?"

"Like electricity—exciting and just a little dangerous if you're not careful." He climbed up next to her and made a show of sitting as far away as possible.

Madeline adjusted her hat and folded her hands in her lap with a perfect show of prim propriety. "I don't know what you could mean, I'm sure."

And so, with the carriage full of laughing young people, Frank took off for the north side of the city. Henry waited until they'd skirted the worst of the congestion before he regaled them with stories of people on the train — from the woman with a pet raccoon in a basket to the man selling shares in the Brooklyn Bridge. "He actually made a couple of sales — gave certificates and everything."

"Did he really?" Madeline turned to face him. "People believed him? Why do you think that was?"

After a moment's thought, Henry removed his hat and twirled it in his lap as he spoke. "I'd say it was his confidence. He told a good story — why it needed investors, why he'd been tasked to sell the shares, everything. Why, he even took down addresses to send people their dividend checks. No foolin'."

"Quite ingenious, isn't it? I mean, there's no way for people to verify information on a train, and knowing he'll get off and make the offer to someone else would pressure people to make a quick decision." Madeline found herself twirling her own hat as she pondered the idea. "Now, did he bring up the subject or...."

"Well, it was like this. We were all sitting in the car. He got on at Cleveland. He sat down and just put his hat over his face — like this." Henry propped his hat over his face and slumped down in the seat. "Just pretended to sleep. But then his valise slid off his lap and spilled over the floor when the train lurched at a junction. That's when someone noticed the certificates. That's how the conversation started."

Her mind whirled as she imagined the scene, and it prompted another question. "And did he seem eager to sell — to tell about his scheme?"

"Not at all. Took a couple of businessmen to pull it out of him — like a dentist with teeth."

Which is exactly what I'd do to get someone to want to invest in my scheme. I'd make them feel like they got something over on me by getting me to tell them about it. It's quite genius.

"What are you thinking, Madeline?" Flossie turned and faced her cousin. "Our Madeline has taken to investigating all kinds of odd things."

"A hawkshaw in a skirt and bowler. That sounds like fodder for one of those detective stories."

"And, had I the skills, I'd create the character myself. Imagine how people would underestimate a woman investigating a murder."

Flossie's shocked expression made it difficult for Madeline and Henry *not* to laugh, but her words proved even more amusing. "Surely, you aren't planning anything of the kind. A *murder!* How unpleasant—and gruesome. Dirty. It might have...." She dropped her voice to a whisper. *"Blood."*

"Strange. I wouldn't have considered blood to be the worst of it." Madeline turned to Henry. "What do you think? Would blood be the worst aspect of murder?"

"I think I'd be most bothered by the body itself rather than just the blood. That used to be a living, breathing, feeling person. Now it's just a shell. I've never been fond of funerals for that reason."

And others, I'd imagine. It proved more difficult to keep her countenance from divulging her thoughts with each passing moment, but Madeline tried. "What do you think, Frank? What would be the worst part of a murder scene for you?"

"Oh, *must* we discuss something so repugnant? Let's talk about the ball! A much pleasanter topic, don't you think?"

As if Henry had never heard of a ball and the delights found at one, Flossie began regaling him with stories of past affairs and what they'd find at this year's event. Henry responded where necessary, but at the first opportunity, he leaned over and murmured, "What about a murder scene would you find most unsettling?"

Though indecorous, Madeline leaned closer still and gave him a

151

very pointed look. "Well, what about it being evidence of a murderer?"

Henry leaned back in his seat, twirled his hat a time or two more, and laughed. "If I'd known you had such interesting friends, I would have swallowed my pride and returned years ago. I predict this will be the best summer I've ever had."

A hat tossed to one corner of the bed, an abandoned skirt and shirtwaist over the end. Stockings littered the floor, and wrappings from a parcel threatened to fall off the dressing table at any moment. With the light blaring overhead, and the window open, Madeline lay sprawled on her coverlet, her wrapper bunched up beside her.

Two photographs lay next to the envelope—one of Amy with the giant Swiss Alps towering over her. She could hardly see Amy for the majesty of the snow-capped mountains. The other showed Amy in a gondola in Venice. Something about it didn't quite ring true, and Madeline suspected the gondola to be a prop. *It captures the air of the place, I suppose.*

But the letter—the letter she read half a dozen times, drinking in each word and reliving each moment as if she were there. *You really are a marvelous correspondent, my dear Amy. I wonder if Russell received a letter as well.*

Beside her on her bed also lay her lap desk, and tucked beneath that was the tiny portrait of Russell. Madeline pulled it out and gazed at it for some time. *It does capture you, doesn't it? I can almost see the juxtaposition of relaxation and wariness. What had I said just then, I wonder?*

Time to reply to Amy's letter. Madeline propped herself up against the bedstead, pulled the little desk onto her lap, and spread Amy's missive out beside her. *The day I learned to use your letters as a template for my own is the day that my correspondence stopped being a complete waste of time for me* and *for the recipient.*

Settled in place, she tested her fountain pen and began the delightful and painstaking task of sending her friend news of home.

Dearest Amy,

How quickly your letter arrived! Each time I hear of you or read a letter, you are in some new and exciting place. Now that you are in Venice, are you attempting to learn Italian? Is it everything you'd hoped it would be? The photograph you sent makes it look opulent and quaint at the same time. Of course, you would likely prefer to hear about Rockland and your friends here rather than my opinions of what you are doing.

Russell visits on a regular basis. I think after that business with Mr. Jackson, he considers it his personal responsibility to ensure that I am not plagued by any more self-important young men who take Mr. Darcy's shocking proposal as a model. If I may let you in on a secret, Amy dear, I rather liked that proposal. For all its faults, it was honest. He didn't pretend to be something he wasn't, which is more than I fear I can say for a certain friend of ours. I grow more and more concerned for her every day.

Vernon Smythe gives all the appearance of a fine, upstanding man, but none of the evidence of one. I've seen him try to evade questions, observed him in suspicious circumstances, and am using the investigation of a project he has proposed for improvements in the Dry Docks quarter as a chance to discern his true character. I hope to learn that I am mistaken in him. I hope more than believe, I'm afraid.

One thing that this investigation has done is made me very aware of the world around me, and in doing so, I have discovered that I am frequently in the same vicinity as a man whom I do not know. He is usually without a hat, wearing a brown plaid suit, and once he carried a cane that he never used. His only other distinguishing feature is a large handlebar mustache. I am certain that, at least twice, he actually followed me, but I cannot determine why. The last time I saw him, he wore a bowler, which I believe was designed to mock or torment me.

You see, I have taken to wearing one myself! Can you imagine? Me! If you find it highly improper, you may lay the blame at your dear brother's feet. You see, he mocked me and my new pastime and asked if I planned to take up the pipe in honor of my hero, Mr. Holmes. So, when I saw a bowler in a shop window, one that looked like it just might fit, I bought it on impulse. Now I wear it more than my other hats. Who knew that purchasing a hat for oneself meant that one would actually <u>enjoy</u> wearing it?

Flossie Hardwick's horrible cousin arrived today. Do you remember Henry the Horrificent? The magnificently horrible Henry? Oh, we did have fun with our monikers, didn't we? Well, he arrived today, and much to my surprise, delight, and tiny bit of disappointment, he's quite improved. That he acknowledged his obnoxiousness and showed genuine embarrassment spoke well of him, I think.

We had a delightful discussion on murder and crime scenes on the way home from the depot. Flossie was properly horrified, of course. Frank turned a little green around the gills, but Henry is a clever thinker still. He just no longer seems to feel the need to inform people of it at every turn.

Speaking of turns, he has promised to join us at the Midsummer's Ball. And here, for the first time, Amy, I must begrudge you that trip. It's just horrid that you won't be here for it! We haven't missed one together since '99 – two whole years! It's a tradition, and you already broke it! For shame! (If you were here, I would wink. I tried to draw one, but failed. I don't have your skill with a pencil.)

For the ball, Aunt Louisa and I went to Miss Ada's. I picked out a lovely dusk rose and returned for a fitting. And here is where you will have quite a laugh at my expense. When I returned for that fitting, Miss Ada had another dress – cornflower – on the mannequin. Oh, Amy it is the most beautiful thing. I wish my new camera could capture the lovely color, but I will have Russell attempt to take a photograph anyway. You can see the style and trimmings. It cost me more, of course. Miss Ada is too clever to make another to suit me and not make it benefit her pocketbook over mine. Had I not purchased that bowler the very same day, I wouldn't have done it, but my dear, I have reached an epoch in my life – one that you will be quite proud of, I am sure. I exceeded my clothing allowance! (Do cheer for me now).

Enclosed is a photograph I took of Russell while on Turner's Pond. I meant to send the photograph in my last letter, but alas, I forgot. You see, Russell purchased a Brownie camera for me! It was kind of him, wasn't it? I believe it was an attempt to keep me out of trouble, but between you and me, I intend to use it, should the opportunity arrive, to provide proof of a certain young man's guilt or innocence to the charge of impropriety.

I've exceeded the limit of the paper. I doubt I'll have much room for a proper salutation, so do be safe my friend. I love and miss you.

Faithfully yours,
Madeline

Madeline blotted the letter, folded it, and slipped it into the envelope. With one last look at the photograph of Russell, she sighed and added it to the letter. "I do wish I could keep that one. It's quite nice, and I don't have one of him."

The words rang hollow in the room — overloud, as though she'd shouted them. *I imagine talking to oneself is not a good habit to develop. Pity.*

SIXTEEN

As a boy, Russell had considered their house on Highland Avenue to be an enormous place, full of perfect nooks for hiding from his friends and his little sister. However, as he'd grown, it seemed to shrink to fit him until, for the past decade or so, he'd considered it quite modest in size. But with his sister in Europe, and his parents spending the summer at Nantuckett, as he seated himself at the long mahogany dining table in a room that dwarfed him all alone, he, again, felt like the little boy he'd once been.

It's too big for one person. I'm used to Paul and Jenny keeping me company at least. Having to fend for myself for the weekend won't be enjoyable, but they've earned it.

Suddenly, his omelet lost all flavor for him. Russell ate it without relish, washed up the dishes, and turned out the downstairs lights as he made his way up the wide staircase and to the study his mother and sister had created out of a little-used spare room. *Lord, not many young men have such a family. I take them for granted.*

Plans for the new arts center called to him. If he could only create the perfect blend of old and new. However, Russell set the tubes of sketches aside, rolled his desk top back, and pulled a sheet of writing paper from the drawer. Two letters awaited his response — one from his mother and one from Amy. Russell picked up his pen, filled it, cleaned, and dried it. The words still refused to come.

"Then perhaps Mother."

157

Dearest Father and Mother,

Rockland is hot and miserable without you. I've sent Jenny and Paul off for the weekend, and so I find myself alone and very much regretting not accepting one of the kind invitations I received this week. But, there is also much to be said for a time of quiet reflection with the Lord, and after I write to you and Amy, I plan to immerse myself in such a time.

Your story, Mother, about the crab who could not seem to evade the curious hands of that child amused both Madeline and myself. She asked permission to copy it to tell her children one day. In her words, "So many children's stories treat them like little imbeciles. I would love a dozen such tales – stories that entertain without insulting the intelligence of children." It reminded me of that educator in England you mentioned. What was that woman's name? I thought Madeline might enjoy learning more about her. I recall the article said something about treating childrens' intelligence with respect.

He wrote of the upcoming bid for the arts center and the Denton offices and the compliments paid to him by Mr. Estershire. He told of the "shower" of blossoms in the middle of Madeline's dinner party and a highly sanitized version of her foray into disguise. That paragraph began a new page, and for a moment, he had the inexplicable desire to tear it up. "Lord, I'm not ashamed of her, so why hesitate as if I am?"

That question prompted him to set aside his mother's letter and pull out a fresh sheet.

My dear little Amy,

Is it time for me to cease calling you "little"? You are, after all, nearly as tall as I am now. Did I tell you that I have determined that European men are all very short in stature and quite averse to women who are taller than they? This is how I keep myself from imagining you fighting off hordes of men who wish to keep you in Venice, Vienna, or Versailles and far from us. I suggested as much to Madeline, and she, being the obliging girl that she is, agreed with me. Don't douse our delusions with the truth. We could not bear it.

All silliness aside, I do wonder that you have not written me of young men. Even the letters Madeline has shared make no mention of Italian gondoliers whispering tender words in a language that, as I recall you saying, "Sounds just as beautiful as love must feel." Do you write of your romantic exploits on a separate page that she can hide from me without breaking the flow of her letter? You wouldn't do that to me, would you? Tell me that Uncle Richard is keeping a close eye on you.

While on the subject of young men, Madeline has met a new one. His name is Henry Hardwick, and I gather you've met him. Madeline seems to find his company congenial, at least for now. I believe she found Delbert Jackson congenial the first few times they met.

Russell stared at the page, hesitating, wondering. Flossie and Edith were both good friends to Amy—not sisterly like Madeline, but still very close. If they wrote letters at all, Amy might find herself inundated with exaggerated stories. He needed to do it. Better to hear from him than the histrionics she might receive from less levelheaded quarters.

The town has been hit with summer fever, it seems. This year, Madeline is the source of gossip. I expect Edith and Flossie will have thrilling tales of her daring deeds and will implore you to exert your influence over her. Well, we both know that neither of us can exert much influence over her. The reverse is usually true, don't you think? So, before you hear these exaggerated stories, I thought I'd give you my account. She's reading a new detective novel. I doubt Mr. Surat will take the place of her beloved Sherlock, but he did stir her to test the theory of disguises.

It took time, but he managed to relate the stories of her foray into disguise, her accidental—he hoped—trek into the Dry Docks, and her subsequent concern for the residents therein. Twice he read the words, checking each sentence. Once convinced he'd told the stories as truthfully as he knew, he signed off.

As you can imagine, gossips like to see such things in the worst possible light, but you know that Madeline has far too much sense to do anything reckless or foolish.

You are missed here, Amy. Maddie and I speak of it often, but we both agree that we envy you this experience. Enjoy every minute, make every memory a treasure, keep filling those journals, and when you come home in February, we'll be waiting to hear all about it. Don't neglect the Lord, though. I pray for you often.

With much love,

Russell

For the first time she could remember, and possibly for the first time *ever*, Madeline looked forward to a meeting at Flossie Hardwick's. The details would be tedious, of course, but she'd heard a little something about Stanley Wakefield just that morning, thanks to a pair of ears attached to a freckled face with overly large teeth. Jimmy Higgins repeatedly proved himself to be a veritable fount of seemingly useless information.

"I heard that rat, Smythe, talking to Miss Edith last night. Isn't she a friend of the Wakefields?" Madeline had confirmed the association and listened with rapt attention as Jimmy grew more and more animated. *"Well, he was all het up about how Mr. Wakefield was out on a bash the other night and got dragged into one of those bawdy houses down in the Dry Docks."* When she'd asked which one, the boy shrugged. *"I just knows it was on Fuller Street, 'cause the fella said somethin' about it. He also said*

he had to go in to drag Mr. Wakefield out, and one of those nasty women accosted him. But miss...." Jimmy had stepped closer and his voice dropped low. *"I was workin' at the Wakefield's that night – had to do some mowing and waited for it to cool, you know. And Mr. Stanley was there all night – had a row with his father. Mr. Wakefield panned him good – read him the riot act. Now how could he be at both places at the same time?"*

Sitting in the Hardwick's parlor, Madeline tapped her toes and forced her fingers not to drum on her skirt as she waited for the usual gossip and various new ideas to be discussed and dismissed before everyone settled firmly on doing things as they'd always done them — proving once again that the meetings were a complete waste of everyone's time.

"Well, that settles it then." Flossie smiled. "I trust we'll all be at the ball on Saturday? Frank and I will be forced to leave early. Grandmother Prisms-and-Prunes is coming for a week on Friday – to see Henry, of course – so we will have to be awake and presentable in time for church." The poor girl fought against tears as she added, "No coming home at dawn for us."

It's that kind of fanaticism that makes the Christian religion a burden rather than the blessing I believe Jesus intended. If we went to balls every week, I would agree that moderation would be necessary, but twice a year – twice – we have an event that makes church the following morning difficult. And it isn't as if we couldn't choose to attend the prayer meeting later instead.

Her thoughts were interrupted by the appearance of Stella's skirt as the young lady passed. Madeline jumped up, looped her arm in the girl's, and pulled her aside. "I heard about Stanley's being indisposed on Tuesday evening. Is he quite recovered?"

"Recovered? Indisposed?" Stella stared at her. "Whatever could you mean? Tues—no, I know for certain he was quite well—hasn't been ill since that terrible influenza in March that I know of."

"Odd, isn't it? Why, I'm quite sure Mr. Smythe was overheard

161

describing how he had to help poor Stanley home that evening." Madeline dropped her voice and tried to force a little color to her cheeks. "I confess I had a selfish motive in asking. I saw him in town that day, you know. He was delivering something for your father, I believe. If it was contagious... with the ball and all...."

Stella's bristled appearance softened immediately. "I can understand that, of course. But I assure you, Mr. Smythe didn't help him home that night or any other. In fact, that night the entire neighborhood likely heard exactly how 'at home' he was. Papa was quite incensed because Stanley said he didn't wish to return to university this fall. You know how Papa gets when riled." Her face flushed. "Indeed, I believe the whole of *Rockland* is quite aware. I'm just thankful it takes something enormous to provoke him."

"Well, Mr. Smythe is new to the area. Perhaps he confused whom he helped."

Eyes darting about the room, Stella pulled Madeline deeper into a corner. "Mr. Smythe knows exactly who everyone in this town is. If he said this, it was to a purpose. I've no doubt about that. I just hope that it was Edith he told such a story to. That might make sense."

"How so?" Madeline blinked and tried to give the impression of full and undivided attention. *And do say what I think, Stella. I would so love the affirmation.*

"Well, if he said it to Edith, then one would surmise that his goal was to warn her off of someone he felt jealous over. As if Stanley would ever be interested in her—too 'peaches and cream and not enough rum,' he would say."

I wonder that you don't consider another reason, Stella. Is it because it would reflect on your brother or because it never occurred to you? I wonder.

The Hardwick home sat back further than any of the other

houses on Sturbridge Road. Speculation ran high as to the reason. Some of the gossips insisted that Mrs. Hardwick demanded it so she could plant a row of trees to overhang the walk—a constant reminder to Rockland that you could remove the belle from the south, but you would not remove the south from *that* southern belle. More charitable suggestions ranged from a desire for privacy, to Mr. Hardwick's desire for his wife to feel perfectly at home so far away from her beloved South Carolina.

Still, the walk, even on a hot summer's afternoon, afforded just enough shade to make it a pleasant stroll to the trolley stop just yards from the corner of their property. *This is likely the reason. Mr. Hardwick wanted to separate the noise of the trolley from his house. Why do people do that — assume the most unpleasant or overly romanticized explanation for anything, when the practical one is likely correct?*

"Madeline?"

On the average day, when lost in her own thoughts and waiting in a pleasant shade for a trolley, the voice of a young man might have proven irritating to the young woman. However, Henry Hardwick had already proven quite interesting, and her errand downtown to replace a few necessary articles of undergarments ruined in the laundry wasn't something she was over-eager to do. With a little more enthusiasm than a young lady *should* show a new gentleman acquaintance, Madeline whirled to face him.

"Why, Henry Hardwick! Does Mrs. Hardwick know you've escaped?"

"She not only knows, she approves. I believe her words were, 'Oh, do walk Madeline home before she takes up a notion to wander through unsavory areas of the city again. That girl!'"

Madeline cocked her head as she listened. But at the words, "That girl!" she shook her head with a disappointed air. "I might have believed you at first, but Mrs. Hardwick does *not* vociferate."

The rattle of the trolley turned Henry's head that direction. "Are you—? You're *not* going home. That's interesting."

"Is it? And why would that be interesting?"

She stepped forward as the trolley came to a stop, but to her surprise, Henry hopped on after her. He settled in the seat beside her, removed his hat, and gave her an inscrutable look. "Well, from my investigation of the right lovely Miss Brown, I have learned that she doesn't enjoy shopping, so that would imply she is on the quest for more information—about *something.*"

"I'm afraid I'll have to disappoint you, then. You see, I *am* going shopping this afternoon." She laughed as he tried to formulate a witty retort and failed. "I will concede that this is usually true. Alas, despite its inherent evils—aside from trips to the booksellers, of course—"

"Of *course,*" Henry echoed.

Something in his tone invited just the kind of camaraderie necessary to affect a change in the Hardwick household as well as gather a bit of insight into her current perplexity. She abandoned her homily on the evils but necessity of shopping and diverted the conversation into a more agreeable track. "I understood you to be a particular favorite of your grandmother's."

"It's shameful, perhaps—on both of our parts. But yes, she does indulge me a bit more than the others. Why do you ask?"

"I just thought that, as her particular favorite, you might be able to *suggest* that it's too bad that Frank and Flossie will miss such a significant portion of our biggest charitable fundraiser of the year. Don't the Scriptures say something about doing for 'the least of these' being rather important? Even Jesus provided food on the Sabbath, and that *is* the ultimate goal of the fundraiser. Food, clothing, and shelter for the orphans."

His laughter rang out and startled an older woman across from them. To Madeline's surprise, Henry apologized and promised to be quieter for the duration of the ride. He winked at Madeline, though, and promised to see what he could do. "Grandmother cares more for the appearance of piety than the reality of it. As long as I can make her see it as a personal sacrifice rather than a selfish indulgence, I should succeed."

"I do so hate that sort of self-righteous hypocrisy." Madeline's eyes widened. She turned to Henry with genuine contrition in her heart and on her lips. "Henry, I beg your pardon. That was unpardonable, but I can't take it back now."

"But of course! And, I might add...." Henry bent a little closer, his eyes earnest, his expression grave. "I echo your thoughts, Miss Brown. When piety becomes *pietistic*, it loses all meaning and then becomes a means of control rather than comfort."

A man on the street prompted her to take her half-spoken reply in a different direction. "—oh! That reminds me. You're a young man."

"Astute observation, Miss Brown."

Impatience mingled with laughter as she insisted he dismiss with the formalities. "I've seen you paddled. I think we're beyond convention, don't you? Now what was I saying?"

"You made the brilliant deduction that I am a man and a young one at that."

With a toss of her head that annoyed her further, Madeline grumbled a self-reproach on being so silly and peevish to herself and returned to the question on her mind "What would make you tell your sweetheart that you saw someone else doing something that the person absolutely didn't do? What would be the motivation?"

"I'm afraid that is a bit too ambiguous. There are just too many variables to consider. Might you be a little more specific?"

When gossip becomes more than an idle pastime of delving into the lives of others, it loses its sting on one's consciousness. The thought removed the few scruples she had left, and Madeline started to explain further. "Oh, dear. This is my stop. I'll have to ask another time."

Madeline started as Henry hopped off the trolley behind her. He offered to take her to a nearby tearoom, but Madeline declined. "I

165

wouldn't wish to be overheard. Perhaps just a stroll down a side street and around the block?"

They took off at a leisurely stroll. "Well, Henry. The situation is this. One young man was overheard telling his sweetheart that another young man became intoxicated and was somehow inveigled into a brothel in the Dry Docks. The man said that he was called upon to go in there and help the poor fellow home again." As she told the story, Madeline's eyes watched passersby in wagons, on walkways, and in the street. "Now, here is the interesting part."

"Nearly faint with anticipation."

"Don't mock me. Now, the interesting part is that the second young man was never in the Dry Docks quarter that night. His entire neighborhood can attest to that. So, the question remains, why would the first young man say such a thing to his sweetheart? Why try to slander another man's reputation? What would be the purpose?"

Henry stopped and stared at her. "If you're the sweetheart—"

"I am not."

"Well, that's a relief." Henry smiled at her inquisitive expression. "I just mean that I had intended to request half a dozen dances and didn't know if your young man would disapprove. He sounds like quite the jealous fellow."

Disappointment flooded her heart. Madeline shook her head. "So that's it, is it? You think he did this out of jealousy—to ensure his sweetheart wouldn't look twice at the other fellow?"

"No, but I assumed that was your opinion." His smile created unfamiliar somersaults in her heart. "I should have known better. I would have said that the first young man concocted a plausible story to explain his own presence in the area—possibly because he suspected someone saw him go into that brothel himself."

Her heart swelled with excitement and filled with shame. *What kind of young lady is happy to hear that a friend's beau is so unworthy?! That's unpardonable!* Madeline nodded in solemn agreement. "That was my supposition, but I couldn't imagine why he would risk such a fine match to go there in the first place. And how does one know what a brothel looks like anyway? I mean, if you were near one, would you recognize it from the outside? I hardly imagine that it says, 'Miss Fancy Woman's House of Ill-Repute' on the sign."

"No, but if I wanted to visit such a place, I imagine I would go to where I knew there might be one and look for the cleanest building around. Dry Docks isn't known for cleanliness, but they would wish to *entice* men there, and what man wants to be so intimate with… filth."

What man indeed? Then again, why would a man become so intimate with someone who may have just been – The thought nearly made her retch.

Henry steered her back onto the main street and apologized. "That was an unpleasant picture to hang in your mind. Please forgive me."

She smiled and turned—just strolled down the street with Henry on her heels, crossed to the other side, and stood before Wakefield's Department Store. "I'm sorry, Henry, but we have to say goodbye here. Thank you for your insight."

"I don't mind sho—"

"But you would, I assure you. Go home." She softened her words with a smile and patted his arm. "But I do hope you ask me for those dances."

$\mathcal{S}$EVENTEEN

The day after her shopping excursion, Madeline received an invitation to a dinner party at the Mertons'. She reread it several times with a curious eye and sent an immediate acceptance by way of Jimmy Higgins. The lad promised to tell her if he saw or heard any other curious things, and over the course of the week leading up to the party, he stopped by half a dozen times to tell her *something* big was happening at the Merton house.

"I just don't know what," he complained. "No one says anything, but they whispers a lot. I can't find a lick of news, but Miss Edith sure gets dolled up every day now just before that louse, Smythe, arrives." Jimmy leaned forward. "I heard he almost did someone in with that Locomobile of his."

As Madeline dressed the night of the party, she recalled the conversations and tried not to imagine what must have happened. *She couldn't – she* wouldn't! *Not so soon, surely!*

Mary stepped into the room. "Mr. Barnes is here. He asked if you would like him to wait for you, or if you wanted to go alone."

"If he's here, I'll be down in just a minute. Thank you, Mary."

Madeline stared at her reflection, her eyes taking in every detail until she couldn't find anything she could improve. *Would if I could, on the other hand....*

At the top of the stairs, she watched Russell check the entry mirror and smooth the top of his hair. He spun the hat in his hands, but as her skirt came into view, he turned and something in his eyes hinted that she must look well enough. Albert Brown stepped from his study as she called out her goodbyes.

"You're looking lovely, my dear. I do love you in that yellow. Your mother wore yellow to our first dance."

You say that every time I wear yellow — anytime I wear anything darker than ivory, in fact. But Madeline didn't remind him. She kissed his cheek, fluffed the tufts of hair on the sides of his head and bade him goodnight. "Don't wait up. I think Edith has a long night planned."

Albert's eyes slid over her head to Russell. "You'll have someone escort you home?"

"I'd be happy to, sir."

Madeline's laughter filled the entry. "He just knows that Amy would have something to say about it if he didn't."

The moment the door closed behind them, Russell suggested an alternative to Amy as a reason for escorting her home. "You could always receive a better offer! I would be on hand to be the first to hear of it."

"Should that happen, Russell, what makes you think I would walk home with *you* then?"

His chuckle — how Amy must miss it — warmed her heart before he quipped, "An excellent observation."

Lanterns lit the walk to the Merton house door, lights glowed in every window, and music drifted down the walk from the open door. Madeline turned to Russell with dismay in her heart and on her lips. "I have a terrible feeling…."

"Madeline! Welcome!" Edith's voice called out from the steps as they neared.

Russell didn't answer, but from the look he gave her, his thoughts ran along the same vein. Furthermore, when they reached the door and saw Vernon Smythe standing there as if he were the host, all doubts — few though they were — dissolved. Russell found

170

his voice first. "Good evening, Edith." He nodded at the man beside her. "Smythe."

"Yes! Isn't it lovely?" Madeline gazed up at a cloudless, moonless sky and marveled. "The stars are certainly... lovely tonight."

"Not as lovely as our Edith is, I trust?" Smythe's familiarity, the way his hand rested on her shoulder—everything about him screamed the coming announcement.

Once more, Russell came to the rescue. "As lovely as the Lord's handiwork in the sky is, I agree that the stars He created when He created Eve are far superior."

I didn't know you could give such a pretty speech. Oh, won't your sweetheart love to hear your piffle? I almost wish I could eavesdrop and enjoy your smile at her pleased blushes.

Edith simpered—or nearly so—in her delighted embarrassment, but Madeline just smiled with the studied vacant expression she'd perfected and remarked that she thought she saw Flossie Hardwick. "Excuse me, I wanted to say hello."

Without waiting for an answer, Madeline hurried into the house and sought out Flossie's company. "You look flushed. Is it as warm as I feared?"

Flossie's pink cheeks reddened. "Not at all. Warren paid a pretty compliment and then went in search of refreshments."

"I'm pleased to hear it."

Her friend pulled her further into a corner and whispered, "Warren proved that Stanley Wakefield lied. I feel like such a fool. "

Warren arrived and arrested Flossie's explanation, but finally Madeline understood her friend's overreaction. Delia Hardwick had married badly because she'd ignored similar warning signs—signs everyone had practically battered her with. Her father forbade the marriage. Still, Delia now sat alone at night with unpaid bills and a baby while her husband ran around town. Of course, Flossie didn't want to end up with the same fate.

171

One mystery solved. It is just so out of character. Flossie is a forgiving creature. I should have seen this much sooner. Now, to convince her *of it.*

A glance around the room showed every friend Edith had — and a few people Madeline secretly knew the dear girl barely tolerated. Mr. Merton stood in the dining room at the head of the table with an enormous grin on his face and a calculating eye to every penny spent. Poisonous thoughts filled Madeline as Ida called everyone to dinner. *Is this dinner worth the investment, Mr. Merton, or should you have considered another market? Time will tell, but who will bear the losses, I wonder.*

Sitting farthest from the window, the heat of the room smothered Madeline until she feared she might actually faint. *You will not do something so idiotic. You're not going to make a fool of yourself at Edith's party.*

Then again, there was the distinct possibility that her inability to breathe might have more to do with the announcement she could feel in the air. It positively sizzled with anticipation and excitement. Across the table, Russell watched her with a touch of amusement and more than a little concern. Madeline tried to give him a reassuring smile, but the effort proved more than she could manage.

This is wrong — terribly, horribly wrong. If I could only articulate why, *I might be able to stop it before it's too late.*

The roast pheasant turned cold as she picked at her plate and tried to plan some way of thwarting an announcement. So lost was Madeline in her own world, that she missed the arrival of the hired waiters to remove their dishes. A plate of ice cream and macaroons appeared before her, and Madeline's heart sank. *All that sweetness with nothing substantial to support it. Well done, Madeline Brown. You deserve every uncomfortable moment.*

172

Vernon Smythe stood as the last plate was set before Reginald Coulter and Edith took a bite. "I'd like to propose a toast, if I may."

Though entirely unintentional, Madeline interrupted the toast by choking on a bite of macaroon. Edith flew to her side. Russell stood. Flossie hesitated and moved her way as well. Flushed with exertion and mortification, Madeline downed the rest of her wine and took a deep breath. "I apologize." The words came out in a rasped gasp. "Do go on."

"Ida?" Edith's eyes searched the room for the maid. "Will you refill Madeline's glass, please? I'll retrieve a cold cloth for her. She looks rather flushed."

Smythe moved to Edith's side and murmured, "Edith, we can pour a glass. Send Ida for the cloth." So quiet was Smythe's voice that only Madeline and those closest to her could have heard it, but no one could mistake the authoritative undertone he used.

"Of course, you are right. Ida, the cloth please. I'll pour."

And in the space of just a couple of minutes, Smythe stood in the same place next to Edith and smiled at the group. "I think it's safe to try this again, or do you need another moment, Miss Brown?"

Do you hear him, Edith? It was inconsiderate and uncouth to draw attention to me choking. Despite her nod of assurance, Madeline's raw throat did not allow her to speak. She smiled and reached for the glass, praying all the while that her smile did not resemble a grimace. *For Edith's sake, I must at least* appear *amiable.*

"Now, a toast to our lovely hostess, Edith. We are all fortunate to call her friend, but soon I will have the great honor to call her my bride. To Edith!"

A great cheer went up around the table. One of the young men followed it with a toast to the happy couple. Madeline sat in her seat, sipped the wine, and counted the minutes until she could excuse herself for a moment.

But as the young people adjourned to the terrace for a cooler evening game of night croquet, Madeline crept toward the water closet to steal a moment of privacy before she became obligated to socialize once more. *I will not play. No one will expect it. I —*

That thought suffered a swift and abrupt death as she passed the parlor and overheard Reginal Coulter speaking to someone she couldn't see. "—solve Smythe's debt problem, assuming Miser Merton gives Edith a wedding gift of a pecuniary nature."

"Might have influenced the speed with which he proposed, eh?"

Though she couldn't place the voice, Madeline felt the keen prick of pain as the truth of the speaker's words pierced her heart. She hustled to the water closet, washed her face, and stood before the mirror blinking back tears of frustration. *She'll never hear a word against him without irrefutable proof. She cares for him, and he has, at least, made an effort to endear her to him. Perhaps it's genuine now.*

Russell met her at the doors that led to the terrace. "I told Edith you might not feel well enough to stay—in case you'd rather go."

Her eyes widened in surprise. "I…." They softened. "You're right, of course. I should. Let me go congratulate her. I'll be back in a moment." She hadn't made it two steps out the door before she returned and gazed up into Russell's concerned eyes. "Thank you for understanding."

$\mathcal{E}$IGHTEEN

After a troubled night of fitful sleep, a lethargic day of discouragement, railing at Edith from several doors down, and yes, a few prayers, Madeline awoke to a Sunday morning as bright and beautiful as any. Sun shone through the leaded windows at Wayfair Chapel, creating lovely light beams that seemed to promise a brighter future than Madeline had envisioned. Indeed, as she listened to the beautiful singing, the encouraging sermon, and the inspiring Psalm read by a young man not yet out of high school, Madeline came to believe that nothing, not even the sight of Vernon Smythe holding Edith's hymnal for her, could mar the perfection of the day.

A stroll home with her father, a lovely lunch of cold chicken, garden salad, and lemonade—she needed the respite. Alas, just as Mary served dainty dishes of sorbet, the door chimed. Madeline's raised her eyes to her father and didn't even try to hide her dismay. "I was having such a lovely day, too."

"Perhaps it's Russell? Didn't he say his expected guests couldn't make it?"

Madeline pursed her lips, trying desperately to keep her opinions to herself, and sighed in exasperation. "Is it ungrateful and unkind that I wish he had someone else to bother—I mean *brother*—now and then? An afternoon free—"

A voice in the entryway stopped her cold. Albert Brown's eyebrows drew together in a decided show of consternation. He

175

stared at his favorite desert, and Madeline urged him to take it to his study. "Hurry."

But, of course, it was too late. Louisa Farnsworth swept into the dining room and took a seat to Albert's left—across from Madeline. "Good afternoon. I thought I would have missed your meal by now. I'm sorry."

"That is quite all right, Aunt Louisa. Would you care for some sorbet? We may be out of lemon, but Cook usually makes strawberry for her and Mary. Mary isn't particularly fond of lemons, which is a shame—so inexpensive this year."

Once begun, Madeline found it impossible to stop rambling about nonsensical things. Louisa stared at her, eyes clouded with consternation, and finally interrupted. "Madeline?"

She choked back a comment on her anticipation of the ball and blinked. "Yes, Aunt Louisa?"

"Do eat your sorbet before it melts into a puddle." She smiled and nodded as Mary brought a dish of strawberry sorbet and held it out for her approval." Thank you, Mary. I do prefer strawberry myself."

For the better part of a minute, the trio ate in strained silence. However, just as Madeline saw her father relax once more, Louisa made the purpose for her appearance known. "I've heard about Edith Merton's engagement. Quite the surprise there. When he was at my house, I thought I saw interest in another direction."

She wasn't supposed to say it. While few others of her acquaintance would have found anything untoward in frankness about the topic, Louisa Farnsworth had assumed antiquated notions regarding propriety—notions that grew more and more rigid and ridiculous every year. But Madeline, her day now spoiled beyond hope of repair, lost all patience with such circuitous forms of conversation. "If you mean that you thought Mr. Smythe showed any particular interest in me, I assure you he did not. In fact, I believe he spoke well of Edith while we looked for your fan."

176

Louisa dropped her spoon onto the plate with a decided air of disapproval. "Madeline, as I have *tried* to explain to you. It isn't *seemly* to speak of such things with such...."

As she searched for the word she wanted, Albert interjected his opinion. "No one but you thinks that it is inappropriate for any young lady to speak frankly with her closest relatives about any young man's interest or lack thereof."

"But this is *Madeline,* Albert. What she does with us, she will do with anyone."

"Anyone? I hardly think so, Aunt Louisa. I may say as much to Amy or Russell—even Edith if the situation warranted. But since it is a moot point now, perhaps we can make it a *mute* one as well?"

Albert nudged her knee under the table—a silent, "Well spoken" encouragement, but Louisa wouldn't let it lie. "Very amusing, Madeline. But now my evening is utterly wasted. You didn't exert any effort to engage either man's interest."

"And you *wanted* me to engage Mr. Gray's interest? You thought that a young man, a temperance fellow, who has stolen cuff links, was the right choice for me? I hardly believe that."

Those words caught the shocked attention of both her father and her aunt. Albert found his voice first. "Stolen? Surely not."

"Then tell me how he just happened to be observing a billiard game the very night that Milty Grueber's cuff links went missing? I mentioned it to Milty, and he spoke to his father. No other set like them has been made, and I went into the pawnbroker's after my shopping trip the other day." A smile broke out over her face before Madeline could stop it. "You should have seen the man's face when he asked what I'd brought to pawn. I assured him I did *not* wish to part with my newly purchased drawers, corset, and things."

"Madeline!" Louisa fumbled for a fan she hadn't brought with her and gaped at Albert as she waited for him to reprimand his daughter. When he didn't, she turned, and produced her severest scowl. "I cannot imagine what drove you into such a place, but then

177

to discuss your *undergarments!*"

"Now, Louisa...."

But Louisa refused to be dissuaded. "This must *cease* before she destroys what's left of her, *and your*, good names."

"Well, I for one would like to know what she learned from the pawnbroker." Albert gave Madeline an encouraging smile. "You implied that what he said is why you believe them to have been stolen?"

"They had to have been. The broker not only had never purchased them and/or resold a pair. He also said that no pawnbroker with any business sense would purchase something with a monogram like that. It's just too difficult to resell. But since he's the only one in the area that Mr. Gray claimed to purchase his, I have to conclude that he stole them and used a manufactured story to explain his possession of them. Had he said they were a *gift*, I could, perhaps, assume that at the least the giver had been the thief. But since he said he purchased something —"

"Yes, yes." Louisa frowned. "You'd think that a *temperance* man would, at the least, be honest."

"He's temperate in his wine consumption but makes up for it in kleptomania?" Madeline took another bite of her now-liquified sorbet and offered her aunt a curious look.

"Klepto — what?" Louisa's head wagged back and forth as she tried to follow a conversation she didn't understand.

Oh, Auntie. You will regret asking. Madeline set her hands in her lap and smiled. "It's the compulsion to steal — a medical condition of the mind. People with this condition do not have a *need* and often not even a *desire* for the object. They only have a need to *take* it."

"And where would you have heard of such a ludicrous notion?"

Albert spoke before Madeline could. "I recall hearing about it as a boy. Do you remember the Walker boy? He was caught stealing handkerchiefs from people's clotheslines?"

"Yes… surely you won't try to tell me that—"

"But that is exactly what I heard mentioned at the time. They did some sort of negative association therapy with him—pain every time he reached for things that weren't his. As far as I know, it was successful. His parents were certainly pleased with the results." He winked at Madeline. "They saved an enormous amount of money when they no longer were compelled to replace stolen handkerchiefs."

"I'm not amused, Albert, and this is beside the point. I came here to tell you that I met a nice accountant the other day—at Mrs. Estershire's luncheon. He stopped in to pay her a visit while in town. As fortune would have it, he's moving here from Louisville—has the most charming accent. His family is in horses."

And you assume that, because I can no longer hope to capture the fancy of Mr. Smythe, I will rush at the chance to be introduced to this fellow. Would it be worth the frustration of trying to explain? Likely not.

So lost in her thoughts was she, that Madeline didn't hear her father speaking until a few words jerked her from her internal raving. "—think Madeline has enough prospects as it is. We certainly wouldn't want her to be branded a flirt."

"Prospects?" Louisa stared at her, a demand for further explanation in the woman's eager eyes. "Why didn't you say something, Madeline?"

"I would have—had I known it myself."

But Albert shook his head and patted her hand. "Go on up and get your book. We understand these… *delicate* matters are a trifling embarrassing—especially at first."

"Wha—" But the look in her father's eyes stopped her short. "Yes, Papa." She skirted the table, kissed her aunt's cheek, and strolled from the room. Once out of sight, she flattened herself against the wall—just as her father knew she would—and waited.

"Louisa. You must not be quite so *pushy* with her. You know how Madeline is. If you push her toward a nice, suitable young man, she's likely to elope with a philanderer!"

Her aunt's protest could have been heard on the walk. "She isn't quite that far gone, Albert! I thi—oh, really. Sometimes I think she's not half as bad as you are. *You* are the true bad influence. Now is there someone I don't know about, or was that just a ruse to extricate her from my clutches?"

Meddlesome clutches. Who's meddlin' now?

"Well, there's always Russell Barnes, of course. I've always had secret hopes there. Amy's year in Europe has ensured she spends more time with him than ever, and it could be that such frequent company will spark something."

"I hardly think—he's like a brother to her, I'm sure."

"For now...." Albert's voice lowered. Madeline strained to hear his next words. "But you are correct. It isn't likely. No, I truly spoke of Henry Hardwick. He's hinted to me that he thinks... *highly* of her." A long pause followed. "They do seem congenial, but nothing will happen if she feels *pressured* into any sort of relationship. So, please. Do all of us a favor and let her be."

Well done, Papa! Madeline skipped up the stairs, impressed by her father's management of the situation and more than a little amused. *Oh, I wish I could have seen her face! She must be feeling so smug. I imagine he saved me from another intolerable evening party.*

But as she reached for her book, a ripple of uncertainty washed over her. *It was an act. Wasn't it?*

The late evening breeze sent a waft of cooler air over the terrace. Roses perfumed the air. Fireflies played tag across the lawn, while Madeline sat in her favorite chair, a cold glass of lemonade at the ready, and enjoyed the quiet that comes just before twilight.

That quiet crashed with the appearance of Mary. "Miss

Madeline?"

No amount of self-control could hide her irritation. "Yes?"

"I'm sorry to bother you, but Mr. Henry Hardwick is here to see you."

"Send him out." Dismayed at the impatience she heard in her tone, Madeline called out to Mary. "I'm sorry, Mary. I didn't mean to snap."

Henry appeared, hat and lemonade in hand and with every appearance of the expectation of a long visit. Before he could greet her, Madeline spoke. "It's in your favor that I am in good humor this evening. If the weather had been even a bit warmer or the breeze had not obliged, you might have found me determined to send you home again."

"It is rude of me to come without an invitation," Henry began.

Madeline stopped him. "Among friends, invitations are a bit formal, don't you think? I am pleased for the company. I had expected Russell Barnes to bring by a letter from Amy, but he hasn't come."

Henry gestured to the chair beside her. "May I sit?"

"I beg your pardon. Please. And do tell me how are you enjoying your visit? Is your grandmother quite pleased with you? Have you scandalized her yet?"

"I've tried half a dozen times, but she refuses to believe that I intend to take up a tramp's life, become a baseball player, or that I want to become an archaeologist on an Egyptian dig."

Something in Henry's voice changed as he mentioned Egypt, and Madeline noted it. "But you do wish to go into archeology, don't you?"

"I should have known I couldn't put one over on you. Yes, I do wish to study." Henry's tone changed yet again—went completely flat. "However, only people with large purses manage to participate. Without Grandmother's support, I couldn't hope to do it."

And there Madeline heard Henry's frustration and

181

disappointment. She slid a plate of molasses cookies closer and insisted he take one. "Cook made these for me today. She'd be most gratified to see them all gone, and I assure you they comfort where nothing else does."

From there, she listened, observing from time to time the differences in his tone and inflections until Madeline grew confident in her understanding of the situation. "I must commend you on your self-restraint. Some young men wouldn't resist the temptation to apply to her for the necessary funds."

"She'd give them to me," Henry said with a sigh that hinted of dreams unfulfilled. "I need only ask, but I can't—not knowing that."

"Very admirable, Henry. Quite. But hardly the way to achieve your goals. What about Mr. Hardwick? Would he, perhaps, consider a loan??"

"Uncle George isn't exactly known for his like of me." Henry slumped back and stared at his glass as if it would reveal the world's secrets to him. "I managed to ensure that ten years ago."

But Madeline refused to allow Henry to remain in a pit of melancholy. "Oh, bother. Mr. Hardwick is hardly the kind of man to hold a grudge against an eleven-year-old boy! If you worded it exceptionally well and with utmost care, you could leave him with the idea that he was doing his mother a courtesy—saving her from the foolhardy release of funds to a grandson who would only squander them. At least being indebted to *him* would ensure that you either proved successful in your studies or they never saw you again." Before he could protest again, Madeline asked about his dreams. "What about archeology intrigues you, Henry?"

Everything in Henry's demeanor changed. His eyes lit up, intensified by the darkening shadows around them, and his voice became animated. "The classes I took at university this spring—they were amazing. Archaeologists are not just finding ancient ruins to explore, they're investigating links from our past to our future. We're correcting misperceptions and recreating entire cultures with every passing day. It's a wondrous time to be in the field, and every moment that I am here, I'm missing another piece."

A thrill filled her as she listened to him speak and imagined his words playing out before her eyes. She felt the sun beating down on her in Egypt as she worked tirelessly in the harsh rays. With a flick of a brush, she found a piece of clay pot, a scrap of linen, a scarab. "Oh, it does sound fascinating!"

"Wouldn't it be thrilling to work together to unearth the secrets buried in those great pyramids? I can just see you there in khaki and that ridiculous bowler hat of yours. Everyone else would be in archaeologist's attire, but I can't imagine you without that bowler. We'd find the tomb of Antony and Cleopatra!"

An unfamiliar feeling washed over her — one of vanity. "I imagine if I wore my bowler, I'd become horribly freckled." She wrinkled her nose. "I wonder why that bothers me so."

"You'd be beautiful as always — freckles or not."

Discomfort filled her, but not from Henry's precise words. No, something in his tone alluded to a deeper meaning than simple compliments. "I've never heard freckles referred to as anything but *unattractive* — by men or ladies alike. I'm afraid you must have singular taste."

"I imagine that any man would find even freckles to be attractive if found on the face of the one he holds most dear."

And if you try to hint that I've captured your heart inside two weeks, I do believe I'll inflict serious harm on you. How annoying.

"But, as for you," Henry continued, "any man who had the privilege of spending so much time in your presence would likely be in love more with your mind than your face. No one could help it."

Madeline sat up and leveled her most studied imperturbable expression on him. "If this is your attempt at flattery — "

"I'd call it flirtation, but flattery works."

She closed her eyes before they revealed more than she cared to share. "I'll amend my words. If this is your attempt at *flirtation* — "

183

But her rebuke fell flat. She glared at him. "Oh, you do know how to ruin a pleasant evening, don't you?"

With that, and no consideration for her rudeness, Madeline jumped up from the chair and stormed into the house. Henry's laughter followed her all the way upstairs and into her room. She looked out over the walk and waited until his retreating form rounded the fence corner. Across the street, a man stood under the streetlight, leaning against the pole with his arms crossed over his chest. She watched, curious as to why he just stood there. Then, without warning, he tipped his hat at her and took off down the street.

Now, Russell Barnes, what was that all about?

Three days in a row, Madeline "ran into" Henry Hardwick, and with each interaction, his flirting grew exponentially more overt. In a moment of frustration, she blurted out to Mary, "He's become impossible! A delicate hint of flirtation can be amusing. This just borders on the vulgar."

So, when she and Edith went to a luncheon together, she almost *hid* from Flossie Hardwick during the program. "Don't leave my side, Edith. *Please.*"

"I don't understand your attitude, Madeline. From all I've seen and heard, Henry Hardwick is as fine a young man as you could hope to meet. Surely it would please Mrs. Farnsworth to see you with a beau."

"I would hope it wouldn't if I didn't care to have him."

Before the conversation could continue, one of the matrons—a patroness of the group—passed by, speaking of the young man in question. "—such a fine boy. I remember how horrid he was as a child. But he's grown into a respectable young man. Winston says

184

that he has aspirations in the field of archeology."

"I heard he's also grown into a fine *looking* young man as well."

Edith nudged Madeline and whispered, "That he has. Notwithstanding my Vernon, I do think Henry is the handsomest young man of our acquaintance."

But Madeline wouldn't hear it. "I was always taught that handsome is as handsome does, and flirting with girls —"

"*A* girl, Madeline. You have no proof of any other flirtation."

Once more, before Madeline could reply, another woman joined the intimate gossip circle nearby. "Oh, are we discussing Henry Hardwick? Did you hear about his work with the youth in the Dry Docks? Why, he's devoting most of his evenings to teaching the boys proper manners, how to recommend themselves to employers, and what *not* to do to avoid being relieved of their positions."

Madeline's heart sank a little and her face flushed. She turned to Edith and whispered, "Well, that is good to hear at least."

"—heard that he is also a part of the temperance league. He won't sign the pledge, as of yet," the voice added with some sorrow, "but he agrees that excessive alcohol is destroying our nation. He's calling himself a temperance moderate."

A wishy-washy man without solid convictions is more like it.

Edith pulled her a little further away before whispering her own take on the issue. "I heard that as well — from Flossie. He drinks wine or cordial with dinner, but won't join a club or accept anything alcoholic when he can refuse without giving offense. He said his objection wasn't to alcohol itself, but to the misuse of it, and he didn't trust himself *not* to misuse it."

It does sound like a fine thing in that light. At least he's not a fanatic.

"Madeline Brown, do come help us with something."

She followed orders and arrived at the side of the aforementioned patroness. "Yes, Mrs. Delaney?"

"You are great friends of this Henry Hardwick, are you not?"

"I wouldn't say *great* friends, no. But we are friendly. Why?"

Mrs. Delaney's eyes skittered between the other two women and rested once more on Madeline. "I wondered at your opinion of him. I had been led to believe that he had paid particular attention to you."

Before Madeline could stop her wayward lips, she formulated a response and let it fly. "I can't imagine why you'd consider the renewing of an old childhood acquaintance to be 'particular attention', but yes, we've spent some time together. I found him intelligent and amiable—a little fresh compared to the other young men of my acquaintance, but I've heard that is a plague amongst young university students."

Though Mrs. Delaney had begun to nod and smile, the woman's entire posture changed in an instant. At Madeline's take on young men, she leveled narrow, hard eyes on Madeline. "I suppose to self-important young women, a young man's frank admiration might be seen as 'fresh.' These silly games you young ladies enjoy make it difficult for young men to share their admiration without opening themselves to the charge of 'being fresh.'"

With that, Mrs. Delaney and the other women strolled off in a carefully hidden, but still evident to Madeline, huff. Edith pulled Flossie Hardwick over to their corner and spoke with uncharacteristic frankness. "Is Henry fond of Madeline, do you think?"

Madeline and Flossie erupted in perfect shocked unison. "Edith!"

"Well, I could spend the next half hour nudging the conversation into a direction that might reveal the answer, or I could just ask. And frankly, I'm weary of that kind of circumlocution. It certainly took enough of that nonsense to bring Vernon around."

And I didn't think you had it in you to put yourself forward. Well said, Edith Merton.

"Well, that's honesty for you." Flossie's tone didn't reveal if she was impressed or insulted, but she answered the aforementioned question before it bore repeating. "And yes, I do believe Henry is growing quite attached to our Madeline. He certainly speaks of her much more than he realizes. Always with great admiration. Always without that careless disregard for a girl's reputation that some of the young men do. I've heard Frank be much less careful of someone he actually had little interest in. I think it speaks well of Henry's improvement."

"Don't you think he's a bit flirtatious, though, Flossie?" Edith leaned forward. "I've seen that tendency in him a time or two."

"I've never known him to be. If he has been flirtatious, it is out of sincere affection, I am sure." Flossie cocked her head in that way she always did while thinking. "It's strange how his admiration for Madeline hasn't changed over the years. Why, I remember Grandmother talking about how smitten he was with her back when we were children. I suppose that would account for his rapid attachment now, wouldn't it?" Her eyes widened. "Why, Madeline! I do believe you're blushing."

Before Madeline could formulate an excuse, Edith spoke. "It is rather a warm afternoon, and we are speaking quite frankly of a young man's admiration for her. I would wonder more if she didn't blush."

Much to Madeline's relief, Mrs. Hardwick called for Flossie, and Edith followed a moment later. Standing alone on the front steps of the musical center, Madeline replayed the conversation in her mind — with some amusement and much thoughtfulness. *Perhaps I misjudged him. I didn't think there could be much genuine interest — more a passing fancy from someone just visiting. But if he thinks he's rekindled some childish admiration, it might not be so unforgivable. Perhaps if I were frank and suggested he be a little less... precipitous.* A small smile crept over her lips and settled there as she took off in a brisk walk toward the trolley. *And, if he is such an upstanding young man, perhaps in time I will receive a better offer. Wouldn't Russell be pleased and relieved!*

NINETEEN

The usual tedium of the junior league's meetings failed to surface as Madeline sat listening to the discussion of the new tables for the library. Hand fans fluttered with enough fervor to create tsunamis on all four corners of the globe in the late June heat, and more than one handkerchief became quite damp from incessant use.

"Well, I think that should conclude our business for this meeting." Flossie Hardwick glanced around the room as she waited for someone to move to adjourn.

Madeline's hand rose. "Did I miss the decision regarding who would contact the carpenter?"

Every eye in the room darted to watch every other one. Flossie flushed. "I suppose we didn't. How strange. Would anyone —"

Before someone else could volunteer, Madeline held up her fan. "If no one objects, I would like to undertake the task. I'm looking for a new dressing table for the guest room on the east side, so I could combine the errands."

The sighs of relief around the room told Madeline that her offer had not only been accepted but was appreciated. *Which, of course, provides the exact opportunity I sought. No one will think anything untoward about me being in the Blackwood District.*

Three of the girls attempted to inveigle Madeline to join them at the tearoom. "Oh, that is so kind, but I really should try to find that carpenter before we leave town. Papa has promised a trip to Lake

Danube after the ball for the Independence Day festivities. We'll be living rough for a few days, but the lake is always so much cooler."

"Oh, won't that be nice! I heard they shoot off fireworks from the island out there!"

I will be tempted to create my own pyrotechnics if you do not allow me to leave! Her aunt's eyes filled Madeline's mind—scolding, exasperated eyes. *I will be more patient.*

But in time, she found herself sliding along the trolley rail into the heart of Rockland. The street where the recommended carpenter kept his workspace and showroom proved harder to find than she'd been led to believe. *If Russell hadn't agreed that this fellow was an excellent woodworker, I might have doubted Mr. Smythe's motives in recommending him.*

The moment she stepped into the showroom, and a bell jingled overhead, Madeline saw that no one had exaggerated the man's skills. A rosewood dressing table caught her eye almost the moment she stepped in the door. "Oh...." The scent of varnish mingled with sawdust perfumed the air, but the room shone bright and clean.

A man entered the room, wiping his hands on a rag, and stepped forward. "May I help you?"

"I'm here about tables for the library...." Her eyes slid toward the dressing table. "And probably that as well."

"I usually sell through a few of the stores around town, but your tables intrigue me. What did you have in mind?"

Not to be dissuaded, Madeline ran her fingers over the smooth, polished wood. "So this isn't for sale? It is a sample, perhaps? Where can I find a store that has one on the floor?"

The man folded his arms over his chest and eyed her with evident curiosity. "If you are serious, this one could be delivered by tonight." He named a price higher than she'd expected but not unreasonably out of reach.

The decision took exactly four seconds. Madeline nodded her agreement. "Excellent. Now, about those tables. I am looking for an estimate. This is a committee project, so it will take three times longer to come to a decision as it should. However, it is a large commission, so perhaps that will make up for the inconvenience."

It took some time to help him sketch exactly what they'd discussed. With an estimate and the drawings in hand, she left her address and turned to go. "And thank you. I had intended for that table to go in the guest room, but I do believe I will be keeping it for myself. It really is lovely work."

"Hiram will be there inside the hour."

"Oh, please don't hurry. I couldn't possibly be home before two hours, and Mary isn't expecting anyone. She'd be quite confused. Tomorrow would even be acceptable." She eyed him. "Is Hiram trustworthy? Can I trust him to treat the piece with care? If so, I'd like permission to hire him to move it upstairs and move mine into the guest room."

With assurances that all would be well when Hiram arrived the next morning, Madeline left the shop and strolled back up the street to wait for the trolley. Passersby nodded greetings. A few messenger boys whizzed past on bicycles. A man appeared across the street.

Madeline first thought it was the same man she'd seen half a dozen times previously. However, just as she stepped into the street to confront him, he turned and faced her. *Not the same man after all. Interesting.*

The trolley arrived, and Madeline noted with interest that the man climbed aboard as well. He sat beside her and waited until the trolley rolled onward before he spoke. "You know this Smythe fellow, don't you?"

Her eyes narrowed. "Pardon me, but do I know you?"

The man shook his head but offered his hand. "No, but I know you. Madeline Brown—the mayor's daughter. You're pals with this Edith Merton, ain'tcha?"

"I'm not sure what business that is of yours, Mr....."

"My name ain't the point." He glanced around him as if to be sure no one was listening before he leaned closer. A near-fatal case of halitosis assaulted her senses as he added, "I can give you information about him. I've heard about you—how you're followin' him everywhere. All I ask is five dollars. I owe my boarding house lady, you see."

Though she had no intention of paying the man a dime for any information—the idea that it might be useful seeming highly improbable—Madeline did have a great curiosity about what the man might think she wanted to know. *How would he know of something that I haven't actually begun! Well, not in* earnest, *anyway.*

But before she could inquire, a man stepped onto the trolley as it stopped to take on more passengers. Her eyes widened. "I'll consider your offer, but first, do you know that man in the checkered suit?"

"Bowler—lot like yours, actually—that one?"

She nodded.

"Nope. Ain't never seen 'im before. Want I should ask—"

"Of course not!" Her voice dropped as the man looked their way. "Now, how do I contact you should I decide to accept your offer?"

Before she knew what was happening, the man jumped up and muttered, "I'll find you," before hopping off the moving trolley.

Madeline stared after him, aghast. "Well, I never!"

Filing cabinets lined the walls of the small room and a small writing desk sat in the middle. In a straight-backed chair, Madeline sat with her hands folded in her lap, waiting for the man behind the table to stop writing. She noted several things as she watched his hand slide across the paper, but said nothing until he set down his pen, blotted the page, and slid it aside—upside down.

"I apologize for the wait. I am Rodney Flint. How may I help you, Miss…?"

"Brown. Madeline Brown, as I said before." She couldn't help but notice a twitch at the corner of his eye as she spoke her name. "I am here to hire someone to investigate a man."

Mr. Flint picked up his pen again and retrieved another piece of paper. "I'm sorry to have wasted your time. We do not take cases that could involve scandal. You may see yourself out, Miss Brown. Give your father my regards."

So, you know who I am. Not surprising, and very encouraging. Madeline watched Flint as he began scrawling across the page but did not move from her seat.

"Excuse me, was there anything else I can help you with?" The question came even without a glance up from his work.

"The man I would like you to investigate is a man who has offered me information about my friend's fiancé. Somehow, he discovered that I have been investigating—and not much as of yet, you understand—this man. I wish to determine if he is a credible source of information. Were I a man, I would do it myself. Were I not my father's daughter, I would do it myself. But as I am a lady and the mayor's daughter, I thought it best to hire someone else to do the work for me."

This captured Flint's attention. The pen rolled to the side and the paper did as well. "You think you are capable of investigating this man? How?"

She considered the wisdom of sharing the information she had already gathered and decided it made sense since he'd need it if he accepted the case anyway. From the moment in Edith Mertons' parlor to the arrival of the man on the trolley, she shared every tiny bit of information she could recall. Once finished, she sat back, relaxed her shoulders, and waited.

Mr. Flint didn't speak immediately. He fiddled with a new-growth mustache and rolled a key over and over in his left hand.

Several of her previous observations proved themselves before he spoke again. "Very observant of you, Miss Brown. Lip color on the sleeve... interesting." His eyes focused on the paper before him before meeting hers again. "And you are certain this other man is the same man each time? It isn't possible that it is several different people dressed alike?"

"He has one shoulder that is just a bit higher than the other, and his jacket sleeve is a mite too long. I suspect to compensate. And, he moves in predictable patterns. I don't imagine that a team of men sent to watch me—an enormous expense, don't you think?—would be trained to respond exactly the same."

"I see. Well observed again, Miss Brown. And tell me, what are your conclusions about the gentleman you have been investigating?"

Her throat closed shut at the idea of sharing her opinions. Madeline steadied herself, took another moment to watch him—see if she could trust him—and spoke the words she'd avoided for so long. "I think he is *not* a gentleman. Lip color on the cuff wouldn't have surprised me at all, but the intimate way he touched her face, spilling the cordial so deliberately on such an unlikely place. Had it been his collar..."

"Yes, I see. Go on."

"Then seeing him speaking to that woman in the Dry Docks. There can only be one explanation for their acquaintance, and an even less savory explanation for him accompanying another young woman inside. With the rest of what I've discovered, and what the woman said the last time I saw him with her, is it any wonder that I am curious about the information this man has offered me?"

"It is not," Flint agreed. "I also find it interesting that you did not rush to accept the information. What was your reason for not taking the information and investigating the man later?"

"If I take the information, he can easily disappear." Madeline watched Flint's hands as she spoke, certain something in them would give away what he thought. "Now he has reason to stay close so you can investigate him before I retrieve the information. Surely it is easier and less costly to investigate a person instead of information that could come from several sources."

Mr. Flint flipped the key again, his fingers deftly weaving it in and out of each one. "You have excellent instincts, Miss Brown. Tell me, what have you noted about me? I cannot pretend not to have noticed your observation of me."

"You write with your right hand, but your left is naturally dominant—"

"What makes you say that?"

"The key." She smiled as his eyes lowered to where he rolled the key through his fingers. "The ease with which you do that implies that. Few people would learn to do something with their non-dominant hand that they didn't *need* to."

"Such as writing or eating?" Flint smiled. "Anything else?"

"You do not need your glasses to see everything—only items up close. You look at me over the tops of them, but you are very skillful at *not* showing that. It took a few times to be certain." Madeline returned Flint's smile and added a smirk. "And you are now considering whether I have the skills to be trained as an investigator." She leaned forward. "I do, Mr. Flint. Of that, I have no doubt. However, I could not do that to my father. It would devastate him. Or rather, it would leave my aunt prostrate with fear that it would devastate him. So, I'll have to content myself with determining if my friend's fiancé is truly the cad I think he is, or if he has left off his...*other relationships* in the wake of their engagement."

The air between them fairly sizzled as they each sized up the other. Flint spoke first. "Should that ever change, feel free to apply to me for training. Now, what else about this man do you not trust?"

"The one on the trolley?"

Mr. Flint's slow wag of his head hid definite amusement. "Your friend's fiancé. I sense it. You do not trust something else about him."

One thing she'd kept from the detective—one thing that she

didn't know the relevance of yet. After a second and then a third start, she shared what she'd overheard Reginald say at the party. "I don't know if there is significance to this charge of debt. Many men do at some point or another, I imagine. With his business interests, surely there are expenses that one expects to be covered by donations once the improvement plan is put in motion—if it ever is."

"But you are skeptical."

Madeline's shoulders sagged. "I am. The man seems sneaky, oily. A weasel would find a comparison between them to be insulting. I am ashamed to admit that I *want* to find something terribly wrong with him. I can't escape feeling like I'd save a dear friend from a terrible mistake."

At the word donations, everything in Flint's demeanor changed, but when she added her concern for Edith, he nodded. "I'll need this man's name—the fiancé."

Hands clenched in her lap, Madeline struggled to decide if it was wise. *With Smythe's name in play, I cannot hope to protect Edith from scrutiny.*

"I guarantee I can find out without your help, but it will only take more time, and I *will* bill you for that time. Are you certain you want to pay extra for what you can give me now?"

"I can count on your discretion?

With pen in hand again, Flint nodded. "Absolutely."

Madeline gripped her hands together and whispered, "Vernon Smythe."

$\mathscr{T}$WENTY

Music reached their ears long before the carriage arrived at the Camden Hotel. As it pulled up to the doors, Albert Brown stepped down and offered Madeline his hand. "The Midsummer's Ball has an advantage over the Evergreen Ball. You don't have to spoil your dress with a wrap."

Madeline smoothed her skirts and smiled up at him. "Well, with such a generous father...."

"Flattery, my dear." He took her arm. "You have mastered the art of it. I actually believe you."

"It isn't flattery if it's true, Papa." Russell stood at the top of the steps, waiting escort them inside. "Oh, look. Russell is already here."

"Do see if you can introduce him to someone, Maddie. He often looks so lonely."

"I suspect he's just missing Amy. They were such chums, and now she's not there for him to torment."

Albert Brown's laughter carried them up the steps. He shook Russell's hand. "Madeline has suggested you're missing your sister this evening."

"I am, but Madeline is an adequate substitute." He winked at her when Albert looked the other way. "Although, Amy is much more circumspect. I would have imagined you'd miss her influence on Madeline."

They stifled snickers as Albert nodded and allowed himself to be swept along with the other guests. Russell offered Madeline his arm and led her into the ball. "Are you eager to dance now, or would you like to circulate for a while?"

"Let's dance first. It's an unobtrusive method to see who has arrived already, don't you think?"

Frolicking dancers waltzed to the childlike notes of the "Rendezvous Valse." Russell's smile implied more than mere politeness. A moment later, he pulled her just a little closer to say, "Is it you or the dress, Madeline? You look particularly lovely this evening. I was tempted to give credit to the gown, but your face isn't shrouded in silk and lace, so...."

The advantage of dancing with your dearest friend's brother is the ability to indulge in a little flirtation without anyone taking it too seriously. "It's the crystals, I'm sure they're sparkling, and I'm enjoying reflected beauty because of them."

"Very prettily spoken. Alas, I find only one problem."

"And that is?"

Again, as they whirled about the corner, he pulled her even closer once more. "It has nothing to do with your crystals. It's you."

This time, propriety overrode camaraderie. Madeline tilted her head, smiled into his eyes, and voiced her thanks. "You look dashing as well, but then you always do."

"I just had an interesting thought. Perhaps in that dress, you'll receive a better offer!"

Just then, Henry Hardwick spun in view. The look he gave her was decidedly complimentary. She saw, in just that flash of a moment, that she'd been excessively hard on him. And while ridiculously premature to imagine any kind of mutual attraction or affection, Madeline did nod. "Perhaps...."

The dance ended at last. Madeline stood near the edge of the dance floor as Russell went to procure punch. *Dancing for nearly ten minutes at a time. It's no wonder that we grow so warm and fatigued. Shorter dances would give people the chance to catch their breaths at more regular intervals.*

Until the supper bell rang, Madeline did not want for partners. Russell danced with a few others, but anytime it looked as if she might be left free, he was right there at the first pull of the strings. In fact, he and Henry Hardwick arrived at exactly the same time to escort her to the supper room. When Flossie flounced past and Warren stood off by himself, looking stunned and a little woebegone, Madeline gave Henry a pointed look. "Take Flossie," she murmured. "Something has happened — again."

Without waiting to see if he did, she turned to Russell. "I'm ready if you are."

Just inside the supper room, Vernon Smythe stood, nearly blocking Edith from a man trying to speak with her. Edith, looking distressed and ready to cry, tugged on Vernon's sleeve, pleading with him not to make a fuss. "He was just being polite!"

"He was overly familiar and crass."

Edith met Madeline's concerned gaze and silently pleaded for help. "Russell, see what you can do. She's going to break down any moment now."

Madeline needn't have spoken. The moment Russell saw Edith turn away, trembling, he stepped in and escorted her to a table. "I'm sure you're quite tired and hungry, Miss Merton. Please join us and have something to eat. Madeline will be so pleased, won't you, Maddie?"

She couldn't help but toss Smythe a derisive look before turning to take Russell's other arm. As they neared the table, she whispered, "He'll not thank you for that."

"As I don't seek his gratitude *or* his approval, it is of no consequence to me."

And this is why Amy and I love you so dearly. You are such a genuine gentleman.

The moment they were seated, Russell murmured, "Are you quite well, Miss Merton?"

"I am, thank you. I don't know what got into Vernon! He was in such good spirits, and then Charley Forsythe said hello. Everything seemed all right, but then Charlie asked if I was going to the mountains again—the heat. And I started to say I was—soon, I think, if this heat continues. And Vernon just exploded! He acted as if Charley had insulted me somehow. It's ridiculous, of course. And so unlike him."

Well, I might have agreed with your statement, but you had to add the appendix, didn't you? I have long suspected it is exactly within his character. But until he proves my suspicions correct.....

Before either Russell or Madeline could respond, Vernon arrived. Concern filled his features as he pulled his chair as close as propriety would allow—possibly just a mite closer—and took her hand. There in front of the entire room's view, if anyone cared to observe, he took it and held it close to his heart. "I'm sorry, my dear. I should have been on hand to prevent—"

"Prevent a friend from speaking to her as he has a dozen times? Why would that be something you should do?" Madeline flashed angry eyes at him and silently dared him to say another word against Charley Forsythe.

"I assure you that there was more to my anger than solicitation for Edith's health. The look—rather, the *leer* he gave her—quite insulting."

Shock filled Edith's face. "Charley Forsythe? Oh, that isn't possible, Vernon, truly. Why, our mothers used to wheel us around in our perambulators together. We've been like brother and sister our whole lives. Charley would never *leer* at me, I assure you." Madeline's pride in Edith's newfound backbone dissolved along with it as she added, "But it is endearing for you to try to protect my honor. Thank you."

Did you leave your sense at home on your dressing table? What he did was boorish and overbearing. Utterly unacceptable.

Fuming in her chair, Madeline couldn't say anything without

losing all sense of decorum, but Russell, as if there had been no unpleasantness, switched the conversation with one perfectly timed question. "I understand you came to someone else's rescue not long ago."

Smythe's eyes narrowed and his jaw went rigid. He threw Edith such a harsh, malefic look, that Madeline found it difficult not to say something. But before he could speak, Edith's eyes widened, and she leaned forward. "Isn't what he did beautiful? I was so proud of him for trying to keep dear Stanley's secret."

"I told you not to say anything to anyone, Edith." The words, though quiet, held a vicious undertone.

"I didn't, of course!" Her eyes filled with tears. "Why are you so determined to be unpleasant tonight?"

Russell stepped in. "Miss Merton said nothing to me of the affair. I actually heard of it from Stanley himself."

Had she not been the mayor's daughter, Madeline would have defied convention, jumped up on the chair, and cheered. *You thought you got away with it after all this time, didn't you?*

Vernon blanched. Edith looked properly sympathetic and slightly shocked. Russell, however, just waited for a response with almost a blank expression. It took a couple of false starts, but he finally muttered something about doing his duty. "I'm surprised he remembered it. He was quite out of his head by the time I found him."

"Whatever made you know to look?" She shouldn't have done it. The moment the words left her lips and felt Russell stiffen beside her, Madeline realized that some questions should be investigated rather than asked. She rose quickly. "Excuse me for a moment, please."

The men rose with her, and both looked much relieved as she turned to leave the room. In the ladies' powder room, Madeline washed her hands and powdered herself—powdered and made plans. *If I can't ask, I'll discover on my own.* She stared at her reflection in the mirror and nodded. "You've done it, Mr. Smythe. I *will* find you out. Tonight's behavior has ensured it."

From their place at the table, Vernon watched as Russell and Madeline found a quiet corner to eat their refreshments. *Are you truly as clueless about your question as you appear? Quite an astute observation from someone who decided it was the perfect time to powder her nose a second later, but Barnes said nothing. His lips never moved.*

Edith touched his hand, allowing hers to rest on it for just a moment. "Is there something wrong with your cake, Vernon?"

"It's perfect. Thank you." He gave her a loving smile and squeezed her hand. "You're very kind to forgive me. I know you wouldn't betray a confidence. Forsythe rattled me."

"You do know he meant no harm, don't you?"

"If you say so, I believe you. Miss Brown and Mr. Barnes agree with you, so it can't be your generous nature... *this time.*"

She didn't respond, but the smile she gave him hinted that his words had struck a place in her heart. *And I do believe tonight I'll allow myself more than a brief kiss at the door.* But Charley Forsythe passed the table with a glance that unsettled him again. *I need to talk to him — see what he was going to say. If he thinks he can drive a wedge between us....*

"—so funny to think of Charley being anything but interested in my trip to the mountains."

Vernon snapped his head back and pulled her hand close again. "You won't go, will you? I can take you for cooling drives of an afternoon. I'll hire someone to fan you and bring great blocks of ice to cool your room."

"But that's so silly! Six weeks in the mountains should be all I need. And you said you'd be busy with work soon. Your business idea?" Edith sighed. "But I will miss you terribly. You couldn't come for a long weekend, could you?"

Which is the best answer? If I say no, will it predispose you to stay? If I say yes, will you look forward to my arrival enough to ignore other men? If someone swept you away....

"Vernon?"

"Sorry, my dear. I think I *might* be able to do that — if everything goes according to plan. I wouldn't like to *promise*, but...."

He saw temptation in her eyes and smiled. *You want to remind me that I can't hold your hand or kiss you if I'm two hundred miles away. And...* A flush filled her cheeks as she stared at the last bite of cake on her plate. *Oh, you think you'll miss those little attentions, too. Well, if I had any doubts about tonight's kiss, they're gone. I think it's time that you learned just how mesmerizing one can be.*

Great silver vases of begonias with delicate pink blossoms filled the terrace, while roses grew nearby as if to provide the perfume the begonias lacked. Paper lanterns lit the outdoors, giving resting couples light to wander through the cooler night air. With stars twinkling overhead, a whiff of the music floating through the great open doors and windows, and the intimate, darkened corners offering the illusion of privacy, couples found themselves in the perfect romantic setting.

Madeline surveyed the night sky as she waited for Henry to bring her a bit of punch. *I think I prefer the two-step to the waltz.*

"Did you say something?"

Must have spoken aloud and didn't realize it. Madeline tried to brush off the unsettled feeling that comes with the realization that one isn't quite as in control of self as one might like to think. "I was musing about the waltz and the two-step. Of course, they'll end with

The Virginia Reel. Have you heard what time?"

"Sometime around two o'clock, I've heard. A nod to Sabbath keepers without providing too much of an inconvenience to our fun." Henry leaned against the railing and turned to gaze at her. "I won over Grandmother, you know. I had to promise we'd go to prayer meeting tomorrow night. You should go with us. You got us into it, after all."

She opened her mouth to say she would but found herself apologizing instead. "I'm afraid of growing fanatical. I hear prayer meeting is the breeding grounds for them, you know." She drained the cup and set it on a tray as a waiter passed. "I should find Flossie and see how she's doing. I think I saw her and Warren talking again."

Henry caught her arm and stepped close. "If I can stick my nose in?"

"Yes?"

"Tell her to demonstrate *confidence* in him. A man likes to feel as though he's impressed a girl."

Madeline hardly remembered to thank him—to smile, even—her mind swirled with thoughts and ideas. She took her time across the terrace and stepped into the stuffy ballroom. At the end of the song, the musicians would take a ten-minute break, but until then, dancers whirled about the room. Flossie was nowhere to be seen.

Edith passed on Smythe's arm, and Madeline asked if she'd seen Flossie. "She went to the powder room, I believe." Edith leaned closer and whispered, "I think she was crying again."

Two minutes later, Madeline still hadn't managed to leave the room. *Oh, why is it that when one wants out of a room, the fates conspire to keep you in, but if you wish to stay, the crush of the crowd will propel you out again?*

The powder room, miraculously and mercifully, was nearly empty. One girl tried to console her, but Flossie refused to answer. "I'll take care of her. Thank you."

"She won't—"

But Flossie flung herself at Madeline, weeping freely. "Oh, it's Warren, of course."

"And what did he do now?"

Only when the door shut behind a now very curious girl, did Flossie answer. "He told me to stop needling him. Needle him! Why—"

"Well, Flossie, you do seem to look for things to criticize. It's hard enough to own up to one's faults without someone you care to impress seeming to find a new one every chance she gets."

"But he—"

Madeline had to stop her. Once Flossie got on a roll, she could find almost anything wrong with anyone. "I wonder, Flossie, if you've ever told Warren what you *do* admire about him."

"Why, of course I—" She frowned. "I—wait. Well, he—"

Madeline took a small cloth and dabbed at Flossie's eyes with the ice water provided. "I was just remembering something Henry told me."

"Yes?"

So I was right. You do look up to him now. Interesting. The cool water made an immediate impact on Flossie's puffy eyes. "He said that a man hopes to *impress* a girl. If you show confidence in him, he's likely to try to prove you right."

"Well, I'm confident he'll disappoint me again."

The time had come for straight speaking. "If you didn't care about Warren, you wouldn't bother with him. So obviously you do— care, that is."

"Well, of course."

Tossing the cloth aside, she settled her hands on her hips and affected her most scolding tone. "Then do him the courtesy of showing him that you care for him at least as often as you demonstrate your lack of confidence in him. Did it never occur to you that he's merely living up to your expectations?"

"But he's being ridiculous and embarrassing me."

Madeline turned to the door. As she pulled it open she suggested, without even turning around to face Flossie, "And you are behaving in exactly the same manner toward him. Do you think he isn't embarrassed and feeling that you are ridiculous when you show the world how little you think of him? He must love you, I think. No young man would tolerate it if he didn't." For once, Madeline had managed to shock Flossie into silence. She released the door, hugged her friend, and whispered, "And if you don't love him as well, do him the courtesy of dropping him before you ruin his reputation for every decent girl. Then he likely would become the rake you make him out to be."

Just inside the ballroom, she felt a hand on her arm and turned. Russell smiled down at her. "Ready to dance, or taking a moment to catch your breath?"

"Both? I was just trying to talk sense into Flossie."

"She needs to know that Warren is not guilty of half the things attributed to him. People are using him as some sort of scapegoat. Why, I haven't ascertained, but they are."

Not until they'd made half a turn around the floor did Madeline speak again. "Well, perhaps they use him because it works." A smile flashed as Madeline shook her head. "Of course, that's ridiculous. Now, what time is it?"

"That's the second time I've heard you ask someone what time it is. I can call for the carriage if you're ready to go?"

She'd made plans to go home with the Hardwicks, but as soon as Russell said something, she nodded. "I would, actually. Thank you, Russell."

"I'll arrange it at the end of the dance?"

"If you would, yes."

Vernon and Edith whirled past as if he had not insulted her and her friends with his boorish behavior less than an hour earlier. Madeline's eyes widened with shock and rose to meet Russell's. "I'm surprised at her!"

"Mr. Merton would not like to hear of Smythe's uncouth behavior; I'm sure." Russell's eyes followed the couple, that familiar crease growing between his eyebrows.

Your crease appeared anytime we did something frightening – climbing atop the wood house or swimming in Turner's Pond after dark. Almost unaware that she spoke the words aloud, Madeline pondered his observation and remarked on it. "I'm not certain he *would* mind, so long as it didn't give rise to gossip. I think he is eager to ensure that Edith takes a new name before Christmas."

The song ended with a great round of applause. Russell promised to return in a moment, so Madeline made her way around the room, saying goodnight to all. A voice she recognized pulled her away from the room and onto the terrace. There, under the lanterns, Flossie and Warren stood arguing. Her heart wrung at the distressed look on Flossie's face, the earnest plea in Warren's tone. All changed in an instant. Flossie said something—what, Madeline couldn't hear—and Warren turned to go. Her hand reached out and stopped him. He kissed it.

"Things are looking up," a voice murmured in her ear. "Look...."

Madeline felt Henry's breath on her ear and cheek as again, he bent to keep his voice from being over heard. She turned and found his face much too close to hers for comfort. "Henry, really."

"Forgive me. I didn't care to interrupt them. Look...."

This time Warren had pulled Flossie close. His lips touched hers for just a moment, but by the expression Flossie wore, that moment wouldn't end for her some time. Madeline turned to go. "I was looking for you. Russell has offered to take me home, and I've accepted. I am quite fatigued."

He led her through the room and out front where Russell's carriage came rolling up the drive. "Well, I think Warren will thank you for whatever you said to Flossie."

207

"How—?"

Henry stifled a snicker as he led her down the steps and to the carriage. "The room is abuzz over some tale about how Madeline Brown finally took Flossie in hand and made her see sense."

"She *just* made up with him. That isn't possible!"

As Henry helped her up onto the seat, he stated the obvious. "Well, it just began, of course. And by tomorrow, the whole town will know."

"Excellent. Now Madeline is meddlin' in more than just business affairs that she can't hope to understand. She's meddling in love affairs as well." Madeline waved at Henry and turned to Russell. "You'd better take me home before I do much more damage. I should have left talking sense into Flossie to someone else. Someone with tact and grace—Edith, perhaps."

The ride home remained quiet. Had she been a year or two younger, Madeline might have allowed herself to rest her head on his arm as they rolled through the streets of Rockland to Beaumont Street. But, despite his close connection with their family, and despite Madeline's well-known disdain for the constraints of propriety, the mayor's daughter wouldn't indulge in such a breach of decorum, no matter the temptation.

That may change someday, however. Someday, I hope to be eighty, sharp witted, and free of caring what convention demands.

"Madeline?" Russell's voice jerked her from her thoughts.

"Yes?"

"You said something about Miss Merton being a better person to speak to Miss Hardwick." He waited for her eyes to meet his before speaking again. With a slight shake of his head, he gave her that look of pride she'd seen him give Amy so many times. "I think you did the right thing. She'd hear from you what she would dismiss from others. Do you think others haven't tried?"

"Well," Madeline cocked her head. "I suppose...."

As the carriage pulled up in front of the house, Russell hopped down and held out his hand for her. They stood at the carriage, her hand still in his, and he tried to explain. "Everyone waited for someone else to say something. You saw how that plan fared."

"This is true. I think my pride is wounded."

"It should be flattered. You made the right decision. If you wish something to be done and done well, you must do it yourself."

Madeline looped her arm through his, and Russell walked her to the door with all the gallantry of a proper suitor. He brushed a mussed lock of her hair out of her face and smiled. "You certainly are beautiful tonight, Madeline. You're always lovely, of course. But...."

"It's a shame your wish for a better offer didn't come true then, isn't it?"

Something in his smile kept her from opening the door. She waited, certain he'd speak when ready, and he didn't disappoint. "That is only true if that *is* my wish." With a squeeze to her hand, Russell Barnes turned and strolled back down the walk. He waved at the gate. He waved again as he hopped in the carriage.

Madeline waited until he was out of sight before she slipped through the door and into the house. *A very good night, I think. Very good — except for Mr. Smythe. I really must determine that man's true nature.*

$\mathcal{T}$WENTY-$\mathcal{O}$NE

As if driven by itself, the carriage slowed at the corner and rolled onto Parkview Way. But as he reached Verdigris Street, Russell tugged on the reins and urged the horse down that street and around another corner. *I can't believe I'm allowing her to influence me like this. It's insanity. Then again, he was ridiculous about the thing with Forsythe.*

That thought sealed it for him. He pulled up the horse halfway down the block and looped the reins over the brake. "You stay put, girl. I hope I won't be long."

With stealth he didn't know he could manage in full evening dress, Russell dashed through backyards, around the corner of the Merton house, and hid behind the hydrangeas, waiting for Smythe to arrive with Edith. *We left early. They were still dancing. But I took my time getting Madeline back here. Surely a man with a Locomobile....* That thought fizzled. *He wouldn't take Edith in that motor, would he? Not to a place filled with horses? But he's into speed. If nothing else, he'd want to prove himself. But with a slow, romantic drive or a speedy one? That'll be the question.*

Several carriages passed, but the Mertons' maple and hydrangeas provided ample shadowy protection against discovery. Time ticked past. Twice, he dashed back through yards to check on the horse—an unnecessary move, perhaps, but it kept him from going half-mad with boredom. However, the second time he

returned, he heard a rustling in the hydrangea. *It had better be a cat —*
even a possum would be preferable. When no barks greeted him, Russell
relaxed and kicked at the bush to try to scare out the critter.

A half strangled, "Oow!" startled him.

In a hiss, Russell demanded that whoever had taken up
residence in the bush vacate immediately. Nothing — no response, no
rustle of leaves — nothing. "I *said* come out of there, or I'll notify Mr.
Merton of your presence."

"And yours too."

The voice. He'd have recognized it anywhere. "Jimmy Higgins.
If Madeline knew…."

At that, the boy scrambled out and gazed up at him, squinting
in the darkness. "Mr. Barnes?"

"What're you doing here?" Even as he asked, the sound of
hooves grew closer. "Shh… back behind there."

"I think we're here for the same thing. Miss Madeline gives me
jitneys sometimes — if I see things or hear things. And this seemed
like a big night — maybe…."

I'll have to strangle her later. As the carriage pulled up to the
house, Russell tugged Jimmy deeper into the shadows. "I've a
carriage around the corner. Go stand with the horse. I'll take you
home once I know — something. Shhh… go!"

It worked. The boy dashed around the house without a word.
Edith's giggle reached him long before they made it up the walk. " —
for a lovely evening, Vernon."

"That you forgave my petty jealousy…. I can't thank you
enough."

Another giggle — since when had she become so fond of
giggling? "I never would have imagined anyone becoming jealous of
Charley Forsythe. Especially in regards to *me!*"

What Smythe said next, Russell could only imagine. Their
voices grew low — too low to overhear. *I can't decide if I'm disappointed*
or relieved. This is ridiculous. I'm supposed to be the steadying influence on

Madeline. *I'm* not *supposed to be influenced* by *her.*

But then he heard it—her invitation to come in for refreshment. Smythe sounded like he'd agree and then demurred. "I should hurry home if I hope to be awake in time for church."

"I hadn't thought to go." Edith sounded uncertain. "Some of us had spoken of going to prayer meeting tonight instead."

"You should do that. I'll try to attend with you."

Yet another sigh. Edith sounded quite lovesick, and it nauseated Russell as well. "You are such a fine example. I really should try, I suppose...."

"I'd rather you didn't. You need your rest. Such a taxing evening, first with the heat and all the dancing, and then my unpardonable rudeness."

I believed you the first time, but now you sound almost Shakespearean in your excessive protests. But Russell couldn't think about it any longer. Just then, Smythe assured her he needed to get home immediately, and if the silence that followed meant what he thought it did, the night had drawn to a sweet close. Russell hurried off, slipping along the wet grass in a couple of places, and dashed up to the carriage. Before he seated himself, Jimmy tossed him the reins. "I had 'em ready for ya. Where're we goin'?"

"West Charles Street."

"Why's that?" Jimmy frowned as he turned the carriage around. "And how come you ain't followin'—"

Russell whipped the carriage down Verdigris and urged the horse to run before attempting to answer. "Because, if I were Smythe, I'd find it unusual to see me sitting over here. We'll get ahead of him along Parkview."

"He won't take Parkview? Most folks don't like riding along Redbrook—the trolley and all."

You're an intelligent boy, Jimmy. More than I realized. Think about it. It took until he reached Parkview Way before he realized he hadn't spoken aloud. "Why don't you tell me why I think he'll take it?"

Jimmy thought for several seconds. "Well, there ain't a trolley at this time. So there's that... oooh. It's closer to West Charles. He won't have to cross back that way. Not with the Mertons' by the corner there."

"Exactly." He had to slow the mare at the corner, but once on Parkview Way, he saw it empty—free of any other carriages—and Russell urged her faster. "Get on, girl!"

He could sense Jimmy's excitement. Had it not been nearly three o'clock in the morning, the boy might have squealed with eagerness. Russell grinned down at the boy. "Won't Madeline be green with envy when she hears about this?"

"You're gonna tell her?"

"Do you think she'd ever forgive me if she heard about it and I hadn't? You can't ever assume that your secrets won't be found out. That's why it's best never to have any you're ashamed of."

The sounds of buggy wheels and horse hooves broke the night's relative silence. With each street they passed, other sounds intruded. A dog barked. A baby's cry tugged at his heart. *When will I have my nights interrupted by colic and damp diapers? Is that in Your plans for me, Lord? I thought so, but I can't help but wonder sometimes.*

"—think someone forgot to tell Mr. Smythe that."

"Tell him what?"

"That thing about not having secrets. From what I can tell, there ain't a fella alive that has more secrets than 'im." Jimmy pointed ahead. "There's an alley up there that cuts straight over to West Charles Street. Should be empty this time-a night. It'd getcha there faster without havin' to run 'er."

Russell flashed a grin Jimmy's way. "And I was grumbling about having to have you along. Good thinking, Jimmy."

They arrived at West Charles Street in half the time he'd expected. Once more, Russell settled the carriage out of sight and around the corner. Creeping through yards and behind trees, they picked a house with plenty of shade and made themselves comfortable… waiting. Jimmy grew antsy within five minutes. "Where is 'e? We drove 'er fast." A loud yawn escaped. "Sorry," he hissed. "Tried sleepin' early, but…."

"Go hop in the carriage. I'll keep an eye out. It'll be a good fifteen or twenty minutes before he can get here — maybe thirty."

"Why?"

"He has to return his carriage. I expect he took one from that livery not far from here, but he'll have to settle his bill and walk back." Russell nudged the boy when he yawned again. "Go ahead. Get some rest."

Jimmy hesitated and then shrugged. "It ain't that far from my house now. I'll go on home. Thanks, Mr. Barnes."

"Are you sure? I can —"

But Jimmy jumped up and shoved his hands in his pockets. "I'll be good. Thanks." And with a barely discernible "I Dream of Jeannie" whistled mostly on key, Jimmy took off down the street. Still, Russell waited.

Not ten minutes passed before he heard the sound of footfalls on the street. They came fast — much too fast to be Smythe. When still fifty feet away, Russell heard his name called. *Jimmy! Shh….*

Panting, the boy leaned his hands on his knees and gasped for air between feeble attempts to tell him something. "Saw — Sm — ythe. Going. Think. Dry — Docks. C'" he gulped. " — on."

They raced back toward the carriage, Jimmy insisting on going as fast as they could. Once seated in the carriage, he pointed. "That way. Two. Streets. Right."

I was hoping you were being theatrical, but the only place you could go at this time of night would be down there. Maybe he hired his horse there?

Four streets down, Jimmy begged to be let out. "I'm six blocks that way. I'll get out now. Thanks, Mr. Barnes. Go get 'im. He's a bad one. I just knows it."

The street was dark — unlit by even corner lamps. Russell

215

glanced up the road, where ahead Smythe's carriage had to be, and turned down the street. "I'll take you home first. If your mother woke and saw you missing...."

"Kinda late for that now. You bringin' me home ten minutes earlier ain't gonna get me outta trouble."

"But it'll keep me out of trouble with Madeline." He grinned at Jimmy and added, "And my conscience will appreciate it, too."

The houses grew smaller, closer together. Lawns disappeared two streets from Jimmy's place. Only the tiniest patches of dirt—mostly filled with vegetable patches, from what Russell could see in the moonlight—separated each house from the next. *Eight of those little things would fit on Madeline's lot — I'm sure of it!*

But Jimmy beamed with pride as he pointed out their little house. "We moved in last year—outta the tenements. Took some doing, but Ma's a hard worker—allus findin' new ways to bring in bits of cash. We've never been late with the rent. Not once."

"Well, I'm glad to hear it." He wanted to offer to help if the time ever came, but the pride in Jimmy's voice stopped him. Instead, he pulled out a quarter and fumbled for more change. "It's all I've got. You'll have to owe me or Madeline an errand or two."

Jimmy stared at it before his fingers plucked it out of Russell's hand. "But what's it for?"

"You got up in the middle of the night to make sure Madeline's friend was okay. She'll want to thank you for that."

"Most she'd give me for that is a jitney! It's too much, Mr. Barnes!" He stared at Russell, searching for something—likely pity. "I ain't takin' charity. We're honest folks."

He couldn't let it stand, even if it meant the boy didn't take it. "Well, it wasn't charity, Jimmy. I just don't have a nickel on me. And you need to know something. There is nothing dishonest in taking charity *if you need it.* Don't let anyone convince you otherwise. You take it, you get yourself out of that situation, and you work hard to be ready to offer it to someone else when the time comes. That's what the Lord would have us do."

"Well...."

"Take it, Jimmy. You earned part of it. And you'll earn the rest. Either that, or bring a couple of dimes to Madeline tomorrow—either way. I should go, though, and you should get in bed before your mother finds you gone and worries."

That's all it took. The boy leapt from the carriage and raced around the house. A moment later, Russell could have sworn he saw a pair of shoes sticking out a window before they disappeared. *So that's how you did it. Wait'll Madeline hears this.*

He drove, winding through streets until forced to make a choice—left toward the Dry Docks or right and back to the livery. Impatience forced his knee to jiggle, but indecision still wracked him. He knew what he needed to do, but something in him resisted. After half a minute of deliberation, Russell turned left. "Okay, girl. Let's see what we can discover. I've already added another hour to my bill. What's another?"

Twenty-Two

If an ounce of prevention is worth a pound of cure, then I say a spoonful of determination seasons the whole pot.

A small paper-wrapped parcel tied in string sat on her lap as Madeline whizzed — at a slow crawl, of course — through the streets of Rockland. Neighborhoods with large houses gave way to smaller homes that crowded the busy fringes of commercial and financial areas. And, in turn, those would soon give way to more industrial areas as they neared the Dry Docks quarter.

A man hopped on and plopped himself beside her. Madeline, focused on an advertisement for Stearns Bicycles and reconsidering her refusal to ride one, didn't notice him at first. But a slow, uncomfortable feeling crept over her — one of being watched. She leveled an indignant glare on him and laughed as Russell's amused eyes met hers.

"What are you doing?"

"I saw that hat and thought, 'I know that bowler — or at least the one beneath it.' So, I hopped onto the trolley, but you were so mesmerized by that advertisement that you didn't even see me. Planning to get a wheel now?"

Her mouth opened to say, "Of course! Just think what I could do and where I could go without being at the mercy of the trolley schedule!" But instead, words that made little sense to either of them spilled from her lips. She smiled at the befuddled expression on his face and added, "Now where are you going this fine afternoon — this fine, *miserable* afternoon?"

"Well, I was on my way to meet with the city council." Russell showed a tube slung over his shoulder. "They're planning a magnificent new center for the arts, you know. The one I told you about." He patted the tube. "I have the plans here. If they approve them, we'll do a scale model before we draw up the blueprints. It's an exciting time to be in architecture, Madeline. Modern buildings will have such clean lines and feature glass in new and innovative ways — like the Crystal Palace from the Great Exhibition."

Madeline's shoulders sagged as relief coursed through her. *Keep him talking on architecture and he may forget to ask where you're going.*

Russell spoke just as Madeline began. "So what are you — ?"

"Does that mean that you — " She blushed. "Sorry. You were saying?" *Oh, there are advantages to being a lady sometimes.*

"I beg your pardon. Continue, of course," Russell insisted. Just as Madeline knew he would.

Her smile seemed to disarm him, and Madeline took advantage of that. "You painted a lovely mental picture of buildings like stained glass — the seams connected by steel instead of lead. They'll be works of art in their own right, won't they?"

The next stop arrived before Russell could answer. "Oh, I'll have to tell you about it later. I'm sorry. But yes, that's a perfect description. I must go." He bent low and murmured one last admonition to her. "Do enjoy your sleuthing, and whatever you do, don't do anything too dangerous. We prefer you alive and healthy."

So stunned was she that he'd figured out her plan, that Madeline missed her stop and found herself heading back up through town again. A new plan formed as she passed Wakefield's Department Store. She hurried to the rear steps, and the moment the trolley came to a stop, she hurried off and back down the street. Once inside the great building, she found her way to the boys' clothing counter, where a clerk stood confused at her presence but eager to help.

"I have a boy who comes to help us at our house, and he's in need of knickerbockers and a sturdy shirt."

"Size?" The young man pulled a few items from a shelf for Madeline's inspection, but she just shrugged. "He's about my height, but a bit broader in the shoulders and the... waist."

"I should imagine. Well...." The young man looked confused. "Well, it's rather unusual, but...."

"As long as they're long enough in the arm and the leg, I think it would do well enough. Perhaps a belt or a pair of suspenders in case they turn out to be a mite large. He could always grow into them."

"Or exchange for a better sizing—if they weren't worn, of course. You could purchase them and have him come in to find the best size." He leaned forward. "It's kind of you, miss. Not everyone cares about the garden boys in this town."

Madeline fingered the shirt in a show of making a decision. "I think I would rather take them with me. Perhaps our Mary can alter if necessary. Should they be too small, however, I appreciate the offer for an exchange. Now, I would like this shirt and those knickerbockers, please. Oh, and the suspenders." A cap caught her eye, and Madeline pointed it out. "I'd like one of those as well, please—in a large paper bag?" One last thought occurred to her. "Oh! Shoes. I do need to get the poor boy a pair of shoes, don't I? Those we'll likely have to exchange, but on the chance that his foot is close to mine, I'll just take one a size larger than I would need."

"We usually box—"

"Yes, I know, but a bag would be much easier to carry, don't you see?" His expression informed her that he didn't "see" at all. "I knew you would. Now, how much?"

Inside twenty minutes, she strolled from the store with a bag in hand and a plan. That plan derailed the moment she climbed aboard a trolley and saw an advertisement. Madeline hopped off again and hurried through the streets. No trolley went to the area she hoped to — not yet.

The stables at the livery Russell always used loomed before her, but Madeline slipped around the back and hid behind an outhouse until the stable boy, working on cleaning out a horse's hoof, led the animal back inside. She crept behind him and found a small space behind bales of hay stacked in a corner. As quickly as possible, she shed her clothes, wrapped her petticoat around her chest as tight as she could, and wove her hatpin in and out of the fabric to hold it in place. Her shirtwaist and skirt came next and proved harder to wrap around and hold together than she'd expected. By the time she pulled on the shirt and knickers, the fit was closer to natural. She attached the suspenders and made strange gyrations to see if the underclothes would stay in place.

Wearing a self-satisfied smile, Madeline stuffed all of her hair in the hat, swapped out shoes, shoved her pocketbook and shoes in the brown bag, folded it up, and tucked it under her arm. In an attempt to test her disguise, Madeline hurried out from behind the bales and up to the nearest boy. "Hey, got me a humdinger of an errand — gimme a jitney when I get this and get another when I deliver. But I don't know where Dermot Street is. Give a fella d'rections?"

"Yer almost there. Jest go down here…." The boy led Madeline out the back again and pointed down the street. "Four blocks. Then goes right on Lincoln Avenue. Three blocks up is Dermot. But yous gotta go a long ways on Dermot. Too bad the trolley ain't goin' that far. G'luck! Wish'd I could earn a few jitneys on the side." He gave her a funny expression. "Smart doin', washing yer face like that." His eyes dropped to her hands. "Yeah. Smart doin'."

Heart pounding, she scurried off with another cry of, "Thanks!" And the moment she got around the corner, Madeline pretended to drop the package and rubbed dirt on her hands as she did. *Why didn't I think of that?* Getting the dirt onto her face without someone noticing — much harder to do. But after wiping the back of her arm across her forehead and scratching at a couple of imaginary itches, she had to decide that it would have to do.

By the time she reached Dermot Street, Madeline was nearly drenched in perspiration. *As revolting as it is, at least I now* smell *the part.*

She made her way into the Dry Docks quarter and rounded the familiar corner. There she waited, wandering up and down the street, chasing after a dog and pretending it stole something from her, and then back again. The day grew longer. Overheated, thirsty beyond reason, and feeling like an utter failure, Madeline circled the block. On her second pass, she endured a verbal assault when she stumbled in front of a wagon. Angry and exhausted, she crept back behind a water barrel at the corner next to the house where she'd first seen Vernon Smythe speaking with that woman.

A man walked past—one she recognized. The suit, that ridiculous mustache, the new addition of a bowler. *What is he doing down here? He can't possibly know I'm here. So maybe it is some strange coincidence.* As she watched the man creeping around the place, talking to people, a new idea formed. *I've seen him since coming down here the first time. Maybe he's searching for Mr. Smythe too!*

Just at that moment, Vernon Smythe rounded the corner and strode across the street. The woman arrived on the step, and Madeline crept closer to hear them talk. Flattened against the side of the building, she heard almost every word clearly.

"I'm settled into the new place in the Blackwood District, and my previous lodgings will forward my messages, so no one will know I've left."

The woman pressed herself close to him. "How much longer?"

"It all depends on this improvement project. If I can't come up with a way to drum up donations, I'll have to leave."

"*We'll* have to leave," the woman corrected. Madeline heard the woman's voice grow dark and ugly. "Don't try—"

The rest of what she said drowned in the rattle of a passing wagon. By the time it passed, the woman and Smythe were gone. Only the man in the plaid suit across the street remained. Madeline stuck her hands in her pockets and slouched through the streets and around the corner. *I need to get somewhere to change again – and get out of these shoes. If I have to try to take another step without limping, I may scream in frustration. But oh, this was interesting. I don't know what it means, but it was interesting.*

It proved easier to change *into* her disguise than out of it. Madeline made it over halfway home before any ideas presented themselves, none of which would work. Of course, the closer she came to Beaumont Street, the more panicked she grew. *Someone is bound to recognize me before long.*

She sat in the corner of the trolley, trying to be as inconspicuous as possible and feeling as though it just made her stand out all the more. However, the closer the trolley came to her neighborhood, the more jittery she became until, several blocks from her destination, she hopped off and scuttled through a few back yards, looking for a tree large enough to hide her movements. Then, she pulled off the too-large shoes and examined her raw toes.

"I'm not entirely sure it was worth this. Not at all." Despite the ridiculousness of the idea, she straightened her stockings, squeezed her feet into her usual shoes, and fumbled with the laces, pulling them as tightly as she could bear. As much as it pained her, the shoe's better fit helped prevent her from limping quite as badly as the boys' shoes had.

How she ached for nightfall. *At least after dark no one would likely see a boy hopping through the back yards wearing girls' shoes!*

At that moment, she heard a familiar whistle. *Jimmy Higgins! This is either the blessing of Providence or the curse of womankind.* She surveyed the area and finally saw him working in the garden at the Morgan place.

As she picked her way across yards, watching windows before moving out of the protection of laundry lines, shrubbery, and trees, Madeline tried to concoct a truthful explanation for her attire. Alas, exhaustion, hunger, and her raw, aching feet muddled her mind until she gave up and decided just to tell him. *He'll keep my secret. Boys like that sort of thing, don't they?*

Hidden behind a lilac in full bloom, Madeline called out to him in a low hiss. "Jimmy! Jimmy!"

His head snapped up and he glanced around him. "Mr. Morgan?"

"No! Behind the lilac. It's Madeline Brown."

He stood and drove the shovel into the dirt. With a glance toward the house, Jimmy scurried around the lilac bush and stopped short at the sight of her. "Uh, whatcha wearin', Miss Madeline?"

"Your new wardrobe. I had to... borrow them for a bit."

Jimmy shoved his hands in his pockets and watched her for a moment. "You went down to the Dry Docks, didn't you?" Without waiting for her to answer, he glanced around and leaned close. "Did you see him? That Smythe rat? He was down there last night! Mr. —" Something in her surprise stopped the boy. "And I saw him kiss Miss Edith today, when he thought no one was lookin'. A real lollapalooza of a kiss, too! Never seen anything like it."

That news derailed her thoughts. "When would this have been?"

"Oh... about noon, I'd say. Why?"

That was definitely before I went down there. I can only assume he kissed her on arrival or leaving. And if it was leaving, he kissed her and went straight to the Dry Docks to meet that woman — the one who expects to leave town with him at some point.

"Miss Maddie?"

Madeline jerked out of her reverie and apologized. "As you can

225

see, I can't exactly go home like this. So, where can I change? Do you have any ideas? If I show up looking like this...." She shuddered. "I can't imagine going much farther without someone seeing me, and that would be infinitely worse."

As she spoke, Jimmy looked around him with a vacant stare in his eyes. Madeline watched as his eyes lit up, and he nodded. "Yeah. Gots just the thing for ya. Over here. I'll keep watch. Use the tool shed. Stay away from the window, though. If someone comes, I'll distract 'im."

Relief washed over her. Madeline kissed his cheek and thanked him with the kind of profuseness that both delights and mortifies boys of his age. "I am so grateful you are such a hard worker, or I would be standing in my father's office getting quite the scolding inside the hour, I think."

Once in the tool shed, Madeline worked with as much speed as she could manage. The clothes for Jimmy she lay on a stack of buckets. Her clothes followed. Even in the dim light of the shed, she could see that her clothes were a wrinkled mess. Someone was sure to notice and remark.

Something skittered across the top of her shoes, and Madeline jumped, squealed, and spun in place, searching for some kind of weapon. A spade hung on the wall beside the door. Madeline grabbed it and waited. The shine of two black, beady eyes glinted in the tiny shaft of light. A twitching nose—in her imagination, anyway—mocked her, but Madeline waited, spade raised and ready to strike. The eyes drew closer. And that's when she remembered the small packet, the one she'd brought from home, in the bag on the ground.

It wants the cookies I'd brought as a bribe. She rehung the spade, worked a cookie out of the parcel, and set it at her feet. Spade in hand once more, she stood back and waited again—waited for the shiny eyes. The better part of a minute ticked by until the rat took a step or two closer. Down she drove the spade into the dirt floor of the shed. A squeak—and nothing. The rat lay in halves at her feet.

Madeline shuddered, scraped the rat out of the way with yet another shudder, and replaced the spade. With one eye on the death scene, she pulled on her shirtwaist, buttoned it quickly, and swapped out the cap for her bowler. She shoved the clothes in the bag and rolled the top shut. Paper bag in one hand, and the parcel in the other, she cracked open the door of the shed and hissed for Jimmy. He popped up so fast it startled her.

"All clear, Miss Madeline. You'd better go fast though. Mr. Morgan should be out soon to inspect my work."

"Here are the clothes. I'm sorry I can't wash them first. It—"

"Right. Good thinkin'. I'm grateful though, miss. I'll work hard for them."

She shook her head as she inched around the corner of the shed. "They're a gift—a thank you for helping me. Oh, here." Madeline passed him the cookies. "You might like a few cookies, too."

"Gee! Thanks!"

Dressed in her own attire, mussed as it was, Madeline took the backyards through the neighborhood to her own and crept up to the back door. She'd just reached for the doorknob when Russell's voice stopped her. "Learn anything interesting?"

Her shoulders sagged. "If I promise to tell you everything, will you please keep cook and Mary out of the way while I get upstairs and clean up?"

Russell stood and made his way to the side gate. "I'll go around front."

Whew! That worked. I never said when I'd tell you everything, did I?

Just as she thought she'd managed to put one over on him, Russell's chuckle filled the evening air. "Should I have asked *when* you'd tell me?"

"Oh, go on with you!"

At Mary's suggestion, Russell waited for her on the terrace. Their silver maple provided ample shade from the sun as it hung low in the early evening sky. *It feels as though you're fighting it – determined not to drop tonight. And, as early as it still is, it's no wonder.*

The thoughts made little sense, but Russell clung to them as he waited. Anything to avoid the words swirling in his mind. *Then again....*

Mary brought out glasses of mint tea with ice chips floating in them and shortbread cookies. "Would you like a sandwich, Mr. Barnes? Miss Madeline said she was 'positively famished', so I thought I'd ask before I make hers."

Though he opened his mouth to demur, Russell heard himself thanking her and agreeing. "I'm dining at Mr. Thurgood's tonight, and they don't begin until nine, usually. A sandwich will keep my stomach rumblings from embarrassing me."

Minutes later, Madeline appeared, carrying a tray of sandwiches and a bowl of strawberries. He jumped up to help her, and to his astonishment, she agreed. "I'm exhausted."

Madeline chose two sandwich halves and half a dozen of the strawberries. "I'll tell you whatever you want to know, but *after* I eat."

"Perhaps I should begin the confessional today."

Her mouth froze open, ready to take its first bite into the sandwich. She clamped it shut, drew her eyebrows together and stared at him. "*You*...."

What he'd dreaded all day turned out to be amusing. Russell described his evening – driving away from her house, sneaking up to the Mertons', finding Jimmy there, taking the boy home – all of it. "Oh, and you may find him eager to earn that other twenty cents."

"So *that's* what he meant about Mr. Smythe being 'down there last night.' I bet he meant the night before. Well, the morning—" She shook her head and took a bite of her sandwich. Her eyes ordered him to continue.

Russell took a bite, chewed, and complied. "Well, after I left Jimmy, I had planned to give up—to return the carriage and ignore it. I knew he didn't do what he said he would, and that was proof enough for you." He leaned forward. "Isn't it?"

"Why do I feel as though you are going to tell me what you think I do not wish to hear?"

"I probably will. You see, I went into the Dry Docks anyway. It took some trying, but I found the brothel you described, pulled up ahead of it, and waited.

Madeline fairly trembled with anticipation. "And?"

"And I saw him half an hour later—just as I decided I'd been ridiculous. I hadn't seen any sign of the carriage he'd been driving, and if I waited much longer, the livery may have sent out a search party for their horse."

"But you saw him."

Russell nodded. "He rode by a few minutes later—with a companion." His conscience rebuked him, so he added the rest of the story in a rush. "A *male* companion. He rode past the brothel without slowing and took the other fellow to a house near the Hardwick's. At that point, I returned the horse, paid my exorbitant bill, and went home."

The expected disappointment never materialized. Madeline sat lost in thought—almost as if confused. "The thing with Stanley...." Her eyes widened. "Do you think he could have met *another* man he *thought* was Stanley? It could have been some grave misunderstanding." Her eyebrows drew together once more. "Then again...."

Sandwich abandoned, Madeline began her tale of the afternoon. From buying the clothes to her aching feet, she gave a highly detailed account of every movement. But as she described the raw flesh,

Russell jumped up. "Take off your shoes!"

"I doubt Aunt Louisa—"

The joke failed to amuse him. Russell interrupted before his desire to shout overrode his courtesy. "I won't look under the table. But I *will* go get you a pan of warm water and mineral salts." His heart squeezed as she leaned to wrestle off her shoe and stifled a gasp. "I'll be back in a moment."

A quarter-hour later, with both feet soaking and her sandwich halves gone, Madeline relaxed against the chair and studied her berry before taking a bite from it. "I saw Mr. Smythe in the Dry Docks today, too. This time with a woman—one who expects to *leave* with him, should he decide to go." She leaned forward and popped the rest of the berry in her mouth. In the time it took her to chew and swallow, Russell thought of a dozen likely scenarios—none of which he imagined she would think much of.

"And this not long after Jimmy says he saw Mr. Smythe kiss Edith—and not a sweet peck on the cheek. He called it a 'lollapalooza' of a kiss."

"He kissed more than her cheek on Saturday night," Russell muttered.

Madeline's face fell. "I don't want him to be the man I'm afraid he is. I want him to love her, cherish her—to be everything she could hope for in a man. Is that wrong?"

Is it wrong that I find your desire for your friend *to be just as disconcerting as it is beautiful?*

"Russell?"

"It isn't wrong at all for you to want the best for your friend." Russell grasped the kindest and most likely scenario for the woman she'd seen with Smythe. "And wouldn't you imagine that perhaps that woman is a relative? A sister or cousin, perhaps? She may be related to the gentleman I saw him with. He may be helping some young woman out of a horrifying life. If you saw no affection…."

"I couldn't really see anything. But he did say something odd."

Russell reached for a berry himself and watched as she shifted her feet in the pan. "Do you need a towel?"

"No, thank you. No, he said, 'I've moved—no *settled*—into the new place in the Blackwood District. They'll forward my messages so no one will know I've moved.'"

Now that *is the most underhanded thing I've heard yet. What an odd*.... His mind whirled. "Well, does he have a business office? Perhaps he can't afford where he was but doesn't wish to give rise to speculation about his ability to manage his affairs." At that moment, Smythe's apology for his behavior burst upon Russell's memory. "I forgot something I overheard as well. He apologized, Madeline."

"For what? To whom?"

"His behavior about Charley Forsythe. He admitted to jealousy and apologized for his boorishness. I...." The memory of it being somewhat excessive crowded in, but Russell dismissed it. "I think we have to assume that perhaps he is what he purports to be."

To his surprise, and great relief, Madeline nodded. "I think you may be correct. Everything is only *slightly* off. Each time I find something unsettling, I or someone else, finds more that isn't or finds a perfectly reasonable explanation."

An hour later, Russell walked up Beaumont Street to the trolley at the corner of Redbrook. As he passed the Merton house, his eyes saw through the hydrangeas right to where he and Jimmy had been hiding. *I wonder if you can see there at night. That would be disconcerting.*

TWENTY-THREE

Flossie Hardwick sat in the Brown's parlor in evident distress. Madeline listened to the tale of woe with a curious ear and discerning mind. "You say that you think someone is trying to malign Warren?"

"And Stanley Wakefield. I'm sure of it. I just can't imagine *whom!* Warren came to the house last night in a terrible state. He was convinced that a policeman was after him!"

Odd.... Madeline moved beside Flossie, despite the horrendous heat, and held the girl's hand. "Now what could he possibly have done to warrant that?"

"That's precisely the problem! He doesn't know. He wanted to tell me up front that if he were accused of anything, he'd tell me right away if the charges were true. If not, he hoped I'd believe him." Her eyes dropped to her lap. "Oh, Madeline. I didn't at first—believe him, I mean. I was sure it was some scheme to try to hide some indiscretion. But then he reminded me about the thing with Stanley Wakefield. And well, one can't argue that it was a gross and false accusation." Flossie flushed. "I know you've received criticism for your...."

"I believe the word is 'meddling.' Papa and I joked about it last night. He said if I wasn't more circumspect he'd give his 'Meddlin' Madeline a paddlin' all the way home.'"

"Oh, dear. Perhaps I shouldn't—"

233

Rude or not, Madeline felt compelled to interrupt. "Flossie, no. We were teasing one another. I tried to make you smile with that story, not give you undue concern. Now, perhaps we could go visit Warren? Is he at the office with his father, or…."

"Why would we visit?" Oh, the panic on her face. If Madeline hadn't known better, she would have been convinced that Warren's father didn't know about their courtship.

"Because I need to know what this man looked like. If he isn't *certain* that the man following was a policeman, then the man must not have been in uniform. That leaves a question of whether the man was police or…."

The alternative rocked Madeline's mind. *Surely, it couldn't be the same man following me. Could Mr. Smythe be behind this — keeping watch on Edith's friends for some inexplicable reason?*

With that thought in mind, Madeline hopped up and hurried up the stairs. She grabbed her pocketbook and hat before rushing back down again. "Very well. We'll do this. You find Warren, and have him take you to the park. We'll find a pasty vendor for lunch — my treat. He shouldn't be seen with both of us in case he *is* being followed. We can meet at that new gazebo. No one will be there during the hottest part of the day, surely."

The moment Madeline left Flossie, she hurried back to the Pinkerton office. Mr. Flint called her in the moment he heard the door open. "Miss Brown. I'm afraid I haven't much news as of yet."

"I just have a question, if you don't mind." She stepped into his office and pushed the door mostly shut. "Have you had Warren Osborne followed in the past week?"

Flint's head snapped up. "Someone else in your circle is being followed?" He stood and offered her a chair, but Madeline demurred.

"Yes. And no, I cannot stay. I'm expected in the park in a short while. But before I questioned him, I thought to ask you." She'd made it almost across the anteroom before a thought brought her back. "Mr. Flint?"

"Yes?"

"What is the likelihood of a detective—out of uniform—following my friend?"

Flint's eyes narrowed. "Not likely. Rockland's detectives usually leave that sort of work to uniformed officers. If someone in plain clothes is following your friend, it is almost certainly *not* someone with the police force."

With that information in mind, Madeline half-walked, half-ran to the park and collapsed on the gazebo bench. With her folding fan working at top speeds to cool her flushed face, her eyes followed every entrant to that area of the park. The man appeared before Warren and Flossie, but by the time they reached the gazebo, it became obvious that he had most definitely followed them.

Interesting technique. I like the subtlety.

"Madeline! We were so swift, I was—"

"Shhh!" Madeline hugged each of them with a quick warning. "The man has followed you again. When we turn around, please check the man seated on the bench by the fountain."

Flossie's hands shook as she pulled away, but Warren waited until a loud noise could explain his perusal of the area. "That's him. He's got to be a policeman."

"I'm quite confident that he isn't. So, that begs the question, who has hired someone to follow you, and why?"

"That's just the thing. I cannot imagine what it could be." Warren's face fell. "If this goes poorly, I could lose the chance at the position I interviewed for. I needed that position for—" His eyes darted in Flossie's direction before he forced himself to maintain eye contact. "—future plans."

Without a word, Madeline fished two dimes from her pocketbook, passed them to Warren, and hurried off with a, "Have a lovely time!"

At the corner of Holbrook and Fielding, Madeline pretended to admire a painting in a curved-glass window. The curvature allowed her to watch the pedestrians along the street—to see the moment that Warren appeared on his way back to work. She went inside the gallery, perused the offerings, and came out again—three times.

"Madeline Brown! What are you doing here?"

Her heart sank at the sound of her aunt's voice. "Aunt Louisa! I could say the same to you!"

"I've come to buy a new carpet—oh, no." The woman's voice grew stern. "Madeline, tell me you are not playing detective again. This meddling of yours is going to utterly ruin your reputation!" Louisa pulled her around the corner and into a back doorway. "I've heard about Henry Hardwick—fine young man that he is. You don't want to scare him off with these crazy ideas of yours."

"Crazy ideas?"

"Albert told me all about your suspicions regarding Vernon Smythe—how you think he isn't telling the truth about Stanley Wakefield. Well, that is simply none of your business."

Relief washed over her at the realization that Louise didn't know the whole of her concern. "Aunt—"

"No more! I'm telling you this now. I try not to put my foot in where it doesn't belong, but I *will* take your father to task if you do not stop this inappropriate meddling."

"I assure you, Aunt Louisa, I am *not* down here on any quest to discover Vernon Smythe's secrets. And, if his flirting is any indication of his opinion of me, I do not think you have to fear that I've destroyed Henry Hardwick's good opinion of me." A cloud covered the sun. "Oh! Exactly what I was waiting for. I wanted to see that painting in a different light." And with a kiss to the startled woman's cheek, Madeline scurried around the corner and stared at the window once more.

Louisa passed with a confused expression on her face, but when Madeline pretended not even to notice, the woman strolled along the street with evident satisfaction in her ability to corral her niece's unconventional pastime. Just as Madeline relaxed, the man appeared in the window—only ten feet ahead of Warren. From the young man's posture and movements, Madeline felt certain that he thought *he* was following the man. She waited until they'd made it a full half block ahead before she strolled along the street behind Warren, her eyes always fixed on the man ahead.

Then he vanished.

Madeline crossed the street and hid behind a tall sandwich sign as Warren wandered the street in search of the man. Once he gave up, Madeline saw the man in question step from a dry goods store and take up the pursuit. Though Warren entered the Osborne building, the man continued, making notes in a small notebook. Madeline continued to follow until he arrived at Merton's bank and disappeared inside.

A slow smile spread across her lips. *Well done, Warren. Very well done.*

Seated at her new dressing table, Madeline brushed and tossed the long curls of her hair until dry and somewhat tame. As she brushed, she opted to say her evening prayers *before* supper as a hope that they would not be quite as rushed. "Who says that evening prayers can't be spoken at any time of the evening?"

Her reflection didn't answer, but she did find some measure of satisfaction in praying when not exhausted and in dire need of sleep. *This may become a new habit of mine.*

Mary knocked and entered. "The Hardwicks have arrived, and I believe Mr. Osborne is coming up the walk now."

"I'll be down as soon as I can pin up my hair. Please offer them something to drink—lemonade, perhaps."

"Not cordial?"

As much as it annoyed her to do it, Madeline shook her head. "I've learned that Henry Hardwick sympathizes somewhat with the temperance union. I think it would be a courtesy to offer lemonade before dinner."

"I'll do that."

Each twist of her hair, each jab of a hairpin, each adjustment—they all conspired against her, until Madeline despaired of ever leaving her room. Once done, she pulled on her dress, buttoned it into place, and slipped her feet into shoes she hadn't been able to wear since her escapade with Jimmy Higgins' new shoes.

Henry stood just inside the parlor as if waiting for her. "You're looking exceptionally well this evening, Madeline."

Before she could answer, Flossie rushed forward and whispered, "We think we were followed again."

"It's nothing, I'm sure. Just do as you usually would do, and all will be well."

"But—"

Madeline preempted Flossie's protest. "I'm confident, Flossie. I wouldn't say so otherwise."

Albert Brown stepped from his office carrying a new gramophone record. "I thought you might like this, Maddie. The salesman said this Edward Favor is all the rage."

Henry accepted the disk and moved to the gramophone. "I've heard this one once. 'A Little Bit off the Top.' He's amusing."

Hat in hand, Albert kissed his daughter, bade the others goodnight, and took off to some dinner party—where, she didn't know. The announcer's voice filled the room as the needle scratched its way around the disk. Flossie and Warren listened with rapt attention, but Henry watched her—and Madeline knew it. The intensity in his gaze hinted at something a little scandalous on the record.

She laughed as the chorus filled the room. "That's 'When Johnny Comes Marching Home'! How interesting." Any further compliment, she couldn't offer. She found the words silly and uninspired. *Likely because my mind is otherwise engaged. I really must stop giving others reason to consider me recalcitrant.*

To her great relief, the buzzer rang—likely Russell. Mary hurried forward, but Madeline waved the girl back. "Tell Cook we'll be ready after we listen to the record once more. Russell may like to hear it as well."

She opened the door to see Russell hiding a smirk—a clear sign he'd overheard her. He pulled off his hat as he entered, and when he handed it to her, murmured, "Why do I fear the offerings of the gramophone?"

"You shouldn't. As far as I know, no one has ever been injured by listening to music on records, despite the fact that so much of it these days offends the ears."

"Very well stated." Henry came and stood close enough to her to appear almost proprietary. "Evening, Barnes."

Even before Russell spoke, Madeline suspected what he'd say. True to form, he offered his hand. "It's good to see you again, Henry. Not tormenting the little girls still, I trust."

Just a flicker of irritation showed before Henry regained control. "I'm afraid not. They all grew up, you see—as did I. I doubt they'd appreciate my boyish shenanigans any more now than they did then."

The words *sounded* well-spoken and proper, but Madeline watched Russell's features to determine what her friend *truly* thought of the young man from Buffalo. Russell stepped into the parlor, calling back to Henry as he did. "I'm pleased to hear it. So many young men never seem to grow out of those childish pranks."

The music played again, and Madeline sensed it—distaste in Russell's stance, the thoughtful expression on his face, in his eagerness to turn it off. "An unusual recording, isn't it?"

Which translates, "Why would anyone waste time and money to create that?"

239

The dinner party began smoothly enough. Warren regaled them with stories of his interview, telling them the answers he'd have given had he not been keen to procure the position. "I've managed to calculate my annual salary, so I think my mathematics skills should be up to par—then again, perhaps not."

"Well, with the price of everything rising by the day, no one can afford not to consider such things," Flossie interjected.

Dear Flossie. For someone as intelligent as you can be, sometimes....

Just then, Frank began to tease her, and in a rush to stop him before he hurt her feelings, Madeline interrupted as if she hadn't noticed he'd been speaking. "I had a—oh. I'm sorry, Frank. You were saying?"

Her eyes met his and he looked away again. "Go ahead. I was just thinking aloud."

"I was just going to say," Madeline continued, "that I had a strange experience this evening. I found myself needing to dry and brush my hair. Flossie can attest to the length of time this can take. And it's rather a tedious exercise."

Henry managed to interject a compliment as Madeline waited for Flossie's agreement. "I can imagine especially tedious for someone with your quick mind."

"Well, that is just my point. It occurred to me that evening prayers needn't be reserved for the last thing of the day. In fact, I'm beginning to think that waiting until then does our Lord a disservice. I found praying to be much more rewarding and well...." Madeline tossed Russell a smile that only he would accurately translate. "Coherent. I must confess that by the time I kneel beside the bed to say my prayers, I am quite fatigued. My eyes droop, my knees protest—it's really quite unsatisfactory for me. And if I find it unsatisfactory, what must the Lord think?"

"An excellent observation, Madel—"

But before Russell could continue, Henry spoke up. "It is, indeed! Your devotion to the Lord does you credit, Madeline. It is encouraging to learn how devout you've become."

Somehow—though she couldn't imagine *how*—Madeline managed a smile instead of a hot retort. Her eyes sought Russell, and she tried to burn her thoughts in his mind. *I'm very sorry to tell you that it appears I was correct the other day. I will* not *be receiving a better offer—even if he should make one it certainly won't be better. How annoying. Do try not to be terribly disappointed.*

But either Russell misread her mental missive, or he found it quite amusing, because his eyes twinkled at her as he took a bite of his roast beef.

The Blackwood District boasted businesses with family dwellings above them and a few tenements. It sounded large, imposing. However, the entire district consumed only two city blocks. And Madeline walked those blocks, camera in hand, taking pictures of everything in sight, while doing her best to stay *out* of sight. She'd lost half a dozen pennies to little boys who all insisted that Mr. Smythe lived in a different place than the last.

One girl, dressed in what appeared to be an older brother's cast-off knickerbockers, adjusted a cap and followed her for the better part of an hour. Sun beat down, but despite the ample protection of her over-sized hat, Madeline felt her neck grow warm—likely red.

She beckoned the girl closer. "Where can I find a soda fountain? I am in need of refreshment."

"I don't know. But my brother would. He takes his girl to get phosphates sometimes."

She fished out a penny and showed the girl. "If you find out where, you can have it."

"I'll find out anyway. You're throwing your pennies away today. Those boys were just being goopy." The girl flicked a braid over one shoulder. "And you fell for it."

"I suspected, but I thought if even one told the truth, it'd be worth the six cents." Madeline smiled as the girl chewed the end of her other braid. "Sometimes you have to be willing to risk the loss."

This time, the girl shoved her hands in her pockets and stared at Madeline with evident suspicion in her eyes. "How come you wants—er *want* – to know about that Smythe fella?"

"Excellent correction." The truth she couldn't hope to tell, but a dozen things she could *make* true flitted through her mind. She landed on the one most likely to appeal to a suspicious little girl. Madeline beckoned her closer and bent to murmur her newly concocted tale. "Well, see Mr. Smythe is engaged to my dear friend. And, I've just learned that he's removed from his previous boarding house to this area. I just don't know where. I thought to send him an official note of congratulations." She swallowed hard at the idea she'd have to waste perfectly good stationery *and* precious minutes on a letter she didn't feel just to keep her words honest. The child's face still looked suspicious, so Madeline added one more truth. "I haven't been exactly... *welcoming* of him. And I think it hurts my friend. I thought I should make the first overture."

There. Now that is true. If he is who he presents himself to be, I am very sorry to doubt him and would like to make amends. I'll send the letter, and I'll pray over every word I write – pray that they will *have a long, rich, happy marriage.*

"Oh, she's a nice girl—not flashy like you, but real keen."

Madeline's forehead furrowed before she could stop it. "She is? You've met her?"

Twin braids danced about the girl's shoulders as she shook her head. "No, miss. I just saw them together day before yesterday. With that kiss he gave her, it *has* to be her."

"Well, you can see why I want to make amends for my...."

The girl's eyes twinkled. "Jealous, were you? Yeah. My sister did that, too. C'mon. I'll show you his lodgings and walk you to the

242

soda fountain."

"If you walk me there, I'll buy you a phosphate. We can drink them together." Madeline cocked her head and smiled. "What's your name?"

"Essie — Chandler."

"I'm Madeline Brown." Madeline turned to go. "Shall we?"

The girl nodded, gave her a curious smile, and took off toward the corner. As they rounded it she added, "Don't think about takin' off with me. I'll kick you, and no boy can run faster than me. Bobby taught me to fight, too. So, I can take care of myself."

"Well, of course you can!" Madeline stared at the girl's knickerbockers. "Can I ask a personal question?"

"Sure."

She glanced around to make sure no one could hear her before asking, "Are those comfortable?"

The girl giggled. "Yeah. Lots better than stupid dresses. Ain't you never — I mean, haven't you ever worn 'em?" She shook her head. "I s'pose not."

"I actually did once, but they didn't fit, and I had my regular clothes wrapped around me underneath them. It wasn't very comfortable, but I thought perhaps...."

"You should try it sometime. Ma likes 'em because she says they're like bloomers, but I can wear Bobby's hand-me-downs. Why make more when we have these?"

Aaah.... Russell, what would you do if I took to riding that wheel you're always teasing me about... in bloomers!

$\mathcal{T}$WENTY-$\mathcal{F}$OUR

Edith, I do hope you didn't mishear. I feel quite foolish walking up and down this street waiting for a woman who may not come. But even as the thought filled Vernon's mind, he saw a chapeau of such ludicrous proportions that it *must* be Louisa Farnsworth. He gave her time to enter the bank and waited a solid minute before following her inside.

Already she stood at a teller window, getting the household money early. *You wouldn't think that one minor holiday would make several days' difference in getting the funds. I happen to know it was nearly a week into June before you stopped in. We met with Madeline and Edith that day, if I recall.*

But as she turned, he strolled past and jostled her arm. "Oh, pardon me—Mrs. Farnsworth! I beg your pardon. I was lost in thought."

"No harm done. I'm nearly trampled on the streets sometimes. A tap like that—hardly noticed it, I assure you." She beamed at him. "I haven't had the opportunity to congratulate you on your engagement. I meant to at the ball, but at the last minute, I decided to stay home—slight headache that surely would have become immobilizing."

"Thank you. I am the happiest of men, I assure you." He gave her a knowing smile. "I've heard hints that you and Mr. Brown will be the next to be congratulated."

So flustered was Louisa Farnsworth, that she made a faux pas that would mortify her once she realized her mistake. "If you mean Henry Hardwick, I don't think it will come to anything. I understand he's a temperance lad, and Madeline is so against the movement."

"Oh, I hadn't heard anything regarding Hardwick. It was something about Mr. Barnes and a secret understanding between them." He ducked his head. "But forgive me. I see now that I wasn't to mention it to anyone. My—I believe the person who told me neglected to share that it wasn't public yet." He bowed ever so slightly and turned to go. "Have a lovely day, Mrs. Farnsworth. Regardless, I hope she'll be very happy in whatever life offers her."

And I hope you'll keep her so busy chasing after that Barnes fellow that she won't have time to go wandering around strange neighborhoods looking for my residence!

Music filled the night air at the Singleton farm just outside the city. Warren and Flossie danced on the makeshift dance floor, spinning and twirling with such abandon that Madeline couldn't help but notice. *Things are settled there. Warren has his job, Flossie has her fellow, and I believe I can safely say I have the satisfaction of being correct in this case.*

Henry asked twice to dance. Both times, she refused. So when Russell came and sat beside her, she prepared herself for a scolding. Instead, he seemed inclined to converse. For several minutes, he asked about the annual August trip with her Aunt Louisa and listened as she described the little cottage up at Lake Vienna. But when he still said nothing about Henry, and didn't even ask her to dance himself, Madeline found herself growing snappish. "Just scold me now and leave me in peace, Russell. I'd rather get the unpleasantness out of the way as quickly as possible."

"And why would I scold you?" His voice held a note of

laughter as he gazed out over the dancers. "Have I missed tales of another of your escapades?"

"You know very well what I mean. I have refused to dance with Henry twice now."

Russell cleared his throat and stood with hand held out. "Will you dance with me, little Maddie?"

He hadn't called her that in months — not since the unpleasantness with Delbert Jackson and the most undesirable proposal. *How silly that sounds — almost like a storybook title. Well, considering the proposal possessed similar qualities to that of Mr. Darcy's first proposal in* Pride and Prejudice, *I shouldn't wonder.*

But even as she thought about it, Madeline stood and gave him her hand. "Please forgive me, Russell. I didn't realize I was in such ill humor. Strange, isn't it?"

"Well, if Henry Hardwick has been making himself unpleasant, I am not surprised. Did he discover the secret to Vernon Smythe's charm?"

"He flirted with me." Though Madeline tried to keep a placid face, she failed. With half-suppressed giggles, she tried again. "That wouldn't have been so terrible. I know how eager you are to have me receive a better offer than...the *last* one, but really. Overt flirtation followed by further evidence that our fine Mr. Hardwick has turned fanatic."

Russell twirled her in slow circles at the end of the song and smiled down into her eyes. "And you've deduced this horrible crime how?"

Arm in his, Madeline led him along the drive toward the highway and away from the other guests. A few would talk, of course, but Madeline knew and was grateful that Russell cared little for the suppositions and gossip of others. "He sympathizes with the temperance league, and then paid a rather lavish compliment regarding my prayer habits. You heard him."

"What a louse!"

Warmth flooded her face as Madeline gazed up at him. "I do sound rather petty, don't I? I just cannot abide that kind of pietistic nonsense — and he's the one who made a comment about how wrong such things are. Hypocrisy is nearly as bad, if not worse. Why cannot people be reasonable about issues such as faith and religion? Too much of any good thing spoils the recipe!"

Several long seconds passed without a response from Russell. She stopped in her tracks and gazed up at him. "What is it?"

"Only that I don't know how to reply to you without having you lose your good opinion of me as well."

Confused, curious, Madeline urged him to continue walking. "Whatever do you mean?"

But Russell didn't speak for the better part of a minute. When he did, she first noted sorrow in his voice. "I had always understood you to be a young lady of faith."

"Why, of course I am! But having faith and parading it as a banner are two very different things."

"So, we should possess a sincere faith but keep it on a curio shelf, only to be taken down at appropriate intervals and then locked away again?"

The words mocked her. Despite knowing she would have made that very claim only moments before, coming from Russell, they sounded off — even wrong. "Well, that might be a bit extreme...." Her eyes filled with tears of vexation, but she managed to blink them away again. "Locking faith anywhere seems a poor way to show appreciation for what our Lord has done. But I can't help but think about that story about not allowing people to herald our giving."

"And yet, in that same book of the Bible, Jesus says not to hide our light from others, but to set it where it can be seen. How can we ignore the direct words of the Lord Himself?"

Madeline ignored the story in favor of another observation. "I had not realized you were so devout, Russell."

The pain that flashed in his eyes wounded her as well. She

248

gazed at him as he struggled to formulate a response and almost cried at the emotion he suppressed as he shared it. "That doesn't speak well to my faith, does it? I'll have to pray about that, but yes, Madeline. My faith is very real, very strong, and I am afraid to tell you it guides every decision in my life."

She couldn't help it—in fact, she almost relished the moment as she asked, "*Every* decision?"

His eyes softened, and a smile, weak though it was, formed on his lips. "Every decision."

Charlie Dougherty played the violin as the group sat in a semi-circle around the fire. The evening breeze blew the heat away from the group as the smoke helped to keep mosquitoes at bay. Voices blended as they sang Foster's dear, "Molly, Do You Love Me?" amid laughter and occasional parodied improvisations by a few of the fellows.

Madeline and Russell joined the singing, but her heart remained quiet and thoughtful as she mulled over Russell's words. *I hurt him. If all sincere, devout Christians were as Russell, this world would be a better place.*

The thought did occur to her that for the world to become such a place, she would have to be just as devout. A scripture came to mind—one about living a quiet life and minding your own business. She flushed as shame filled her to think of how much she had been focused on others' affairs of late.

But Edith....

How swiftly the heart hardens when one finds justification for one's actions.

Russell nudged her. "Are you well? I can take you home if you prefer. I brought a carriage since I had to come so late."

She'd ridden to the farm in one of the hay wagons, and though she truly had no desire to leave so early, the opportunity to speak alone with Russell did tempt her. "I'm well, yes. But if you would take me home later...."

He rarely did it. Propriety being such a harsh taskmaster made him unwilling to show affection for her when his sister wasn't close by. But seeing her distress must have prompted further concern. He patted her hand, squeezed it, and offered a reassuring smile. "Of course," he murmured. "Sing. It always brightens your spirits."

With her questions filed away for further perusal later, Madeline tried to enter the spirit of the evening. Three songs later, after the first wagon drove off with those needing to be home early, she agreed to Russell's second suggestion that they leave. "You're too good to me. I must write and tell Amy that she should come home. I think her brother is missing having a little sister to spoil."

"It could be." However, despite his agreeable tone, Russell looked perfectly content with life as it was. "But I wouldn't wish her away from this experience for anything."

They hadn't quite reached the carriage when Warren's voice rang out behind them. "Madeline! Wait."

He and Flossie rushed up to meet them. "We thought you'd gone." Warren waited for Flossie to catch her breath before he continued — something that didn't seem necessary even as thoughtful a gesture as it was. "I just knew you'd enjoy a laugh at my expense."

"Oh? So did your 'detective' prove you to be the upstanding young man we know you to be?"

Oh, the stunned expressions on Flossie and Warren's faces! Flossie found her voice first. "How did you know?"

"With the recent rumors, unfounded, of course, surrounding Warren lately, it is only logical that a new employer should wish to discover if the young man he wishes to hire is trustworthy. And a man like Mr. Merton wouldn't waste the funds to investigate if he were not certain he wanted you. I knew you'd have the position and a cleared reputation in no time."

Even Russell stared at her in evident amazement and admiration. Warren just chuckled, shook his head, and took Flossie's hand. "We'll let you go. I should have known you'd figure it out. When you didn't tell me to be concerned, I was confident all would be well, but this...." He laughed again. "Well, I know if I ever need anything riddled out again, I'm coming straight to you!"

Again, uncertainty roiled within her as Russell helped her into the carriage and urged the horse to drive off out into the night. They'd gone half a mile before he spoke. "Something still seems to be troubling you."

"Do you think my 'meddling' is counter to Scripture?

When he didn't offer an immediate answer, Madeline concluded he'd come to a rather unsatisfactory—for her, anyway—conclusion. But his words surprised her. "I think it's a little more complicated than right or wrong. Some things are very straightforward. Murder is wrong. But other things rely on looking at motive because the action may or may not be. Is it wrong to try to protect a friend? I don't know. But I do know...."

Madeline fought hard and failed to stifle a sniffle. "Oh, bother."

Russell stopped the carriage in the middle of the road and turned to face her. With the moon behind them and little light from the carriage lantern, she couldn't see his expression, but every vowel and consonant blended into the kind, understanding tones he always used when instructing Amy. He turned her head in a feeble attempt to meet her gaze. "Madeline, you care about people. You're intrigued by them, yes, but you care. I can't imagine an unkind motive behind your concern over Edith's choice of young man. And whatever you did to help Warren was kind. He certainly appreciated it."

She heard the expected disclaimer in his tone. "However...."

"Those who love you are concerned. You cannot think that people will not be upset or offended when their carefully hidden misdeeds are revealed? Surely."

"So I should sit at home with needlework and novels to content me until that better offer just waltzes through the door on the feet of some stranger? Is this what my existence is reduced to? I cannot go to college. Aunt Louisa would make Papa's life miserable with her constant harping about how horrible it is. I cannot take up a position or a profession. I'm too 'common' to do anything truly astounding and too 'aristocratic'—at least in Aunt Louisa's mind—to do anything but be an ornament on some man's shelf!"

Russell's low chuckle soothed rather than irritated her. "Poor Madeline." He clicked his cheek and the horses pulled forward. "She's too traditional to be a modern young lady and too independent to be traditional."

"And that is precisely why I think young women are joining these movements in droves. There is nothing else for them *to* do. I cannot even hope to teach a classroom full of unruly students."

"Which you would despise."

She nodded so emphatically that her hat flew off and nearly out of the carriage. "You have that just right, Mr. Barnes. I would." A sigh escaped. "But it would be a pleasant thought to know that I was at least *useful*."

They'd traveled over a mile—perhaps two—before Russell spoke. "Madeline. You're useful in ways that aren't as tangible as a child who learned to read or an ill child nursed back to health. Instead, you keep your father happy and from being alone. You give your aunt the closest thing to a daughter that she's ever had. You help your friends with their little troubles and influence a young boy to be a better person." At her sharp look, Russell laughed. "Yes, I know about your little project with Jimmy Higgins. You are not the only person who can extrapolate information from actions and deduce motives."

"I see." Madeline waited for her cheeks to cool a bit more before she added, "Thank you, Russell. I needed the reminder that all duty is worthwhile—not just the more exciting ones."

TWENTY-FIVE

Jonas Merton spoke with someone in the study—a voice Madeline didn't recognize. But with the door cracked open, and neither man even attempting to be quiet, she dawdled on her way to retrieve the hat she'd left in Edith's music room. The fact that she'd been careful to leave it behind meant little to anyone but her.

The man's voice sounded concerned—panicked even. "—is planning to keep *open* the brothels. I overheard him speaking to the woman myself!"

"I understand your concern, but I've spoken to Brown, and he insists that the police will manage that aspect if the rest is attempted. Smythe is only being practical."

Didn't you hear him? He said that he saw Mr. Smythe talking to that woman! *Isn't that proof enough of a connection?* A new thought sent her thoughts whirling. *Do men invest in such ...businesses? Could he have financial interests associated with that...?* Bile rose in her throat at the thought. The other man spoke again, distracting her from unsavory ideas.

"I've read of similar improvement projects around the country. Most are expensive. Most fail."

"Well, if we fail, it isn't for trying. As for me, I have no interest in the project. If people want to live in squalor, let them. But Smythe seems to think it will benefit the city's business interests, and I cannot ignore that this could be true."

The man would be coming. Madeline dashed for the hat. Hidden behind the great curtains that adorned the entry to the music room, she waited. "Edward" stepped from the office, agitation fairly rippling over him, and strode toward the front door. Madeline followed. Without a word to Edith, she raced to the front door, watched from a window, and then followed the man as soon as he'd stormed out of the gate. Jimmy caught her at the corner of the yard.

"Goin' somewhere, miss?"

"Want to help me?" Even as she asked, Madeline dragged him alongside as she walked. "Run up ahead and see where he goes. Then circle back as if you forgot something."

Without waiting for further instruction, Jimmy rushed ahead of her and the man. He stopped to tie his shoe and then vanished. Madeline's heart strangled her as it tried to escape from her throat. But just as she passed a darling bungalow on the corner of Windemere Lane—one she'd loved for years—Jimmy's hand shot out of an overgrown lilac bush and touched her. "Shhh… it's me."

"What happened? I thought you were following him?"

"Don't need to. I saw him pull out a train schedule and his watch. Then he skedaddled quicker'n a hound after a coon."

I can't imagine where you heard that one. I'll have to ask later. Madeline fished a nickel from her pocketbook and passed it into the bush. "Rush to the train station and see which one he gets on, please. I'll follow and meet you by the porter's booth."

"Yes, *miss!*" But he didn't take the nickel. "I only owe you and Mr. Barnes one now. That's good enough for me. Now I can give that quarter to Ma."

She wanted to protest, but time wouldn't allow. She urged him to hurry. "Oh, and be sure to tell Edith that I commandeered you *before* she has a chance to scold. Tell her I said I'm very sorry but it was urgent. Now go!"

The boy disappeared one second, appeared the next, and then a blur of brown and blue streaked across the street and disappeared around the corner of a woodshed. Madeline followed "Edward" but lost sight of him half the time. Only on the trolley, did they come and stay in close proximity. But Madeline busied herself fidgeting with her fingers as if some great calamity were to befall her at any given moment and never looking around her at all. Had the man known her well, those actions would have been unusual enough to arouse suspicion.

The closer she came to the train station, the more nervous she became. *I can't exactly climb aboard a train for who knows where and follow a strange man simply because he is opposed to a plan that has the potential to improve the lives of many of Rockland's most unfortunate citizens. Is he right? Is the idea foolhardy? Is there reason to be concerned? I should tell Papa, at least.*

By the time she arrived at the station, Madeline was overheated and flushed. Jimmy met her at the porter's booth with an excited gleam in his eye. "He's headed to Boston—track four. I heard him say he is meeting someone. He went over to the pasty stand."

"You get on back to the Mertons. Good work, Jimmy." Madeline beamed down at him. "*Very* good work."

Before she could decide what to do next, the man in the plaid suit and bowler appeared just across the platform. His gaze couldn't be mistaken, and in a fit of sauciness, Madeline tipped her bowler to him and turned away—turned, and plowed straight into Vernon Smythe's chest.

"Oh! Pardon—Mr. *Smythe!*"

"Are you all right, Miss Brown? No injury?" Despite the solicitous words, Smythe's tone snarled and snapped.

"None at all. I am so sorry! I thought I saw someone I knew and wished to say hello before boarding."

A sneer twisted Smythe's lips before he rearranged them into some semblance of a smile. "I hadn't heard of your travel plans."

"Just a quick trip to Chicago. A friend there isn't well. I just received news today."

The skepticism in Smythe's eyes couldn't be imagined—not even by the most gullible of people. But Madeline just waved and hurried off with a plea for him to "Give Edith my best!" She rushed to the train where a conductor made the last call for Chicago and climbed aboard. At the nearest window, she seated herself, waved at Smythe, and settled herself in for the ride.

Curled up with her favorite Sherlock Holmes story, *The Final Problem,* Madeline nearly jumped out of her skin when the doorbell buzzed. Though she often answered the door to save Mary rushing through the house, Madeline hardly stirred. Her racing heart blended with the story as a man, wielding a truncheon, attacked Holmes. Lost in the excitement of the action, the sound of approaching voices registered only when Russell exclaimed, "She *is* here!"

"As I said, Mr. Barnes." Mary's giggle pierced through the last of Madeline's story-armored shield.

Without disguising her reluctance, Madeline dropped her story and leveled an impatient glare on both of them. "I am where?"

Confusion and suspicion clouded Russell's eyes as he moved to sit beside her. "There is a rumor around town that you were seen climbing aboard the train to Chicago this afternoon. Vernon Smythe, Adeline Engels, and a few others insist they *saw* you climb aboard that train. So when I come to ask your father why you'd taken an abrupt departure to visit an unnamed *sick friend*, I must say that I'm astounded to discover you sitting here."

Seconds passed as Madeline debated within herself. Propriety insisted she answer the question without illustration or embellishment. The throbbing of her calf suggested perhaps just this once. She untucked her bare feet from beneath her and pulled up the hem of her skirt just enough to show the nasty bruise forming.

"Jumping from a slow moving train is easier than I imagined. Unfortunately, I jumped one second before I saw a rock half-hidden by grasses. I almost missed it too."

His eyes, wide with either shock or dismay, remained glued to the bruise until she remembered the basics of modesty and recovered it. "Oh, Madeline."

"I wasn't going to tell Mr. Smythe *why* I was at the station. That lie flowed so easily that I'm still stunned. I'll be stuck in this house for at least a day or two more. Papa and Mary know, of course."

"And I'm supposed to keep your secret as well, I assume."

"It would be preferable."

He picked up her magazine and eyed the story in it. "Another Sherlock Holmes? No, an older one. I've read this."

"As have I. It's my favorite—I think. I sometimes think that having favorites is a waste of time. The more acquainted you are with something, the more or less you are wont to appreciate it." Madeline stood. "I think Cook made lemon cookies. Would you like some? We have cold mint tea as well—possibly enough ice not to annoy the queen of the kitchen if we steal some."

Russell stood. "I'll go forage. We wouldn't want someone to look through that back window and notice you're home."

It took all her poise and self-control *not* to throw a pillow at his retreating back. Still, just as he reached the doorway, Madeline aimed and fired with remarkable accuracy. Russell's voice reached her from the hall. "I wondered what took so long."

And you've developed a terrible habit of allowing your sentences to trail off. Be a man. Commit to your words. A snicker escaped. *Now I sound like Aunt Louisa, "Commit to a thought and speak with confidence, but don't lose sight of your femininity."*

Russell arrived with a tray so quickly that Madeline realized Mary must have anticipated their needs. "I don't know what we'd do without her sometimes. That harridan we had before her...."

"She was a drunk, Madeline." At her stunned expression,

Russell apologized. "I'm sorry. I didn't realize you didn't know."

"Oh, I knew! I just didn't realize anyone else did!" Her eyes narrowed. "How did you guess?"

"I caught her with a bottle outside once. I informed her that I'd get her fired myself if she ever got drunk when you girls were home alone again."

That must have been years ago – when we were quite small! Madeline accepted a glass and peered over it. "Just when was that?"

"A few weeks after you moved in here. Your father was working on some project and wasn't home much. I came to get Amy one day, and she was out there in the back yard hiding behind a bush with a bottle of something."

She couldn't help a smile. "And I always thought you didn't like me in those days."

His eyes met and held hers. "I was still of the foolish opinion that young men shouldn't actually *enjoy* the company of their little sisters and their friends. So I tried to hide it with obnoxious behavior and bossiness. But imagining either of you in danger because of that woman…."

This time his trailed sentence ended with a suspicious-sounding choke. Madeline handed him the cookie plate. "Let's sweeten those memories, shall we?"

His eyes met hers once more, and with a slow wag, Russell shook his head. "With pretty little speeches such as that, you should have no trouble receiving a better offer, Madeline. Be careful whom you share them with."

The room spun a little as she drank in the intensity of his gaze. "Of course."

Between bites of cookie, Russell complimented her on the tea, the cookies, even the arrangement of the tray – all things she'd had no part in whatsoever. She waited for him to say what he really wanted to – ask whatever question truly occupied his mind. It came as he finished his cookie and relaxed. "Madeline, why did you go to the train station today?"

Aaah, this is the question I'd expected the moment I said I'd jumped from a train. She shifted, and the bruised calf bumped against the edge of the sofa. "Ouch!"

"Have you arnica for that?"

"I put Cook's salve on it earlier. I'll do it again before bedtime. I must be more careful, though. It'll be black and blue for weeks if I'm not." A sheepish smile escaped before she could stop herself. "But you asked about the train station. I'd discovered information and wanted to learn more. So, I went in search of it."

"And how did you know that Vernon Smythe would be there? He said he didn't know he was going himself until he received news that someone was coming in on the four-twenty from Chattanooga."

Oh, the delight in seeing Russell's face as she frowned and said, "But, Russell, I didn't know *he'd* be there at all!"

News of Madeline's last-minute trip to visit a friend in Chicago made its way to Louisa Farnsworth two days after the train pulled out of the station and Madeline rolled down the gentle sloping grassy hillside—right into that rock. No one seemed to know the name of the friend and so applied to her for answers. And that's where things became intolerable.

All along the trolley route, Louisa twisted a handkerchief in her hands, fighting the temptation to practice her speech aloud. *I may not be able to say what I want now, but just wait until I get you alone, Albert Brown. Why my poor sister should have to endure eternity watching these shenanigans, I do not know.*

At the corner of Redbrook Avenue and Beaumont Street, Louisa stepped from the trolley and began the short walk to her brother-in-law's house. Mary opened the door with surprise and a fidgety air that she found quite annoying. "Is Albert home?"

"Um... he is. He's in his study. I—"

"I'll see myself in there." Before the woman could stammer out the question, Louisa added, "And I would appreciate a cool glass of water. Thank you."

"Yes, ma'am. Right away." She seemed to wait for something, but when Louisa didn't speak, Mary scurried off toward the kitchen.

Albert jumped at the sound of her voice in the doorway. "Louisa. What are you—?"

"I have heard some strange rumors around town, Albert."

The man sagged. Had Madeline's reputation not been on the line, she might have felt a twinge or two of remorse, but Madeline had to come before their comfort. She waited. Waited, and he didn't say a word.

"Is it true? Madeline has gone to Chicago to visit some sick friend—*alone?*"

Albert ran his fingers through the tufts of silver hair on each side of his head and leaned back in his chair. "Two afternoons ago, Madeline did board the 4:20 train to Chicago—something about a sick friend, but I haven't spoken to her about that."

"She went without your knowledge or permission then?" Louisa dropped into the chair opposite him and threw up her hands. "Really, Albert. You *must* see why this can't be allowed any longer. People are *talking!*"

"People *always* talk, Louisa—particularly about a politician's family. It's what they do. Better that she give them cause to speculate about the horrors of disease she may encounter than to focus on how she is lacking in civic-minded adherence to things like suffrage."

"You cannot be so obtuse! People are talking about her *behavior*. Young ladies do not ride trains alone to Chicago!"

His tone shifted to the one Louisa called "stubborn resolve." She'd never get through to him unless it changed. But before she could try another tactic, he spoke. "No, young ladies climb aboard trains and ride them across the country to colleges, to marry strange men, to work in Harvey Houses. Is that what you would prefer? My daughter should do something like that rather than *visit the sick when they ask for her?*"

"Well, no, of course not. I just—"

Mary arrived with the water and a plate of cookies. "I thought you might be hungry, ma'am."

"Thank you, Mary. *Someone* in this house knows how to behave, anyway." The moment the woman left, Louisa pounced with her next question. "And what friend *is* this? I didn't know she had any friends there."

"I don't know, Louisa. She didn't say—likely too in a rush to get out the door to realize she forgot to tell anyone. I'll learn all about it when she gets home." Albert leaned forward. "Note that singular pronoun? I said *I* will learn. *You* will leave her alone. I'm losing all patience with your constant interference. You make yourself a nuisance, if I may say so."

Fingers hovering over a cookie, Louisa gasped and dropped her hand. "Why, Albert Brown! How can you say such a thing? I—"

"Don't get all huffy. Just leave the management of my daughter to me. She wouldn't be as well-loved as she is if I had done the reprehensible job of bringing her up that you seem to think I did." His face and his voice softened. "She loves you, Louisa. I want that to continue." He leaned forward and rested his hands on his desk. "But if you continue to harp on her about every little outdated notion of propriety that you can find, I guarantee you'll ensure she wants nothing to do with you. Young people don't like to be scolded like little children when *they have done nothing wrong.*"

A dozen retorts flew out of her mouth at once, resulting in an incomprehensible stutter of syllables and vowels. She jumped up, grabbed her pocketbook, and stormed out the door. Three steps from the stairs, she froze in place as Madeline skipped down barefooted and carefree.

She froze at the bottom. Louisa stared. There they stood—two ice statues. Madeline found her voice first. "Why, Auntie! I didn't—"

"I was told you were in Chicago, Madeline!" She turned and, without regard for propriety at all, shouted across the house. "Albert Brown!"

"Oh, don't blame Papa. He just agreed to keep my little secret as a kindness to me. I did get on a train to Chicago." Madeline smiled. "But only to keep someone from knowing why I was there."

Louisa's eyes narrowed and her breath came in great huffs. "Vernon Smythe has every reason to be annoyed with your constant—"

"I didn't even know he'd be there, but the man is quite arrogant. He assumed I'd followed him. I could see it in his eyes. So I made up a story—something I'm *not* proud of—and then decided to make it at least *look* true to protect Papa's reputation."

A voice cleared behind her. "Louisa, as I just stated…."

But Louisa couldn't leave without a parting warning. "Madeline, if you are not careful, Russell Barnes will change his mind about you. His mother loves you almost as her own, but she won't approve of an alliance with a lying, meddlesome girl. You *must* see that. I understand why you didn't choose to encourage Mr. Smythe. He clearly is not the man for you. But if you continue in this manner, you will lose *all* of your prospects."

And with that, Louisa sailed out of the house. Madeline stared at her father, blinked, and swallowed hard. "Do you know what she is talking about?"

"It seems she thinks you and Russell have some sort of understanding."

"That's what I heard. I just couldn't imagine where she would get such an idea." Her heart pounded. Perspiration beaded on her upper lip, her nose, her forehead. Madeline scurried off to the kitchen for a drink of water, muttering something about people minding their own business.

TWENTY-SIX

With the slight kick of her foot, the front door shut behind her. Madeline stood before the hall mirror and pulled the bowler from her head. Her hair, mussed from too much resettling of said chapeau, frizzed all about her head. The solution—a simple one. She popped the hat back in place and strode toward her father's study with only the merest trace of a limp.

Albert Brown sat in his favorite chair. It occupied the brightest corner of the study and provided optimal natural reading light. So, it did not surprise her when he looked over his newspaper and smiled at her before returning to the afternoon news. "Have a nice time?"

"Listening to half a dozen young ladies who shouldn't be allowed to open their mouths? Why, of course, I did. Such a thrilling way to spend a muggy afternoon."

This time, Albert folded his paper with much care and laid it aside. "Something has you unsettled. What's wrong?"

"I overheard something today—something I am confident *certain people* would not wish me to know."

Concern drew the man's silvery eyebrows together until they nearly met in the middle. "Madeline, you know I don't like to restrain you. You've never given me reason to doubt your judgment, but after the affair with the train, I must admit to being leery of your...." He winked at her as if to soften the blow of his next words. "...*meddling.*"

"Now, Papa. I don't know anyone who has any reason to *harm* me. I just said I didn't think some people would like to know that I overheard this particular discussion." She hesitated. Telling him *what* she'd heard and what she thought it meant might make him more comfortable, but it would leave him in an awkward position.

"There are more ways to harm a young woman than to physically assault her. The most damaging injuries are rarely ones visible to the casual observer."

Madeline drew up the ottoman her father rarely used and perched herself on it. With elbows on her knees and head propped in her hands, she smiled up at him. "Well, what I have to tell you isn't going to get me hurt at all."

"Then what is it?" Albert leaned forward himself, hands clasped in front of him and eyes nearly piercing through her.

"Mr. Smythe's plans for the Dry Docks quarter? I would recommend distancing yourself from it."

Albert drew back into the chair and folded his hands in his lap. He eyed her with evident interest, but Madeline saw the faintest flash of anger in his eyes. "And why is that?"

"I—" She swallowed the explanation that only made sense to her own ears and shook her head. "I just don't think you should." Madeline reached for his hand and held it fast. "Please, Papa."

She saw it in his eyes, the way he held her hand—even the way he pursed his lips. But Albert shook his head. "I'll look into it further before I give it any support. That's the best I can offer."

Despite his words, Madeline heard his intent behind them— nearly as good as a promise to stay out of the plan. She kissed his cheek, whispered her thanks, and hurried to the door. "You do indulge me. Thank you."

"I feel as though I should reprove you for your dislike of the fellow, but I can't help but recall other instances where you noticed things the rest of us missed. If you're uncertain of him, I can't help but be cautious. The sudden fascination, I suppose, is to be considered."

His words carried her through the house and to the stairs. *Maybe it's not as meddlesome as it seems — not if I really have seen something. I just wish I knew what it was — had some proof!*

At the top of the stairs, she sighed in relief and strolled to her room with a carefree lilt to her step. Seated at her new dressing table, Madeline removed the bowler, sailed it across the room to her bed, and picked up the brush.

Only when she'd managed to tame half her head did her mind illuminate the deeper meaning of her father's words. Madeline dropped the brush in her lap and stared at her reflection. "Why is everyone so intrigued with this idea? When I first asked about it, people were shocked at the mere mention. Now Mr. Smythe comes along and suggests it needs 'improving' and suddenly it's the talk of the town."

Fireflies dotted lawns like nighttime's dandelions as Russell strode down the street and into the Brown yard. Mary sent him out back the moment she opened the door. "She's swinging out there — trying to cool herself."

"Is everything all right, Mary?"

The woman shook her head. "No, sir, I don't think it is. She's been out of sorts all evening." Mary sighed. "And, of course, it's not my place...."

"I'll talk to her. Thank you."

The heat of the day lingered in the house and even out onto the terrace. But as he neared the great tree where her swing provided respite from the miserable temperatures, Russell felt the air cool a little. "I should have known you'd be out here. Amy says nothing soothes more than a turn in your swing on a muggy summer's night."

He grasped the ropes and held them fast. "Ready?"

"Oh, Russell. You don't have—" But her words dissolved into the wind as he pulled her back and let the swing fly. "Ooooh…. it is so much more soothing with greater speed."

Russell pushed again. "I thought you'd be interested in something I saw today."

"Oh?"

For a moment, Russell reconsidered discussing the strange scene that had played out before him. "I was down by the Newcastle Hotel at lunchtime. Who did I see, but Mr. Smythe and Edith."

"Oh, that's right. She did say they were planning to meet her father for luncheon today." She stopped and twisted the ropes to stare at him. "What happened? Something did. I can hear it in your voice."

Once more, Russell grabbed the ropes, this time allowing her to twist back, and then pulled hard. She flew into the air again. "Well, that's what was so interesting. They'd just started up the steps when he led her away again. She seemed confused and quite unhappy about it. So, I looked around, and who do you think I saw coming down the steps?"

Russell gave her one good shove and moved so he could try to see her face. Madeline watched him as well, but he must not have given away the answer she sought. "I can't imagine."

"Charley Forsythe."

That stopped the swing once more. She jumped from it, almost landed in a heap at his feet, and pulled her arm through his as she started back toward the house. A second later, she snatched her arm back again and strode faster. "I wonder why he did that."

I wonder why you are suddenly awkward with me. Do I address it or hope it corrects—oh, no. This is you. I know better. "Madeline?"

She didn't even look his way. "Hmm?"

He caught her hand and held it fast until she turned to him, ready to demand that he release her. "Why did you pull away just now? Have I offended you?"

Impatience, frustration, chagrin. One after another, thoughts and emotions flickered across her face, but Russell could think of only one thing that could have caused it. "Or is this your Aunt Louisa's idea? Somehow, it is no longer proper to allow a gentleman to escort you somewhere? Will you be sporting an ever-present chaperone?"

A giggle escaped almost simultaneously with a sigh of exasperation "It *is* Aunt Louisa." Madeline looped her arm through his once more and nudged him in an arc back toward the tree. "I believe she's heard *somewhere* that we have some secret *understanding,* and she's convinced my horrible behavior is going to make you break it."

Perhaps it was rude. Russell couldn't have objected had someone made such an accusation, but he laughed. "So, Madeline doesn't like her name coupled with mine any more than she does Henry Hardwick or Vernon Smythe."

"That's not it at all, and you know it! I just—well—it surprised me. I don't know where she got such an idea. No one else of our set thinks anything of our friendship." Madeline sighed and faced him. "It was just as if she was there that night we talked about Mr. Jackson. I didn't know how she could—"

"I'm still surprised that you'd allow her to bother you so." But he saw it—unease still in her eyes as she tried to assure him it didn't. Russell racked his brains, searching for the one thing that would help her forget such awkwardness, and settled back on Charley Forsythe. "I wondered what you thought of me talking to Charley—asking what might have made Smythe overreact to his conversing with Edith."

Immediately, she began making plans to do it herself, but mid-sentence, she stopped. "He would likely be more open with you, wouldn't he? Especially if Aunt Louisa is going around town acting as if I'm half-engaged to someone."

"Well, since you *aren't half*-engaged to anyone, I think you're perfectly within your prerogative to say as much, but no, I think Charley would be more likely to open up to a man—especially over a game of billiards."

"That is true." She sank back onto the swing seat and sighed. "Would you? I know it is probably distasteful to you, but if he knows *anything*...."

"It might take me a few days—a week or more. But I'll do it. I want it as natural as possible, so he doesn't feel like he's been primed and pumped."

Her eyes met his and he saw it—*his* Madeline. Not the girl made uncomfortable by meddlesome busybody aunts, but the one who didn't care what others said or did—the one who cared only for what was right and good. "Thank you. Now, if you could please make my guilt vanish, I'd be just fine."

"Guilt?"

Her toes walked her backward before she swung forward again. "I've become a terrible liar, Russell! The stories I've told—the things I've had to do to make as many of those as true as possible. If I'm to discover the truth about Mr. Smythe's character, I can't do it at the expense of my own."

That he didn't know how to answer. When nothing came to mind, Russell said the only thing he could think of—and the one thing he knew would likely drive a wedge between them again. "I'll pray about it, Maddie. I'll look at the Bible and see what I can find. It's the best I can do."

But her reply surprised him—surprised and humbled him. Madeline nodded, flashed a genuine smile, and thanked him. "I knew you'd know what to do."

$\mathcal{T}$WENTY-$\mathcal{S}$EVEN

After a week of looking forward to a relaxing Saturday afternoon and evening party by the pond, Madeline found herself standing at the parlor window, watching the deluge that Mary insisted on calling "a little rain." Jimmy Higgins, unable to hoe their garden or do any of the other outdoor work, stood on a stepladder in the dining room, cleaning the wires that ran to the light fixture. Cook did the week's baking. Her father, however, Madeline hadn't seen all day.

It hasn't been that long since I would have gone out and swung in the rain. Of course, at nineteen, one cannot indulge in such foolishness. Someone could come calling, and oh, the rumors that would fly! Papa's career — destroyed in a moment of carefree frivolity. I do believe age is the most malefic entity women must endure. First, in arriving before we're ready for it, and then piling on us, year after year, until we drown in it.

The doorbell rang, but Madeline ignored it. Russell was sure to be there, ready to try to cheer her after such a disappointing afternoon, and in a fit of uncharacteristic contrariness, Madeline didn't *want* to be cheered. *Sometimes, a person just wishes to enjoy a few minutes of misery for the sheer novelty of it.*

"Miss Madeline, there's a gentleman to see you."

She didn't move. "Show him in, of course. I'm surprised he didn't waltz in with a—"

"I can waltz if you like, but I will look rather silly dancing alone,

269

don't you think?"

Madeline whirled and stared at the picture of Henry Hardwick standing in the center of the parlor, one arm in an arc, the other extended. "Which tune would you prefer?"

Mary's giggle reached her from the hallway, but Madeline ignored it and urged Henry to sit. "I thought you were Russell, here to scold me for begrudging the farmers the rain. I'm sure it's most appreciated by someone, anyway."

"I wouldn't imagine he'd be available to play reprover this early in the day." Henry seated himself—in her favorite place, no less—and urged her to sit as well. "Then again, I have noticed that he is often free to join our little amusements at times most working men are not. He must have a very understanding employer."

Or, perhaps you miss the obvious answer. He works long into the night after our frolics have ended. If Amy only knew the trials she puts him through to keep me entertained.

"He's highly regarded at his firm, so I don't imagine they find his work lacking."

"I would expect no less. My aunt implied that you have a very *close* relationship with him."

Twice Madeline adjusted herself in her seat, a weak attempt to hide her irritation, and redirected the conversation to less unnerving topics, but Henry just as easily circumvented it. A more direct diversion became essential to a peaceful conversation. "Would you care for tea, Henry? I believe Cook also made tarts today. She might be persuaded to part with one or two."

She saw it in his eyes—amusement and something else. It took half a dozen seconds to identify it. *You are disappointed. You take my diversions as a sign of... my secret affection for Russell, perhaps? You might learn to look at people with a little less presupposed mystery. Anyone knows my affection for him. But you imagine it to be something much more than it is, and that's where your creativity overrides your observational skills.*

"Madeline?"

"Oh, yes. Tea. I'll be back in a moment."

How she managed to escape before he spoke again, she didn't know, but after her disaster of a proposal in recent months, Madeline saw the signs of budding interest much clearer than she had before. *You're a pleasant young man, Henry, but I still haven't determined if you have a sincere, devout faith, or if you are the self-important orthoprax I suspect you to be.*

Minutes later, she found him relaxed and reading the *Christian Endeavor. Oh, my. He must have brought that with him. We certainly never subscribed to it.*

"Interesting reading?" The moment she asked, Madeline regretted it. *You know better! What has gotten into you?*

"There's an article on eschatology that I found fascinating. I tucked it away in my pocket for reading on the trolley, but I had such a nice conversation with a man there, that I never opened it."

Madeline pounced on those words in a desperate attempt to divert the conversation once again. "And what did you discuss with this man?"

"Sabbath keeping. I've been studying it." He accepted his cup of tea and gave her a smile she knew all too well. "You're looking exceptionally lovely today, Madeline."

She swallowed an ungracious retort and gave him the merest hint of a smile. "Thank you."

"Have you an opinion on keeping a Sabbath?"

"I don't, no." Though still overfull from lunch, Madeline served herself a tart and held her fork ready to eat a bite should the conversation grow more tiresome than it already had.

Henry began explaining his "investigation" into the intricacies of Judaic Sabbath keeping as compared with modern practices in the Christian church. "It seems to me that we do a poor imitation of the Jewish adherence to the law. Either it is an example for us to follow, or something we are free from with the law fulfilled. Is our salvation

271

the *true* Sabbath rest, or do we observe a Sabbath as a reminder of what the Lord did, does, and will do for us?"

On he rambled, until Madeline's head began to ache from the constant drone. *I now see the little boy he once was, now. He's much improved. No one could doubt it. But here in this fustian monologue, I cannot but wish him gone from here.*

A slow smile formed. *Oh, Russell. I have thought you might consider him the perfect candidate for a better offer, but I am afraid that, should one come* — Madeline couldn't help but send a plea in the negative winging its way heavenward — *it won't receive much more favor than the first.*

Quiet — the kind she'd longed for and now dreaded — broke her from her thoughts. Madeline looked up at Henry, determined to preempt any romantic silliness and found him gazing at her with such earnestness that it drove all sensible thought from her mind.

"Madeline, do you never think that life with someone who shared your passion for the Lord and His teachings would be the closest thing to heaven we will ever find on earth?"

Much to her dismay and disgust, Madeline choked on her tart.

Never had a day felt quite as long. Madeline read by the light of a lamp on the parlor sofa and tried to enjoy the rain splashing against the window. *Perhaps if Papa were home.*

At that moment, the doorbell rang, and Madeline dragged herself to the front of the house to answer it. Mary skittered toward her, saw her crossing the foyer, and dashed back to the kitchen again. *Perhaps that means they're making ice cream. That would be a refreshing change. And if this is Henry again, I could always dump mine on his head if he begins his baptized sentimental nonsense all over again.*

Russell stood under the portico, shaking out an umbrella and looking quite pleased with himself, despite his bedraggled appearance. When he didn't step inside, Madeline grabbed his coat sleeve and tugged him into the entryway. "Whatever made you come out in this?"

He reached into his suit coat and withdrew a letter. "I received news from Amy today. I don't believe she's received our letters yet, but someone has been writing her."

And you would come out in the rain to share with me. It's who you are. But I see it in your eyes. You are predisposed to scold me tonight. I wonder what I've done now.

Despite her misgivings, Madeline busied herself making Russell comfortable. She brought him hot coffee, a warmed-over tart, and her father's spare slippers. "Your feet must be soaked."

Russell watched her as she carted off his shoes to the kitchen where the heat of the stove might dry them faster, and he watched her as she tidied the parlor with nervous energy she couldn't explain. "Madeline...."

"So, you've had a letter?"

"And you've had another offer." Had she not been listening with a keen ear for every tonal inflection, Madeline still couldn't have missed the flat tone.

Well, if you've guessed, then you must have wished for me to find Henry more congenial than I think I can.

"Maddie?"

She turned to face him. "I have not. Thankfully, Henry Hardwick has more sense than to offer *marriage* after such a short acquaintance. One cannot say as much for other men."

"Well, I can see *something* happened with Henry."

But Madeline chose to ignore the implied question and asked one of her own. "Why is it that knowing *you* have a deep faith encourages me the more I think of it, but Henry's ever-increasing fanaticism revolts at every occasion?"

"I would hope," Russell said after consideration of her question.

"I would hope you know me well enough to see how I live it. Henry can only *tell* you about his until you've known him longer and he's grown comfortable in it himself."

He speaks sense, but I cannot hope to understand Henry anyway. Madeline seated herself beside him and folded her hands in her lap. "Will you read Amy's letter to me? It's not quite as wonderful as hearing Amy's voice would be, but it's a pleasant substitute."

She hadn't fooled him. Madeline could see that, but Russell unfolded it, hesitated, and after her reassurances that she much preferred hearing him read it, began from the beginning.

Dearest Russell,

Greetings from Rome! The world feels smaller with each city. However, at the same time, it feels even larger. I wish you were here to take me to the Colosseum and St. Peter's. Why didn't you come again? I think being an architect would have meant you would have <u>wanted</u> to see the beauty of these magnificent buildings.

Madeline's last letter was full of stories about everyone in our set, but there was little of herself. Is she well? You are visiting her, aren't you? May I remind you that you promised not to leave her alone? With Mr. Brown busy with his new position as mayor, she'll be so lonely. Flossie and Edith are dears, but Madeline needs companionship with an interesting and clever conversationalist.

We both know what happened the last time you were away on business. My dear brother, do not force me to abandon this tour and come home to take you to task for failing your duty to my friend. Nee, <u>our</u> friend. I can almost see her accepting someone like Delbert Jackson in order to dull the pain of boredom.

While on the subject of Madeline, I must bring another matter to your attention. You see, our mail preceded us, and I received a very concerned letter from Stella. She intimated that there is some animosity toward Madeline over some visit to the Dry Docks quarter? Why would Madeline go to such an unpleasant place? It's shocking!

Russell paused and smiled at her. "Can you imagine what Stella must have written?" His voice scaled an octave. "'Oh, Amy, dear. Madeline wandered into the Dry Docks. I'm positive we'll never get the stench out of her hair. Do come home from your unimportant little trip and give her something to amuse her again.'"

The irritation that had welled up in her heart dissolved as Russell spoke. Madeline leaned back, closed her eyes, and sighed. "Read the rest. Poor, Amy. I must write her immediately, of course."

Do you know if she has kept up with the junior league and our other committees? There should be projects enough to keep her occupied and out of trouble. If you would take the time to visit of an evening, or take her for a walk or drive on a Saturday night. For pity's sake, play that horrible chess with her! But to read Stella's account, Madeline is destroying her reputation!

Then again, this is Stella, and we all know how she cannot keep her own counsel. She does tend to talk and then exaggerate. I only recount this in case this is one of those times that the story is mostly accurate. If she is consumed by her usual histrionics, then have a laugh with Madeline at my expense and still visit more. I sense she says little of herself because she's lonely.

There is so much to tell you – the things I've seen! However, my love for Maddie spurs me to post this immediately. I will write again in a day or two. Perhaps, by then, I will have finally heard from one or the other of you.

All my love,

Amy

The room became enveloped in one of those delightful silences that turn a house into a home. Madeline hated to break it, but Russell seemed to have no such scruples. "She sounds happy."

"Except for the part where I've scandalized the town with my forays into the seedier side of life."

Madeline felt his hesitation. She tried to find something to say that would reassure him of her intention to keep herself safe, but Russell reached for her hand and held it fast. "You know I wouldn't presume to say what you should or shouldn't do."

"You've never hesitated in the past." Her joke snuffed itself out before she finished speaking it.

"Well, I'm asking you now — not *telling*, asking. Next time you're tempted to investigate something that seems strange to you, please reconsider."

A joke — one about how he feared the wrath of Amy, should anything happen to her — sprang to her lips, but a choke chain jerked it back when she saw the earnestness in his eyes. Again she conceived a bit of teasing about his mothering skills. It too refused to vocalize. Instead, she squeezed his hand and nodded. "I promise."

The moment held — much longer than she would have expected, but at last Russell nodded and released her hand. He folded the letter, pocketed it, and stood. Madeline expected him to go — why, she couldn't say, but instead, he carried the chess table across the room and set it before her. "Amy did say we should play more chess...."

$\mathcal{T}$WENTY-$\mathcal{E}$IGHT

Fans fluttered in frantic unison all over the church and did little more than ensure the even distribution of unpleasant body odors. Madeline fiddled with her handkerchief and tried to listen, but it had the irrational and improbable tendency to muffle the minister's voice as he droned on about the duties of Christians. Flies buzzed about and somehow the constant sound, combined with the heat and the monotonic quality of the minister's voice, produced a soporific spell over the entire congregation.

" — the least of which is forgiveness. Our Lord demonstrated forgiveness in every moment of His ministry. Can we forget the words of our Lord to the woman at the well? 'Go and sin no more'? Can we forget His graciousness to the woman caught in the very act of adultery? 'He who is without sin'? And then, of course His gracious love to us, that while 'we were yet sinners' He died for *our* sins."

The words reverberated in Madeline's mind as she struggled to remain awake. *"He who is without sin." "Go and sin no more." "Woman caught in adultery." "Woman with five husbands...."*

Her eyes slid up two rows and to the left, where Edith sat between her father and Vernon Smythe. *I wonder at you, Edith. What do you see in him? He can be charming; it is true. When it suits him. And he is quite handsome. He is obviously an intelligent man.* Her forehead furrowed until she had to make a conscious effort to relax again. *Then why have I always found him so unpleasant?*

That question startled her. Until that moment, Madeline hadn't been aware she'd always disliked the man. Once more, she felt her forehead wrinkle as she tried to recall what had set her against him—and how she hadn't noticed it. *He does remind me a bit of Mr. Bennett's assessment of Wickham. "He simpers and smirks and makes love to us all." Alas, I'm not "prodigiously proud" of him at all.* Her eyes slid sideways just in time to see Edith give Smythe such a caring smile. *But Edith is.*

Another glance that way showed Mr. Merton sitting there without his eyes moving from the front, where minister had begun the wind-down to the final prayer. *But you, even without looking, are most definitely "prodigiously proud" of your daughter's conquest. Is it merited, I wonder?*

Everyone around her bowed heads and the voice of Reverend Whitmore filled the room as he beseeched the Lord for favor and forgiveness for the manifold transgressions of his congregation. So caught off guard was she, that Madeline nearly snickered. *Do you know how manifold they are, Reverend? I can't help but think you are as blind to our faults as we are ourselves.*

However, worse than being trapped in a pew in a stifling building is the impossibility of escape once the permissibility has been granted. With each shuffle of her feet toward the door, Madeline wished herself further and further from humanity in general. She tugged on her father's coat sleeve. "Papa?"

"Yes? Unbearable today, isn't it?"

"It is." She tried to keep her voice as quiet as possible, lest someone overhear and offer to "escort" her. "I think I'll take a long walk home along Kensington, just to enjoy those trees and the shade."

"That sounds lovely. I'd offer to go, but I think I understand you." With a squeeze to her hand, Mayor Brown nodded at a gentleman across the way. "Hugh! I had a question for you."

It worked in ways she'd never grow accustomed to. People

always made a path anywhere her father wished to go. *As if he couldn't possibly wait until* business hours *to do that little thing called... business.*

But once she made it to Hugh Jacobson's side, Madeline saw exactly what he'd done. The door was only another ten feet or so, and not a person blocked the path. With a squeeze to his arm and a whispered, "I'll see you at home, Papa," she strode from the building.

Once outside, she hurried down the sidewalk. For a moment, she thought she heard someone call her name, but Madeline ducked around the corner, hid behind a large shrub, and when a repeat call didn't come, she took off toward the beautiful tree-lined street otherwise known as Kensington Avenue.

A message came for her early Monday morning. The words — simple. *Please visit the office at your earliest convenience. Rodney Flint.*

In half the time it usually took, Madeline dressed, popped her bowler atop her head, and flew down the stairs. "Have you a biscuit, Mary?"

"A — oh, no. You need a proper breakfast, Miss Madeline. Now it's sitting at the table, and Cook'll have my hide if you don't eat it."

It had been years — a decade perhaps — since Madeline had felt the temptation to bolt her food, but she not only felt it, she succumbed. It took less than three minutes to eat her soft boiled egg, toast and jam, and small slice of ham. "It was delicious as usual!" Madeline called the words out just as she opened the door to leave. She flew down the steps and out to the sidewalk. She didn't quite know what to expect, but her mind whirled at the possibilities before her as she waited impatiently for the trolley.

Nervous energy drove her to the next stop — and the next. At last, near the third, she rushed to meet it before it took off without her and she was forced to walk the rest of the way into town. Once more, Madeline seated herself across from the bicycle advertisement and tried to imagine if she would enjoy having the freedom of quick locomotion without the inconvenience of waiting for trolleys. *I would think it would be a fine thing. No one would consider it untoward. Everyone has a wheel these days. But....*

A familiar man climbed aboard and his eyes met hers. *What are you doing here?*

Once seated beside her, the man waited until the trolley jerked forward and then murmured, "Been waitin' to talk to you. Are you ready for th' information?"

"I thought you assured me you would find me when I wished to meet with you."

"I did."

"Well...." Madeline stared ahead at the trolley operator, waiting to be certain they couldn't be overheard before she turned to face him. "Well, I'm afraid I have little confidence in your ability to deliver. I most certainly didn't wish to meet with you right now, yet here you are."

All the way to her destination, off the trolley, down the street, and into Mr. Flint's office, Madeline reveled in the satisfaction of putting a man she felt certain to be of dubious character in his place. Mr. Flint rose to offer her a seat—a good sign, she thought. Alas, when he seated himself, his expression gave him away.

"I'm afraid I cannot give you the information you sought. We have found and followed the man half a dozen times. We've conversed with him on three separate occasions. He either knew you came here and is careful, or he is guiltless of anything too nefarious."

Madeline pulled out her pocketbook and reached inside. "I suspected as much, especially since he approached me just a little while ago."

The man's eyes narrowed. "You do realize," he said at last,

"that it is... *concerning* to have someone so intimately acquainted with your movements."

"Of course, I do. I'm not a fool, despite my inability to shake the constraints of my sex and position in this town."

"I wouldn't have implied otherwise. I just..." Mr. Flint shrugged and nodded. "I concede your point. It was a bit condescending. Unfortunately, I can find nothing about this man that even hints at him being anything other than someone who has lived in Rockland almost since birth. He has little family left, and a few money troubles, but nothing severe enough to cause undue concern."

Madeline stood and rolled a few coins in her hand. "What do I owe you, Mr. Flint?"

"For the amount of inquiries we had to make, the fee is ten dollars."

She counted out several coins, passed them across the desk, and turned to go. "I appreciate the significant discount; however you do make it difficult for me to feel free to return. Is that deliberate, I wonder?"

Without waiting to hear a reply, Madeline stepped through the office door and into the waiting room. To her relief, he didn't call her back as she opened the door to the street. *That would have been most awkward. It's one thing to hire a hawkshaw, but another to be in his debt.*

As she passed the window of a large toy store, a reflection caught her attention. Madeline ducked inside and beckoned a shop clerk to the window. "That doll there. Is it German?"

With the eagerness of someone whose livelihood depends on each sale he makes, the clerk rhapsodized about the maker — French, of course — and their superiority to the Germans in the doll making world. Madeline nodded at all the right inflections, asked about the cloth of the dress, but all the while, she watched the man across the street. The man in a bowler with a checkered suit, stood speaking to the very person she'd just paid Flint a few pennies to investigate.

Her heart quickened as she saw something exchange hands. It

seemed… yes, the way the man examined it and put it in his pocket implied that Mr. Checkered Suit had given the man money. *You won't be offering me information anytime soon. You were either paid to do so, or you're being paid to stay away now. Either way –*

" – wrap it up for you?"

"Why yes, of course. Thank you." The moment she spoke, Madeline groaned inwardly. *Of course, you would purchase a doll. What has gotten into you?*

And at the counter, when she pulled out her pocketbook, Madeline found herself even more chagrined. "I'm afraid if I'm to take the doll, I'll have to ask you to deliver it to my father's office and present him the bill." With an apologetic smile, she explained. "I fear I've just given away my last dollar. I don't know what I was thinking!"

"Where is your father's office, miss?" She could see it – hear it in his voice. The young man didn't believe the bill would be paid.

"City hall – the mayor's office. Just ask for Mayor Brown and tell him his daughter Madeline sends her love and apologies for, once again, overspending her allowance."

As she turned to go, the young man asked if she wouldn't rather take the doll with her. "We can send the bill by courier later. There's no reason – "

"Oh, but Papa will so love to see what I've purchased. Do add delivery to the bill, won't you?"

And with that, Madeline stepped from the store. She paused, nodded at the man across the street, tipped her hat, and strolled uptown with a carefree gait that belied the excitement welling in her. *Something's coming. I just know it.*

TWENTY-NINE

Mary knocked on Madeline's door as she dressed for dinner and carried in a familiar envelope. "Telegram, Miss Madeline. I do hope it isn't bad news."

Madeline took the missive and opened it with a churning in her stomach. The contents, however, proved less disastrous and more interesting than she'd expected.

HAVE LEARNED OF VERNON SMYTHE'S ATTACHMENT TO EDITH MERTON. PLEASE CONTACT WMS & SONS IN CHICAGO FOR IMPORTANT INFORMATION. LETTER TO FOLLOW. M. SEMPLETON

"So, Amy has run into the Sempletons on their honeymoon. And Michael has sent information regarding Mr. Smythe via letter? Or is the information only through this office of Williams & Sons, I wonder."

"Yes, miss?"

She turned to Mary and promised to be down in a moment. "Is Papa home yet?"

"He is. He said something about inviting Mr. Barnes, but I didn't understand him. I *think* he meant to say that Mr. Barnes couldn't come for dinner, but he would be here later." Mary paused at the door. "Should we delay dessert for him, do you think?"

Madeline gave her skirt a final tug, tucked the telegram into the pocket, and followed Mary downstairs. "Do that. If I find Russell *is* coming, I'll let you know. And thank you."

A glance in the dining room showed only two places set. Her father appeared in the hall before she could reach his office. "Did you say that Russell *is* or is not joining us for dinner? Mary wasn't confident in your answer."

"He said he likely won't be out of his consultation before then. I told him we'd wait dessert, though." Albert rubbed his rotund belly and winked at her. "It will leave me more room for a larger piece of cake if we delay an hour or two."

All through dinner, Madeline fought the temptation to share the contents of the telegram. She wanted her father's opinion, of course, but he might be predisposed to forbid further inquiry, or worse—do it himself. *I can just hear the response. "Oh, you say he is not the gentleman he pretends to be? He drinks spirits and attends vaudeville acts? I see. Well, thank you for your insights."*

The moment those thoughts filled her mind, Madeline flushed with embarrassment. *You've grown acrimonious in your "old age."*

"I think it is over-warm in here tonight. Should we sit outside, do you think?"

"Warm?" She stood and opened a window. "Is that better, Papa?"

Albert eyed her with curiosity and then amusement. "I spoke because of your reddened cheeks, but now I wonder if they aren't because of my mention of Russell." He watched her with the eye of a father most desirous for his child's greatest happiness. "Have you grown... *fond* of our favorite guest?"

Heart racing, cheeks flaming, Madeline shook her head with a decided snap to it. She stared at the empty plate before her and protested with unguarded vehemence. "I'd say not, Father! I am fond of him, of course," she conceded when Albert coughed, as if dubious at her excessive denial. "But he has been the brother I've never had. I can't imagine thinking of him—or truly, any man—with such *personal* feelings."

Madeline raised her eyes, determined to put an end to any meddling her father might do if he thought his little girl appeared to have romantic interests, and found herself staring into Russell's amused, twinkling ones. "Oh, good evening...." She swallowed hard. "Russell."

Her father's eyes widened and his face drooped. An apologetic whisper preceded his overly effusive welcome. "Aaah! You are finally here. We were just talking of you. I was about to ask Madeline when your sister would return and release you from your... duties as Madeline's... companion?" He mopped at his forehead with his napkin and stood. "I'm sorry, but the heat in here really is quite intolerable. I'll ask Mary to serve dessert outside."

Russell moved to her side to hold her chair for her as she rose. She turned to him and barely stifled a snicker. "Your timing, Russell...."

"I cannot decide whether to be relieved that you are not eager to 'snag' me as a husband, or relieved that you have no thoughts in other directions either."

"Both, perhaps?"

He offered his arm with exaggerated fanfare. "Perhaps." As she took it, he nudged her toward the doorway. "Shall we join your father?"

With a quick glance around her to ensure Albert wouldn't return, Madeline reached into her pocket. "First, would you look at this?"

Russell took the telegram and read it. "Chicago...." A slow smile formed as he read it once more. "It seems you had the right idea in taking a trip there after all. And, had you continued, you might not still be hiding that bruise."

"It doesn't hurt much anymore!"

He returned the telegram and led her toward the doorway. "No? Only when you forget and cross your ankles in your usual fashion."

285

"Well! Look who has turned detective!" They stepped out into the night, and Madeline had to concede that, despite some mugginess in the air, the breeze was far cooler and the air more temperate than inside. "Why, Papa, I think you are positively brilliant. I didn't expect much difference at all, but it is truly lovely out tonight. And the fireflies are sending their little love notes to one another already!"

Normally, such a comment would have been of no consequence, but after being caught discussing her heart—or rather, the lack of any flutterings in it—the words seemed excessively flirtatious. She turned from the table and strolled out into the grass. "Or so they say. Such a silly turn of phrase, don't you think?"

Of all the things she could have done, Madeline realized that this was the *last* she should have considered. Russell followed her, of course, and her father jumped up from his seat. "I just remembered that I'm supposed to receive some important papers to peruse. I'll eat my dessert in my study. You two have a nice evening. If you play chess, I would like to see the final moves."

She watched his retreating back with both eagerness and dismay. "Oh, bother! Now he will suppose we have some sort of secret understanding. How could I have been so foolish?!"

"You will show him the nature of your heart—sometime in the next year or three, surely? I imagine when you've lived so many years alone, all your romantic leanings tend to pile up until you can't help but allow them to spill over onto your only child."

Madeline turned to Russell and searched his face for some hint to his meaning. "You think Papa has been lonely all these years?" Her forehead furrowed, despite her aunt's admonitions never to allow it to happen. "*It'll spoil your complexion, my dear. Dreadful wrinkles....*"

But before Russell could answer, her shoulders drooped. Unexpected and uncharacteristic tears sprang to her eyes. "Oh, how could I have been so blind? Why hasn't he remarried?"

"Perhaps he has no desire to. Some men love once. Would it be right for him to marry someone else with his heart still devoted to your mother — presuming that is the case, of course?"

Once more, she gazed back up at Russell, searching his face for some answer as she questioned him further. "Do?" She blinked. "Do you think men really do that? I somehow imagined that a more feminine accomplishment — that fatalistic — "

"Don't, Madeline. It isn't that at all." He shook his head as Madeline began to pounce on those words. "No, I *don't* know. But I can imagine. And I think that if I were in his shoes, and if I hadn't been able to let go of my previous love, it wouldn't be out of some sentimental, fatalistic nonsense. It would be because I had been so content with what I had that no one else could tempt me."

They strolled toward the back garden, and her arm slipped through his once more. "I recall the day I overheard him talking to Aunt Louisa. She wanted me to go off to the east somewhere for further schooling. Wherever it was, it had an excellent program in elocution. A perfect science for the daughter of a man with political aspirations at the time, is it not?"

"I believe I remember that. He came to talk with Mother and Father about it one evening. Mother was decidedly against it."

I hadn't realized that. Madeline sighed. "You should have heard him, Russell. His voice cracked, I know he was crying, and I couldn't even go to him." She gave him a saucy smile. "I wasn't supposed to be listening, of course."

"Of course." Russell steered them in a nice U and led her back toward the house. "So, what did he say that still has you so upset?"

"He said, 'She's all I have left of Lily, Louisa. How can you ask this of me?'"

Russell's hand covered hers as they strolled up to the table where pieces of cake waited for them. "Madeline?" He held her chair. "I hope you don't believe your father doesn't wish for you to marry yourself...."

"Of that, I am certain!" She smirked at him. "I wish you could have seen the absolute delight in his eyes when he decided I was mooning over you at the table. He most certainly does *not* think I should remain a spinster to cater to his whims."

The conversation had grown uncomfortable again. Despite Russell's apparent lack of offense at her indifference to his reputed charms, Madeline decided she preferred a less personal discussion. "So, if the letter doesn't come in the next few days, what would you think of me taking a day trip to Chicago — to speak to this Williams and Sons?"

He stiffened as he seated himself. "That could be a dangerous proposition." When she protested, he leaned forward and stole her fork. "Please, Maddie. If you go, allow me to go with you. I don't know what Sempleton was doing sending a message like that. He had to know that you would want to investigate. And this just sounds dangerous."

She gazed at the fork before plucking it from his hand again. "Has Amy mentioned the Sempletons?"

"Not that I recall."

"Could you send her a telegram? Ask if she has seen them? Perhaps if she's mentioned Edith's engagement?" The moment she asked, Madeline realized how foolish she sounded. "Never mind. The expense...."

"Is worth it if Smythe is unsavory. But the telegram doesn't give enough information to say *why* there is information, if you should retrieve it, or wait for the letter. One could *infer*...."

"But one doesn't like to." Madeline nodded. "But still, an international wire...."

"I'll do it first thing tomorrow if you promise to notify me before you hop a train to Chicago."

Against every instinct, Madeline nodded. "I promise." She jabbed her fork in the direction of his cake. "This really is the fluffiest thing she's ever baked. It's like eating chocolate air!"

With Russell successfully distracted, Madeline took another bite of her cake and smiled to herself. *I did not, however, promise when I would inform you or how. If a messenger takes off for your office at the same time I climb aboard, well....*

"I'd prefer to know in time to join you if you decide to go."

Madeline's eyes flew up to meet his. "Honestly, Russell! You are almost prescient sometimes!"

"I know Madeline Brown better than she thinks. She isn't so difficult to read if you know how."

At that, Madeline choked on her cake.

$\mathcal{T}$HIRTY

After the third pass up and down Waterbrook, Madeline hailed a taxicab and asked for him to take her to the nearest street to the Dry Docks area that she imagined the man being willing to go. He turned and eyed her with alarm. "Are you certain? That's getting near a rough area, miss."

"If you would prefer, I could find another—"

"I'll take you." With a second glance back at her, he clucked his tongue in his cheek and the horse jerked them forward.

Her plan—still undecided. She knew what she *wanted* to do, but desire does not ensure gratification. *If one can pay a certain kind of woman for certain kinds of favors, perhaps she might accept payment for other, less... unsavory ones.*

So, with that idea in mind, Madeline paid her driver and strolled up the street and around the corner. The rapid clip-clop of a horse's hooves hinted that the driver might have followed, so Madeline ducked into a rather miserable-looking tearoom. *An establishment such as this should, at the least, be clean....*

A man in an ill-fitting suit and with effeminate manner stepped forward and offered to seat her. Madeline offered an apologetic smile and stepped back toward the door. "I'm sorry. I just...." The memory of the recent ease with which she fabricated stories to suit her purpose stopped her from yet another foray into falsehoods. "Didn't want someone to see me. I'll remember your establishment if I am down here and in need of refreshment, though. Thank you."

Before he could try to importune her to stay, Madeline hurried from the room and up the street again. With every step, it seemed as if the world became a much more drab, dreary, dirty place. *How do people survive here?*

Boys, running from a paunchy man with a filthy beard and leaving a stream of harsh words in his wake, nearly knocked her down, but Madeline managed to hop out of the way just in time. Wagons rattled past and splashed mud that barely missed her skirts. Still, Madeline charged forward, determined to find the woman she'd spoken to again. *If I can just inquire....*

The morning passed, and Madeline grew weary and thirsty, but still she trudged onward. Twice, a barrel of water tempted her, but seeing the sorts of people who stopped to dip a drink stopped her. *Why have I never considered that at the train station?*

Just as thirst nearly drove her to take just a small drink, she saw someone—the young woman Vernon Smythe had so intimately led into what she could only imagine was an establishment of ill repute. Madeline scurried across the street. The young woman, pretty enough and dressed in clean clothes at least, stared in horror as Madeline rushed up to her. "Oh, can you help me?"

"I—"

"I've been wandering around here for hours. I'm so tired and thirsty, but every time I think I've found my way out, I end up right back here." She dug into her purse. "I'll *pay* you if you'll—"

But the young woman drew back. "You don't want to be seen with me, miss. People might think—you just don't."

"Please, if you're helping me, of course I wouldn't be ashamed to be seen with you." Even as she spoke, Madeline's mind whirled with possibilities. The most direct won out over more complicated things that could be derailed by the young woman becoming spooked. "I should never have come, of course. But I saw a man I know and tried to follow him. Then he just disappeared!"

"It ain't hard to do in here, miss. People what know the place could stay hidden for days if'n they wanted to."

That's an interesting bit of information. I wonder if Mr. Smythe is aware of it. That thought solidified her plan. "I just don't know why Vernon would be down here at all."

By the way the young woman started and tried to repress a gasp, Madeline knew she'd found the right woman. Her new plan became paramount in that moment. "Oh, do you know Vernon? Vernon Smythe? Perhaps you know where he is? I'm sure he'd see me home and save you the hassle."

She slipped her arm through her new companion's and smiled. "What is your name? I—"

"Abby, miss. But you can't walk like this. And I don't think Vernon is here today. He said—" As she broke off the sentence, Abby turned away from her. "I should go."

"But if you're a friend of Vernon's, surely we should know each other, too. Have you been friends long?"

It took some time—almost to the far outskirts of the Dry Docks, but Abby opened up to her. "We're engaged, you see. He has promised t' marry me so many times, but somethin' allus prevents it. He'll say, 'We'll go on Friday,' but then business or somethin' takes 'im away agin."

Oh, the dilemma of choosing between immediate disclosure and further investigation! Madeline considered every angle as she slowly drew out the girl's confidence. They reached the tearoom the moment she reached a decision. "Abby, I like you. You seem such a sweet girl, and I wouldn't want you hurt."

"Thanks, miss. You're awf'lly nice."

"Now, Vernon isn't exactly pleased with me right now. He thinks I'm interfering in his business affairs." She shook her head. "I'm not, of course. I just want to understand them. But you know how men are. They always think we're incapable of understanding more than how to arrange our hair or press a fine crease."

293

Abby nodded with an understanding smile. "That's how he is when I asks about 'is work. He says, 'Abby, don' you worry your pretty head about it none.'"

I doubt he tacks on that unnecessary "none", but otherwise, I can just hear him say it, too. She pulled a quarter from her pocketbook and pressed it into the girl's hand. "I promised to pay you for taking me out of there, and I keep my word."

"It ain't—"

"It most certainly *is* necessary. My papa would not think well of a daughter who didn't keep her word. Now, I'm going to make a few inquiries and then I'll come back to see you. I'll have a boy find you for me, though. I wouldn't want to get lost again!"

The horror in Abby's face at hearing Madeline intended to return, dissolved at the promise of sending a boy. "That would be best."

"But if you would just keep our meeting a secret for such a short time." Madeline pretended to duck her head. "I wouldn't want to encourage you to hide things from your fiancé for long. It wouldn't be right."

"No'm."

Madeline squeezed the girl's hand. "But a short-term secret to ensure everyone's happiness. Surely, that isn't inappropriate."

And without much effort at all, Abby walked back into the depths of the Dry Docks after promising not to say a word of their meeting. Madeline strolled toward town, her eyes on a constant lookout for her checkered shadow, but the man never showed himself. *Are you feeling under the weather today, or have you decided to try not to be visible?*

The six-ten train to Chicago rolled into Union Station at twelve-fifteen. Madeline and Russell bustled off the train and found themselves swept up in the sea of passengers eager to make it to the taxicab stands out front. "There's such energy here." She smiled up at him. "If I didn't love Rockland so much, I would be inclined to reconsider my rejection of a profession and take up some secretarial course, or perhaps accept Mr. Fl—" She swallowed the name and pointed. "That one. It's a bit further, but perhaps if we dash...."

Russell grabbed her hand and helped weave her through the passengers looking to find something closer to the front. The cabbie grinned and welcomed them. "Smart of you. Must be seasoned trav'lers. Most folks waits for us to move up in the line."

"We're looking for some kind of firm—Williams and Sons. I only know that they're somewhere on Carroll Avenue." He glanced at Madeline. "Or, at least that's what I've been told."

"I'll find it for ya. If there's somethin' I'm good at, it's findin' places."

As they rode through the streets in search of the elusive Williams and Sons, Madeline thanked Russell once more. "Once this is over, I can repay you for the fare and this ride. I just didn't like to ask Papa.."

"Let's just see if your concerns have merit. You still haven't told me what precipitated this trip."

"Why, I thought—"

Russell's shaking head cut her off. "Sorry, Madeline, but our discussion left a visit open ended, and two days later, we're in Chicago?" He chuckled. "It's just fortuitous that I worked extra all last week. My employer was happy to allow me a day off."

When she didn't reply, his laughter filled the taxicab. "You counted on me not being able to go, didn't you?"

"Well, I did think a young man who is trying to make his mark on a company might not be at liberty to take a frolicsome trip to Chicago on the whim of his little sister's bosom friend."

The cabbie broke through their conversation. "Sir, I think I knows someone ahead who kin tell me where to go. You might want to hold on."

They had less than a second to grip the handles before the cab zipped forward and around another one. He wove through the streets at such speeds that Madeline ached to call out, "Faster!" However, a glance at Russell hinted it might not be a good idea. The man looked ready to shout for the cabbie to slow down. "He knows what he's doing. Papa says there are no better drivers than the taxi drivers in Chicago and New York City."

"If he overturns us...."

"Won't do it, sir. That I kin promise." The words came shouted back at twice the volume necessary.

And then it happened. He pulled up beside another taxicab, shouted a question across the way, and nodded at the reply. Seconds later, he urged the horse down one street and up another. "We're almost there. Sorry for the deeter."

They'd arrived at the proper building before Madeline translated the word. *Oh, detour. His speech is... unique. Reminds me a little of Abby's yesterday.*

Russell helped her from the taxicab and would have sent the man on his way, but she stepped forward. "Can you wait? We shouldn't be long. I'm famished, though."

"I kin getcha to a fine place to eat. I'll jest wait right here."

Russell hurried her inside before stopping and staring down at her. "Are you *trying* to get us killed?"

"I'm trying to reward someone who found what we needed in a timely fashion." Madeline pointed to a sign that marked the Williams and Sons office on the fourth floor. "And look, there's an elevator. I think our City Hall could use one. It would make carrying things from floor to floor so much easier. Why, I saw them carrying a desk up the stairs the other day. Someone is going to get hurt!"

All the way upstairs, Madeline chattered about the kinds of inventions she'd heard of. "Why, it's only a matter of time before we manage to create a way to fly. Can you imagine looking overhead and seeing someone gliding down from the sky to stop and purchase a pound of sugar?"

"It isn't likely, Madeline." As he spoke, the elevator rumbled its way up the shaft. "While I don't doubt the possibility — even the *probability* — of flight, I doubt we'll use it to do things so mundane. It would be more likely that we would fly from Rockland to Chicago for this trip. What took six hours by train might only take three or four in the air — with no stops and the potential for the wind to aid in achieving higher speeds."

As practical as his words were, Madeline couldn't help but hope that flight would become so simple that it might make the need for trolleys and their unhelpful routes obsolete. The elevator let them out on the fourth floor. Three doors down, an etched glass door with gold lettering announced the firm of Williams and Sons — lawyers. "I wonder why Michael Sempleton would send us to law offices. I had expected private investigators or something of the sort."

Russell opened the door and gestured for her to enter. "Well, let's find out; shall we?"

A young man with ink-stained fingers listened to their mission and asked them to wait. Russell suggested she sit, but Madeline shook her head. "We've been sitting for so long already."

The young man appeared moments later. "Mr. Williams — Senior — will see you. Please come this way."

Walnut paneled walls with built-in bookcases and an enormous desk gave a hint as to the success of the firm. A thin, wizened old man stood, shook their hands, and fumbled through a stack of files before he found the one he wanted. "I expected you after receiving Mr. Sempleton's telegram. Are you...?" The man offered an apologetic smile. "I'm sorry, but I do need some confirmation that you are the intended recipient."

"Madeline Brown. My father is Mayor Brown of Rockland, and this is my friend, Russell Barnes."

"Well, Mr. Barnes isn't mentioned, but I am pleased you were intelligent enough to come with an escort."

Russell stepped a bit closer, and Madeline wondered at it. "We don't exactly know *why* we are here. Perhaps you can enlighten us."

"Did you bring Mr. Sempleton's telegram?"

Her fingers trembled, just a bit, as she fished it out of her pocketbook and passed it across the desk. "He only says you have information for me, but not why or regarding what."

"But you have suspicions?" Though he answered Madeline's question, the man addressed his words to Russell. And in the space of less than a minute, Russell took over the conversation. Madeline murmured a couple of questions, but twice Russell preempted her.

Just how much have you discerned already?

And then it happened. The man slid the contents of the file in a large envelope, wrapped string around it, and passed it to Russell. "I believe the information in here will answer any general questions you may have. Young Edward out there was up half the night copying it for you. I'm pleased he finished before you came."

Less than ten minutes after they entered the building, Madeline and Russell stepped out onto Carroll Avenue — with no sign of their taxicab in sight. "I can't decide if I'm thrilled about the information or irritated at the loss of our driver!"

"Because," Russell teased, "it certainly cannot be both."

THIRTY-ONE

The clock struck eight-thirty just as Russell and Madeline entered the Hardwick parlor that evening. Madeline had taken a moment to change her dress and re-brush her hair, but Russell had insisted he wouldn't have taken the time to change if he'd been at work. "I know how you want to watch Smythe. Why wait for something that'll only attract attention?"

Russell's words had buoyed her spirits right up to the moment that Mrs. Hardwick had opened the door. The knowing look in the woman's eyes nearly inspired a scream of frustration. But Russell's hand gently squeezed her elbow as they moved into the parlor, and it had a surprising, calming effect on her.

"Madeline! We were growing worried!" Though Flossie didn't say it, the question hung in the air. *Why didn't you come alone?*

In the corner, Vernon Smythe stood behind Edith, a smile she couldn't help but feel was sinister growing on his lips. But Edith, with her characteristic sweetness and an extra dose of obtuseness, patted the seat beside her. "Do come tell us what you've been doing that would keep you from us."

"It was a series of diabolical events determined to ruin my evening. I'd regale you with witty stories, but I fear the men don't care about or understand the contrary nature of a woman's hair, or how easily a dress can be spoiled by a spilled drink. Needless to say, Russell saved me from a lonely walk over." A few more eyebrows

299

rose and reminded her of *why* she'd begun the story in the first place. "Shall I tell Amy to give him full marks in the brotherly department for tonight?"

"Well," Flossie announced, "we were just about to begin a game of 'Who Am I?' Would you like to begin?"

Madeline turned to Russell. "You begin for us. I am going to avail myself of a glass of cordial first. The walk...."

Twice, in the space of as many minutes, one of her friends hinted that she'd made quite a conquest in Russell. Stella's murmured, "My mother says he's not 'catchable', and you know she's always right. So for you...." required Madeline to exhibit more self-control than she knew she possessed.

"He's my friend's brother, Stella Wakefield. I should have thought you knew that." The snappish quality of her tone sounded overly offended, even to her ears. "I'm sorry. It's been a long day, and I'm a little tired." When Stella didn't respond, Madeline leaned closer and whispered, "I wouldn't want to place Russell in an uncomfortable position—needing to keep his word to his sister, but people supposing his affection to be greater than it is."

"But—"

"What if he should meet someone he *does* care for in that way." She prayed he'd forgive her and added, "Perhaps Elizabeth Denton? I've always thought he showed particular interest in her."

That's all it took. Stella turned to watch the amusements, her eyes fixated on Russell. A moment later, she whispered. "I think I see it...."

By the time they seated themselves, shouted guesses filled the room. Madeline leaned close to Edith and asked, "What was the last clue?"

Edith shrugged and gazed up at Smythe. "What was it? I didn't hear. Russell's things are always too clever for me."

"I believe...." The intimacy of Smythe's hand on Edith's shoulder, the way he leaned so close his lips could brush her ear, the husky tone of his murmur — Madeline struggled to physically restrain herself from turning and accusing him of everything before the entire room. "I believe it was, 'Of my many inventions, only now is there hope of my favorite being realized.'" Smythe gave Madeline an indulgent look, but the tone beneath his words sent shivers through her. "I don't imagine Miss Brown is adept in the field of inventions. She's far more interested in fairy stories —"

Madeline lost all patience and turned to Russell. "Would that be da Vinci and his flying machine?"

The groans around them told her she'd been correct long before Russell turned and yielded the "floor." "Well done. I should have known, with your fascination with flying, that you would know the answer to that one. Whom will you choose? I wonder."

In her peripheral vision, Madeline saw Smythe stroke Edith's neck with his thumb, and whatever self-control she'd mustered flew out the window. She stood before the room, hands clasped in front of her, and eyed the guests with a saucy smirk on her lips. "I gave all the appearance of honor and none of the evidence of it."

Guesses flew at her, but Madeline shook her head. In the corner, standing just behind and to the side of Smythe and Edith, Russell gave her a look that clearly said, "You are playing with fire, Miss Brown" but instead called out, "I believe we need another clue."

Her eyes flashed at him. "I was trusted with much and faithful in little."

Without a doubt, he knew exactly who her mysterious person was. Russell gave her a slight nod to acknowledge the fine hint she'd left but said nothing. Flossie guessed Brutus. Again. Smythe glared at her.

Ah, so you know whom I mean as well. Well done. "Did you have a guess, Mr. Smythe?"

"I would prefer another clue, I think."

The room echoed the request, but before she could offer it, Edith's nose wrinkled and her voice, confused and predictably vacant-sounding, reached Madeline's ears as she turned to Vernon. "Why, it almost sounds as if she speaks of Judas Iscariot. The biblical reference, you know."

"Well done, Edith!"

Madeline moved to find a seat and found the only open space to be a small chair next to Russell. Several tossed her knowing looks as she seated herself. With fingers fidgeting and a mind whirling with ways to stop the speculation, Madeline didn't hear Edith's first clue. However, since the entire room erupted in the same answer, "George Washington!" she doubted she'd missed much of a challenge.

Twice, Russell answered first. Twice more, he offered his own question. Both times, she could have chosen to answer his riddle, but the constant silent teasing and presumption of understanding by the others quelled any desire she had to join in the fun. After the third time as questioner, Russell bent low when he arrived at her side and whispered, "Since when does Madeline Brown care what others think of her?"

She answered the very next question almost before Henry Hardwick finished asking it. "Why, that would be Alexander the Great, wouldn't it?"

"That's my girl."

She didn't know if she actually *heard* him say it, or if she only felt it, but Madeline smiled anyway. *He's quite right. Why would I allow them to spoil my fun? So silly….*

The evening breeze coming off the river cooled the night air. The Hardwicks enjoyed the blessing of large trees that whispered cooling sweet nothings into the ears of the guests. Madeline stood just outside the door to their terrace and waited for Russell to finish his discussion with Stanley Wakefield. *Please do hurry, Russell. I'm*

truly exhausted.

"Tired?"

Oh, Henry. Don't annoy me tonight. I'm not in sufficient humor to be cordial. Please just go away. Of course, despite her true thoughts on the matter, Madeline said only, "A bit, yes."

He disappeared without another word—something that irrationally annoyed her. But less than a minute later, he arrived with a glass of lemonade with a few strawberries at the bottom. "It'll refresh you while you wait." As she thanked him, Henry moved in front of her. "Madeline, would you allow me to escort you home? There's no reason to wait for Russell if you're tired, and he shouldn't leave if he wishes to talk with Stanley." As if he realized his invitation lacked warmth, Henry added, "You know I enjoy your company, so it is no inconvenience to me—only my pleasure."

Refusal—such a temptation—but coming weeks of obnoxious attentions from a young man she'd already decided should remain merely a general acquaintance would likely prove more than she could bear with grace. *It would be prudent to avert an unpleasant exchange in the future.*

"Madeline?"

She turned a smile his way and passed him her tumbler. "I'll tell Flossie to explain to Russell. He'll likely appreciate *not* having to escort me home and return back to this side of town again." At Henry's delighted reaction, her stomach churned. *He will surmise my purpose, Henry. You haven't bested him by any means.*

"I'll see if we have any carriages available. It would make it faster and more comfortable."

Flossie showed much more excitement about the turn of events than Madeline could have wished for or anticipated. Despite a strong desire to demolish any romantic notions in Flossie's already overly romantic mind, she kept such desires in check. *She'll only think them a diversion to distract her from my purported interest in Henry.*

Bessie, the Hardwick's maid, arrived to inform her that Henry

303

had procured a carriage. "He's driving up to the door, miss."

"Thank you, Bessie. I'll meet him out front and save him the trouble of finding me."

"He don't think it no trouble, miss. I know it." She gave Madeline a sweet, shy smile and skittered off to attend her usual duties.

Oh, dear. When household help know of a guest's personal interests, then it must have been discussed amongst the family. I must not be derailed.

Henry met her halfway up the steps. "I apologize, Madeline. I'd meant to fetch you."

"Well, as I am neither a bone nor a pocketbook or gloves, I think I can do my own 'fetching' if you don't mind." The words, if spoken in a snide tone, would have been rude in the extreme, but with her smile and the teasing quality, they teetered between lighthearted and flirtatious. *Perhaps a mistake....*

"Well, in that, you speak truth. You most certainly are 'fetching,' Madeline."

The groan she stifled might have been better vocalized. *He definitely perceived it to be modest flirtation. Poor choice, Madeline Brown. Very poor choice indeed.*

Henry murmured something about not wishing to be offensive, and Madeline snapped at him. "Where is the charming young man who amused me on the way home from the train station? He seems to have vanished and left behind someone I don't recognize."

He helped her into the carriage, climbed up beside her, and urged the horse forward. Her words hung over them as he pulled out onto the street. "Flossie said something similar today." He sat rigid, eyes forward, voice tight. "I confess, it is why I hoped you would agree to allow me to see you home. I knew if anyone could help me, it would be you."

Oh, bother! How am I to discourage you when you intrigue me?

"Or, we can discuss the upcoming dinner party at the Mertons'.

Will you thwart him announcing the date of the wedding by fainting from the infamous Merton heat?"

"I wouldn't care to think of it. It is too lovely of an evening for that. And, I am not in the habit of fainting. I leave that to others with more theatrical inclinations." A prayer for wisdom and plea for prevention of awkwardness bubbled up in her heart before Madeline could resist it. Such impromptu petitions were not a particular habit of hers, but with the thoughts formed, she allowed herself a moment of reflection before turning her attention to Henry's words—a story of something amusing that had occurred before she'd arrived with Russell that evening.

"Henry?"

"I'm boring you, aren't I?"

"Honestly?"

She heard the discouragement in his hesitant, "Yes."

"I'm more intrigued by what you think I could possibly do to help *you*." Bumbling, fumbling, she suspected he also had a ruddy neck as well as Henry tried to explain. A lengthy moment of silence followed until Madeline felt obligated to encourage him to continue. "I'm inclined to assist in any way I can, but if you don't tell me, I fear I'll disappoint."

The words then spilled from him. "I've been a Christian since birth—I thought. But then I came here and a fellow over at Wayfair spoke to me after church one Sunday. He...." Henry stopped the horse in the middle of the road and stared at her. In the darkness, she saw little, but his confusion rang through every word. "He showed me just how important a sincere faith is, but I...."

Had he been Russell, Madeline would have wrapped her arm through his and offered some comfort. Instead, she folded her hands over her lap and struggled to find just the right words. "You *have* said some rather startling things lately."

Once more, things grew quiet. He clicked his tongue against his cheek and urged the horse forward. "I know I've made myself a nuisance of late—" When she stirred to demur, he broke off his own sentence and contradicted her. "I have. I know. I wanted to apologize." The lengthy pauses became part of the cadence of the ride. "I was sweet on you all those years ago. Did you know?"

A string of recent semi-untruthful statements and outright falsehoods pricked her conscience and prompted strict honesty. "I didn't—until just recently. It explained your... precipitous show of interest now."

"Only I would wait for years to return and see if the fascinating Maddie Brown still knew how to mock me and make me smile—all at the same time." When Madeline didn't respond—couldn't, really—he cleared his throat and urged the horse to move swifter. "I'm sorry for the distraction. What were we discussing?"

Madeline choked out a half-whispered, "Bible."

"Yes. That is correct. I was trying to explain that I—I am excited about what I'm learning in the Bible. When Paul says it's alive and powerful, he speaks truth, but...."

That single, diminutive word opened a world of alternatives to avoiding "Henry the Biblicist" or something equally revolting. "So, what is the other side of that coin, Henry?"

"I fear it's repressing what I believe—what I feel. I fear it is hiding my faith in an attempt to avoid making a show of it. We discussed that once, if you remember."

"Yes." Madeline offered him a smile she knew he couldn't see and relaxed. "You called it *pietistic*. I thought that a perfect description. All the appearance of piety without the substance of it."

The horse's hooves sounded their path through the outlying streets of Rockland to Parkview Way. Night critters serenaded their path to Beaumont Street. A cat yowled. Dogs took up barking at something—who knew what?—and the breeze rustled leaves overhead. Madeline sat in the buggy lost in thought.

One doesn't like to promulgate such things, I agree. And he was great fun before he... well, before. Even I was excited about my new prayer idea

306

and shared it publicly without thinking how it could sound. If only.... And that thought gave Madeline the answer she realized he needed.

"Henry, I think you should speak to Russell. I know no one who has such a sincere faith as he. I should have realized it, of course. It shows in everything he does, but he is careful of sermonizing or excess in his speech or public behavior. I truly had no idea how devout he was until we discussed it once."

"I'll speak to him." Henry stopped the carriage in front of her walk and hopped down to assist her. "I'll have time to be a careful pupil, you see."

Excitement and dread mingled in her stomach until Madeline couldn't decide which was preeminent. "You will?"

"Uncle Hardwick has offered to fund my archeological expedition if I first finish my education at Rockland College."

Dread dissipated in the wake of his words. Madeline took Henry's arm as he led her up the walk. "And how will you like that?"

"Well, it is a small college—not much known. But I would stay and be close to Grandmother. She's growing feeble; I think. That's why she's come—to stay, it seems. Being close if these are her last years would ease my father's heart, for sure." At that moment, Madeline heard it. The excitement almost bubbled from him, but rather than the boyishness he'd shown at his arrival, she heard a maturity in Henry's words and tone.

"It sounds quite lovely. I know Flossie dreaded your leaving. And you've made yourself such an indispensable part of our set, that the only thing others will begrudge is the going away party we cannot have."

Her teasing fell on deaf ears. Henry stood in her entryway, the lights blazing about them, and gazed down at her. "Few people are afforded a second opportunity to make a better impression. I hope I may be one of them."

"I don't know...." She tossed him a saucy smile and, without regard to what her Aunt Louisa would say about it, folded her arms over her chest. "Are you prepared for *three* more years in the company of such a *livewire* as me?"

What he said, she never remembered. He backed toward the door, winked as he grinned at her, and bade her goodnight. Madeline wandered through the house, turning off lights, and made her way upstairs. She didn't look in on her father, despite his open door. Instead, she stepped into her room, undressed, and began the tedious task of brushing out her hair, all without conscious thought of her actions. Only one thought permeated her mind and, she feared, her heart. *How could I be happy to hear he's staying, when only an hour ago, I wished him away?*

THIRTY-TWO

His nose wrinkled and eyes smarted at the pungent waves of sulfuric gasses wafting through the Dry Docks. Vernon held a handkerchief over his nose as he passed the corridor that received the worst of the stench. *The factory is in fine form today. I'll be glad when I do not have to come down here anymore.*

Just at the edge of the quarter, a man appeared. *Jim. I wonder what he knows.* Vernon beckoned Jim to follow and strode toward his machine. He grabbed the starting iron and waved it. "I'll be back in a moment."

Starting the vehicle — always a nuisance. He held the iron over a smithy's fire and waited. Once it grew red-hot, with the iron over his head, he dashed back to the car and thrust it into the boiler. *Come on, now. Take... take...* The boiler roared to life. Vernon grinned. "Hop in. We'll talk on the way."

With the discretion the man was known for, Jim hopped into the passenger side and waited until Vernon took off down the road. "She's not down here today, but she was gone yesterday with that Barnes fellow — arrived in Rockland at seven-ten on the one-twenty from Chicago. I don't know if she went the whole way or not. I didn't see her leave."

"Chicago! She couldn't have gone all the way there and back so quickly. It leaves at six o'clock."

"Six-ten to be precise." Jim twirled his finger around the end of his handlebar mustache. "I checked. But there was a nine-thirty to Bloomington that might have made a connection. It's possible that she gave me the slip then. But I spent all day looking for her and didn't see a thing."

That would account for her arriving late, but she couldn't have gone there and back and done much more than have a decent meal. It's a six-hour trip each way.

Vernon steered more sharply around a corner than he meant to and took the vehicle up to nearly twenty miles an hour once he turned onto Westbrook Boulevard. Jim clutched at the ridiculous bowler he'd purchased as a way to mock her and laughed. "Vern, if you didn't want me to wear the thing, you could have just said so."

"I still say you shouldn't have mocked her."

"She knew I was following. I thought it might put her more at ease — make her less likely to feel threatened."

"Perhaps if she felt a bit threatened, she wouldn't have taken another trip to Chicago! What could she be doing there?"

Jim shook his head. "I don't know, but I do know I don't want some cop coming to me about bothering the mayor's daughter. That's asking for trouble."

Everything is asking for trouble. Edith did have *to have such an inconvenient friend. Well, we'll see about that!* Vernon pulled over at the corner of Jefferson. "Try down by City Hall. I got the distinct feeling she'd be visiting her father today."

The moment Jim hopped from the machine, Vernon whizzed toward the quiet, lovely neighborhood where Edith lived with her father. "I also need to convince you *and* your lickpenny of a father that living at your house would be preferable." *We'd save so much money, and he's never home. We could move to rooms on the opposite side of the house, even. It's large enough not to see him except at meals — if we chose to join him at all. Ida's a lazy thing. She can learn to step lively and bring our meals upstairs. Yes....*

He found Edith languishing in the parlor with windows open

310

but the shades drawn almost all the way down. Vernon opened windows at the front of the house and raised the parlor windows just a little higher. "A cross breeze will cool you much better, my dear." Her eyes thanked him even as she mopped at her forehead. "And, I think a bit of ice water." He eyed the powder blue weskit she wore and shook his head. "No, no. That won't do. It's lovely; it's true. But you need something thin and light. Even if it's excessive, it would be better than over-warm. Why don't you go put on your lovely ivory dress? You'll be much cooler."

It worked. Her eyes lit up, a smile formed, and she paused beside him long enough to press a kiss to his cheek. "You do take such care of me. I knew you liked this weskit, but...."

"It's much too warm." With a darkened room and an eye to privacy, Vernon pulled her just a little closer and allowed his lips to linger on hers much longer than he usually did. "But you choosing it to please me is so very wonderful of you."

She hesitated, unwilling to leave, but Vernon knew she'd become irritable if she remained in that unnecessary extra layer for much longer. Irritable wouldn't lend itself to supporting his ideas. So, Vernon left the room in search of the ice water, knowing she'd hurry down in the dress he'd recommended. *It might be more elaborate than is usually supposed as appropriate for an afternoon, but the sleeves are sheer, the neckline a little lower, and if she's smart, she'll leave off all but the most essential petticoat.*

And she did. The limp skirts, the hint of shoulder shown at the top, and the fainter pink to her skin all proved that he'd made the right choice. "You look more comfortable already, my dear."

"I confess to having confiscated Father's atomizer for his ferns. I often refresh myself with it. The fine mist...."

"Well, whatever you did, you look lovely and much less miserable." Once more, Vernon pulled her close. With infinite tenderness, he stroked her cheek, gazed into her eyes, brushed her lips with his. "I missed you today."

311

Her blush deepened as she relaxed against him and whispered, "I thought you weren't coming until late. Don't you have a dinner engagement?"

"I do." Vernon smiled into her eyes. "But I couldn't stand to wait so long to see you, so I thought to visit for an hour or so before I have to change. I hoped you wouldn't be out with one of your friends."

It worked—how, he couldn't imagine, but Edith spoke the words he most hoped to hear. "Madeline and I did have plans to go to the soda fountain down by City Hall, but she sent Jimmy over a while ago, saying she wasn't up to it today."

Take care.... she's a loyal little thing. Vernon allowed himself the pleasure of an arm slipped around her waist as he led her to the cozy settee. "Well, I know how dear she is to you, but I can't help but be glad for less time with her. I do worry about her influence."

"Madeline! Why? She's a lovely girl."

He debated. Distance himself or appeal to her vanity. Vernon saw the beatific expression on her face and chose the former. He leaned back and clasped his hands in front of him. "I didn't mean to imply she wasn't, but her reputation is becoming injured with her meddling, Edith. I wouldn't want you to suffer by association."

Edith stiffened as well, but a moment later, she relaxed again. "I know you mean well, Vernon, really. But so does Madeline. She's a wonderful girl."

"I'm sure you know best." He wrapped her hand in both of his and raised it to his lips. "Just think about it. Please."

"And Vernon says he doesn't want to wait until autumn for a wedding. Of course, any sooner would show undue haste." Edith sipped her tea and nibbled on her cakes between sighs that threatened Madeline's composure.

"What does your father think?"

Edith blushed and gave away her answer long before she managed to whisper, "He thinks that I should marry as soon as may be."

I imagine he does. The sooner someone else takes over the management of your affairs – and your spending – the sooner his bank account benefits.

" – ink I should do?"

It took a moment for Madeline to recreate the probable question, but she managed to look properly thoughtful as she did. "Well, I wouldn't do anything with much haste. And besides, you know how uncomfortable it would be if you were to have a wedding before the weather cools. I wouldn't care to see you faint before you could make your vows."

"Oh! Can you imagine the horrible things people would say?

Oh, no. I must wait. And...." In a rare moment of filial disloyalty, Edith sat up and offered Madeline an embarrassed smile. "Besides. When Father sees that Vernon is not as changeable as he fears, it will be a bit of a triumph. I do so grow weary of him always treating me like my lack of quickness means I do not understand the things he says about me."

And I underestimated you as well. I have never seen evidence of your understanding them either. Madeline filled her cup again and reminded herself *not* to lean back against the sofa cushions. *I am growing quite lackadaisical in my habits.*

"May I have another cake, Madeline? Your cook does make the finest little teacakes I've ever had. Why, I do like them more than even the ones at that little room downtown."

She urged Edith to take both, but the girl slid just one onto her plate and toyed with it for a moment. "I suppose I should learn to do something useful. I don't imagine Vernon has quite the resources to pay for a full time cook."

And the opening Madeline had been waiting for presented itself with great fanfare. She took a sip of tea, a bite of cake, and set her cup and saucer on the teacart. "Well, with his business interests, he should be prepared to provide someone – at least for special dinners. And you really should learn how your cook plans those things. It wouldn't do not to understand exactly what goes into a successful party."

Edith blinked twice before understanding filled her eyes. "Oh, that is true, isn't it? I've always left it to Mattie. She's such a fine organizer, and we both know I'm hopeless with those things." She took another bite, lost in thought. Just as Madeline thought she'd have to be more direct with her hints, Edith's eyes widened. "Oh, goodness. That would never do! Do you remember what happened when the Wakefield's cook died, and Mrs. Wakefield left everything to the new cook for that dinner? Mr. Wakefield lost that account over it. Dortmann's Dry Goods has the exclusive right to sell those horrible stockings!"

"Horrible or not, they're excellent sellers. I *still* hear him cast that up to her at opportune moments."

That would be all she needed to do. Nothing hurt Edith more than to have her past failures held against her. Madeline offered a sympathetic smile and waited. Edith spoke sooner than she expected. "Oh, I do need to study this. Perhaps they have a book on home keeping at Gardner & Henley's."

"They might!" Madeline sat forward. "It's an excellent plan. And with autumn just around the corner, you haven't any time to lose!" She waited, hoping. *There you have it, Edith. Now suggest a practice party.*

But instead, Edith planned a list of parties. "I can arrange everything for Mattie to approve." An excited light filled her eyes. "I could save them! Wouldn't that be a fine thing? I could just choose one for the right number of people, and whomever dear Vernon hired to help me could use it as a guide."

Desperate measures – it was time. Madeline arranged her

features into an awestruck expression and sighed. "You are such an inspiration. Why, I would never have the courage to hold an important dinner party just from a paper plan! Of course, your cook is a genius at these things. I'm sure she knows best. But how brave you are!"

Her words sounded excessively effusive, even to herself. But it worked. Edith chewed her lip and stared at the last bite of cake on her plate. "It would be wise to try it a few times." Then it happened. Edith's face lit up like a ray of sunshine and her eyes sparkled. "I'll do it! I'll have a party. I'll invite my friends, and we can all have a laugh when I serve two main courses and no soup. Or I forget napkins!"

"Splendid idea! Although," Madeline added with a squeeze to Edith's hand. "No one would laugh at you for inexperience. We should all be impressed with your desire to be a good wife to Mr. Smythe. And he would appreciate such an effort, surely."

Hesitation — Edith seemed to ponder something, and that made Madeline nervous. She raised eager but troubled eyes and asked, "Would Friday be too soon, I wonder. I shouldn't like to before next week, but it occurs to me that Father's dinners are often last minute affairs. I wouldn't like to be thrown off guard...."

If Madeline could have done a jig without concerning her friend, she would have. Instead, she jumped up and dashed for the stairs. "I'll escort you down to Gardner's myself!"

*T*HIRTY-*T*HREE

As Madeline wrapped a little-worn dress that few would recognize, she debated the best course of action. If she used Jimmy, she'd be certain of the success of the errand, but Madeline didn't like to think of her little friend wandering down in the Dry Docks looking for a young woman such as Abby.

That thought determined her course. She tied string to hold the paper in place and snatched her hat from her dressing table bench. Without a word to Cook or Mary, she slipped through the front door and out onto the walk. Jimmy stood outside the parlor window, soaping it with such energy she suspected he meant to douse himself liberally as he worked.

"Going somewhere, Miss Madeline?"

"Yes."

He dropped the rag and sauntered to her side, drying his hands on his knickerbockers. "I could take it for you. It's gonna be a scorcher today."

"Yes, but I don't think my friend would take it if I didn't bring it myself." Madeline leaned close and whispered, "She's shy." Her conscience tried to protest, but Madeline refused to listen. *It's true — in this area, anyway. If Jimmy arrived for me, she'd never take the dress. I'm sure of it.*

"Well, you should go to the soda fountain and get yourself a phosphate. It's a perfect day for it."

If she hadn't known him better, Madeline would have been convinced it was a hint. But he turned to go without even the slightest hesitation and added as he crossed the yard. "Ma got one for me and Clemmie the other day. Lemon. It was a real humdinger. You should try it."

Despite every effort to show some sort of self-control, Madeline found herself following Jimmy to the window and fishing out a nickel. "When you're done here—when that window sparkles like it was brand new—you go on down and get yourself another one. You'll need something cooling by then."

But Jimmy refused to take the nickel. "Oh, no, miss. I can't. That wouldn't be right. I wasn't angling for a jitney!"

Madeline made a show of setting the nickel on the walk. "Take it or don't. I'm sure a delivery boy would be happy to have it." In her mind, she saw him picking it up and leaving it on the hall table. "I appreciate your reticence, Jimmy, but it isn't polite to refuse an appropriate gift."

She'd nearly made it to the corner before she heard rapidly approaching footfalls. Gasping for air, Jimmy dashed past her and stopped short. "Thank you. I didn't say thank you."

"Well, you did now. But...." She waited for him to stop fingering the nickel and look at her. "Walk back home. It's too hot to run in this heat."

"Oh, it's not bad. I just tried to see how fast I could make it. Fifteen seconds!" He shuffled backward. "Did you know it ain't easy to count slower than your body moves?"

He was gone in a moment. And Madeline, feeling quite silly, found herself walking as fast as she could but counting slowly. "Hmmm... it *is* difficult."

But Jimmy's words followed her all the way down to the Dry Docks. If she found a soda fountain, they could have a nice, cooling refreshment as they talked. *And we will also have less privacy.* That one word stopped her. No matter how much more agreeable a phosphate might be on a hot summer's afternoon, a tearoom would be quiet. *And the propinquity cannot be undervalued.*

By the time she reached the tearoom, Madeline had nearly reversed her decision. She watched for fifteen minutes until a boy of the right age and apparent intelligence surfaced. Madeline called to him. "You there. Will you help me?"

For a moment, she thought he'd run. But he inched his way forward, dashed around an approaching wagon, and eyed her as he approached. "Yeah?"

"I wonder if you'd like to earn a little money."

The boy's eyes lit up and something in them unnerved her. *So, you think I'm easily fooled, do you?* With a new, revised plan in mind, Madeline shifted the package under her other arm, pulled out her pocketbook, and fished for a penny. "The errand is simple. I will give you this penny now as a sign of good faith. You go in there and find Abby at that large yellow building across from that—"

"I knows the one." He eyed her with frank curiosity. "You know it's a brothel, right?"

"I suspected, yes. Well, there's a girl in there. Her name is Abby."

The boy nodded. "I knows her. Everyone knows Abby."

"Well, good. You tell Abby I'm waiting here for her. I'll wait for one hour. But...." She leaned close and whispered, "You have to tell her where no one else can hear. That's very important." Madeline let her words sink in for a moment before she pulled out a dollar coin. "When you arrive back with her, I'll trade your penny for this dollar."

All doubt drained from the boy's face. He took one look at that dollar, glanced at Madeline, and dashed away. "Be back in a lick."

You just got taken in by a budding swindler. He'd have done it for a "jitney." But despite her inner scolding, Madeline found herself seated in the shabby little tearoom with the dollar coin before her on the table. The proprietor tried to serve her, but she asked to wait.

"I'm expecting a friend, you see."

Everything in the man's face changed. His eyes narrowed, his shoulders squared. "We don't like unsavory—"

"If you're maligning my character, sir, I will have something to say about that. My friend is a young woman, and there is nothing untoward about our meeting!"

The obsequious expression fell back into place and apologies flowed. Madeline almost sagged in relief as someone else entered and the man scurried away again. *And now I wait. Again.*

Not for the first time, Madeline wished she'd asked for that watch pin she'd fancied at her birthday. *The waiting is likely developing some sort of virtuous character quality that I cannot hope to understand.*

But after the third time the proprietor came over to ensure she didn't wish to order tea while she waited, Madeline asked how long she'd been there. "You came in at half-past, miss."

"And the time now?"

He checked his pocket watch and nodded. "Quarter-past."

Fifteen more minutes. Should I wait? Perha— But before her thought could materialize, the door opened and Abby stepped through. "Oh, there's Abby now. Excuse me. I'll be right back. We'd like that tea now, please."

Madeline scooped up the dollar coin and hurried to the door. She gave Abby a smile and pointed to their table. "I'll be right back. I just need to pay the boy."

"I sent him on his way. He knows better'n to take advantage like that."

A glance outside showed the boy gone—vanished. Discouraged, Madeline made her way back to the table and slid the dollar across to Abby. "Please give this to him. I offered it of my own accord. It's ... excessive, yes. But it could have been difficult to find you."

The girl hesitated and then slipped it into her purse. "I'll give it to 'im. His mother kin use it." She eyed Madeline for a moment.

"You're... differ'nt."

"Well, I'm at a loss, if you want the truth. I'm here because I don't know what to do." She retrieved one of her photographs from her pocketbook and passed it to Abby. "Is that your Vernon?"

Abby barely glanced at it before she passed it back. "Yes. How did you get it?"

"I took it just over a week ago. It finally came in yesterday's mail. He met with another woman that day—I think you know her. From your...." Madeline stumbled over her words but corrected herself. "Employer?"

"Lucille was there? That's strange. She don't usually go out with men—not wheres she kin be seen." The girl eyed her. "Why'd ya come agin?"

The reality of what she was about to do physically assaulted Madeline's lungs. The breath left her in a *whoosh* of air, and her eyes smarted. "I still find it difficult to believe that you're engaged to *our* Vernon."

The words—all wrong. She knew it the moment they left her lips. But before she could apologize and try to explain, Abby drew up and pushed her chair back. "So a girl like me can't expect to meet a nice man like him. Is that it?"

"No...." Madeline took a deep breath and prayed for some kind of Providential help. "It's that he's engaged to a friend of mine."

Abby wilted before her eyes. Had she shown any hint of surprise, Madeline might not have gone through with her plan. Indeed, as they'd sat there, she'd decided it was too risky—too public. But seeing the dismay and pain on the girl's face was all it took. Madeline pulled the parcel from beneath the table and passed it to her.

"Take this. Wear it on Friday night. I want you to come to this address...." She pulled out a calling card with her address written on the back. "At eight-thirty. We'll walk over to Edith's together."

"And why would we do this? I can't go to no party in that part

321

of town. They'd call for the cops!"

But Madeline shushed her and insisted she come. "No one will call for the police; I assure you. My friend is a kind girl. She wouldn't even if she wanted to. And I assure you, she won't wish it."

Abby fingered the string on the package. "Why are ya doing this, miss? Ya don't haf to."

Madeline heard herself answering with truth and sincerity she hadn't been aware of until that moment. "Because, if Vernon is who he has presented himself to be, you should be very happy with him. He can't possibly be Edith's Vernon. But if he isn't...." She frowned. "Abby, if he is who I am very desperately afraid he is, then you and my friend—or both of you—will be very unhappy. I just want to prevent that unhappiness."

*T*HIRTY-*F*OUR

Lights blazed in every window of the Merton home as Madeline and Abby strolled up the walk. *I do hope Mr. Merton doesn't see this. If he did, he'd never consider electricity!*

Abby tugged on her arm. "Maybe I shouldn't go in. This is too grand—"

"Nonsense. You're here as my guest. Edith will understand. I told her I might bring someone." To herself she added, *And if she chose to think of that "someone" as a gentleman, well, that's her own misapprehension.*

"I don't know...."

Madeline stopped halfway to the door and turned to face Abby. "Do you love Mr. Smythe?"

"I...."

Oh, dear. If you convince yourself you don't, I won't have you for evidence. Madeline attempted to appeal to the girl's conscience. "Even if you don't, he's led you to believe he'd marry you. Would you have my friend's heart broken when he does this with some other young lady? If not for yourself, will you please come in to save my friend?"

She hadn't thought it would work. Nothing in the girl's demeanor hinted that it would. But Abby slowly nodded and turned toward the door once more. "I kin do that. And maybe it ain't my Vernon. That'd be nice, wouldn't it, miss?"

"Yes, it would."

Ida let them in with a second and suspicious glance at Abby. "They're already eating, Miss Madeline, but I'll bring you both a plate. I guess that's why there are two empty places at the end."

"I told her I might bring someone."

"Yes, miss."

Those two words conveyed more meaning than an entire dictionary. Much to Madeline's relief, Abby seemed unaware of it. Ida led them into the dining room and all heads turned their direction—all but Vernon Smythe's. He finished slicing a piece of meat from his roast and raised his fork to his mouth. It never entered. Never had Madeline seen a man's face so white.

She stepped forward and led Abby to one of the empty chairs. "Hello, everyone. I apologize for my tardiness It's becoming a terrible habit of mine." She turned to Abby and asked, "Do you know everyone?"

"I—"

"Well, everyone, this is Abby Cooper. I suppose you are new to our set." Madeline turned her gaze to Vernon and smiled broader. "But, of course, you know Mr. Smythe, don't you?"

"I—" Smythe's glare cut Abby off before she could speak further.

Edith, on the other hand, urged them to sit. "And how do you know Vernon, Miss Cooper?"

Abby looked at Madeline, back at Edith, and over at Smythe. The abject fury on Smythe's face had the opposite effect intended. She lowered herself into the chair, sat up quite straight, and turned to face Edith with frank honesty. "We're engaged."

A collective gasp, followed by a ripple of murmurs, filled the Mertons' dining room. Smythe's face grew redder and redder, until he looked ready to pop! But Edith, dear, sweet Edith, blinked as she took in the words and tried to make sense of them. "I don't think I understand. You see...." She reached for Vernon's hand and squeezed it with evident affection. "*We* are engaged. I think you must mean some other man? We were asking how you met this one — Mr. Vernon Smythe."

Under her breath, but loudly enough for most of the table to hear, Abby muttered, "T'ppears just *one* of us ain't enough for *him*."

Jaws sagged with collective uncouthness, but Edith still shook her head. "I'm sorry, but I still don't understand who you mean. I'm engaged to Mr. Smythe. Who is your fiancé?"

Smythe found his voice and used it with poignant rancor. "I think this meretricious creature is out of place here. You should leave."

But Edith protested with such gracious gentleness that Madeline almost regretted the manner in which she'd decided to make Vernon Smythe's true character known. "Oh, don't send away Madeline's guest. I'm certain she's just a little confused. It is awfully warm in here tonight."

Under her breath, but loudly enough that even Edith could hear it through all the fluff filling her head, Madeline said, "Because women are often confused about whom they have agreed to trust their hearts to for the rest of their lives."

This time, Edith stiffened. She gazed at Madeline, over at Abby, and back at Smythe. "I do see your point, Madeline...." Though she tried to catch his gaze, Vernon refused to look at her. "Vernon?"

An entirely different demeanor came over him. He moved closer to Edith and covered her hand with his. Leveling a malevolent glare at Abby, Smythe shifted his attention to Madeline and shook his head, as if in disbelief. "Miss Brown may find such jokes amusing. I do not. It is quite inappropriate, and...." He turned to Edith. "I don't think you should allow something like this in your father's home. You've allowed your meddling friend to tarnish his hospitality."

Madeline watched in disbelief as Edith drew up and withdrew her hand from Vernon's grasp. She folded them in her lap and met his surprised gaze. "I don't think you should speak of my friends like that, Vernon. In fact, I think it would be best if you would go discuss this misunderstanding with my father."

Whether something in Vernon's expression enlightened her, or if the truth of the situation finally made itself clear, Madeline couldn't tell. But Edith's entire demeanor changed once more. "If it *is* a misunderstanding." With a slight shake of her head, she dropped her gaze and half whispered, half gasped, "Actually, Mr. Smythe, I think I've changed my mind. I think you should leave." Smythe's protest lasted only long enough for the entire table to hear her add, "And I don't think you should return."

But he didn't. Smythe stood and moved behind her chair. With hands on her shoulders, he bent low, and only the absolute silence of every guest in the room made it possible for Madeline to hear him speak. "Edith, you're overwrought. This girl is playing some —"

At that moment, Russell stood and beckoned Frank Hardwick to follow. They moved to either side of Smythe and insisted he leave. In a huff, and wresting himself from their grasp, Smythe stalked from the room and out the door, slamming it behind him. Abby rose as if to escape, but Russell stopped by their seats and murmured, "I wouldn't leave just yet. You wouldn't want to meet him in the street. I'm certain Miss Merton would be happy for you to stay a little longer."

Abby protested and rose, but Edith had already risen as well. "Please, come and sit with me. Ida will bring you a plate, of course. And one for Madeline, too." In the corner of her eye, Madeline noted movement that hinted Ida had been a witness to the entire thing.

There will be some interesting gossip in the kitchen tonight, Edith. And well done! I've never seen you so magnificent. You may not be the most brilliant mind I've ever met, but you do have quite the gracious disposition. Why, I fully expected you to fall into a fit of weeping, or worse.... Madeline almost shuddered. *Faint. I absolutely expected you to faint at the news.*

The meal continued but with much less animated speech than usual. Conversations remained quiet, sedate. And with each passing minute, Abby looked more and more miserable. It took exactly fifteen minutes for Madeline to give up and offer to escort Abby home, but Russell objected. "I'll take her." As they passed her chair, Madeline stood and murmured her thanks to Abby.

"If you hadn't come...."

"If you hadn't shown me." Abby gazed back at Edith. "I'm so sorry, miss. Really."

Madeline walked them to the door, but as he stepped through, Russell leaned close and murmured, "Please just stay here. *Please.*"

Despite his pleas, the authority in his tone rankled, but at the concern on Russell's face and the memory of Edith's kindness and graciousness, Madeline nodded. "I will. Thank you for escorting her. I'll be sure to save you a plate of refreshments."

Ida arrived with dessert not two minutes after Madeline took her seat. The silence at the table unsettled more than just Edith. However, as they finished their plates of ice cream and macaroons, one by one, the guests rose, bade Edith goodnight, and left. Each time, they gave Madeline such looks of confused disapproval that she began to doubt her method of disclosure.

However, once they were quite alone, Edith led her to the parlor and offered her a glass of cordial. Had she expected her friend to be distraught—and she did—Madeline would have been quite surprised at the calm demeanor Edith exhibited. Indeed, she was. They sat in silence until Madeline could stand it no longer. "Are you much disappointed, Edith? At first you seemed upset, but then...."

Edith met her gaze and blinked. "Why, of course I'm upset. I planned to *marry* him, Madeline."

"You loved him, then?" Oh, how it hurt to think of the pain she'd been forced to cause.

This time, Edith shook her head. "I don't think I loved him *yet,* but I would have in time, I think." She sighed. "I admired him, though. He was so kind, said such lovely things to me, admired me — or pretended to, I suppose. I thought he would be kind and treat me well."

"Oh, Edith."

Her next words tore at Madeline's heart. "I thought he would have, at the very least, been faithful. Of course, he wouldn't have been. I see that now."

For some time, they sat together, each sipping at cordial, lost in her own thoughts. Madeline imagined Edith to be planning how to tell her father, but one thought repeated itself in her mind. *She's showing more backbone than I ever knew she had. She, well, she is quite splendid, isn't she? And as public as this display was — ugly thing, that — others got to see just what a marvelous girl she is. Why, I expected her to be pertinacious in her opinion of Mr. Smythe, but when she saw through his smooth words....*

The memory of his rebuke of her brought a smile to her lips. *And it may have worked, had he not tried to insult me.*

Russell appeared just as she tried to decide what would be the best way to share the information they'd gathered. He offered to walk her home, but Madeline resisted. "It's kind of you, but I don't like to leave her alone."

As if she hadn't just overheard a whisper clearly not meant for her ears, Edith rose. "I think it might be best. I... well, I think I could use a few moments alone before I tell my father. He always said Ver—Mr. Smythe would lose interest. I suppose, as is usual, he was correct."

Madeline hugged her friend and whispered, "I have proof of other indiscretions—many. If you have need of them, just send someone to us. I'll be happy to show your father." Though it took some effort, Madeline added, "And if you find you don't care to be alone after all, send someone down then, too. I'll come stay with you."

The true state of Edith's heart and mind revealed itself as Madeline and Russell walked themselves to the door and down the walk. Through the windows, the faint sound of crying reached her ears and wrung her heart. "Oh, Russell...."

"I will probably get my ears boxed for saying it, but I'm proud of you. I know what a sacrifice it was for you to offer to stay with her. She'd likely chatter all night to drown out her thoughts."

"Considering I was the cause of her pain—"

But Russell interrupted her. "No, Maddie. Smythe was. Although, I do wonder at how you chose to reveal his true character."

She didn't speak until they reached her gate. Madeline stared at the latch as if somehow it would unlock all the answers to questions she'd been afraid to ask herself. "I feared that if we didn't produce Abby, Edith would never believe it. And, if we did it in private, he would find a way to discredit her, or worse."

"Surely, you don't think he'd harm either one of them!"

"No...." She'd started to raise her eyes to his but dropped them again. "Russell, I thought Edith too easily led. I was confident he'd be able to convince her that she'd misunderstood—that I'd grown set against him. He'd appeal to her gentle nature and...."

In a move he hadn't made since the night Delbert Jackson had informed Madeline of his intention to marry her despite her deficiencies, Russell pulled her close, hugged her, and whispered, "Edith was marvelous, wasn't she?" He stepped away again and smiled down at her. "I always wondered if there wasn't more to her than she shows. Sometimes it seems as though it's there, but she doesn't know how to unveil it or something. Tonight, however...."

This time, her eyes did meet his as enthusiasm filled her. "She was magnificent." Madeline unlatched the gate and stepped through it. "Thank you for seeing me home, Russell. Goodnight."

"Try to sleep." He waited until she glanced back at him before he added, "I'll see you tomorrow after work. We'll go for a walk."

She whispered her thanks, but as Madeline reached the steps she turned again. "Russell?"

The latch clicked once more and the steady, rhythmic sound of his shoes on the path grew nearer until he reached her side. "Yes?"

"Would you care for some coffee? Tea? Cordial? I think Papa even has bourbon somewhere if you prefer it."

To her great relief, he offered his arm and led her up the steps. "I'd be happy to. Besides," Russell waited until they entered the house before he added, "I still want to know what hand you had in the Sempleton letter. I can't believe you are as innocent in that as you pretend."

With goblets of cordial in hand, and the parlor lights turned low enough not to invite curious visitors, Madeline admitted to leaving the possibility open. "I didn't know the Sempletons would be there, of course, but I did leave a line in a letter to Amy about how the young man behind you in the photograph seemed to be transferring his interest from the unknown woman to Edith. I thought if your uncle had ever heard of Vernon Smythe—anything untoward—he might warn Amy. You know how she is." Madeline smiled at Russell's nod.

"Yes, she would immediately go to him and ask for a magnifier so she could see better." Russell returned her smile with a grin. "You couldn't have imagined such a history, surely!"

"Well, no. I didn't." Madeline traced the bottom of the goblet with her finger as she worked out the best way to explain. "But really, is it such a surprise? I saw him in the Dry Docks with that woman, and he went inside with his arm around Abby's waist." Wrinkle cares aside, Madeline's forehead furrowed into deep rows. "Of course, I didn't know who she was at the time."

Russell drained his goblet and set it down. Leaning forward, he rested his arms on his knees. "You mean, I suppose, that if he was keeping company with a woman of dubious morals, then why should stories of girls' reputations destroyed surprise us?"

Her eyes flashed, and all trace of wrinkled brow disappeared. "He left young girls with *child*. Just left them—*three!* Two of those girls were from good families, simple but honest and Christian. Now their lives are ruined, and the worst that will happen to Mr. Smythe is that he'll lose all hope of an inheritance when Jonas Merton dies."

"You don't think he'll suffer business setbacks with this breach of character?"

Despite all attempts, Madeline couldn't hide a decided sniff. "Oh, Russell! Really? A man is forgiven almost anything but scandal in business. If his personal life includes indiscretions, once they're forgotten, few will care that their money is braided together with that of a man who cannot keep his word to a woman."

"But surely it is a sign of a deeper rooted problem—that lack of honesty." Russell eyed her with such curiosity that she couldn't decide if he were truly that gullible or if he tried to discern her understanding of the situation.

"One would think. I know that I would never do business with a *known* philanderer. If he cannot be true to someone he claims to love, how can I expect him to be true to any business arrangement? People are careless with their reputations the moment love or money is involved."

"I'm sorry it is so, but I believe it is." Russell shook his head. "It's a shame that Edith will bear the brunt of this."

With a little shrug, Madeline jumped up. "I'll get us some refreshments. I feel decidedly pinched."

Russell followed as she made her way to the kitchen. "It isn't any wonder. You didn't have dinner. You arrived late, and everyone left shortly afterward. Ida probably had your place cleared before you knew what happened." As she lifted the lid on a cherry pie, he coughed. "And I do believe you promised me dessert when I returned from taking Miss Cooper home."

She slowly laid out a spread enough to satisfy the hungriest of young people. With tall tumblers of milk set before them and great slabs of ham and cold potatoes to cut from, they seated themselves for a late repast.

"Russell?"

"Yes?" Russell watched her as she cut her meat into small pieces much as she might have done as a child.

"Why did I have to be right about him?" The words escaped from her lips in whisper.

"That is his fault, Madeline. Not yours." Russell dug into his pie, eating half before he spoke again. "You were bothered by him that night at Edith's — the one before you started all this 'meddling.' Something about his sleeve?"

"Well, as I said at the time. Edith doesn't wear lip color. She considers any cosmetic to be quite vulgar. So, when I saw him brush something from her cheek — quite brazen of him in such a public setting when they weren't engaged."

Before she continued, Russell brushed a crumb from Madeline's cheek and nodded. "My cuff touched your lips. I see."

"Exactly. But the color on his sleeve wasn't the cordial he claimed. It was lip salve. He'd tried to cover it with a bold move — for what purpose? No one would likely have noticed, and without attention drawn to it, if someone *did* see it, they — even I — would have assumed it to be the cordial."

"I'm not sure I follow your reasoning, then."

Madeline leaned on the table and propped her head on her hand. "Russell, only a guilty man would try to *cover* something so unlikely to be seen." She frowned. "And there was one other thing. When I saw her in the Dry Docks that day — the other woman from the brothel. She remarked on my dress."

"Which one was it?"

The question was quite unexpected. Madeline peered at him over her teacup before shrugging. "My poplin — with the gingham waist." He stared at her with the blank expression most men wore when discussing feminine frippery. "Lace?" When nothing illuminated his face, Madeline continued. "Well, as I said, she remarked on my dress, and of course, when that happens, one tends to notice the other person's apparel as well." She dashed from the table and returned with a small photograph. "See that?"

Though he looked at the photograph with great interest, Russell shook his head. "What am I looking for?"

"That inset in the skirt—stripes forming a chevron pattern. She wore that in the Dry Docks *and* when I saw them meet this day. And here she wears it again when they meet again. She is connected with that brothel. I believe this is Abby's 'Lucille.'"

Pie eaten, Russell rose and carried his plate to the sink. He pumped water into a large pot and set it on the stove. Madeline followed his example, covering uneaten dishes and returning them to the ice box. They worked in silence for some time. With the water heated, Madeline washed and Russell dried the dishes. A sense of contentedness washed over her as they finished. *It has been a good evening – difficult, painful, of course, but a good evening. Edith is spared....* She turned to face Russell, her heart pounding and tears stinging the back of her eyes. "You don't think Mr. Smythe could have—that he *did* persuade Edith to...."

Russell shook his head and hung his towel over the little rack by the sink. "I can't imagine she could have been so calm for so long had it been so. And Edith, for all her apparent dullness, is a good girl. She wouldn't allow herself to be too far tempted."

He cleared his throat. "I suppose now is a bit late to tell you, but I finally spoke to Charley Forsythe today."

"Oh? And what did he say?"

"He knew about Abby and at least one or more others. Smythe overheard him tell George Denton that he planned to warn her. But Smythe overreacted to it. He didn't stay to hear Denton mention the engagement. Charley didn't know about it, you see."

"Oh! So, are you saying Charley *wasn't* going to say anything?"

Russell grinned. "No, he wasn't. Again, the guilty conscience strikes and creates a problem where one might have hidden. Charley decided that if Smythe had proposed, he must have given up his other...*relationships.* Had he been pleasant, no one would have been

333

the wiser. Charley had considered speaking to Edith ever since then—concerned that Smythe's reaction might be indicative of a brutish manner."

"Is that so?"

They stood there, just feet apart, each lost in thoughts neither seemed eager to share. At last, Russell gave her arm a little squeeze and murmured, "It's late. I should go. Let's go rowing tomorrow. I should be off work by six o'clock."

"I'll fill a picnic basket."

She followed him through the house and to the door. There he smiled down at her and added, "Try to get Edith to come."

Madeline hadn't done it in the better part of a decade, but she stood on tiptoe and kissed Russell's cheek. "Thank you—for everything."

Thirty-Five

As he tore around the corner, Vernon watched as Essie Chandler kicked a perfect drive up the street. All for naught, too. The boys scattered at the sight of his car, but Essie just turned and glared at him. *If you were ten years older, little girl.... Oh, how I'd like to recruit you.*

He pulled up in front of his building and the Locomobile shuddered to a stop. Vernon beckoned her closer. "I've got a nickel—"

"Not doing anything this late for less'n a quarter." Essie waited a moment and turned to walk away.

"Fine. A *quarter*. You'd better hurry, then. I need you to go to Fremont Street and find Jim Weston. He—"

"He's the fella that follows that Miss Brown around. I know 'im. I'll get 'im." Essie stepped closer. "My brother Bobby will give you a pounding if you try to cheat me." With that startling warning, she took off down the street, braids flying out behind a cap too big and boyish for a girl like her.

Vernon watched her feet fly across the ground and resentment grew. *Not all of us had a carefree childhood like that. Some of us had to make our own way.*

Despite adherence to his silent entrance protocol, his landlady stepped out of the parlor, knitting in hand. "Mr. Smythe. I must remind you that your rent is now four days past due. I'll have to—"

As much as he hated to do it, Vernon pulled out the amount owed as well as the rest of the current week's rent. "I do apologize. I should have thought to leave it in my room with a note. I'll do that next time."

The woman's pursed lips relaxed and her face gentled as she nodded. "I should have known you weren't trying to skip out on me. So many..."

"Don't give it another worry, Mrs. Nester. I shouldn't have left you waiting." He slid one foot toward the stairs. "If you'll excuse me, I need to do a few things before my friend arrives."

"Mr. Weston? Certainly. Would you care for a little refreshment? My treat to make up for being so unpleasant."

Oh, you are easy to manipulate, Mrs. Nester. Much too easy. He demurred, waited, and then agreed with a show of reluctance. "If you are quite certain. I know how hard you work...."

"I wouldn't like to see my boarders going to bed hungry. And with you working until all hours!" She patted his cheek and hurried off to the kitchen, the knitting still in hand.

Just don't drop that in the teapot.

His room welcomed him with its lumpy mattress and smoking oil lamp. "This is why we need electricity in every home. That stupid lamp is a health hazard; I'm certain of it."

His tie, he tossed on the bed. Dinner coat followed. Shirt unbuttoned, shoes off. Vernon wriggled his toes on the thick, ugly carpet. *If it has to be ugly, at least it's comfortable.*

And then he paced. With fists balled at his sides, Vernon wore a discernable path in the large, plush carpet as he searched for some way to get back into Edith's good graces. *I have to discredit Abby. She'll have to leave.*

Lucille would want him to pay for Abby's ticket, but his purse wouldn't stretch that far—not for a fare to someplace far enough away to ensure she'd never return. *I need money—fast. But how? It's too soon to leave, especially if we can get Abby out of the city and Madeline focused on someone else's business for a while. Edith will come around. She's too gullible to believe this for long. I just have to be patient, sincere....* A few expletives filled his room. *This is Madeline Brown's fault. None but hers.*

A knock startled him from his thoughts half an hour later. Jim stepped through the door, that obnoxious bowler spinning on one finger. "The kid —"

"Did you pay her?"

"Are you kidding? She demanded a quarter. I told her to take it up with you —"

But Vernon didn't listen. He snatched a quarter from a tray on his bureau and jogged downstairs in his shirtsleeves. Essie stood on the porch, staring out into the night. She didn't even turn when the door opened. "Thought you'd make me go get Bobby."

"Here's your stupid quarter. It's robbery."

She turned and Vernon winced inwardly at the flash of the girl's eyes in the moonlight. "It's a contract. We made it. You kept it. We're good. Goodnight."

A cooling breeze rippled through his shirt. Vernon stood on the steps, enjoying the evening air. The steady pulsing in his head grew into an obnoxious pounding. Still he stood there, waiting, resting, thinking, seething.

"Smythe, are you coming in?"

He shook his head and sank to the porch steps. "We've got a problem. And it's cooler out here. Let's talk."

Jim leaned against the post and folded his arms over his chest. "What's up? I thought you were having a practice dinner at the Mertons'."

"I was. Until that meddling Miss Brown showed up with Abby in tow."

"Uh, oh. Did —"

Vernon shoved his hands in his pockets and once more, paced. "She found out — somehow. *You* were supposed to keep her away from Abby. You botched that, too."

"She didn't go down there! I watched. I couldn't just follow her at ten paces all over town. Her father is the *mayor*. The cops would be on me in no time."

"She must have sent that boy Jimmy in there." The words he muttered under his breath as Vernon continued his pacing. "But now it'll take me longer to get my hands on Edith's money. I've got to figure out how. But first, Abby goes."

The front door opened. "Mr. Smythe? Did you want your refreshments out here?"

Perspiration beaded on his forehead. *You have to be more careful. If she overheard you....* Vernon rushed to take the tray she'd retrieved as she awaited his answer. "You should have called me. I would have carried it for you, Mrs. Nester."

She beamed at him. As Vernon carried the tray to the small table at one end of the porch, Mrs. Nester spoke to Jim. "He's such a polite young man—thoughtful. Not like those college boys who want something every few minutes without so much as a thank you or a please." She reached for the tray and urged them to eat. "I'll come get the things later."

But Vernon held fast to the tray. "I'll bring them in. You have enough to do, and we could be out here for hours. A businessman never sleeps, you know." He propped the tray against the table legs and led her to the door. "You should rest. It's been a long day, hasn't it?"

"It has. My feet ache something terrible." She smiled. "I think I will turn in if you're sure. Just put the things in the kitchen. I'll wash them up in the morning." Mrs. Nester smiled at Jim. "Good night, Mr. Weston."

"G'night, Miz Nester. Thanks for the victuals." Jim moved to the teapot and sniffed. The moment the door shut, he poured a cup of steaming coffee. "I never can understand how you get people to do these things."

"You tell them what they want to hear. People will believe anything if spoken with conviction and compassion." Vernon grabbed one of the sandwiches and sniffed. Roast beef. Exactly what a man who hadn't had a solid dinner needed. "Meanwhile, I need to talk to Lucille. First thing in the morning."

Jim reached for the other sandwich as he shook his head. "I wouldn't. You can talk Abby into anything. Why waste the connection? If you set her loose, you'll have to cultivate another or pay like the rest of us." He shook his head. "Only you could convince a 'woman of the night' that you'd marry her."

"Again, I told her what she wanted to hear. I showed compassion. Now… now she'll regret listening to Madeline Brown. Lucille will see to that."

"Why should Lucille do anything for you? What's in it for her?" Jim reached for a strawberry and stared at it. "These look kind of puny."

"They're tasty, though—sweet." Vernon grabbed one. "Lucille knows I'll keep her interests in mind when working on my projects. I'm not about to put her out of business. Everything I do will benefit her in some way. But if she crosses me…."

Jim's face showed the fear that Vernon hoped to instill in the man. *You are useful. I need you to remain loyal. For a man like you, fear is the best choice.*

"She won't. No one would who knew you. So now what?" Jim reached for another strawberry. "If you send Abby away—"

Without regard for Jim's observations, Vernon began speaking. "I'll need money. A good amount, too. Quickly. I'm running low."

"If you hadn't bought that motor…."

You think I actually paid *for it. How unusually naïve of you.* "What I did changes nothing about what I need to do now. I need money. I might have to push this project ahead. If people donated to clean up the Dry Docks, that would keep me until I can win Edith back. Just a few dollars off the top of each donation…."

Jim didn't speak. For the better part of a minute, the only sounds Vernon heard were those of crickets, night birds, and the occasional banged door or yowling cat. "Go ahead and say it. I know you have an opinion."

"How can you be sure people will donate now? When they hear—"

"Because the only thing people like almost as much as compassion and confidence is the opportunity to commiserate. If I get to people first—leave a few well-timed words about how broken I am that Edith believes sordid tales about me...." A new thought occurred to him. "Or, I could play the penitent man. It worked for Warren Osborne. We'll have to see."

Vernon paced again. "I'd planned to live at the Mertons' as long as possible, but we'll likely have to leave. I need a plan in place—a way to get enough money together to keep us in reasonable comfort." He smiled at Jim. "Again, another way to keep life pleasant. Don't make your wealthy wife feel deprived by her modest lifestyle, but do make her eager to apply for help whenever those little financial troubles that plague marriages just 'happen' to befall."

"And how many wives have you had to know this?" Jim didn't bother with just one strawberry this time. He grabbed a handful and popped them all in his mouth at once.

"I've observed, my friend. With the right inducement, a woman will do anything for her husband."

The longer he spoke, the more confident Vernon grew. *It's a minor hindrance to my plans. Edith will forgive. She assumes her matrimonial prospects are slim. Everyone knows her father isn't likely to give much of a wedding gift. I convinced her that I wanted only her. She doesn't know I'm aware of her mother's money. Keeping that quiet is a good way to ward off fortune hunters.* A slow smile formed. *I can appeal to her, and once she knows Abby has gone, she'll eventually believe that the girl played up to Madeline Brown's dislike of me. She may even cut Miss Brown's society after that.*

"Hey, Smythe?"

"Yeah?"

Jim waited for him to look up before asking, "What about the electrical thing? If you set it in motion, you might gain some respect in the business circle. You could work through Mr. Merton that way. He'd see you as a sound businessman."

His mind swirling, Vernon nodded. "And at that point, it would be easy to convince Merton that I was set up by an unscrupulous young woman who used an indiscretion of mine to her own advantage. Her fleeing the city would be proof of my story...."

The men planned long into the night. Vernon, after taking the dishes indoors, washing them, drying them, and putting them away, climbed the stairs to his room and began the long, tedious task of designing certificates for the printer in Bloomington. *I'll have to waste the fare to get them. But the printer can mail them once they're printed. That'll save a return trip.*

As the sun rose over Rockland, Vernon stood leaning on his windowsill and watched. *You will regret interfering, Madeline Brown. I'm not beaten yet.*

ℰPILOGUE

Mayor Brown dropped a newspaper at Madeline's breakfast place a week and a half later. "Despite your usual excellent judgement of character, my dear, it seems that now Mr. Smythe has a new plan in mind."

Madeline unfolded the paper and read the headline with disgust and more than a little disapprobation. *Edith will be so hurt and embarrassed.*

SMYTHE HAILED AS SHREWED BUSINESSMAN

"It grieves me to hear it." Her eyes scanned the article and her heart dropped into her stomach, leaving little room for breakfast. Madeline pushed away her plate and read the article with more care. "To think that otherwise intelligent men could know of his true character and still consider his ideas.... What did it say?" She scanned the article again for the words. "'Revolutionary — ready to bring us fully into the twentieth century.' It's unbelievable."

"Perhaps they haven't heard yet. It's been less than two weeks."

"Gossip, Papa. You know it spreads faster than disease and is twice as virulent." She glared at the headline as if it would impregnate the ink with sense.

The doorbell rang and Mary scurried past on her way to open it. A minute later, Russell stepped into the dining room, newspaper in hand. "I saw the headline and brought one straight over." He flushed. "I thought perhaps Mr. Brown had already left for the office."

"I would have, but when I saw that, I waited for Madeline to eschew sleep in favor of our presence." Albert bent, kissed Madeline's forehead and bade her have a nice day. "Go buy yourself a dress or a book or a library! I might have been taken in by him myself if not for you."

Madeline waved goodbye and gestured for Russell to sit. "Stay long enough to eat some toast and let me read this. I'll walk you to the trolley."

He hesitated, and it was no wonder. He was already late for work. But to her surprise and great delight, Russell seated himself and stopped Mary on the way to the kitchen. "Would you mind? I think I could use another cup of coffee this morning."

"Certainly, Mr. Barnes. Terrible business that," she added. Two steps from the doorway, she turned again. "Ida, over at the Mertons', says that Miss Edith is brokenhearted over it—started going to the Methodist prayer meeting and everything. She's joined the temperance movement, too!"

Russell's eyes widened in surprise. "Has she?"

"I'm afraid so." Madeline sighed. "She's quite committed to her cause, as you can imagine. I receive at least one plea per day to reconsider. I believe someone has convinced her that the 'demon liquor' is the cause of Mr. Smythe's indiscretions." Madeline pursed her lips in a feeble attempt to restrain herself. "As if mankind needs the aid of alcoholic spirits to indulge his carnal nature."

"I can't imagine Mr. Merton is pleased about that."

A giggle escaped before Madeline could repress it. "Oh, if you had only been there the day she threw out his expensive whiskey! I think, had I not been in the room, he might have paddled her like a child!" A new thought changed her demeanor in an instant. "But you know, this affair—or perhaps the influence of the temperance union—has given her a strength I never saw in her before. That is good, I suppose."

"Without a man to help strengthen her, the Lord will have to do, is that it?" Russell tried to repress a smile, but Madeline saw it hovering about the corners of his lips as he buttered his toast.

"Perhaps. But I think a nice temperance man with a strong faith and a desire to protect her would be the perfect balance, don't you think?" Madeline sipped her breakfast tea and added, "If you were more inclined to the movement, I would have suggested you as the perfect candidate."

It worked. Russell nearly choked on his toast at her words. With eyes half-bugged from straining, he took a sip of coffee and spoke with the kind of dispassion that any man clearly not interested in a young woman would display. "I'm afraid that, as sweet and kind as she truly is, Edith's... *simplicity* would ensure we were both miserable, but I thank you for the consideration. That you consider me worthy of such a lovely young woman is quite the compliment."

Article finished, Madeline stood. "Shall we go? You'll get called on the carpet by Mr. Thurgood if we don't get you downtown post-haste!" She grinned. "Wouldn't Jimmy be proud of me. 'Called on the carpet.'" She frowned. "I did say that correctly, didn't I? It's so frustrating to have to question the appropriate use of *slang*."

As they strolled down her front walk, Russell pulled her arm through his and gazed over at her. "So you truly don't mind Miss Merton's new 'fanaticism'?"

"Of course, I do! It's ridiculous! She is making quite the display of herself in an attempt to hide her embarrassment. How is that any credit to our Lord? But...." Honesty forced Madeline to concede a point. "It has improved her some. I can't deny that. And at least she is finding a way to redeem her reputation, while mine...."

Russell shook his head and covered her hand with his. "No one blames you for what you did, Madeline. I've heard it spoken of only with great respect."

"And much censure as well? Aunt Louisa has waxed eloquent about my utter lack of decorum and propriety." She gave him an arch look before adding, "Did you know my prospects for matrimony have dissolved into nothing better than a boot blacker or, if I am very fortunate, a wagon driver making two dollars a day if the Lord blesses us with a generous employer?"

"I don't know. I doubt it'll be difficult for you to get a better offer than your last."

The trolley rumbled toward them, but Madeline ignored it. She met his frank gaze and shook her head. "Better than my last?" A slow smile formed. "I disagree. However, I will do my best." Just then, new thought changed things. "Then again, perhaps my recent interference... my *meddling*... will make that an impossibility. Aunt Louisa is correct, you know. It worked out this time, but few people appreciate having their carefully hidden secrets exposed."

He didn't answer. Only a smile, a wave, and a jaunty hop onto the trolley signaled his departure. Meanwhile, Madeline strolled back home again, a small smile playing about her lips. *It may have been a bit... unconventional, my so-called meddling, but it was so much more entertaining and rewarding than endless committees and the suspicion that I should learn to play an instrument or something equally uninspiring.*

As she stepped into the house, a fresh determination washed over her. Mary appeared in the dining room just as she reached for the paper once more. "Do you know, Mary? I believe I've learned something about myself in all of this."

"What's that, miss?"

She snatched up the last small bit of toast from her plate and popped it in her mouth. "I need a more constructive use for my time than committee meetings and afternoon teas. I think I'll take my Brownie about town today and see if I can learn something about composing better pictures."

"That sounds like a fine thing." Mary filled her hands with Russell's dishes. "I'm sure Mr. Barnes will be pleased to see them."

I'm sure he will.

CHAUTONA HAVIG'S BOOKS

The Rockland Chronicles
Aggie's Inheritance Series
Ready or Not
For Keeps
Here We Come
Ante Up! (Coming 2016)

Past Forward: A Serial Novel (Six Volumes)
Volume One
Volume Two
Volume Three
Volume Four
Volume Five
Volume Six

HearthLand Series: A Serial Novel (Six Volumes)
Volume One
Volume Two
Volume Three
Volume Four
Volume Five
Volume Six

The Hartfield Mysteries

Manuscript for Murder
Crime of Fashion
Two o'Clock Slump
Front Window (coming 2016)

Noble Pursuits
Argosy Junction
Discovering Hope
Not a Word
Speak Now
A Bird Died
Thirty Days Hath…
Confessions of a De-cluttering Junkie
Corner Booth
Rockland Chronicles Collection One
(Available only on Kindle: Contains *Noble Pursuits, Argosy Junction,* and *Discovering Hope*)

The Agency Files
Justified Means
Mismatched
Effective Immediately
A Forgotten Truth

The Vintage Wren (A serial novel beginning 2016)
January (Vol 1.)

Sight Unseen Series
None So Blind

Christmas Fiction

Advent
31 Kisses
Tarnished Silver
The Matchmakers of Holly Circle
Carol and the Belles

* * *

Meddlin' Madeline Mysteries
Sweet on You (Book1)
* * *

Ballads from the Hearth
Jack
* * *

Legacy of the Vines
Deepest Roots of the Heart
* * *

Journey of Dreams Series
Prairie
Highlands
* * *

Heart of Warwickshire Series
Allerednic
* * *

The Annals of Wynnewood
Shadows & Secrets
Cloaked in Secrets
Beneath the Cloak
* * *

Not-So-Fairy Tales
Princess Paisley

Everard

* * *

Legends of the Vengeance

The First Adventure

T 88541

CPSIA information can be obtained
at www.ICGtesting.com
Printed in the USA
LVOW04s0346120816

500068LV00014B/162/P